CHAINS

Hounds of the Reaper MC

S.J. Rowe

S.J. ROWE

Cover Design: Frauke Spanuth

Editor: Hot Tree Editing

First printing: July 2022

www.sjrowe.com

Special thanks to my alpha and beta readers. Can't do this without the red, purple, and sometimes blue pens.

Thank you to Eddie. Without you, half the facts would still be wrong.

To Rodeo, thanks for keeping me smiling.

As always: Cin-Cin-ohh-La-La

Maddy —

I don't do commitments. And I don't stay in a place long enough to get attachments either. But now I've got two after my only friend calls in a favor that's long overdue. Hiding myself is one thing, but hiding with two kids who have never known happiness is harder than expected. Especially when *he* comes knocking. Well, more like demanding and riding a Harley.

Chains —

The system failed me. Got me locked up for a crime I didn't commit. Five years is a long time to want justice, but all I want once I get out is to find my sister's kids. She died while I was locked away, and I refuse to be separated from my family a minute longer.

I can't believe this chick won't give me my kids. That's fine. I can wait this out. I learned how to play nice behind bars for five years. What's a few more days of pretending to be the good guy before I get what I want? And I always get what I want.

Just never expected that I'd want *her* and would be willing to go to war to keep her.

Prologue- Maddy

"**W**ant to tell me why the hell I'm here?" Izzy needed to start speaking or hand me a cup of caffeine quick. I didn't drag my ass down here at 4:00 a.m. just for *any* best friend.

"Madison, thank God." She jumped from her bent-over position, probably waking up from a mini nap at her desk, and rushed me as I leaned against her office doorframe. I had eyed it when I first came in, debating if I could sleep standing up. But as I was pulled into a hug that more crushed my bones together than anything else, thoughts of sleep vanished, replaced with the desire to breathe.

"Sit, sit, sit." She pushed me into the chair before giving me a chance to decide on my own. Probably because she knew I would have protested a bit, not being a fan of sitting when others stood. One firm push on my shoulder had me falling into a chair as my knees gave out at the same time.

Okay, she could win this round. I'd blame my tired ass later for letting her manhandle me, something I absolutely hated and a fact she knew.

"I'll be right back."

With a speed I didn't know existed for any animal outside the cheetah family, Izzy ran out of her office, closing the door with a thud. I had a thousand questions for her. Okay, I only had one when she called me three hours ago, waking me from one of the best sleeps I'd had in months and telling me to get my ass down here or lose her number forever. Her words, not mine.

I didn't try calling her on the way over, choosing to focus all the five brain cells that were awake on driving my truck down to her place without running off the road. It wasn't like the towns I drove past were awake, but I had the luck that I would hit the only bird flying and run right off the road, flipping the car seventeen times before it came to a stop and exploded.

The only question I had while driving over here was why the fuck I was there. And I already asked that. Not that she answered. My body sank into the chair. The five active brain cells were now down to two, and when did someone turn off the lights in Izzy's office?

"Here, coffee with a shit ton of cream and sugar."

The bang from the door hitting the wall woke me more than the smell of bad office coffee. I jumped but caught myself from hitting Izzy and the only caffeine that was within the vicinity. Grabbing the Holy Grail before me, I chugged the sludge as Izzy sank back into her office chair. It was crap coffee, but the extra helping of sugar made my gagging only last for the first ten seconds after I finished it instead of twenty.

"Girl, when you run this place, please tell me the coffee machine is the first thing you'll replace. I can't keep coming down here and drinking that unless you're trying to kill me. 'Cause that is the only way I would drink it again, if it was my last cup before I went under. Even then, I might not take it, and you know that's saying something about me."

I was a self-proclaimed coffee addict. Would go to meetings for it, but apparently those meetings didn't serve coffee. I needed the meetings that recognized you as an addict and helped you embrace it. I wasn't saying I couldn't go without it, but I hadn't tried, and for everyone's health, they hadn't recommended I do.

Looking to my friend, I expected to see her rolling her eyes at my comments, but I was surprised instead. Before me wasn't the vibrant woman who'd grown from the ashes that were burned around her. *This* was a disheveled shell of the woman I knew.

While she and I shared the same body type, which was great for clothes sharing, everything else was opposite. I had the long dark brown hair that was too thick to do anything but fall flat, kind of like my green eyes that always seemed more muddy than lively.

Her blue eyes, those that usually matched the dark depths of the ocean, even seemed dulled out on her heart-shaped face. The lighting, or maybe just the defeat on her face, had her looking hollow.

And this was the type of girl who'd never even had a hair out of place since birth. We both had shitty pasts, and we didn't compare who had it worse 'cause we would both lose and win at the same time if we did. We'd both lived our own horror flicks as kids, and shit went downhill for us for a long while. Some days, it still felt that way, but we were crawling back to happiness. Izzy was more determined than me, but she kept me on a short leash so I didn't fall too far back when she climbed that uphill battle.

Probably why I was here. She knew I owed her. *I* knew I owed her. And if she was calling me, she had no one else to go to. We might have been ride-or-die bitches for life, but most of our qualities weren't good ones.

Fuck, this was going to be bad.

Leaning forward, I tossed my foam cup in the wastebasket, mentally high-fiving myself for making it, and reached for her hand across the desk. "Tell me."

One of the best parts about Izzy and me, we didn't bullshit around the stuff that needed to be talked through.

"I've got a mess, and I don't know how to fix it."

"What did you do?"

She shook her head and stood. Pacing was the way she thought, so, despite how uncomfortable I was, I sat and watched her tower over me as she walked around the room and spoke.

"It's not me. Jesus, I shouldn't have called you. I should just place them."

"Place who?"

"Teddy and Grace."

I blinked. I mean, what else was I supposed to do? Surely she wasn't asking what I think she was asking.

"If you've seen them, God, five minutes with them and you know they're special."

Damn, she is totally asking. Deflect, Maddy, deflect.

"What's the problem?"

"It's complicated."

No shit. I wouldn't be here at 4:00 a.m. if it wasn't. "Complicated how?"

She stopped pacing to lock eyes with me. I could feel the tension in my shoulders from that look alone, warning me this was going to hurt. "They're Jennie's kids."

Cold sweat ran down my back. There was only one Jennie Izzy and I knew. We hadn't spoken to her in years, but we never forgot her.

"Did she…?" I couldn't bear to ask. I knew the answer from the look on her face, but I was begging in my heart for it not to be true.

But Izzy didn't maintain eye contact, and I knew the answer. She was dead. Fuck. The girl was no saint. She was in some bad stuff when I met her. But there was something about her that just made me want to be a part of her life, for however short a time that was.

"How long?"

"Eight months ago."

"Shit. Any family?"

"A brother in prison, and her mother just passed yesterday. The kids came to me when the police called."

"And the father?"

"It listed none on the birth certificates for either."

Double shit.

"Look, I know there are a million reasons why I shouldn't ask, but you've taken the classes. You're certified."

"No, not, uh…." I knew what she was asking. I couldn't. It would be no good. I took the foster care classes on one of my many whims of what I wanted out of my life. But that was where it ended.

Izzy worked in child protection services. She hooked me up with everything I needed to get cleared. But then we both knew my heart wasn't in it, so I never had a family placed with me. I was the backup that Izzy swore she would file away and never search for. Guess she lied.

She shook her head. "Look, I wouldn't ask if I had another option, but I don't. I need them off the books."

"Off the books"? That had my alarm bells ringing. Izzy's main reason for going into this field was to make sure there were no "off the books" moments. She liked rules and orders,

and she enjoyed living in the laws that kept her and others safe.

While we might have been best friends, that was where we differed. Izzy clung to the law with both hands while I ran and hid from it.

Okay, I'd stopped running. Sort of.

"Izzy, this isn't like you. You're a rule girl. When things get bent, it's because *I'm* bending them. You are a strict black-and-white, 'follow the little white line on the ground in front of you path' girl. You don't do things 'off book.'"

"Exactly, *I* don't. *You* do. You might not outright break rules, but you don't necessary follow them either. Look, I'm not asking you to do anything illegal. You *are* certified. I just can't use my usuals. They'll know."

"Who are 'they'?"

"I don't know. I just don't like this. The kids have been through hell. Hell like you and I grew up in. They need a good place that they can feel safe. I can't guarantee they'll be safe if I send them to the usuals."

"What makes me safe and the usuals not?"

"You don't like cops."

Fuck, this was bad. I hated cops. Had some serious issues with them—mostly daddy issues.

I quickly stopped my mind from tumbling down that dark path. We didn't have time for my breakdown, which would be me crying and rocking myself for hours at a time, maybe even days if I really spiraled.

But was I willing to take on two little ones for Izzy? For Jennie? Anyone else and the answer would be an easy "Hell no." This was anything but that.

"Fine, let me meet them. I'm not saying yes, but I will at least meet them. If we talk and I'm not a good fit, we look at a different option. I won't force these kids into my home. If what you say is true, if their paths match our own, the last thing they need is to be told to stay with someone they hate."

"Deal."

Wow, she answered faster than I thought. Either she was that desperate or knew I would fall for them instantly, like she already said. I really hoped she wasn't right. I was a mess, but she knew how to get me involved: pull at my past childhood strings and I was like a Malibu Barbie, doing whatever you wanted.

Before I could set any more terms, Izzy was out the door and across the hall, pulling open the door and leading two little munchkins back to me.

Crap.

One look. That was all it took.

Dammit, Izzy.

The little girl, Grace, clung to her brother, Teddy. She was adorable and dirty, with a smudged face that, even despite being moved around at 4:00 a.m. still looked up and smiled quickly at me before hiding in her brother's arm.

Teddy seemed serious and cautious. I really just wanted to pull him in for a hug, but I doubted he would appreciate it.

Izzy smiled down at them, then looked at me. "So this is Grace. She's three and a half. And this is Teddy. He just turned six last month."

I gave them a finger wave. "Nice to meet you all."

"Are we going to your place?" Teddy asked.

There was no beating around the bush with this little dude. Straightforward and to the point. He was smarter than any six-year-old I had met before. Not that I'd met a lot, but from his stance and expression, the kid was already in his late teens. And with his background, from what Izzy hinted at, I bet he had to grow up fast. Which was the last thing any child should ever have to do. I would know.

"If you want to," I replied. "You get to call the shots, little monkey."

He looked at me, then Izzy, then back to me. "Okay."

El Dorado Correction Facility- CHAINS-

"One more year and I'm out of this fucking place. City of gold, my ass. This joint fucking sucks. Can't get out of here soon enough." I was griping to my boys on the other side of the glass, trying to keep things as normal as possible. But what the fuck was normal about being locked up for five years? Only thing keeping me going were these monthly visits from the boys. Sometimes I was lucky and got two in a month, like now.

"We got a problem, brother."

Fuck, of course we do. Wonder what it is now. Am I about to get another visit from a rival club that just likes to poke a bear and see what happens? Or is it bigger this time?

"Gran's dead."

I didn't ask Bulldog to repeat himself. Didn't even look at my lawyer, who was sweating in his six-grand suit next to him. I just asked the simple question, the only one I was focused on. "Where's my family?"

"We don't know." I watched the straight line form on my lawyer's lips as my friend sat next to him in a deep frown.

I could sense it, the thing that made me who I was, rise through me. Every Hound of the Reaper member had it. The need and urgency to sink my teeth into something and rip it to shreds. But unlike the past, I had no name, no person standing in front of me with the answers I needed. Not yet.

"You find them. Find them now. And I want out. Not a year from now, not a few months from now—*now!*"

Fuck this place. I've served my time. Don't need to waste any more of it when I got family that needs me.

Chapter 1 - Maddy

Five weeks have passed since I became a single mom—of sorts—and things are finally getting into a routine. I didn't know how the kids would react to me. And let's be honest here, I was clueless about what I was doing. I still don't know.

Grace has been easy. The girl stole my heart immediately and had no problem letting me in. From her blue eyes looking into my soul with so much hope for a better life to the way her cornfield-blonde hair curled into ringlets that bounced with each step she took. She's a genuine princess to the core, despite that she refuses to be called one, preferring to be known as Supergirl Grace, or Gigi for short. It doesn't make a lick of sense, but when I first called her that, she couldn't stop giggling. Even Teddy showed one of his rare smiles. She's still so young, which helps me on so many levels. I try not to think about how she has no mama anymore, but I don't think she remembers her much.

From the way Teddy speaks occasionally, even though Jennie died less than a year ago, I get the feeling she wasn't around a ton. It makes my heart ache to know they were alone so much. They had their grandma, at least. She might have forgotten things, but at least she was around. That had to count for something.

For today, Grace is all about superheroes. But with the way I keep showing them new things every day, I'm sure my little superhero will change into something else by the end of the month. Heck, she was all about solving mysteries the first two weeks, and we watched nothing but *Scooby-Doo.*

It took some time, but she soon moved from clinging to her brother to me. Not sure what I did to deserve the love of the sweetest superhero ever, but I cherish each hug, each cuddle with my entire heart. It's made for some difficult times when she refuses to be out of my arms, proving more than once she has abandonment issues. On nights that the cling monster comes out, we usually order in, as there's no way I can cook with one hand. I'm not that talented yet. But I'm working on it.

I have no illusion that I can keep Teddy and Grace, but I willingly live in denial that the day won't come soon.

Teddy has been harder to get to warm up to me. He's a tough nut to crack, and I'm in no rush. He's been through hell. Might weigh the size of a peanut, but he seems to carry everything on his shoulders. Or at least he tries to. He watches over his sister more times than not, and he's started even watching over me. I can't tell if it's his concern for me or being wary of me.

Even without getting the dossier on him that Izzy sent over after the third day, there was sadness in his hazel eyes that no little boy should ever have. His hair matches his sister's in color, but he likes to keep it short. In his words, he wants to see what's coming at all times.

I will admit that I don't have a ton of experience on how to handle trauma kids. Google searches have helped a bit, but mostly they've made me think I've been screwing it all up with what I've been doing. Apparently buying everything the little boy wants, or what I think he wants, is a bad thing. Well, too damn bad. The boy needs happiness, and I'm trying to give it to him, even if that means I have to buy a new Lego set every day. The kid is wicked smart and able to build anything I put in front of him.

The routine is simple for us. Kids wake up at the ass crack of dawn, pulling me out of bed to turn on cartoons. They enjoy a few snacks while watching silliness while I try to wake up after drinking a few cups of coffee. Then breakfast, followed by another cartoon or two, depending on the time. By ten, I usually have them outside. I have nothing really awesome in the backyard. The house is a fixer-upper, in and out. Most of the areas inside are decent enough, which is why we focus on the outside for an hour or two. I try to get them into planting flowers and mowing, which usually works for ten minutes, and then they're off exploring the area, which isn't that large but big enough for them based on the smiles they have. It's great watching them play together.

By half past eleven, we head inside to wash up and eat lunch. Gigi goes down for a nap, and Teddy, who constantly says he's too big for one, will look at one of his books before crashing out for at least an hour. I crash then, too, as the kids wear me out all the time. We typically fill the afternoons with Teddy building something. Gigi was off being a superhero that gave tea parties to all her stuffed animals. And yes, if I get Teddy a new Lego, Gigi gets a new stuffy. What can I say? I've already admitted I'm clueless. Who cares if the girl has about forty different stuffies already? If she spots another one, I know I'm going to buy it for her.

Dinner is early—well, for me anyhow. Before the kids showed, I usually worked on the house till well past eight before calling it quits, but I soon realized that one great asset the kids have is they love to sleep. Bedtime is at 7:30 p.m. for both, which is awesome, but makes dinner at six fun, especially since I have to wrap up my stuff at five. Who knew cooking for three took so much time?

I'd like to believe that once the kids go down, I live it up. That I'd focus on the house, get back on schedule to get things done in the timeframe I planned to sell the place in the next few months. But honestly? I usually spend way too much time googling how to cook something, or buying something new I think they would like. Even looking up ways to coax Teddy out of his shell a bit more. He's said little unless he's trying to protect his sister.

That first day was interesting. After our little coffee talk—always making sure I have one in hand to keep the smile on my face—we did breakfast, then went shopping. I asked them a million questions about what they liked, and they didn't answer, so I just chose what I thought looked good. When I piled up the baskets full of clothes at the first store and bought everything without blinking, they soon realized that if they wanted something, it was theirs. I'm not loaded, but a few delayed installments in my renovation were worth the smiles from Gigi. I even got one out of Teddy when I found his love for Legos while we took a turn around the toy aisle. Books were in the basket already, but kids have to have toys. It's a must.

I'm just cleaning up the cereal bowls as the kids finish the latest *Scooby-Doo* when I hear the grumble of bikes. Both kids notice as well and look at me in alarm. This isn't the first time we've heard the noise of a motorcycle going by. A few times we went into town, one would pass. Both kids freaked at the sound. Gigi usually gets over it quickly with a distraction, but Teddy remembers enough to have nightmares about them.

That's another routine we've gotten into. His nightmares are getting less frequent. Not nightly, like when he first showed up, but a few times a week. He wakes up screaming, and I run to his room asking what's wrong. He never tells me, so I just hold him and tell him it'll be okay. That's the only time he lets me hold him. The boy might pretend he's a man, but those nights, he needs a mama, and I'm always happy to oblige, for a little while at least. The only way for him to drift back to sleep is reading him *The Cat in the Hat*. I don't argue if he wants it nightly, or repeated three times before he sleeps. It's what he needs, and with all my Google searching, that's one thing I learned: do what they need to feel safe.

A quick glance out the front window shows five motorcycles pulling in. My heart's in my throat as I hear the pounding their engines made.

I smile at the kids, faking it so much my jaw aches. "Do me a favor and let me know who the shark ghost is. I'll be back soon."

Teddy does the cutest chin lift ever, saying he has my back without words.

Buddy boy, I got yours. Don't you worry about it.

Opening the hall closet, I angle my back to the TV so the kids don't see what I'm doing. I reach for the top shelf and pull down my Remington. Loading it quickly, I walk out the front door, pushing the screen door open with the barrel as I smile down at my guests, who parked in front of the porch.

"Good morning. Can I help you with anything?"

Not going to lie, I totally think I'm smug as shit when they all hesitate to get off their bikes.

Yeah, dumbasses, I ain't letting you take my kids.

Wait, "my kids"?

Shit, I'm already claiming them. That's one rule for being a foster parent: don't get too attached.

Too late, looks like I already am.

My smugness dies as the biggest of the bunch—and probably the sexiest man I have ever seen in my life—slides off his seat, as graceful as water rolling off rocks, and stalks toward me.

My mouth's drier than a dryer sheet and tastes fouler. The man has bulk from what I can see, and it's all in a yummy way. His sunglasses are the type that cost more than a reasonable person should pay, but damn, do they look good on him. I only notice he has no helmet, like the rest of them, because I'm drawn to his hair more than I should be. I have no idea if it's 'cause I'm turned on or just jealous as shit that his dirty-blond hair—emphasis more on dirty—is silky and has a wave to it as it drifts just past his shoulder blades. That and his full beard have me wondering if he's more lion than anything. I mean, it's a lot of hair in one area, like a mane. *Is this guy some kind of king of the pack?* He definitely has the alpha male thing going on. As well as the hunting prey part, especially since he doesn't seem to stop or take his eyes off the house for a second, only halting when I cock the shotgun.

"Where are they?"

His growl sends a shiver over me. I hope he sees it as fear. I would rather him think I'm scared than the fact that his deep, husky voice has another effect on me.

"And who might that be?"

"Don't play dumb with me, bitch. I know they're here. I want to see my niece and nephew right goddamn now."

Yeah, fuck the lust. This guy is definitely on my shit list. I can just scroll the internet and find a Thor lookalike to cure whatever draw I had for him for a second. The second before he spoke, that is.

"First off, don't call me bitch. And second, I don't know who you are or who your niece and nephew are."

"Quit with the bull, honey. We know Teddy and Grace are here. If you know what's best for you, you'll let their uncle see them before we stop playing nice," one of the other bikers still on his ride jumps in, speaking for the group.

I spare the guy a look, not foolish enough to take my eyes off the man before me for more than a second. He wears the same glasses. Big fucker too. But while the god before me has more hair than I do—which is a fuck-ton—this one has his hair slicked back to show a widow's peak. Just enough 'stache and beard on him to be more than noticeable but less than using some special gels to maintain.

"Nice? Pretty sure I'm the one with the gun. Now tell me who the hell you are."

"Think that will stop him?" From my periphery, I see his head bob to the beast man before me, the one claiming to be the kids' uncle. "Don't think you want to try it."

I should stand my ground, but against my will, my eyes travel up and down the man who hasn't backed down. His fists are tight at his sides. Wonder if he's contemplating using them against me. I might have the gun—well, the only one with it out, anyway. I'm not an idiot. These boys are packing. But despite my show—for really, it's all show, because I can only get off one round, two if rushed—we all know they can overtake me.

"Doesn't matter," the beast growls in response to my question about who he is.

Is he seriously playing this stupid game with me over what his name is? I might be one against half a dozen, but I will shoot first.

From the clench in his jaw, he must realize I'm not backing down without knowing some idea of who he is.

"Chains."

I barely control my eye roll. "Legal name, dumbass."

"What the fuck did you say to me?" He takes a step forward, hands clenched even tighter, and the men get off their bikes as if in a dance sequence.

I don't hesitate. Pulling the trigger, I fire into the dirt at his feet. He pauses and glares up at me as I cock my shotgun again and aim it at his center mass. "Damn right, I want a legal name. Only two people know who I have inside, me and my friend, and you don't have tits. Now stop acting like a pussy and prove to me you're their uncle. We'll start off slow. Your name, asshole. What is it?"

Through clenched teeth, he snarls, "James Randall."

"And what was your sister's middle name?"

"Are you kidding me with this shit?"

I don't hide my sarcasm. "Does it look like I'm kidding you?"

"Fine. It was Janet."

"No, that was what was on paper. What did the family call her?"

Taking off his sunglasses, he tilts his head to the side as he pauses and looks me over slowly. "You knew Jennie?" His voice changes tone for a moment.

"The name." I hold firm. I'm not about to show I'm anything but badass, but come on. The guy did that slow look up and down on a girl. I'm practically a puddle of goo on the ground from that look. Especially from the intensity that his light brown eyes have right now. So light they're almost yellow. Not yellow like the sun, more like a metallic gold, ones I would have no problem looking at for a very long time.

If things were different, of course.

"Dammit. We called her Dammit Janet."

A twitch of a smile touches my lips. "She hated that movie."

"Who didn't?" He doesn't smile, but the intensity isn't rolling off him as much. I almost feel like I can breathe, as his anger had been choking me even with him off the front steps.

"We done?" His eyebrow quirks up. It's a neat trick, one I've always wished I possessed.

"One more. What was her favorite ice cream?"

He shakes his head before he even speaks. "Trick question. She didn't have one."

"Not as kids, but she did. What was it? If you are who you claim you are, then you know this."

I watch as his eyes draw together before he looks down and then back at his friends, who just shrug. I'm not trying to trick him, but I need to know if he's legit. Jennie may have been a lot of things, but getting tied to trouble was her well-known trait. And from what Izzy showed me of how she died, and what we knew of her activities prior to death, the kids weren't safe. That's why they're with me. The people she associated with were known for many things, but none for being a loving parent. More like stealing kids *from* loving parents.

"Vanilla." He pauses, and I almost pull the trigger on him before turning it on his friends. "Two scoops of vanilla that she topped with a can of Diet Coke and five cherries on the stem and called a cherry float. Tasted like shit."

"Don't knock it. We trademarked it when we invented it."

His eyes widen when he realizes who I am. I never met him, but Jennie and I were pretty close for a while. There was no doubt he would have heard about me and I him. I doubt he got my name, but that ice cream shit was something we created during a semester of community college finals when we were tired but needed the sugar to keep us up.

"Great. Now that we did *that* song and dance, let me see my family."

"Not so fast, dumbass. I might agree you are who you say you are, but that doesn't mean I'm letting you see my kids."

"They aren't yours, bi—" My head twitch has him changing his word. "—woman. They're mine. Jennie always wanted her kids to be with family. With Gran dead, that leaves me. So get out of the way."

"Again, not going to happen. And before you piss and moan any more, I'll tell you why. First off, Jennie didn't leave a will."

"What?"

"Exactly, which means they belong to the state. Also, no way in hell will the state give custody of her kids, family or not, to a felon who just got out of jail. How long have you been out, anyway? Like a week or something?"

"Try three hours."

My brows fly up my forehead. "You got out today? Are you fucking insane?"

"No, just want my family. You get it? *Mine.* Not yours. Don't think I didn't hear you claim them. They ain't yours, so get that out of your head. They belong with me and are coming with me."

Oh my God, I can't even believe this guy. He's a one-track-mind asshole. Did he even think this through? He's right that they aren't mine, but I'm not about to let someone, even if they are family, just take them from me without knowing they're safe. I wasn't instantly a queen at this whole parenting thing, but even I know the basics that are needed with kids. Does he? Ten to one, he has no fucking clue.

My anger at the audacity of this guy has me venting more than I probably should about the personality traits I've learned from the last few weeks of being Teddy and Grace's sole provider.

"Sure, and where will they stay, huh? You got a place? Or do you live with these guys? You got somewhere for them to sleep? 'Cause Grace and Teddy can't sleep in the same room. And Grace needs to have lullaby music to fall asleep to that you have to reset twice for her to stay asleep. Teddy, he might not need music, but he does need a night-light. And when he comes in your room at night, 'cause it will happen with the nightmares, you better not have anyone with you. The last thing that six-year-old boy needs is to see you finally getting your dick sucked by, I'm sure, the willing groupies you have around your place."

With the way his cheeks hollow, he must be biting them to keep from screaming at me, or just at his lack of planning. I know I won the bet. Wish I'd put money on it; could have used the extra cash. Seriously, did the guy really think he was just going to roll out of here with them?

"Besides, how the fuck are they supposed to come with you? Do you have car seats that strap to the backs of those bikes of yours?"

Breathing deep, I lower the gun, not putting it down completely. I'm not that stupid. But I have to see it from his side. They're his family, but he needs to know it all. Well, not all, but a little more, at least till I trust him completely.

"Besides, motorcycles terrify the kids."

"What the fuck?" This comes from the biker who spoke earlier.

I nod to the group, taking my time to look them over. They're in various leather, clean enough but definitely falling under the scruffy definition compared to clean-cut. "I don't know why. We've seen some in town. The noise bugs the shit out of them, but I usually can get them settled after a bit. But seeing one, that really sets them off. Grace ends up clinging to me like a monkey for hours, if not days. And Teddy shuts down completely, and his nightmares are the worst." I shake my head and feel the pangs of sadness just thinking about the night I'm sure Teddy will have after this. "If you care for them, which I'm sure you do if you came here before thinking twice about getting laid first, like most people do after they get out of prison, then think this through. They don't know you—I mean, not really. You're a name, nothing more right now. Teddy recalls you from what Jennie has told him. Grace, well, she has a picture of you as a kid, but that's about it. Their lives have been shitty lately. I'm not saying I'm making it all sunshine and rainbows, but at least with me, they can count on someone who will have their back."

"I'll have their back." His growl is back again, but his glare isn't half as intense as the first time.

"I'm sure you will, just not right now. I'm not trying to replace you. I'm just saying think it through."

"She's right, man," the other one mutters.

Chains runs his hand through his hair. Why is that such a turn-on? "Shit. They're the only family I got left." I can hear the exhaustion in his voice. I've known that type of exhaustion. The kind that eats at your soul, making you feel helpless but knowing you have to keep fighting even if it's taking more strength than you ever knew you had.

"And *you* are the only one they have left." Fuck, I need to compromise on this. Not for me but for them. "Look, how about we plan for a dinner in a week? You come back in a truck or something, spend some time getting to know them. We do that for a few months and see where it leads."

He takes a moment to look at the ground before he raises his head and puts his sunglasses back on. Nodding once to me, he walks back to his bike, sliding his leg over it smoothly.

Wow, okay, didn't expect him to agree so easily. Guess this guy can see sense after all. Just have to break it down for the big ox.

"I'll be back tonight."

He starts his engine just as I take a step off the porch. "Wait, what? Tonight? No, a week or something. Give them time." Panic is setting in. I need time to prepare for this guy at my house. I know my body is sending me all the signals that it wouldn't take much for me to hump his leg. He's pretty with a capital *P*. I want him, and my body is saying it's *craving* him in such a short time of knowing him. But my head—thank God—knows it's beyond bad. I need more time in my head to get my body under control before I spend any length of time with this guy.

Even with his sunglasses on, I can feel his eyes lock with mine. "Tonight."

As the group peels out of the drive, I really hope someone heard me scream that we eat at six. Otherwise, the guy's going to be extremely disappointed if he shows up after eight and we're all in bed.

Chapter 2 - Maddy

"You did what?"

"I said I invited him for dinner." Okay, that's a lie. James—or I guess he prefers Chains—invited himself, but I'm not going to tell Izzy that part. She's highly protective of me, though she doesn't need to be—well, not anymore. I know how to take care of myself now. The hell she helped pull me out of before will *not* happen again. I'm a big girl now, can tie my own shoes and everything.

And it's about time I remind her of that too.

"Are you crazy? He's a criminal. How can you even trust that he is who he says he is?"

"For one, I saw his picture before he showed up. Two, Teddy looks like him all the way. And three, hell, who else would come to a woman's house to claim them? And if he wasn't who he said he was and was only trying to take them away, then he wouldn't have stopped when I stood in front of him. The odds were in his favor, not mine. I was outnumbered, and yet he didn't storm the castle. Yeah, he did say some not-nice things, and he was kind of a jerk with the way he spoke to me, but the guy did just get out of prison. I doubt he was practicing his manners behind bars."

Not sure why I'm defending the guy. Probably because he's the kids' uncle. Yeah, that makes more sense than me *wanting* to like him on a personal level and all.

"Shit, I don't know about this."

"What could go wrong?" I joke, expecting her to giggle at it.

"So many things."

I know her whispered response wasn't meant for me. I doubt if she even knows she spoke out loud. The hairs on the back of my neck rise.

"What aren't you telling me, Izzy?"

Just silence. I don't speak either. I know she hates silence, and I'm not letting her off the hook.

"I, ah, I never told you that Jennie got in touch with me about a year ago."

"She did what?" Now it's my turn to yell at her.

"Yeah, she was scared and didn't know where to turn. She was worried the kids wouldn't be safe if something happened to her. She asked if I could watch them in case things went south."

"Izzy, you tell me now. Was Jennie... was she murdered?" I whisper the last bit, more afraid to ask than for the kids to hear me.

Another beat of silence. "Yes. But I can't prove it. Cops ruled it an overdose, but when I talked to her, she told me she had been sober since she found out she was pregnant with Teddy."

"Why didn't you say anything? Why didn't you tell me earlier?"

"She begged me not to. I really thought if I could keep the kids with you that no one would have to know. Thought Chains had a few more months, even a year left on his sentence. I honestly thought I had time to sort this all out. Jesus, I don't know. I was scared too. I didn't know what I was agreeing to when she asked if I could help, and then it happened, and it took me so long to find them that by then,

I was only thinking about hiding them, and then you, and then—"

"Izzy, calm down. Take a breath, chica. Jesus, no wonder you've been so wound tight lately."

She let out a forced laugh that was more pitiful than anything. "Yeah."

"Look, I need to process this all. And don't think I won't come back to you on this. I know you. I know you grilled Jennie and have more info on this than what you're telling me. But I'll let you get away with it for now. You're right, at this moment, I doubt anyone needs to know. Not yet anyhow. For now, the kids are safe. We'll keep it that way. But if things get weird, if things start to not add up, that's when your time is up. Okay? You get me?"

"Yeah, I get you." She sighs in resignation, but I hear the relief in her voice. She might not be up for telling me things right now, but I know she hated keeping the secret from me. She always has. "Sorry, Maddy. I really am. I didn't mean to lay this all on you, but shit, I had no one else I could trust."

"I'm just happy you have me. And that they have me now too." I glance at the kids in the living room. They're coloring pictures and have been relatively quiet. In such a short time, they've wormed their way into a heart I thought died a long time ago. "I'm going to let you go. I got to cook. No idea what, but I've got to at least attempt to look like I've got this foster parenting all figured out."

"Make spaghetti. The kids will eat it, and it's not that hard to burn."

"Oh, you got jokes now."

Her laughter dies down after a bit before her tone turns hesitant. "Maddy, one thing before I go. You might think you know when things get bad, but in case you don't, you see a Devils Damned, you call me."

"What, like a demon?"

"No, they're an MC that has taken over a ton of places south of here. They call themselves the Devils Damned. They're bad business, and Jennie was mixed up with them. Not sure if they've gotten up this far north yet, but I know they're trying."

MC? Motorcycle gang? Shit, is Chains part of them? I saw the group roll up with all-black vests, but I didn't pay attention to the names.

Fuck, who the hell did I invite to dinner?

By the time Chains drives up in the biggest truck I've ever seen, I'm in a panic, clutching my phone to my chest. I already typed out a text to send to Izzy to get her ass here and bring the cops if I find out that Chains is one of those Devils guys. Or was it Demons? Fuck. I'm freaking out so much I'm confusing myself.

I watch from the screen door as he steps out of the big blue cab, hair pulled back in the sexiest man bun ever. Dark jeans and a white shirt do sinful things to his body and send just as sinful thoughts through my head.

Get it together, Maddy. He could be someone who killed Jennie or knows something about her murder.

My stomach's in knots. The quick spell of desire I had for him vanishes at the thought of Jennie. I'm going to throw up soon if I don't get an answer.

"Are you a Devils Damned?" I have to admit, I'm surprised I just asked like that. I should have been more tactful or some shit. But no, I just blurted it out the first chance I got.

He stops dead in his tracks. Even from here, I can tell his eyes are narrowed on me as I screamed the question from the front door, not even opening the screen. Not that it would keep me safe. Shit, I'm nervous.

"What the fuck did you just call me?" He may have been pissed this morning when I told him he couldn't have the kids, but he looked almost jolly then compared to now.

"A Devils Damned?" I squeak, not loud enough for him to hear me, but he must read my lips.

"I ain't a fucking cunt. And that's what a Devils Damned is. Why the fuck would you ask me that shit?"

I shrug. How can I tell him without having him completely freak and take the kids away from me, thinking they would be safer with him when he has nothing lined up for them? "I heard of them, but I know little about you. You just showed up, and then you were gone. I'm assuming you're in an MC, but hell, you could just be a weekend rider for all that I know about you."

I have no clue where my confidence is coming from. I'm also super proud that it sounds like I know what I'm talking about. I'm pulling at every straw to even put a full sentence together.

"I ain't no pussy weekend rider, and I ain't no cunt."

I really want to say those are the same thing, but I guess in his mind, they're different.

"I ride with the Hounds of the Reaper." He grins as he watches the recognition play across my face. They're everywhere in this town and about every town in a hundred-mile radius.

Shit, they're bad.

Okay, I actually have no idea, but everyone knows to walk on the other side of the street when you see them in town. I've never had dealings with them, but I've seen them around. They're hard to miss. Not only from the loud bikes but they're all hot. Like *hot* hot. Firefighters holding puppies on a calendar hot.

And Chains is no different.

Sliding the phone into my back pocket, not sending any text to Izzy, I open the screen door as Chains comes closer. He only grunts as I hold the door for him to pass through. I don't know what to expect. There's definitely an awkwardness about this whole situation.

"Where're the kids?"

I jump at his words. He probably didn't bark them, but I'm so lost in my own thoughts, his voice sounds like a megaphone in my vacant foyer.

"Playing in their rooms."

He nods once before looking for them.

"By all means, make yourself at home," I growl, but a grunt from him makes me think he's laughing at me.

Teddy's room is first, and he's so deep into building his Legos that he doesn't even notice us come in.

"He's gotten so big." His voice sounds rough, and the way he clears his throat softly has me staring anew at the large biker in my house. Seeing a big-ass man get emotional over a child does something to a girl. Specifically, it does something to her uterus. Mine seems to pulse with need for the man over the simple act of watching him look over at a nephew who he hasn't seen in years.

"When's the last time you saw him?" I whisper, not wanting Teddy to know we're there yet. I want Chains to have his fill of admiring the little boy before him.

"He was nine months old. I got locked up after that and didn't want Jennie coming to see me with the kids while I was in there. We talked a few times on the phone, but it's not the same."

Teddy finally senses us and glances up, looking Chains over for a few seconds before he asks, "Uncle James?"

Chains only nods once before Teddy jumps into his arms. The tears just slide down my cheeks before I even know it's happening. They don't talk, just grip on to each other. They know who the other is, but being able to hold, to touch for the first time in years is different.

A small hand grabs mine, pulling me from Chains and Teddy to see Grace looking at them.

"Up?"

Without hesitation, I have her in my arms.

"Who dat? My uncle?"

I nod, still too choked up to say anything.

"Hey, princess. I'm your mama's brother." He looks at her but doesn't move to let Teddy go, and the boy makes no move to get down.

She smiles and waves as she tucks her head into my neck.

My heart and uterus just keep pounding in time together at this happy reunion.

Dinner's uneventful, but what did I expect from a biker who just got out of prison? To be shanked five minutes into the meal over a roll? Yeah, I guess I did. Probably explains why I made so many. While no fights break out, it seems nothing else is going to either. The kids are quiet. Grace is her shy self around new people. Teddy just stares with hero worship. Not sure if it's 'cause Chains is his uncle, a badass, or just because Teddy had heard about him all his life but never really met him. Probably all three.

I didn't want to, but I send a silent prayer that the big guy doesn't break the little ones' hearts. He seems the type. And yes, I'm totally putting my baggage at Chains' feet, but it's what I know. Fairy tales don't exist, at least not from where I sit on the bleachers. I'm not going to be the one to burst any bubbles, but I'm also not the one making any for their delight.

"Are we going back with you tonight?"

Teddy's question has everyone pausing. The pregnant pause I heard about all my life but never felt until this moment. I open my mouth but shut it quickly as Chains glares across the table at me.

What's he going to say? Has he found a place for them? Is he going to take them away despite what I said a few hours ago? It would be considered kidnapping. He isn't their legal guardian, even if he is family. But could I do that? Could I turn him in, send him back to prison, when all he wants to do is be with his family?

"Not right now, Teddy."

The wind couldn't have been knocked out of the kid's sail faster. Despite my feelings toward the man, the fact that he's thinking about more than just his own thoughts, that shit does something to me. And when he continues to talk to Teddy like an adult, never taking his eyes away from him? Well, that does something to my ovaries.

"I ain't got shit ready for you and your sis to come live with me yet. But I'm working on it. And trust me when I say this, you will be coming to stay with me. This is just temporary. We're family. We always will be. Right now, shit, we just need to wait a bit. Give me time to find a place for all of us, and also give us some time to get to know each other before we live under one roof. You good with that, little man? Think you can stay here for a bit longer, watch out for your sis, keep this place on the up-and-up till we get our own?"

I bite my smile back as Teddy straightens a full head taller at being does the a man. Yup, the boy idolizes his uncle and eats up everything he says like a dog after table scraps. And now that he has a job to do? Take care of this place? Well, hell, you would think Chains asked him to watch over the most precious Lego that was ever invented.

"Yeah, that works. I can make sure this place is good till we get our place." No longer is a six-year-old sitting between Chains and me but a very happy young man who seems to have aged in pride by seven years. Who knew a little responsibility is the way to dealing with kids?

"What about you?"

It takes me a full minute to realize Chains is talking to me. Even then I have to blink a few times for my brain to recall what he said.

"Yeah, that works. I, um, I think we can set something up so you and the kids can get to know one another. I'm not sure how the paperwork will work, but I got a friend, and maybe she can make some calls to see about custody and stuff." I'm lying through my teeth about the paperwork, but I'm not about to tell him there is none really keeping the kids to me.

The look he gives me isn't easy to decipher. He either hates that I have a friend, the word paperwork, or he just thinks me an idiot. Probably all in one. "Don't need to sign shit to see my family. You do what you need to do to make yourself happy, but once I'm settled, they're coming with me. Don't care what the court says. Got it?"

How can this man go from sweet-talking to threatening in a few seconds depending on who he's talking to? And why the hell does it both scare the crap out of me and turn me on?

I have *soooo* many issues.

I don't know how to respond to that, so we all go back to eating and no talking. Thankfully, the kids actually eat their food and it's not a battle tonight, so we don't sit here for over an hour to finish, just ten more minutes.

As soon as everyone is done, Chains starts saying his goodbyes. I see the hurt in both kids' eyes, but the promise of seeing them soon fades it a bit. They run off to get ready for bed, and I walk our guest out. It's habit more than anything to make sure a person leaves my house. Don't need that nightmare to occur again.

"See you tomorrow," he tells me.

"Tomorrow?" I get that he wants to get to know the kids, but I didn't know it would be so soon.

"Yeah, you got a problem with that?"

His challenge has me prickling for a fight. Hell, he's had me prickling all night for one. "Yeah, maybe I do."

"Too damn bad, Mama Bear. I'll be here every night till I can get them moved out."

"Every night?"

"Yeah, and maybe try to cook something that isn't shit next time. I was in prison, remember? Spaghetti was every Wednesday night, and they sure as hell made it better than you did. Maybe think about that next time."

What. The. Fuck?

I stand flabbergasted on the front porch for who knows how long. He left in his monster of a truck at one point, but it isn't till Grace starts asking for me that I turn and go inside.

A smile creeps on my face as I lock the door.

Oh, he'll get a better meal next time. One that's definitely not on any prison menu.

Chapter 3 – Chains

"Hey, man, want to go get some beers at the Flying Monkeys with me and the boys? Club is thinking about picking it up as an investment, and I need to do some on-site intel to see if it's worth it or not."

"Nah, got dinner."

Bulldog raises his eyebrows but keeps his comments to himself. He gets me. I don't like to be questioned. But Bass, even if he knows me, still likes to open his mouth every chance he gets.

"Dinner? This early? You're out of the joint, man. No need to stick to those rules anymore."

I don't realize I'm growling under my breath till Bulldog pushes Bass behind him. I usually only make that noise right before I bust in a head or two.

Goddammit, this woman keeps fucking things up for me. I can't even get along with my boys anymore. And no, that isn't because I've been behind bars for most of the last five years. I know how to interact with others. This isn't some shit about welcoming me back into society. I knew I wouldn't have a problem at all when I was released yesterday. But that goddamn woman has everything mixed up.

First she says I can't get my kids back, and then she makes me look like a fucking pussy who runs to her at six every night. Last night, after I finally got some sleep, I played it over in my head so many times to see how I could get Grace and Teddy to me full time, but I didn't see it. In the light of day, I don't see it either. It isn't like she's refusing me access to them. If she did, she would be six feet under already.

No, she had to talk common sense to me, explain shit I didn't see at first, and hell, she had to treat them better than I can at the moment. It isn't the money; I have a shit ton. The boys never went without cutting me in for my share, no matter that I was locked up. I also knew, even if I didn't have the cash, they would front me what I didn't have, no questions asked. But she's right, as much as it pains me to admit, and it fucking hurts to think that.

I have no plan. Outside of getting out of the joint and finding them, I didn't think past that. My room is one of the many at the clubhouse. We have spare rooms, sure, but what kind of uncle will I be if I raise a six- Color me sand three-year-old in a house full of sex, drugs, and rock 'n' roll? Probably a badass one. Still, I don't want that for them. Granted, Jennie and I grew up like that, and I turned out fine. Going to prison wasn't because of how I was raised; it was because of a stupid cunt who I still have to deal with.

Jennie, well, she was in and out of rehab. She was always with the wrong guy and had no stability. Even when she had the kids, I thought she would stay in, like she'd talked about, but she was raising them on her own. No matter how much I begged for her to bring them to the club, she never would. Stubborn was what she was. I respected her wishes, though I wish like hell I hadn't. The moment she died and they declared it an OD, I got thrown into solitary for two weeks. I went apeshit on anyone who talked to me that day—didn't care who it was, just pissed at the world, you know?

The kids need better than what I have right now if I want to guarantee they won't turn out like their mom. Parts they can have: her strong will, determination, even some stubbornness. But drugs? Fuck no. They also will *not* be getting mixed in with the wrong crowd. I get it, things happen no matter how people are raised, but shit if my kids are going to be like that. I have no problem going into any place and dragging them out, kicking and screaming if needed.

So till I find that spot for them, for all of us, they need to stay with *her*. The woman who's raising my kids, providing like hell for them, giving them what they need. Not sure if she has money or had things lying around, but I get that she cares for them. They don't seem like a meal ticket to her, like some foster parents. Hell, she shot at me to protect them. Yeah, that totally had my dick springing to attention for her. Fuck, the woman is a bombshell. Anything she does has my dick looking up at her.

I'd like to think it was just because she'd been the first woman I laid eyes on in a while, but when I got back to the clubhouse after our little introduction, I grabbed the first thing walking and went to my room. It wasn't quick. Not that I didn't want to get off, but I couldn't till the woman faced away and I could close my eyes. Once I let my mind wander to the replay reel to get myself there, one look of *her*, and I was lost.

I didn't need time to realize I was fucked. I knew it as soon as I was shooting off my load into another cunt and thinking about someone else who'd threatened me just thirty minutes earlier. What really pissed me off was that I felt like I did something wrong. Like I cheated or some shit. I threw the slut out and took the longest shower ever, burning off the skin that other woman had touched. Did no good; still felt like I needed to scratch away at my skin.

Till I went over there and she called me a fucking Devils Damned. Fuck. That. I really thought that sealed her fate for me, but then, once again, surprise was on my side. She showed me Teddy, then Grace. I ain't some emotional pansy, but I felt like a fucking woman holding back my tears as I hugged them both to me. They looked just like their mama, and I missed Jennie so much. I hated that I missed out on so much of their lives. I swore it wasn't going to happen again. No matter what, I would get my shit together, find us a place, get me a steady job—hell, I'd even started looking into one of those real expensive daycares that ranked the best in the state for Grace to go to while Teddy went to an equally expensive, supersmart first grade. I had a fuck-ton to do. But I also needed to get to know them.

They've been through a lot. I had the boys check in on my family while I was away. I knew Jennie wasn't the best of parents, was gone a lot, and now I knew why. Addiction was hard as hell for someone to quit. And when they got sent to Gran's, well, she was old. She had Mom when she was young, and Mom had *us* when she was past her prime. She died when Jennie and I were kids, Pops shortly after that, and Gran was all we had left. She was old when we lived with her, and she forgot things even then. A lot. I didn't know it was that bad till the boys told me last night, after I threatened to cut off their dicks and then smash their bikes. I know they held a lot back while I was in, but now that I'm out, I need it all. The good and the bad, no matter how ugly.

Apparently Gran had dementia, forgot shit all the time. The day of the week, the house she lived in for forty years, that she even had kids, much less grandkids and great-grandkids, and even to feed them. The boys found out about that when they took a peek in one day. Guess Gran never went shopping, and the kids were eating cat food. *Cat* food. God, I really hope it was just that one time, but I have no clue.

I want to ask, but I also secretly hope they forgot about it or don't even know that's what they were eating when my guys saw them.

The club went shopping every week after that, picking things up and putting them in the house once everyone was in bed. At first, it was just everyday groceries, but once again, they realized Gran wasn't cooking anything for the kids, so they picked up things that didn't require it. Bread, Lunchables, fruits and vegetables. I doubt the kids had a home-cooked meal till Madison came along.

Madison, or Maddy. I had the boys run a check on her the minute we knew she had my kids. I didn't read beyond her name before we went out hunting for her, but I looked over it today. It isn't much, which set alarm bells off. I had no clue about her family, but she was apparently left the house she's in by an aunt. The boys' minor dig only went back to when she was eighteen; nothing before that was found on the simple check they ran.

But what they did find is a woman who's floated through towns and career choices, never seeming to stay in a place long. I can't tell if she can't find something she likes or if she's running from something—or someone.

Just another thing I need to get done.

"Kids eat early. I'll be back in a few."

"See ya, man." Bulldog chin lifts his goodbye as I walk out to my ride.

Another thing I hadn't planned on—not being able to ride my bike all the time. That was one thing I *had* dreamed about since I got sent to prison. Freedom on the open road. Not being stuck inside a fucking cage again. At least I'm in control, and the drive only takes fifteen minutes. Color me surprised when I learned how close my kids were to the compound. I doubt their foster mama knows, especially the way her face drained of color the other night when I told her I'm part of the Hounds of the Reaper MC. I ain't about to tell her. Well, not yet anyway.

Stomping up the porch, I don't even ring the bell before I walk in. The house is quiet, which freaks the fuck out of me. This house has kids in it—scarred kids, but kids nonetheless. There should be some kind of noise from them.

I double my pace as I look in each of the three bedrooms and both bathrooms. The blocked-off kitchen and garage are also empty. Last place to look is outside, and I should have tried that first. It's a breezy eighty degrees today, perfect for kids. And *her.*

The one woman I can't get off my mind, no matter how hard I try. And my eyes seek her out first of their own accord.

Fucking hell. She's on her goddamn knees doing some gardening shit, and hell, it's a fucking turn-on.

I try to pull my eyes away, but damn. She's got a little dirt on her cheek, a braid in her hair, and fuck if she isn't what I'll use as spank bank material later. Her purple tank rides up a bit as she leans forward to pull a weed, and I see a bit of her back dimples. Her shorts are low, and when I say short, I mean mini. Fuck, it's more like what the vamps wear to get a guy to fuck them at the club, but she must use them as her gardening ones. I can see the fray all around them, worn from use, and man, I want to go over there and pull them down a bit to see if her ass is really the shape of a peach like it looks from here.

The kids screaming hi to me has me jumping to look at something else as Maddy glances over her shoulder at me in my periphery.

I watch, in mild fascination, as a bright smile crosses her lips before she speaks. "Right on time."

"Really? 'Cause you look like shit. And why the hell was the door unlocked?"

Her face drops like a ton of bricks.

Shit, I didn't mean to say that bit about her, but she's got me so riled up. The last thing I need is some chick thinking she can control me with a cock of the hip. That's what got me locked away in the first place. Ain't going to happen again.

"First off, I saw you drive up. And thank you so much for the compliment. So happy Teddy has a role model who can show him how to treat a woman. Get the kids inside and washed up, would you? I've got to change."

The sass she gives me just increases the size of my dick. Thank God she's too pissed at me to even notice I'm tenting in my jeans.

"Uncle James, Uncle James!"

My name tears me away from watching the swinging of Maddy's hips as she goes inside. The full-on knockdown to the dick, in the form of a little girl running full force and hugging me, does the trick it needs. Talk about a kick in the pants. Literally.

"Hey, sunshine."

Her giggle does things to my heart. "I not sunshine, I Gigi the Superhero!"

"Oh, is that right? And are you going to protect me from the big and bad?"

Her face grows completely serious. "Yes, so you no go away again."

Well, fuck! Maybe I haven't learned my lesson. This girl could look at me and I would do anything she wanted, as long as it brought a smile to her face. She has me; I'm completely gone. And if I wind up back in prison, I won't even be mad about it.

Looking up, I watch Teddy. He's slow to come to me, and I'm not sure if it's a kid thing, a scared thing, or something else. I hold his gaze, letting him know I ain't about to overlook him and I'm here now. I'm in his life for good and ain't going away. The kid just met me yesterday, so I really should cut him some slack for being cautious. Hell, I should be proud of him, and also concerned that my little Gigi just ran so willingly into someone's arms. Granted, they're mine, but I think I need to talk to her about strangers and all that shit.

"Should we call you Chains or Uncle James?" Teddy questions.

"Whatever you want, little man." I don't mind my legal name, just haven't used it in over a decade. Even before I became a prospect with the Hounds, I was always known as Chains. But I ain't about to force something like that on the kids.

"Mom called you Chains. Think I will too."

"Sounds good, but I'll answer to anything whenever you need me. Got it?" I watch him close. The kid has been through hell and needs support. Maddy's been that for him before I showed, but I'm here now.

He nods solemnly.

"Dinner's ready," Maddy calls.

The kids run in, and I take a beat, damning Jennie for leaving these sweet souls behind but also praising her for having them. She might be dead, and so is Gran, but both got me out. And now that I am, I ain't going back in. I have little ones to look after, ones who make me a pussy as I force back the sudden tears that want to break over the bow. I ain't a pussy. I don't cry and shit. But these kids make me want to.

Walking back in, I should have guessed something was up. Maddy looks far too innocent as she and the kids sit at the table, waiting for me. Then I see what's for dinner.

"What the fuck is this?"

"Dinner."

"But...."

No words. Literally no words.

"You asked for something off the menu of the last place you ate. Doubt they had this. Eat up." The large grin she gives me doesn't reach her eyes. Eyes that harden, daring me to call her out on it.

I will admit I was a dick yesterday. Okay, I've been a dick since I met her. But can anyone blame me? She's the fucking woman taking care of my kids, looking hot as fuck in everything she wears, and the woman *can* cook. Last night was amazing. Tasted like no other spaghetti I'd had before. I knew I was in trouble after taking one bite, which explained why I told her it was crap. Not sure what I expected her to do, but this was not it.

Salad. A fucking variety of salad. Even then, it still looks amazing. Pasta salad, fruit salad, potato salad, and just regular leafy salad.

She drops her smile and pointedly looks at Teddy. The little man's watching me, not taking anything till I do.

Fuck! She planned this. Even if I am new to this whole parenting thing, I know veggies are good for kids. He needs to eat them, and if I don't, he won't.

"Well played," I comment under my breath as I heap all four types of salad onto my plate.

"I know." *Now* her eyes sparkle and match her grin. It stuns me for a second, but I force myself to look at my plate and stick food in my mouth before I say anything else.

Dinner's a quiet affair, much like the night before. Not really sure what the hell to talk about with them. Gigi babbles on about the villains she took down today: a fuzzy bunny by the name of Evil Carrot Top and another called Mr. Potato Head. The kid needs some originality. Thankfully, she has me. I have originality in spades, not that I can think of a better name at the moment. Being put on the spot doesn't work out for me unless it has to deal with a woman and what position I'm putting her in.

"Thanks for dinner," I say as I pass Maddy another dish from the table to put in the sink. The kids already were excused to clean up their rooms.

"Wow, a compliment. How much did that hurt?"

I sigh at her quick response. *Wonder how long she's been practicing that one.* "Don't do that. You ain't a bitch, so don't act like one."

It cuts her smile in half, but at least it doesn't die out completely. It's clear that she likes what I said, and she isn't like the girls who hang out at the club. Nothing about her is bitchy. She disagrees with me, but that's only when she's going into mama bear territory. And no matter how many times I tell myself it isn't sexy as hell, it's a lie. Something about it has my dick taking notice and my chest getting warm.

"So... did you like it?"

Her back's to me cleaning the dishes, so she can't see me war with myself on how to put my words together. "It didn't suck."

She snorts her reply. Goddamn, even that's cute on her.

"Well, at least you didn't think it was shit."

Ouch. Guess she's still upset about last night.

Rubbing the back of my neck, I wince as I apologize—sort of. "Yeah, prison did a number on me. Sometimes I say shit without thinking. Don't take it all that hard. If it helps, I rarely give a fuck what comes out of my mouth to remember what I say anyhow."

Once again, my mouth isn't doing me any favors. The glare she turns on me should shrivel up my dick if I didn't also see pure unadulterated desire fill her eyes as she takes me in. I don't move. Call me a prick, but I like that I do that to her. Having her move from anger to lust in seconds. Getting her so overwhelmed from the peek of skin I'm showing of my V-shaped abs with my shirt pulled as I keep my hand on my neck that she's speechless.

I don't play fair; I know that. I was in prison, after all. Fair isn't a word I use anymore. Using both hands, I gather my hair up. I always had it long, but prison really brought it home for me, and even though I've been back only two days, the chicks fucking love it. They say so every damn minute I see them. And Maddy's no exception.

Hands still soaked with soap, resting in the sink, she turns her body at an odd angle to see all of me, Those beautiful moss-green eyes trace over every inch, and she watches with bated breath as I pull my hair into a bun and secure it at the top of my head. I linger a while to give her one last look of the goods before moving my arms down, my shirt covering the front of my jeans once more.

I break the spell as I smirk. Then that glare comes back. I half think it's directed at herself more than anything.

Turning back to the dishes, she focuses on scrubbing the bowls. "Well, you need to start remembering. I can get over shit, been doing it all my life. But those kids in the other room need someone who will think before they act. One who will remember and care about what they say. Words hurt just as much as anything."

Fuck, why does she have to make so much sense all the time? And why can't I stop being such an asshole to her?

"Noted." I need to get out of here. The itch to grab her ass and grind into it is getting too strong. Does she know she wiggles it a bit when she washes each dish? Is she doing it on purpose? Fuck, life isn't fair. The one woman who gets my dick hard in years, and I can't have her. "I'll see you tomorrow."

"About that...."

"What?" My glare goes unnoticed with her back still turned.

"You sure you want to do this every night? You just got back. Maybe you would prefer to spend time with your friends. We can do dinner every other night, or even two or three times a week." She squeaks the last bit, making me tilt my head a bit to see her profile. One that's an adorable shade of pink as she pretends to not see me notice her blush.

"Ain't happening. As much as I hate them not being with me, you had a point."

This gets her attention. Turning off the faucet and grabbing the towel to dry her hands, she turns to face me, surprise clear in her wide eyes.

"Kids need stability," I continue. "Till I can get that for them, they can get that from you. But they are family, and I've missed too much already. I have no clue how to do the parent thing, but I'll figure it out. Even if we move in together, there will be a learning curve, but this way, we can learn who we are together without stepping into each other's space."

"Wow, that's actually pretty smart." Shock fills her voice.

"Ain't just brawn, baby. I got the brain parts too. I'm the whole fucking package." I make a point to flex as I point to my head.

She rolls her eyes but does so with a smile.

"Fine, dinner nightly. Any requests?"

"All for kids eating their veggies, but they're growing too. Next time, some meat wouldn't be out of the question, would it?"

Nodding, she puts her hands behind her, resting them on the sink. She did it for comfort, I'm sure, but fuck, if I don't notice it pushes her tits out, alerting me that they would fit well in each hand. "I can do that. Not a fan of going without meat for long myself. I'll stay away from spaghetti, though. Anything else you had too much of at your last place that you want off the foreseeable menu?"

Fuck, she's going to make me say it. I hate when chicks do this. Get all sweet and shit and make me want to be just as nice back. Maybe not nice, but at least tell the truth.

"Nope, nothing is off the menu, to include your spaghetti."

Her eyebrows dart to the middle of her forehead in question. I want to pull her toward me so badly and smooth the wrinkles there with my lips.

"Everything you make tastes a million times better than what I had in the past, even before prison. Everything." I don't look away till I see the realization on her face.

Yeah, *that's* my apology.

Chapter 4 – Chains

Three weeks later

"**W**here the fuck are they?"

"I don't know, man. I've checked every hospital I can find, and they ain't signed in anywhere. Her phone's off, so I can't get her location, and her truck is so old there's no tracking system in it. Are you sure she didn't tell you they were going to be out for a bit or something? I mean, it's been less than an hour. Maybe they're just late or some shit."

Flint needs to shut the fuck up right now. I'm not losing my mind. They didn't go someplace and forget to tell me. Even though I made that crack weeks ago about not remembering what's coming out of my mouth, I remember what I hear. And I ain't heard nothing about this. They're just gone.

We've been having dinner every night since I got out. I show up right at six, we eat, and then I leave. That's never changed. But now it's four minutes to seven, and they still ain't here. I've walked around the place, even broke in after the first time I called Flint to find her. Nothing seems amiss, but they scattered things about like they rushed out of here a few hours ago. There's coffee still in a cup. That's my sign that something's off. Maddy never leaves a cup unfinished. Never.

The rumble of a truck on gravel has my head coming up.

"That them?"

The growl penetrating my voice is all Flint gets as a confirmation.

"Good. Tell that woman of yours to turn her phone on."

"Ain't my woman, and I will. I want a full mockup of her place with surveillance. I'll go over it with you when I get back."

"Roger that."

I hang up but keep my movements slow. I don't need to break my phone because I'm pissed. The fuckers got expensive since last I had one; ain't about to buy another one soon.

I stay on the porch as I watch Maddy pull in. Her face looks grim, but I'm not sure if it's because of the day she had or seeing me, arms crossed and mad as hell. She pulls parallel to my truck, and soon all I can see is Grace waving with glee from the back seat.

I have no fucking idea how to get her out of that damn car seat, and I really don't want to yell at Maddy with the kids present, so I still my movements. That's till both Maddy and Teddy round the bed of the truck, Teddy heading into the house and Maddy to get Grace out. Then I lose it.

"What the fuck is this? What the fuck happened?"

"Hey, Uncle Chains." He's so defeated, but I would be too if I had a splint on my arm.

"Jesus, what happened, little man?"

"Broke my wrist," he huffs as he climbs the stairs.

"It's nothing. Just a hairline fracture at the radius. They said it would heal in a few weeks after the cast gets put on. Nothing to it, right, Teddy?" Maddy chimes in as she lifts Grace down.

Teddy nods but says nothing.

Grace bounces up, pulling my arm until I'm bent over, then grabs my face and kisses my cheek. "We got pizza!"

I look up, seeing Maddy holding a gigantic box as she ascends the stairs, and realize my calm side is completely gone.

"Teddy, go inside with Grace and watch some cartoons, would you? I want to have a talk with Maddy."

I don't take my eyes off Maddy as I hear the kids opening the door and going inside. It's still unlocked from when I was looking at things.

I want to see everything. Every emotion on her face, her entire body language. I need to see if she's about to lie to me, but all I get is a pale face.

"You broke into my house."

"Yes."

"You can't do that. It's against the law."

"I did, Mama Bear, so get over it. What I want to know is why the fuck didn't you call me?"

"Call you?"

"Don't act dumb. Yeah, call me. Teddy got hurt. His arm is fucking broken, and I got nothing from you. Not one goddamn call or text. I tried to call you, but you turned your fucking phone off. Listen, lady, those are my kids. *Mine!* You playing house with them is only temporary. You ain't keeping them, and you sure as hell ain't keeping me locked out of their lives. I should have been told immediately, not after the fact. Hell, you even stopped for fucking pizza. What kind of bitch are you?"

I watch her stand there, stock-still, as I lay into her. Her jaw's open for most of it till the last part, which forces her to shut it as the glare she usually has for me returns.

"You really want to do this?" She grits out between clenched teeth.

"Yeah, I sure as hell do."

Shaking her head, she tunnels past me. The screen door closes, but the main one's ajar. I watch from outside as she puts the pizza on her coffee table, tells the kids to eat, then comes back out, shutting the door as she exits.

"First, I already told you not to call me a bitch. Second, the pizza was for you."

"What the fuck is that supposed to mean?"

"Exactly as you heard it. You come for food, so I brought you food. If you don't want to eat it, fine by me."

"I don't come for the food."

"Really? 'Cause you could have fooled me. You get here right at dinnertime, eat, barely talk to the kids, and then you're gone, and the rest of us have to do all the cooking and cleaning."

"That what this is about? You want someone to help you fucking pick up?"

She rubs her hands on her face, and I see the red splotches from the amount of force she uses as she pulls them away. "Jesus, you aren't listening. You claim you want to get to know these kids, but you don't know shit about them. You think showing up for dinner and staying for less than an hour is being there for them? You say you want to get to know them, but other than knowing that Teddy likes green beans and Grace likes corn, do you know anything else about them?"

"Don't put this shit on me. If you want me here more, just say it. Hell, pick up the phone and call me. You obviously don't want me here, so I keep away from you 'cause the kids need a happy home, not the shit that happens when we get in the same room together."

"I never said that." Her hands move faster than her mouth as she gestures at me and then herself. "If you want to be around them more, then do it. I'm a grown woman. I can deal with shit, including you showing up for hours at a time, if I have to. I can even play the perfect cheerful hostess."

"Really? Then why not call? Why not call me when you need help? Or when you think the kids would like to see me? I ain't no mind reader. How the hell am I supposed to know this shit?" I flex my hands, just now realizing that I've been gripping them so tight to avoid strangling her.

"'Cause that's what parents do. If you want to be one, you need to realize they come first, always. You're tired at work? Too damn bad, because you got kids now. You don't get to go drink with your buddies. You stay and watch the kids and maybe have a beer, not seven, while watching a silly cartoon. Or you play dress-up and have to deal with making weird noises all day on repeat 'cause it makes them smile. I shouldn't have to tell you to spend time with them. You should want to. If you don't, then let's cut this off now. You and I both know Jennie didn't give them a ton, and I'm trying to make up the lost ground that's been handed to me. They need to feel wanted, and right now, you being here for thirty minutes a day just shows them you're reliable for only those thirty minutes. So congratu-fucking-lations. You're Uncle of the Year!"

I open my mouth to lay into her more when she stops me by holding a hand up.

"And another thing. I would have called you. I would have called you every time Teddy runs into my room with a nightmare. Every time Grace asks where her mommy is. You would have been the first phone call once Teddy fell off the swing and started crying. But I can't call you. I don't have your number."

I roll my eyes at that. "Yeah you do."

"No, asshole, I don't." Her hands move to her hips to emphasize the point. "You never gave it to me. I know I sure as hell didn't give you *my* number, so it's weird you know my phone lost power and shut off after we were waiting in the emergency room for over an hour because I had the kids playing games on it to keep them entertained while we waited. And that says it right there. This isn't working. Every time I attempt to have a normal conversation with you, even ask for your phone number, you open your dumb mouth, say something shitty like 'You look horrible' or 'the food sucks' or whatever, and I shut down and forget to ask. But you never gave it out, asshole. So as much as you want to blame me for not calling, blame your own fucking self for not giving me the chance to keep you in the loop. Now, your thirty minutes are up. Go home."

I'm stunned. The woman has stunned me. I grasp on to the last bit she said and focus only on that, 'cause the rest is too much for me to fucking deal with right now.

"What about dinner with the kids?"

"Kids are probably done with theirs. You'll have to get yours on your own. I ain't your maid, no matter that you treat me like one."

I stomp off, pissed as hell. "What a...."

"What?"

I turn around, wondering why the hell she's still outside and not inside like I thought. "Huh?"

"What were you going to say? What a... bitch? Cunt? Pain in your ass?" She steps forward as if she's going to come off her porch. "I want to know what you were going to say. What am I to you? 'Cause I know what I see. I see a woman who had no plans to take care of two kids six months ago, but as soon as she saw them, she dropped everything and did what was needed. Not for her but for them. I see a woman who's struggling to do a job that most people prepare for and one I was thrown right into without a lifeboat or anyone I can rely on to help me when things like today happen. I see a woman who's scared shitless that one wrong thing will send Teddy into an internal spiral where his count of speaking words to others will go from a hundred to zero. Not sure if you saw he doesn't say much. Been like that since before you came. He doesn't talk, like he's afraid he'll get cut down or something and just avoids it altogether unless he's protecting Grace.

"And Grace, that girl could have the world burning down around her, and it has, and she still shines on. But I have no idea how much more crap can be thrown at her before she just gives up like the rest of us and lets that part die inside.

"I also see a woman who doesn't call social services, hell, even the cops, when their uncle shows up and threatens, on numerous occasions, to take them away no matter what the courts says. A man who just waltzes in and demands to be fed the best of the best but doesn't lift a finger to provide for it. And through it all, this woman rolls with it. Not 'cause she wants to, not 'cause she can't possibly think that a guy who's been in prison for five years can't be dangerous at all. I have no reason to think you're even safe to have around children, that you won't attack us if you're provoked. I know nothing about you. But guess what? I'm trusting you. For them. So before you go on a rant about how I'm such an inconvenience to have around, realize I ain't here for you. I'm here for *them*. And I will continue to be here for them and do what they need so they don't have to worry about it."

Time beats away as we stare at each other. I have nothing to say. She gave me too much to think about, things that make me pissed off that I didn't think about before, and I'm still too pissed about Teddy's arm to focus on any one thing.

She gives up waiting for me to talk and walks back inside.

I get in my truck, but it's not the same. I need to think, and this cage isn't doing shit for me.

Driving toward the club, I pull in next to my baby. Don't even say hi to the guys as I hop from one motor to the other and head out of the gate that's still open from when I pulled in.

Two hours of driving around did shit for me. I thought I would see clarity, find the peace I was looking for and the answers I needed. I found the peace, just not the answers. No, the bike gave me what it always did   freedom to escape. My brain was zen'd out, and nothing mattered but me and the bike. I should have known no answers would be on the road. There never are. The bike, she only gives me the reprieve to feel free till it's over.

Which is why I'm looking for the answers at the bottom of the bottle next to me. It isn't helping either.

"Come on, baby. Let me put a smile on your face."

"Told you to get lost, Christy."

The vamp huffs but doesn't get the fucking clue to leave me the hell alone. "But why? We're good together. I know you don't get with the other girls. Just me. Look."

She leans in and gets too close for my liking. She got too close about five minutes ago, but now she's really agitating me. I've never laid a hand on a woman in anger, but this bitch is about to get strong-armed away if she doesn't back the fuck up soon.

"I know it's been a while for you, and maybe you have a few things going on, but hey, I'm willing to try anything. Whatever you need, baby, to get you there."

No. She. Didn't.

"What the fuck did you just say?" I stand up from my seat, and the bitch gets that she messed up. Big. "Do you really think that 'cause I ain't sticking my dick in you, it's because I can't get it up? Ever think I had you and it wasn't that good? Huh? Maybe I'm looking for something a little tighter than that flabby shit you got between your stems. I did you. Now move the fuck on, bitch. I said get lost, so *get lost*. My dick works fucking fine for something I'm interested in. And it ain't you, so get gone."

I don't care that she stumbles away, on the cusp of crying, before I turn back to my drink. The vamp will find a willing brother to fill her hole, but it ain't me. Doing her after I got out was a mistake. Not 'cause I was thinking of Maddy the whole time, but I knew Christy before I was locked away. She's a needy bitch, and using her for that first time went to her head. But she was closest. Biggest mistake I made since getting out. I've tried to stay away, been polite about it, but she needs a wake-up call. It ain't going to happen again.

Ever.

"You look like a man on a mission."

I grunt as Bulldog takes the barstool next to me and eyeballs my bottle as he grabs a glass from the other side of the bar before pouring himself a very generous amount of *my* whiskey.

"Start talking."

I want to argue. I really do. I want to rave and scream that it ain't his place. But he's the VP. And as much as I think I can do this on my own, one thought has become clear. I need the club. Even if it's just to have my back, I need them. If there is a custody battle, they'll need to be in on it. Not that I think for a second that Maddy would ever deny me my niece and nephew, but she really doesn't have a say. The court is the one that decides, and with my record of assault charges, it won't be a cakewalk to get them. No matter if I'm the only living relative they have. Besides, unlike the rest of the fuckers in here, except Prez, Bulldog has a kid. He'll at least get half of what I'm going through.

"Teddy's arm's broken."

"What the fuck?"

I can't hide the smile on my lips. Goddamn, I love my club. Every member gets pissed at the same things for the same reasons. We all have one another's backs. "Yeah, apparently he fell off a swing or some shit."

"He okay?"

I shrug. "Don't know. I think so."

"What do you mean, you don't know? What did the doc say?"

I hang my head in shame and give it a little shake. "Wasn't there."

"Come again?"

"Maddy never called and told me. Only found out about it after the fact."

"That bitch needs to include you in shit like this."

This time I wince. "Apparently she doesn't have my number."

"Come the fuck again?"

"Stop saying that. You sound too fucking proper for your own good."

"I'll stop saying it when you start talking. You've been out for about a month. You basically have a baby mama, and she doesn't have your number for emergencies? Shit, what the hell do you guys talk about when you go over there every night?"

I rub my face, knowing once I say this out loud, I'm going to sound like the biggest ass ever. And maybe I am, but shit, I didn't even think about half this shit till Maddy brought it up. Which makes me an even bigger ass for not thinking it was a problem till now.

"I never gave her my number. Didn't even think about it. Had Flint program hers into mine, but I've never called her before. Hell, I can't even remember asking for it from her. Just told Flint I needed to track her, and bam, her number was in my phone, and that's it. We don't talk, not much. I show up for dinner, we eat, and I leave. Not much time to do the whole 'How was your day?' speech when kids are clamoring for your attention."

Okay, they never are begging for my attention, but Grace is a talker, and Teddy usually pipes up a few times, enough for me not to even notice that he doesn't talk unless his sister pulls him out of it or I say something to him.

Shit, I *am* a fucking ass.

"That it?"

"What you mean?"

"You go for a meal and that's it? Hell, even if your girl had your number, I doubt she would have called when the kid got hurt."

"What the fuck?"

"Calm your undies before they get all twisted and answer me this. Why the fuck do we have weekend riders?"

I grunt. "'Cause they're pussies. They play at being one of us. Never will be with only doing it a few times a month or a year."

"Exactly. You, sir, you're a weekend uncle."

"I'm there every fucking day!" I yell, shocked that my brother would ever compare me to those weekend pussies. It was a poor-ass excuse, but I don't like being told I did something wrong.

"No, you're there for food every day. You ever bought them a gift? Ever just sit and watch them play and see how their little minds work? Ever been pulled out of bed at three in the morning to a screaming kid who's having a nightmare? Puked on? Peed on? Have you lost your temper or had a yelling match with a toddler? Got to say, that happens all the time, and you haven't lived till you argue with a kid about a teddy bear at midnight and lose the match 'cause you're so dog-ass tired from taking care of them all day since they have zero off button."

I blink once. Twice. Nothing like a brother to drive it home. Maddy may have spelled it out, but Bulldog put it in words that sent my system into overdrive for how badly I'm fucking up.

"Fuck!" I bang my head on the table, half conscious to do it away from my drink. "I'm an idiot."

"Ha, nothing new." He slaps me hard on the back, and I grunt through it before I lift my head and see him pour another glass for himself.

"But now that you know, you can pull your head out of your ass and fix it. Trust me, I make a million poor decisions with my little princess, but I'm still around, and so is she. Kids are resilient. You can fuck up for days, then have a great day, and they remember that over the bad. But from what you already told me, they've had more than a few bad days already. And I'm not just talking about when you walked into their lives. They need more good than not. You might fuck this up, but what about the woman, Maddy? She good for them?"

"Yeah, man, she really is. Dropped everything the moment she saw them, she says. Got no reason to doubt that. I might hate the fact that she has them, but there's no denying the love she has for them. Would claim them as her own if she could, I know."

"Then what the fuck is the problem? She sounds like one awesome bitch. Pretty hot from what I remember and the way the guys speak about her when you got back that first night." He grabs me before I even make a move to stand, already knowing what I'm thinking. "Easy, no one's claiming her. But the way you just about took off my head makes me think you want to. Got something for the baby mama?"

"Mama Bear," I grind out as I lean over the bar again, not looking at him

"What?"

I pass him a glance. "It's Mama Bear, not baby mama." I finish the bottle with a deep gulp.

"Oh shit. Already got her a biker chick name? You're screwed."

He might laugh at me, but I'm huffing at the fucked-up nature of it all. "Tell me about it. If it wasn't complicated enough, I can only get hard when thinking about her."

"Shit, man, we ain't women. I don't need to hear that shit." He takes a moment to sip at his drink, and I glance at it longingly, wanting more but knowing I've had enough. "But I get it. That can fuck with a guy's mind. Maybe you need to take a step back and see what it is about her that's got you all mixed up."

I shake my head in denial. "Don't need to think about, I know. Her braid."

"Her what?"

"She wears her hair in a braid all the fucking time. It hangs over her shoulder, and after a long day of doing whatever the fuck she does, little pieces frame her face that I can't stop looking at. Which pisses me off 'cause she makes me fucking flustered, and then I usually end of saying shit which is not what I mean. So, of course, I come off like a jackass."

He nods but looks off in the distance, as if a memory has caught his attention more than me. "Had that once. Cherry lip gloss. To this day, I smell that cheap shit and it gets me rock hard."

I hesitate to ask, but I got to know, hoping there's a simple solution to all of this. "You ever think if you just get one of the vamps to wear it around here, it would get that chick out of your system?"

He shakes his head but is still staring off in the distance, not seeing anything. I know it's a memory floating around in his head. "Nah, man, that shit's sacred. That woman was one of a kind. Not about to drag her memory down with the sluts around here."

"What happened to her?"

"Don't know. Summer ended, and she went home with her family."

"The fuck? You chasing jailbait now, man?"

"Nope. I was seventeen. Best summer of my life. We knew what it was, no promises to each other after it ended. But man, if I don't think about her every now and again."

"Seems like a long time to remember something."

"Like I said, best summer of my life. Moments like that don't just go away with time. When a woman can get you forgetting yourself over something as simple as what she sees as an everyday thing, it's got your boys knocking at you to fuck it out of your system, but you know it'll never happen, so you stay away. That's one hell of a woman."

"Yeah, one hell of a woman."

"If I had her again, I wouldn't let her get away."

I look at my hands as I whisper, "What the fuck should I do?" I'm at a loss.

"Fuck if I know. I complicate my life enough as it is without trying to solve your shit. But I would start with the kids. Figure that shit out first before you focus on the woman. Kids always come first. That's one thing you need to get and one thing I can guarantee. This chick might be the one, but if you fuck it up, you won't be able to walk away, not as long as she has the system on her side. If she's something you want, that you really want, make sure the kids aren't a factor. Be at a place that they come first, and then, if it's meant to be, then shit, you'll finally be able to know how that braid feels wrapped in your hand, if you catch my drift."

I shift on my stool. Yeah, I got his drift. Big fucking hell yeah, I did. I thought about it more often than not. Wanting to know if I was able to wrap the strands in my fist once or twice. Would I do it during our first kiss? When I take her from behind? Or when I finally have her on her fucking knees and she's begging for my cock?

So many possibilities with that hairstyle. So many.

Chapter 5 – Maddy

Yesterday sucked, on several levels. Teddy and his arm was the main reason. I was a total basket case, not knowing what to do until Grace started screaming that we needed to go to the doctor. Hate to admit it, but I didn't even think about that till she said so. What kind of foster mom am I? I totally suck at this.

At least I got him seen with only minor questions. The last thing they, or I, need is to raise flags. Izzy's many things, to include amazing. She was able to get the kids under my alias, and no one even looked twice at our insurance card. Hiding by myself is one thing. Hiding with kids make things complicated, but Izzy didn't let me down. Hell, she never let anyone down, ever. That's just how badass she is. I need to call her and give her a heads-up, but coffee comes first.

After getting home last night, I knew it was inevitable that Chains would be here waiting and that we would fight. We rarely speak, and when we do, he's usually insulting me. He's a dick. One that makes my lady bits want him a hundred percent of the time, but my head knows it's just the hotness factor. I mean, the guy's ripped. Muscles in all the right places. And his arms? I'm a complete bicep girl. The idea of being wrapped up in them while I sleep, caging me in as I do the dishes? Hell, having them bulge as he holds me against the wall to fuck me? Yeah, I'm a shameful slut with all the wicked ideas I have about Chains. We might not get along, but damn, he's pretty to look at and fantasize about.

I replay the night's conversation in my head for the fifteen millionth time. It happens every night since he came into our lives; it's the only time I allow myself to just let go and think up completely impossible scenarios about us that end in happily ever after moments. Or ones that just end with a smile on my face. But last night, I was freaking out that maybe I pushed too hard. Maybe instead of telling him all that shit to show him ways to be better at being involved with the kids, he saw it as too much work. What if he isn't going to show up anymore? It would devastate the kids, and it would completely be my fault.

Story of my fucking life.

A knock at the door has me cursing myself for not charging my phone the night before. It's still at the bottom of my purse, probably covered in fruit snacks, as Grace went through at least ten mini bags while we waited at the hospital.

Before six months ago, I used a cell phone as a paperweight in my house more than anything. I wasn't a popular person. No one called me but a select few, and they knew that, more times than not, I would forget where it was. They accepted that about me, or at least they got over it.

But now that I have the kids, I really need to charge it. More so for when emergencies happen, so I can call someone if needed. I don't like the police, but if I have to, and I really have no other options, then I would call. Which is why I have the cameras set up around the property. Aunt Jan had them when I was a kid, so it was more like I just turned them back on and had the service updated to alert me on my phone when the motion sensors are triggered, as opposed to the alarm chirping inside the house like when I grew up here. But with the way I keep forgetting to have my phone on me, much less charged, maybe going back to the chirping would be better than me walking toward the door with trepidation to peek through the peephole.

Not that I have any reason for anyone to cause a problem. No one knows I'm here. At least, I don't think so. The will that left me Aunt Jan's house was so encrypted, it looked like they left it to the bank and some random person bought it to fix up. The lawyer got everything signed off with the alias I've been using for the last few years.

Checking the peephole, I tremble for every reason *but* fear. Just the sight of him has me weak at the knees and my hoo-ha screaming for him. I really need to get a grip. Or just get laid. Actually, a new battery-operated toy might be best. No need to bring a man into the kids' lives when I only plan to use him in the bedroom to work out a few things.

Pulling open the door, I push open the screen and step out. I don't close the main door, but I'm not letting Chains inside if he's only here to yell at me again. The kids don't need to see that.

"What are you doing here?"

"Man, Teddy was right. You really aren't a morning person."

I just glare 'cause there's no way I'm giving him the satisfaction of being right. He can guess it and I won't deny it, but no way in hell will I voice it.

He chuckles, and his smooth voice does something that only the third cup of caffeine ever does—it pulls a sigh from my lips.

"Easy, Mama Bear. I actually came here to apologize. Don't want another fight. I want a truce."

I cock an eyebrow. Or I think I do. I'm sure I just look odd. Never was very good at doing it the right way like they do in the movies.

We stare at each other for what feels like an uncomfortable amount of time, but maybe I'm just the one feeling uncomfortable. Chains, like always, doesn't look the least put out as he continues to stare at me.

"Well?"

"Well, what?"

"Apologize!" I flare my arms out, and I'm definitely looking on this side of crazy now.

Jesus, it's like pulling teeth. He's worse than the kids.

"Oh, right. Sorry." He smiles sheepishly as he rubs the back of his head and looks down. It shouldn't be cute, but of course it is. "Look, I did some thinking, even had one of the guys talk to me about it. I get it. I've done shit, and that ain't what I want. Don't know how to do this sort of thing. I always wanted to be part of their lives, but I always figured Jennie would still be around and be able to walk me through things that didn't make sense. I never wanted to be a dad but thought a cool uncle was something I could work with. But now she's gone. I'm still trying to get my feet under me after being locked up, and, well, I honestly never thought that if the worst happened, I would have to deal with, well, um...."

"Me." No use in denying it. I'm the *X* factor in all of this.

"Yeah. Like I said, sorry."

Okay, so the rant was completely adorable. Seeing him all flustered does something to my heart. I just want to hold him and say, "Good job," but I'm not his mom. The last thing I want to be is related to him. I have too many kinky ideas floating around in my head for that to be legal in any state.

"I'm sorry too. You needed to hear what I said yesterday to get your head out of your ass, but maybe I could have broached the subject better. Or hell, talked about it with you from the start and not let it fester. I tend to do that."

"You wouldn't be a woman if you didn't." Chuckling, he quickly adds, "No offense."

"Offense taken." I don't even last a full ten seconds with a stern face before breaking into a fit of giggles that he joins in on. Our shared laughter destroys whatever tension is between us. "So, why are you here? Thought you said you work on Friday mornings."

"You remember that?" His eyes are sharp on my face as a hidden smile plays across his lips.

Shit, I'm blushing now. I want to throw out a comment like "Of course I remember that. I need to know where the kids' uncle is," but it's really because I'm becoming borderline obsessed with him and remember everything he says. Even if he said it sixteen days, seven hours, and twelve minutes ago in a passing comment to Teddy, when I was meant to be out of the room.

Yeah, I have it bad for this guy.

"Right, well, I took the morning off. Figured we could hang out. I mean, if that's okay with you. Thought I could start making up for the time I lost out on."

I tilt my head, making sure he understands it doesn't work like that. "One day isn't going to make it all better, you know."

"Yeah, I plan to change up the schedule starting next week. I want to make this right for everyone. Figure we could plan for more time together. Not just dinners, maybe even a few sleepovers type of shit."

"You got a place?" I'm quick with the question. Panic runs through me so fast I have to unlock my knees in case I pass out. I'm not ready for them to leave. For *any* of them to leave.

"Nah, not yet, but I got a few friends who have the space and would offer it to me to bring the kids around so we could get accustomed to each other."

My panic rescinds a bit, but not completely. I keep forgetting that this is just temporary, that it can all be gone as quick as it started. I bite my lip to keep my emotions from showing as I mumble, "Yeah, I think they would like that."

His smile really should be illegal with the way he's flashing it so freely right now. And wow, I had no idea he had such pretty teeth! His grin is wider than I've ever seen on a grown man before. Maybe more appropriate for a kid getting a new toy.

"Good, maybe we can plan for something or some shit like that. I really am trying to work this out, but I got to admit"—his snicker at his own lack of knowledge is somewhat charming—"it's like learning how to walk. I'm going to struggle in a few places. Going to need you to let me know when I'm screwing up, as I tend not to notice, if you haven't figured that out yet."

I really am not trying to read too much into things, but I swear the heat level coming off him went up ten notches as he stared me down for that last part. All those "yous" rolling off his tongue have me thinking that even if he has a place to go tomorrow, I won't be left out in the cold.

"Ha, yeah, don't worry. I'll call you out on your shit." I'm light-headed from reading too much into his words, and my voice sounds too high even to my ears.

Does he notice I'm freaking out a bit?

"I have no doubt you won't."

Wow, okay, I totally didn't misread that. His voice drops so low as he steps into my personal bubble, and I almost bite my tongue off to keep it from rolling out of my mouth and panting like a dog in heat.

"What if I did?" *I totally just squeaked that.*

His grin is megawatt again, followed by multiple eyebrow raises. "I would bribe you."

My libido can only take so much hotness rolling off this guy. I'm seconds away from jumping his bones, and that's probably not the best move for me right now.

"Really? For not calling bullshit when needed?"

"That or if you didn't accept my apology and let me in the house." He shrugs as he leans back enough for me to see the bags behind him.

Yay, me. I love treats.

"Ooh, well, now you got me curious. What do you plan to give me?"

"Not just you. The kids too."

Ahhh, so sweet.

"Wow, pulling out all the stops, are we?"

"What can I say? When I see I fucked up, I try to make up for it quickly and efficiently. Besides, I get that you ain't like the usual bitches—I mean chicks I hang out with. But I doubt you would turn down free shit."

"Depends on the shit."

"Let me in, woman, and you'll find out." His growl isn't half as bad as yesterday. He's still sending my lady bits into a frenzy, but at least he's doing it with a smile.

My own smile crosses my lips as I open the door, letting him pass. Bags of tricks included.

"Nice outfit, by the way."

Wait, what? Oh shit!

I look down and freeze. Why the hell didn't I notice what I was wearing till now? And why couldn't he have just let me live in la-la land and be oblivious. But no. No matter that he was all sweet and apologizing seconds ago, Chains is a bona-fide jerk. 'Cause only a jerk would point out that I'm still in my pj's. Pj's that might be appropriate for being around toddlers who don't notice certain things, but definitely not for said toddlers' uncle. Because he doesn't miss *anything*. Not one bit. Like the fact that my shorts are shorter than appropriate and hug me in areas that leave nothing to the imagination. Or that my tank, while not see-through as it's light gray, doesn't hide the curve of my breasts or my hard nipples peeking out.

Talk about saying good morning, because even if I'm not saying it, I'm pretty sure my girls are.

I grab a sweater off the back of the chair and put it on before noticing what he pulls out of his bag. "You bought me a phone?"

"Yeah, well, you said you didn't have my number."

I'm sure his shrug is meant for me to see the obvious here, but I'm not. "Um, so just give me your number."

"See, the thing is, I have a lot of numbers. I wanted you to have my cell, the club, and the shop. As well as a few key members in the club, in case you can't reach me there." He doesn't even look at me as he talks. I'm not sure if it's just complete bullshit or if he really believes what he's saying. "Besides, I tried calling your phone this morning to let you know I wanted to stop by early. It's still not on."

He doesn't see me watch him as I remark offhandedly, "Yeah, I know. I'm horrible at charging it."

"That's the other beauty about this one. Charges in half the time, and the battery life is double yours." His megawatt smile is back as he glances at me for the first time since we started this little dance.

"It's also twice as big as anything in my purse, so I doubt I'll lose it." Not that I'm complaining about the size. God only knows how many things I lose in my bag.

"That too."

"And that you can track this one, even if it's off, isn't half bad either, huh?"

It's cute how his eyes get bigger, and he just stares at me. Does he really think I'm that big of an idiot and don't know things like this? No way would a guy fork over a few grand on a phone for a girl, even if she's watching his kids, unless he planned to make sure it stayed safe. Now to see if the big man will admit to it or pussy out. I'm sure my smug grin at reading through his bullshit of "I have a lot of numbers to plug into it" isn't helping him come up with a better lie.

"Yeah, that too."

He says nothing else, just holds my eyes over the kids, who are going bonkers for their own gifts. Teddy got a new Lego set. A motorcycle, of course. Got to admit, if Chains wants him to get over his fear, this might help. And Gigi's a mess with excitement over her new costumes, and thankfully there's a variety. Ever since the emergency room visit, Superhero Gigi is out and Doc Gigi is in. At least she kept the name.

"Thanks."

My reply clearly surprises him, but he tries hard not to show it. Ten to one, he was expecting me to throw another fit. And maybe I should, but come on. It's the nicest phone I've ever had. I don't care if he can track me. I'm always with the kids, and if he needs to know they're safe, well, that's fine by me.

I said I knew nothing about him when I yelled at him the night before, but that isn't true. I know he's determined, pigheaded, and has love at the center of everything he does. He didn't need to come and claim his sister's kids, but he did. He didn't need to have dinner with them every night, but he does. We're still working out what all he needs to do, but the base of it's there, the heart of the matter. And that's what I see and trust.

"So, what's the plan for today?"

I think he's asking me, but I'm not quick enough to answer, and Grace beats me to it.

"Oh, can we go to the zoo?"

I sigh inwardly. "Gigi, honey, we went to the zoo last week." And it was an exhausting trip. I thought it would have gotten rid of some energy. Boy, was I wrong. Doubled it when we got back. Nap time didn't even happen that day for our little doctor.

"That's the small one. She wants to go to the one we saw on TV." I'm shocked Teddy is even paying attention with the amount of focus he has on his latest Lego.

"Which one is that, little man?" Chains asks.

I'm already exhausted mentally, 'cause I know exactly which one they're talking about. If the small one caused twice the excitement, I don't even want to know what the one double in size and animals would do to them.

"If it's the Kansas City one. Sorry, kids, that's too far." Far because there is zero way I have the patience to last in the car there and back plus the two- to three-hour walk around. I love these kids, I really do. But they have *no* off buttons. I swear they siphon my energy into their souls. Why else am I so tired and they never are?

"No it's not."

I don't fake my surprise at his response. Does he know how long a drive it is? "That's over two hours, one way."

He nods. *Typical.*

I move away from the table, grab my cup and his hand, and head toward the coffee maker. Damn, his hands are large and warm and as strong as can be.

"Have you ever done a long trip, or anything over ten minutes in a car, with a three-year-old? They get restless. Even Teddy will. Especially with his arm wrapped up." I try to keep my whisper low, but I have to talk over the sound of the delicious brewing of a fresh cup of coffee.

"Been meaning to ask, when does he get it cast?"

I glance at him as I pour my sugar and cream. "Um, tomorrow, midmorning."

"Okay. I want to go with y'all."

I have to stop stirring my coffee to digest what he just said. "Um, sure." He wants to spend time with us two mornings in a row? Okay, this guy is really not the same Chains who left last night.

I hear his deep chuckle over the last tapping of my spoon on the side of my mug. I don't turn around, but goose bumps rise up my arms and my breath hitches as I feel him at my back and see both hands grab the counter, boxing me in.

"Relax, Mama Bear, I just want to be there and talk to the doc so I know how bad it is. Not saying you didn't tell me, but I want to make sure our Teddy gets the best treatment. I've broken my arm a few times before, so I know what I'm talking about. I might not have experienced a long trip with kids before, but if you give me half an hour and the keys to your truck, I can make sure we all have a great time. Going and coming back."

Did he just purr those last words?

"You want keys... to my truck?" I look over my shoulder. Damn, he's close, but still far enough for me to see his entire face and not just focus on his lips. His plump lips that are parted slightly. "My baby? The one thing I've been able to rely on for the last five years?"

"Yeah, Mama Bear, I really do." His raspy voice has me thinking he and I are talking about two different topics right now. "Hand them over. Trust me, I know what I'm doing, and I promise not to break her. I'll treat her just like my girl. Won't even get a scratch on her."

Yeah, my girl bits are having a seizure. *What did he say about treating right and scratches?* My head is in the gutter as I try to grasp what he said in full sentences. And in the order he said it.

My head rears back and my eyes pop out as my mind replays it at half speed. "You have a girlfriend?"

Of course he has one, silly. The man is a freaking sex god walking. He probably has a dozen, or even a couple dozen, one for every hour. So you can stop with all the fantasizing about him. He is taken. Taken!

His chuckle and shake of his head are not clearing things up for me. "Don't have an old lady, just my girl. My Harley."

"What's an old woman got to do with anything?" I am so confused and not nearly caffeinated enough for this conversation.

"Fuck, you're cute. Old lady, babe. It means girlfriend but in biker terms, and it usually means a serious one at that. I don't have one of those, and before you ask, I ain't got a nonserious girlfriend or anything else either. I'm free, in every sense of the word."

Yeah, I'm back to seizures again. Only this time, not only is my hoo-ha convulsing, but my damn heart is about to beat out of my chest. He said it so matter-of-factly, but the way his eyes are boring into me, I feel like he's letting me know it's a big thing. Like he needs me to know how unattached he is.

And ladies, before you ask, I can already tell you there is nothing wrong with the man. Nothing. Sure, he went to prison. Sure, he's in a motorcycle club that might be or might not be dangerous as hell. But if you saw his ass in jeans as he walks away, you would know what I know. Especially since he's walking away to play with the kids.

The guy is *fine* with a capital *F*.

Chapter 6 – Maddy

"So...?"

"So what?"

"Was I right?" His smug grin as he stares at the road has me wanting to punch him, but I don't want to get in a wreck. We already have enough people in the truck with a sling on, thank you very much.

"You're really going to make me say it?" I grumble as I cross my arms and sink lower in my seat.

"Damn right." His smile pisses me off and has my stupid heart doing doubling beats again. Damn thing's been doing it so much today that I think I might have a heart attack soon.

"Fine, you were right. Letting them each have their own DVD player installed in the truck was a great idea." And it was. The drive there was mostly quiet, and now on the drive back, well, it was *peacefully* quiet, as both kids are asleep. "I still think they aren't needed. Kids shouldn't be glued to the TV all the damn time," I gripe, but the quiet is actually really nice.

He shoots me one of those looks. You know the one. The kind that says "shut the fuck up and sit quietly." Guess I'm rubbing off on him if he doesn't say it outright with the kids in the car. I can bet my life he would have said it if we were alone.

"Hush, woman. They ain't glued. It was a couple hours. Won't kill them. Hell, I doubt even having the TV on all day will hurt. Cartoons have come a long way since when we were kids. They're all educational and shit now, learning shapes and numbers. No more shows simply about farting."

"Thank God for that," I mutter under my breath.

"Should have figured you weren't the type." He relaxes a bit as the little traffic we hit eases up and it's just us and a handful of other cars on the road now. He even goes as far as taking a hand off the wheel to rest on the back of my seat.

And yes, he's driving my truck. Don't even get me started on that bit. Took ten minutes of arguing and debating before he just hopped into the driver seat and refused to get out, even to help the kids get into their car seats. Well, first he installed the DVD players on the backs of the headrests, but then he just hopped in like he owned my baby.

"So tell me, what did you watch? What was your favorite cartoon?"

A cold sweat breaks out all over me. No idea why. It's a normal question. One I can easily lie to, and hell, probably have a million times. But I'm so tired of pretending to be someone else all the time. With the kids, it's nice not to have to pretend. I don't need to have my guard up so much. And then Chains came into my life, and, well, I don't *want* to pretend with him either. He's from the other side of the tracks. My past shouldn't affect our future 'cause it isn't connected. It's in two different worlds. There's no reason for me to lie, but... telling the entire truth might not be good either.

"I was a *Scooby-Doo* fan all the way. And yes, before you ask, Grace has already gone through the Mystery Machine phase. But I hope it comes back. Her finding clues around the house was super cute. Even Teddy got into it for a while but then stopped when he decided that if there was no dog, it wasn't going to work."

"Already had the dog conversation too? Damn, I missed that one."

The comment is probably meant to appear as a joke. A smile stretches across his face as I eye him in my periphery, but the hitch at the end is the giveaway. He really wants to be more involved. Damn, if that doesn't melt my heart a bit.

"I'm sure it'll come back around. Next time when he asks, I'll point him to you so you can tell him no."

"Fuck that. If the kid wants a dog, he gets a dog."

"Um, no."

"Um, yes." His tone mimics mine as he glances over with a pointed look that does funny things to my stomach.

"First off, who would keep it? Last time I checked, you don't have a house yet, and Teddy would want it with him every second of the day, and my house is a mess already. And second, what kind would you get? 'Cause if you bring in an animal, then both kids are going to want to play with it, and Grace might seem like a big girl, but an energetic puppy will grow quickly, and it might scare her if it pounces on her. Or hell, she might want to make it play dress-up, and if that goes anything like the time she took Teddy's dinosaur and painted the toes pink—her way to make them girls—then it'll be a disaster."

He shrugs. "Don't know. Never thought about it before."

"Well, think about it before you just buy one. And realize I won't pick up after it. Already got two to do that for. Don't need a third." I cross my arms to emphasize my point. *No way are we getting a dog.*

"Noted." He takes a beat, and I fall for it, thinking we're done with this asinine conversation. Should have known better when his smirk rises on his perfect face. "Besides, I could always just get Grace one of her own. Or hell, a cat. They don't do nothing but lie there."

"Not true. Cats are awesome!" No clue why I'm getting so defensive over a cat. Never had one. Couldn't even keep fish alive, but I'm not about to tell him that. "They curl up in your lap. They play with yarn. They also go to the bathroom in a contained area that's easier to pick up than going outside and not looking and bam! Instant poo on your shoe."

"Of course you're a cat person." He rolls his eyes, which just has me grinning like crazy. *Why is this so much fun right now?*

"And of course you're a dog person. Imagine my shock that we can't even agree on the same animal."

This is nice. We're arguing, but no harsh words are being thrown. No evil looks. Hell, we're both smiling and laughing. But of course, this isn't going to last.

"So, what's with the house? You fixing up to sell or just fixing it up?"

I'm not surprised at the change in subject. We've been hopping from topic to topic more times than not to have a steady conversation almost nonstop since we left this morning. More surprised it took him this long to ask.

"To sell."

He makes a noncommittal grunt in the back of his throat that has me checking on the kids, making sure they're still asleep before I dive headfirst into telling Chains more than I should. But after a day like this, with the way he showed up, in more than one way, I feel like I owe him more than a two-word answer. Or maybe it's just the excuse to talk about something that's beyond superficial between us.

"My aunt left me the house. She passed a few years back, and I'm just now finding the time to get to claiming what she left me. The house is in a prime real estate area. I should just mow it down and sell the land, but I grew up in that house, or at least I spent enough time there to call it a home. It might not have everything—doesn't even have a basement, which is probably why I didn't get a lot of bids on it. But I got one, and now I'm just making it prettified."

"You already have a buyer?" His tone gives me nothing to work with. Not sure if any of this shocks him. Even his face is giving me zero clues on his feelings on the matter.

"Sort of. I got someone interested, but they're only interested in the plans I showed them of what it will be like when I'm done. They put in an offer contingent on it matching what they approved."

"When you supposed to be done?"

I hesitate to answer as I glance sidelong at him. "I got some time."

"Ha, that's BS speak for you're running out of it." There's the emotion now, though not what I expected. But at least he's laughing—at me, of course, but it's better than a scowl. "Guess having some kids thrown at you put a wrench in the schedule, huh?"

Okay, he really needs to stop the laughing. It's getting to be a bit much now.

It's his laughter that puts my hackles up, and I reply with more fire than I need. "If we want to be technical about it, yeah, I'm off schedule by a few months. But I have been in contact with the buyer, and they're willing to move the date back a bit."

"How far is a bit?" he asks skeptically

I don't want to let him win, so I shrug it off. "Actually, they didn't say, and I didn't ask."

"You need help?"

I look over wide-eyed at him. He's trying to be all nonchalant about it, but wow. This is an enormous step for him, for us. "You offering?"

He shrugs as he pays the tolls. "Not me really. I work better on bikes than making things pretty in a house. But a few of the boys own a construction company. Could have them come over and do a few parts of it and get you back on schedule."

"Thanks, but I'd rather do it on my own." Yeah, that sounded believable even to my ears. *Not.*

The look he tosses my way says it all. He reads between my bull and calls me on it next. "It would be free, Mama Bear. Ain't about to let you pay for something I'm offering."

"Why do you call me that?"

"What, 'Mama Bear'?" His glance at me has me thinking he's more uncomfortable answering it than I am with accepting help.

"Yeah."

There's that damn shrug again. The man has nice shoulders going for him, but I swear he's working out right now with how often they keep going up and down. "Don't know, really. First time I met you, shotgun and all, you were like a fierce mama bear protecting her cubs. Everything you do is about protecting them. Just fit and stuck, I guess."

I notice he doesn't offer to stop calling me that or even offer me a choice if I like it or not. But I do. I secretly love that I have a nickname with him.

God, I'm so pathetic.

"The kids know you're leaving?"

"No. Like I said, I'm behind schedule. Didn't think it would be right to mention it to them till I signed on the dotted line. Even then, I doubt it matters."

"Why do you say that?"

I shrug, not sure if he's looking at me or not. God knows I'm not looking at him anymore for this conversation. Things are getting murky, complicated. I can't look him in the eye right now 'cause I know he'll see I'm hiding things. Or he'll see I'm secretly not wanting to let the place go yet. Maybe I never was.

"The rate I'm going, you'll have found a house before I'm done. The kids will be gone before I finish." I look out the window, dreading that moment.

Don't know when the kids became the most important thing in my life, but they are. I'm sure I see some of myself in them. Both parents out of the picture. Death, a shadow cloaking their pasts, and even an unknown enemy they know nothing about. It's almost kismet.

"Hey." His voice penetrates through the fog, but his hand that reaches over and lies on top of mine pulls me to look at him. "You don't have to go."

I can't contain my snort of laughter. "Oh yeah? You got a lawyer in that biker gang of yours to get me out of it, buddy?"

He gives me a self-indulgent smile. "It's a club, not a gang, and yeah, Mama Bear, we got one of those too."

"I need to sell." The whisper my voice makes lets me know more than him how desperately I need to let go of the past. He might think it's because of fond memories, but they aren't. They're dark and cruel and have been following me for so long that it's hard for me to turn my back without fearing I see them.

"Then sell, but you don't have to leave. When the kids come stay with me, maybe you can too."

"What? You want to live together?" Jaw is on the floor, ladies. Literally on the floor.

"Ha. Actually I don't know. Just sort of slipped out there." At least he's as shocked by what he said as I am, causing us both to chuckle in disbelief. "But—" He glances over, going as far as squeezing my thigh by flexing my hand that's resting on my leg. "—I could look for places that have those attached apartment thingies so you'd have like your own space and all but also the ability to see the kids every day."

"Careful, Chains. With this sudden change, I might actually think you care, and not just about the kids."

He chuckles again, but a grin appears and sticks to his perfect face. Giving one last squeeze of my hand, he moves his to turn the music up a bit. I miss the warmth even with the heat on in the car. It's the first time he's touched me, and I'm trying so hard not to act like a twelve-year-old girl with a crush on a boy. But I'm losing the battle.

"Got to ask you something."

"Okay, shoot." I'm being overenthusiastic, hoping to hide the giddiness I feel, but it's not working. Damn, I really hope he can't read me so quickly, but I doubt he misses anything. He's a man, a sexy man at that, so he probably knows the power he holds over women and how just simple touches and glances can send a woman over the edge into crazy worship town.

"We got a family BBQ going on at the club tomorrow. Want to know if y'all want to come."

"What time?" I can't help the smile on my face, seeing that I totally caught him off guard again at how quickly I responded.

"After two."

"That should work. Teddy's appointment's at nine to get his cast on. I should be able to drop off the kids after that, as long as you give me directions to where I'm going." Might even get a few things done if I time the drop-off and pickup right.

"The invite was for you too." He passes me a look but keeps going as my brain freezes on making plans for my party of one. "Figured you would want to get the lay of the land on who I plan to let the kids spend time around. Also, might be good for you to meet a few of the brothers, talk to them about your construction." He mows over my attempt to cut him off. "Ain't telling you to hire anyone, just saying you can talk shop. Might even pick up some ideas to move things along quicker if that's what you want. Just a thought. But I think it would be good for you to meet the boys. You know, for the kids' sake and all."

I look out the window, more wide-eyed than a doe in headlights.

Am I ready for this? Meet the entire club? Be brought into his group of friends? I really don't have a choice, do I?

"Right, for the kids."

"I'm happy to report that no tears were shed during the casting."

"Including your own?"

"Why would I be crying?" I'm paying more attention to the GPS than what I'm saying back to Izzy.

"You're a mama bear now. Don't they do that when their cubs get injured or something?"

"No idea why I told you he calls me that. And Teddy was already injured. This was just to make his boo-boo go away." I take a deep breath, more to steal my nerves as I pull up to the gated compound. "Besides, I already cried when it happened. Not that anyone but you knows that."

"Ha, pretty sure everyone knows that, Mama Bear."

"Shut up." I look back once more at the kids. They're completely oblivious to my words or the phone call I put into my headphones so they couldn't hear Izzy go on and on. The DVD players really are awesome to have in times like this. You know, when you want to talk reality and not spell out every other word so little ears don't know what's going on.

I called her on the way over from the house. I was a complete mess. What does one wear to a biker's BBQ? Specifically where you're only invited because you watch kids who are related to a club member but whom you refuse to give guardianship to until said club member proves they can handle the kids alone? A dress? I really hope so, 'cause that's what I decided on. A sundress with pretty daisies all around it. At least that's how Grace describes it. And if she likes it, then who else cares? I'm only going for the kids anyway. Has nothing to do with the long-haired, blue-eyed, big guy who's been amazing this morning.

He met us at the doctor. Actually he was waiting for us to arrive. We texted a few times last night after he left, as well as this morning. I don't know if it's to check in on the kids or just confirm I'm still keeping my phone with me at all times. He mentioned the phone several times when we were at the zoo, the whole importance of it. I get it; I mean, I'm not an idiot. It just hasn't been a priority until now. And now I'm being forced to make it one. Not that it bothers me. The phone's wicked awesome, and I can upload my favorite apps with ease, including the perimeter surveillance one.

Just another thing he does well.

I'm getting whiplash from him. He literally changed overnight. The man does something all the way when he puts his mind to it. I really want to meet the person he talked to so I can say thanks. Hopefully there will be a neon sign over his head to point out who the guy is.

The phone's one thing, the zoo another, but the hospital almost brought tears to my eyes, despite what I'd told Izzy. He was right on time, came straight from the shop, but he'd cleaned up enough not to get grease on everything. He held Grace's hand and put an arm around Teddy as we walked in. I just followed like a lost puppy till we hit reception.

Chains is obviously used to taking charge, but when he opened his mouth to say who was there for their appointment, I jumped ahead and spoke over him. I almost passed out from holding my breath so long after I said we were there for Teddy "Fox's" appointment. I begged Chains with my eyes not to freak out since I wasn't using Teddy's real last name.

His eyes flared before they glinted. I breathed out in a push of air. I knew that look. Didn't need to go to school to understand it. He would keep his mouth shut, but only for a while. He's going to ask later, and I'll need an answer. I have no choice.

After that tense moment, everything else went by with ease. Chains even asked if it was okay that only he and Teddy went back. I really wanted to protest. Teddy looked so sad and dejected. Chains had leaned into me, and I hate to say that at the moment his hot breath touched my neck and ear, I almost fell to the floor in pleasure. I had to close my eyes so tight and make my body rigid straight as he whispered, "He's scared. I've been there. The last thing he wants is to be alone, but he wants to be brave. Let me take him back. I want to show him he can rely on me, and I'll also show him it's nothing to be scared about since I've had it done before. Trust me, Mama Bear."

All I could do was nod. I mean, I was basically goo standing. Everything was jelly after he'd spoken to me so intimately.

"Come on, little man. Let's get this over with. I always loved being able to watch when they cast me."

"You had a cast?" I can still hear the aw in Teddy's voice, as well as remember the look in his eyes as he walked with Chains toward the nurse who called him back.

"Actually, my arm was broken three times. Had to have a cast every time, just like you. Guess it's a family tradition, huh?"

And that's all it took for Teddy to fall in line.

After an hour, they came out, and we parted ways. We still had a few hours till the BBQ, and Chains had a few more jobs, or whatever, to do at the shop. I wanted to get Grace home for a nap anyway, so we left, and the butterflies started almost immediately after he texted me the address and told me to just tell the guy at the gate who we were when we got there.

And here we are. The guy at the gate doesn't ask questions, just gives me a chin lift and continues to block the way in. Guess that's his way of asking?

"Um, we're here to... um... see Chains?"

He stares at me for a minute longer than I feel comfortable with, then looks in the back seat. "Pull up on the left, next to the other cars."

"Wow, who was that? Are you there? What does it look like? Are they all hot like on those TV shows? Can you see what the women look like?" Izzy's voice in my ear isn't helping anything as I slowly pull in. I take to breathing through my mouth, hoping slow breaths will stop the pumping in my chest.

"Um, yeah, it's big. Okay, I, ah, I think I need to let you go."

"Right, call me after. Tell. Me. Everything!"

"Right. Bye, sweetie." I'm freaking out and do not need Izzy in my head any more than I need my own thoughts.

"Bye, Mama Bear."

Seriously, why the hell did I tell her that name?

Chapter 7 – Chains

"Chains, you got guests."

Hell yeah. I'm pumped. I jump from my seat, not even caring that it falls back, making a hell of a noise as it hits the patio.

"Easy there. We might have to change your road name to Bullet if you keep that shit up."

"Fuck off, Bulldog."

I say it, but I actually slow down. The asshole's right; I don't need to seem too eager. I'm like a fucking kid being told they can have any candy in the store.

Shit, I need to get my act together. In the last forty-eight hours, things have changed; even the boys notice it. The talk with Bulldog at the bar did it. Didn't take much of the bottle of whiskey to see my error, and it wasn't that hard to change. Just had to be there. That was it. Be fucking there for the kids. And get along with Maddy.

Shit, that was the easiest part. Things would have been different now if she hadn't forgiven me or if she hadn't let me in.

Yeah, okay, I know the effect I have on women, and I totally used it on her at some points when I saw the indecision in her eyes.

Like this morning. She wanted to tell me no. She was all mama bear when I said I wanted to be the only one with Teddy during the casting. But damn, my play on her did a number on me too. I was hoping the soft words would turn her to my way of thinking about wanting to man Teddy up, since that's always how he acts when we're together. Hell, he even said he was the man of the house to me a few times—well, when I'm not there—so I wasn't about to let my little guy feel like he couldn't be the big man on campus.

But the first shiver that went over her body when I spoke to her had me stilling. I thought I was good, but hell, being this good, having this much of an effect on *this* woman, had me savoring the moment longer. I spoke more words than I intended. Kept looking at her beautiful neck, mesmerized by the little freckle at the base that played peekaboo with the wisps of her hair that were free of her braid and blew with the AC on them.

I should have realized last night that I was in way over my head. After spending the entire day with them, I came back to the club and texted her. Like a fucking teenage girl. And I smiled about it. The whole damn time.

Yeah, I'm screwed, and I honestly don't know if that's such a bad thing.

The chick has been under my skin ever since she pulled a fucking gun on me. I tried to fuck her out of my system, but after that first time, I knew it wouldn't work. Felt like a fucking asshole afterward too. And doesn't that say shit about how fucked-up in the head I am about this girl?

There I was, just out after five years and had a chick under me. Nothing wrong with Christy's snatch. It was willing, ready, and I glided right in with how much the vamp wanted me. She made the right noises, said the right things to get me hard, but fuck. I really expected the first time after being locked up would be quick. I was banging the club girl for twenty minutes and nothing. Changed positions so many times I knew she was sore from it. I even thought about pulling out and finding someone else 'cause it wasn't working, but Mama Bear popped into my head and that was it. One sight of her and I was unloading like crazy. I barely kept her name from leaving my lips that night. I might be a dick, but I'm not dick enough to call out another girl's name from the one I'm banging.

Might have fucked for over twenty minutes, but it only took twenty seconds to feel disgusted with myself. Threw the vamp out and took a shower to clear my head, wondering why in the hell I felt like I'd just cheated. Did that once when I was a kid, hated the feeling it got me all wrapped up in even then, hated it even worse now.

It was fucking stupid; one look and a part of me claimed a woman who wants nothing to do with me and my life.

Okay, maybe that shit isn't completely true. I affect her. The pebble of her nipples that show in her thin shirts are signs of that. A sight I never tire of seeing, but I really have to make sure I'm not caught. Last thing I want her to know is that her outfit choices do little to hide her arousal for me. I love her in tanks.

Even if her body wants me, I know her brain's at war, just like mine is. The kids complicate it. No one wants them hurt, and Maddy's a class above every woman who shows up at the club. She ain't like the vamps, looking to score with any willing brother. She also ain't like the onetime flirts who want a taste of the bad side to warm their minds while they're fucking the boring banker they married instead to have the perfect 2.5 kids and picket fence.

She has secrets. Ones I'm dying to know, but I respect her enough not to invade. *Yet.* If she doesn't talk to me soon, like the whole claiming Teddy under her last name and not as a Randall, then I'll use every bit of the arsenal I have at my disposal to find out everything there is to know about her.

Had Flint do the usual check when we learned she had my kids. Nothing popped, and I didn't ask for a bigger dive till I had eyes on her. The offer to go deeper is always on the table for Flint, but we're both holding off. I actually prefer not knowing everything about this woman from the start. Fucking dumb as shit, since she has my kids and all, but dammit, parts I thought died long ago are leading me around. My fucking heart is playing the game, arguing with my mind that it'll be better for her to tell us instead of finding out on our own. That she's earned that much since the kids are happy and healthy with her.

I round the side of the club's main building, and swear to fucking Christ, Maddy looks like a fucking angel. The sun is literally giving the woman her own spotlight. It's been cloudy most of the morning, but the rays are finally poking through. And they're right on her. Not the car, not the kids, just her. Shit, it's like fucking Jennie's trying to say something from her resting place. She always was a nosy sister.

Her sundress clings to that sexy little hourglass figure she's got going for her. The woman ain't big, but she ain't small. Just right. *Fuck, now I sound like fucking Goldilocks.* They don't see me yet, which is good, so I can push down my dick that always wants to say its own personal hello when Maddy is close. The fucker is needy for this chick. Damn needy.

"Uncle James!" Grace spots me first and barrels right into me. All of me. If that doesn't kill a boner, nothing will. Serves that fucker right, but it still hurts like shit to get rammed in the dick. Again. Grace has a way of doing it on repeat.

"Hey, my sweet girl. You ready for a BBQ?"

"Yup. Maddy even says I can show you my tumbles 'cause I have shorts on."

"Gigi!" Maddy shouts. "Put your dress down!"

I chuckle as my niece lifts her pink dress to show me the shorts underneath. It's cute, for about five seconds, till my brain registers that she can never do that around a boy ever again. Dread crawls up my skin the instant I see a flash of my little Gigi with a boy doing just that. I stumble. Didn't expect that image, ever. But now I can't get it out of my head.

A soft giggle breaks into my thoughts as my eyes travel up long legs, over the curve of a pale pink dress with daisies going up in rows till they taper off just below a few handfuls of breasts that, for once, aren't pebbling under my gaze. Either I'm losing my touch or her bra is thicker than the ones she usually wears.

"Don't worry there, Uncle. She has a long way to go before you need to worry about her doing that for a boy in any way that isn't completely innocent."

I raise my eyebrow at her. She was the one to yell first, and now she's contradicting herself.

She rolls her eyes with a smile. "Doesn't mean I'm not going to correct her still."

"Hey, Chains, what'd you bring me?"

I turn and glare at Flint, wanting to flip him off but conscious of little eyes on me, happy to see him just keep walking instead. See? I'm learning, and fast. Seventy-two hours ago, I would have done it without thinking. What can I say? I was an *A* student in my day. Doesn't mean I won't punch the smirk off his face the moment I'm out of eyesight of certain youngsters. Especially with the way he's eye-fucking Maddy. Yeah, that asshole is going to get it.

"Oh shit, should I have brought something? I didn't even think about that. But of course I should have. I mean, you don't come to a BBQ without bringing something. Especially a family BBQ. 'Cause that's what this is, right? Didn't you say something like this was family day or some shit so the kids would have others to play with?" Maddy rambles, throwing her hands in the air. "I totally messed this up. Okay, there's a gas station a few blocks away. I'll be right back. Going to get chips or ice or napkins. Crap, just text me."

I move quickly, untangling Grace from around my leg, the place she'd been clinging to, and grab Maddy's arm, pulling her back against my front, forcing her to stop before she can make it back to her car.

"Easy, Mama Bear." My tone is harsh, and my grip on her is hard, but I'm not about to hurt her. "I don't expect you to go get ice or napkins. Didn't invite you for that. Family day means family can come around, not that we expect family to bring shit. We might be a rowdy group, but we can buy our own fucking ice without a woman telling us how."

I doubt she knows she relaxes into my arms a bit, and I'm not about to correct her, 'cause fuck, it's amazing. A part of me feels at peace with just that. She isn't just some vamp who'll cuddle up to me for the night. Isn't just some girl batting her eyelashes at me so she can suck my cock and tell everyone she did. She's Maddy, the mama bear to my kids.

I'm completely screwed.

"Right, sorry." Her soft laugh shows more than anything how nervous she is. "Guess I'm just a little wound up. Didn't really know what to expect, and I feel like a fish out of water."

Her confession does things to me, and I turn her around to see her face. The image of her biting her lip does *other* things to me, but I will it away to focus on her. I brush a strand of hair behind her ear, and her eyes clamp on mine as I follow my fingers that are trailing the braid that falls over her shoulder.

"Just be you. Ain't asking for anything but that. The guys don't bite, and those who do ask first. But if anyone doesn't, let me know, and I'll deal with it." I watch the fire flicker in her eyes at my possessive words toward her. "You ain't a fish out of water, but you will get some looks."

Her eyes go wide. "Why? 'Cause I wore a dress? Fuck, I knew it was too much. I've never been to one of these things before and totally asked my friend, and then, well, Grace said it was pretty, and I—"

"I need to meet your friend," I cut in.

Hurt flashes over her face quickly. I don't hide my smug smile.

"And thank her for the suggestion," I continue. "I like it. And Grace is right. It is pretty. But that isn't what's going to cause them to stare."

"Then what?" Her tilted head has me just barely swallowing down the lust. The sun is full-on shining on her now, and she's just too fucking amazing for her own good— and has no clue.

"'Cause you are fucking stunning. No matter what you wear, you are stunning." I turn to give a nod to one brother who passes us, but I can't help to add a bit more. "And your braid is fucking hot as hell."

"Oh, um...." She's saved from saying anything as her phone goes off. But the pink on her cheeks lets me know I hit my target.

"Oh crap, I need to take this. Can you watch the kids for a second?"

"Yep." I nod as she takes a few steps away and answers the phone, turning away to give me a marvelous view of her ass.

"Wondered what was taking you so long. Now I know."

I barely pull my eyes away from Maddy's ass to see Bulldog grinning like a fucking idiot and ogling her as well. I can't be mad. Her ass is fine as hell, but it still burns me that he's looking.

"You ain't got anything better to do?"

"Nope."

"Fucker."

He laughs and walks away, but only a few cars down to his own truck. No doubt getting something for his little princess. His baby girl has him wrapped tighter than a coiled rope.

"Shit." The softness of her voice draws my attention to her.

"What's up?" I already know I'm not about to like what she has to say. Her entire demeanor has changed from shy flirtation to total devastation.

"I can't stay. Um, something's come up, and I need to go handle it."

"It can't wait?" *Or I can't handle it?* I really want to ask that but know I have no right. Not yet.

"I asked, but no. Sorry, but would it be a problem if I left the kids here for a bit? I can come pick them up after." She doesn't make eye contact with me, which just pisses me off. Can't fix shit when things aren't told to me.

"Or you could just come back. We'll be going for a while." I'm trying, I really am. I'm used to people just telling me what I need to know. Not much song and dance from women in the past. They usually like to tell me more than I want, always expecting me to do something about it. But not Mama Bear. Apparently she isn't ready to trust me with those details yet.

"No, um, it's probably for the best, actually. Family day and all. Think only family should attend."

I can see she isn't wavering, and something happened on the phone to throw her off. Everything in me is pinging to demand what it is, but I hold off.

"Right, okay. Why don't I just drop them off afterward? Give you some time to deal with whatever you got going on?"

I leave it open, hoping she'll offer something up, but she doesn't. "That would be perfect, thanks. Let me just take the car seats out."

I nod, but my brain is already trying to fix the issue. I really wanted Maddy here today, but I'm not about to tell her no. I'm torn 'cause I want to go with her, but I know she won't agree. Seems like I will be upping my background check on her now. I can't not know anymore.

Sending off a quick text, I look back at the car and see her struggling. "Need help?"

"Yeah, actually I do. Izzy put these things in here, and I honestly have no idea how to get them out."

"Not a problem." I put my fingers into my mouth and whistle for the one man who can help us. The noise draws his attention, and just about every damn idiot in earshot. A wave has him jogging over.

"What's up?"

"Maddy, meet Bulldog, our VP."

"Hi."

He chin-lifts her a hello, then turns back to me, knowing full well I'm not introducing them for fun.

"Think you can get the car seats from her car to mine?"

He nods. "Sure. Do it for my princess all the time when I switch the cars in the shop."

"You got kids?" Of course she would ask. Fucking Mama Bear is just that.

"Yes, ma'am, I do. She'll be five in another month."

Can't fault the guy for adoring his little girl and talking about her, but does he have to take his damn time getting the seats out?

She smiles at him. "Thanks for this. I really should know how to do this on my own, but I've never had to move them before."

My hands are in fists, and I keep them that way. Dammit, does Maddy even know she's flirting, or does she really think she's just having a normal conversation with another parent? 'Cause the way Bulldog keeps flashing her a grin, I know he would be calling dibs if it was an option.

Which it ain't.

"Not a problem. I'm always available for things like this."

Motherfucker. He's going to show me how to install these things tonight. Hell, I'll YouTube it. Damn fool would probably refuse for the fact that he knows it might get him more time with her.

"Yeah, well, this will be your first and last time, hot shot," I cut in. "Keep it moving. Here are my keys. Truck's over there."

"Watch who you're talking to, boy." He drops the smile, and I pick mine up as he walks away.

"Are you going to be in trouble for talking to him like that?" Maddy asks.

Cute as shit that she's worried. Cute as shit.

I laugh. "Nah. I was the VP before I was locked up. Bulldog took over when I was in."

"You going to take it back?"

"Don't know, haven't thought about it much. Wanted to figure other shit out first, if you know what I mean." Wonder how she would feel if I did. I really have no idea what I want, and till I do, I ain't rushing decisions right now.

"Yeah, I do. Hey, thanks for watching the kids. I'm really sorry about this."

"It's okay, I got them. We're going to have fun, right, guys?"

Grace is the only one jumping up and down, Teddy just kicks at the dirt. Shit, a moody six-year-old. This will be my first solo trip with them, and they ain't all happy. *Talk about learning to swim after being thrown into the deep end.*

A beautiful smile crosses Maddy's face, one that has me forgetting to breathe. "Grace, remember to listen to Uncle James. And if you need to go potty, ask him so he can take you. Don't go off looking for the bathroom on your own. This is a big place, and I don't want you to get lost."

She tosses me a look, letting me know that Grace might just do that.

Great, I have an adventure on my hands with her today.

"And, Teddy, it's okay to smile today," Maddy continues. "It's just a cast. We talked about this. It'll be off before school starts. And...." She rummages in her purse before pulling out a pack of permanent markers. "I'm pretty sure your uncle can help you put a few cool designs on it. And if he can't, a few of these guys have some awesome tattoos. Maybe one of them is even a tattoo artist and can do something amazing with it. What do you say?"

Wow, this woman is incredible. Teddy's entire face lights up at the idea. "Do you know anyone who can do that, Uncle Chains?"

"Yup. Domino and Jumper are our resident tattoo artists. Pretty sure they would love to design something for you."

"Awesome."

I chuckle as the kids hug Maddy, now both bouncing with glee.

I pull her in, too, unable to resist. "Bribery?"

Her eyes sparkle. "Learned from the best."

"Ha, I bet."

The moment we share is quickly taken away as her eyes flicker behind me and her entire face drains of color.

"What is it?" I turn around but see nothing out of the ordinary.

"No-Nothing. I should get going. Have a good time." Faster than I've ever seen a woman move in heels, she's in the car and pulling out.

"Wow. She late or something?" At least Bulldog is as confused as me.

"Or something," I mutter. I look over my shoulder again but still see nothing that would have caused Maddy to be spooked. All I can see are a few brothers and some women walking around the backyard.

My phone rings, and I answer it as I watch Maddy drive out the gate and turn right.

"Still want me to follow her?"

"Yeah, keep me posted." I pocket the phone and take another moment, waiting till I see the prospect's car drive by before turning to my niece and nephew and introducing them to my world.

Chapter 8 – Maddy

My phone chimes with a movement alert. I look over and smile as I see Chains' truck pull around the curb. The kids are back, and they're the distraction I need. It's after eight, but I bet they'll still be up. I already planned for popcorn and a movie. Anything to get me out of my head.

Guess the kids didn't get the invite as I head to the front of the house to help them get out of the truck.

Spotting a sleepy Teddy walking up the stairs as I open the door, I reach him quickly, and he just leans into me. Fuck, this kid can make my heart hurt in all the right places. I pick him up, and he wraps both arms around me tightly and doesn't move other than to find a comfy place to rest his head. I look up at the sound of a car door shutting to see Chains in a similar position with Grace.

My day has been completely crappy since getting that call at the clubhouse, but seeing a big, sexy god carry a sleeping little girl is both ridiculous and panty melting all at the same time. I can't help the huge smile on my face.

"What did you do, drug them or something?" I whisper, but the kids are so out of it, I bet they don't even care if I yell.

"Or something."

I realize I'm going to have to drill him with questions. He looks almost as exhausted as them, but a badass biker couldn't tucker out so early. Could he? Then again, kids have a way of sucking the energy out of you.

I hold the screen door for him, but he takes it from me and nods for me to go in. *We have a gentleman, ladies and gentlemen.* I couldn't even hide my smile if I wanted to, but at least I keep the laughter at bay. Don't want him to think I don't like it, and I really don't want to wake up the kids.

"Take her to her room. I'll get Teddy settled and into pj's, then come help."

He nods and wanders to her room. I get Teddy through the motions. Even get him to pee before bed. The kid barely even registers he's moving, much less changed.

I see the hunk of a man just rocking Grace when I enter. I make an audible gulp. I mean, the man is basically walking sex. And a little one in his arms looks good on him. Real good.

He turns and looks sheepish. "Sorry, didn't know where anything was, and to be honest, I have no clue how to even get her out of the dress."

I don't laugh, but my smile must give something away, as he visibly calms that I don't make a fuss. Taking her from him, I do the same with her as I did her brother. She's a little easier, if putting pj's on a statue is easy. The kid's a dead weight. No potty break for her.

Closing the door behind me, I go to the front door, expecting to find Chains heading out. But he isn't there, and a quick look shows his truck in the yard. Moving through the house, I stop at the kitchen. Well, it's more like kitchen/dining area with the hole in the wall now.

He looks over his shoulder at me, away from the wall, eyes bright with questions. The one he asks is not the one I expect. "Having a party?"

I follow the gaze that flickers to the counter and see the not-so-neat kitchen counter covered in my awesome margarita ingredients.

"You know, I had planned on popcorn and cartoons tonight."

He shrugs. "That works too."

Right, so he isn't leaving. Don't know if the butterflies in my stomach are because I recognize I'm going to have to explain a few things or the fact that this is the first time we'll spend time together without the kids. I'm going to need something stronger than cartoons and popcorn to get me through this.

"Get me a drink, will you?" I go to the pantry, grab a bag of chips, and pull the chunky salsa from the fridge. I pour a generous amount into a bowl and go out the back door, not saying anything more to Chains, but I know he'll follow.

The man is full of surprises. Not only does he get me a margarita in a tall glass, one of the biggest I own and filled to the rim with a nice straw for decoration, but he got himself one too. Took him more for a beer guy, especially since he told me he was. Worst part is, once I heard that from his lips, I went and bought the kind he mentioned he likes. How pathetic is that?

I'm munching on chips and sipping on my straw, more to keep my mouth occupied so it doesn't start yapping away. I know we need to air some shit, but I'm nervous about his reaction. And I have no idea what I'm going to say. How far into the truth department am I going to go with him? Can I trust him a hundred percent or just with the kids?

Why the hell is this so complicated?

"That the clubhouse?"

He breaks through my self-argument, and I follow his gaze to the hilltops in the distance. It's far enough away that you can't make out people's silhouettes, but you see the building's outline and the lights on.

"Think so."

"Huh, didn't realize you could see it. I shouldn't be surprised. We chose a higher plane than most of the houses around here."

I just nod, not really sure what to say.

"Got to admit, the margaritas surprised me."

Shit, he's going to make me feel bad for drinking. And alone at that. Crap, I *do* feel bad about it. This doesn't look good for a foster mom. He probably thinks I drink all the time, but I really don't. It was a shit day, and screaming was getting me nowhere. So I chose the next option: a good strong drink and a sledgehammer.

"Figured you would be one of those who drinks coffee at night since you drink so much during the day."

A snort of laughter bursts from my mouth as I swivel my head to look at him smirking at me. I smirk back as I reply, "Done that too. So you weren't too far off in your thoughts."

I see the questions brewing in his eyes and jump in with my own to hold them at bay. Coward's way out? You betcha.

"How was the BBQ? I take it the kids had fun if their dead-to-the-world antics are any sign to go by."

"Ha, yeah. They don't have off switches, that's for damn sure. Didn't take long for Teddy to get his own group of admirers after Domino and Jumper put a few art pieces on his cast. Hell, the two even fought over it, which, got to admit, made that little man smile bigger than I've ever seen. And Grace, well, she took to Bulldog's princess like peas in a pod. They literally ran circles around us."

"I bet."

"It was nuts. Princess never had another girl at the clubhouse before, and she loved it. Bulldog acted like he was cool with it, but I think he was just as much a mess as I was after we saw them run close to the bonfire twice. After that, we made a circle of brothers that they could run between. They all bitched about only getting to talk to the ones next to them, but I didn't give a shit. I know I felt a million times better when we contained them. We need a cage built, I think."

"Or just get a play set added. Grace rarely gets off the swings unless it's to go down the slide. Maybe that other girl, Princess, is like her."

He nods, and I can tell the idea has stunned him. "Great idea." He pulls out his phone and texts away for a few minutes. "Got the guys looking at sets now, and we'll get one installed before the week's out."

Wow, talk about manpower. Totally jealous that he just decided, and it's getting done. I take a while to choose, and when I do, it takes longer to get it done since it's just me. Not that I would ask for help. This place is my home. It's special to me. It's got stories and secrets in the walls I don't want to share.

"So...."

My heart triples in speed at that one word, and I refuse to look at him, even though I can feel his gaze on me.

"Either the place you had to go to over the BBQ set you off, or you really hated that wall. Want to let me in on it?"

"Yes."

"Yes?"

"To your question."

"Which one?"

"All of them. Yes, the meeting I was called to set me off. Yes, I hated that wall. And yes"—I look over at him—"I'll let you in on it."

I take a breath and a big drink. Need all the courage on this one.

"It was the bank. I told you I had a buyer lined up for this place. Well, I thought I had time. But they pulled out. And the bank, well, they were willing to front me a loan for repairs and all when I had a prospect for paying it back. But now, I have no buyer, no job, and no way of getting another loan."

"How much you got left?"

Okay, so this is the part I was really hoping he wouldn't ask. "Look, I am not telling you this to get anything out of you. I need you to get that. This is not me looking for money from you. This is not me throwing a pity party to get money tossed my way. You asked, so I'm telling you. I'm treating you as I would any of my friends who ask how crappy my day was. That's it. Ain't looking for a fix, just talking, okay?"

"Maddy, how much?"

Why does his growl always get to me?

He's already being stern with me, and he's about to get pissed. I just know it. "I took the loan out in January for sixty grand. It was all meant to go into the house with the appliances and supplies for the remodel. Ten went into the house before April. Then things changed, my priorities changed, and I used the money on other things."

"Other things...."

I nod, even though it's not a question.

"The kids," he softly whispers as he realizes what I'm saying.

I don't nod this time, even though it's true.

"I don't regret for one minute spending money on them. They needed their own rooms and things to make them feel like kids in a home they could call their own. Never saw it as a problem—still don't. I don't go crazy on the spending, but I don't turn down anything if I think they need something. I got enough left to get food and stuff set up for us through the summer, but that's it. By the time Teddy goes to first grade, I need to have a job and daycare set up for these kids. It's either that or sell the place as is and move back to Texas. My prior gig is always open for me there, and it's a simple job that pays well."

He's quiet, and I fear the wrath that's about to explode, but it doesn't. He takes it all in, looking at his drink over me.

"Do you want to move?"

"I don't know," I huff as I sink into my chair in defeat, lost over what to do. "Before the kids, well, I had no reason to stay here. But now, I don't know if I can be apart from them. But if I have nothing keeping me here, there's no reason to stay. If the house gets sold, and you find a place for you all, why stay? This might be the home I grew up in, but I've got to admit, outside of this house, I don't have great memories here. I would never have come back if I didn't feel like my aunt would rise from the dead to beat me with a shoe if she knew I passed over on her house. She took pride in this place, and it was amazing when she had it. But it got neglected over the years, outdated. Figured I owed it to her to make it grand like she and I envisioned it all those years ago."

"A vision that didn't include the wall between the kitchen and dining room?" His eyes twinkle as they meet mine, and I appreciate how he's trying to keep things light. I'm about a second away from being swallowed by a black hole of terrible memories and doubt.

"Ha, well, yeah. When I drew up the plans, it was originally an open design. But the buyer liked the formality of a dining room separate from the rest of the house, so I kept it. But once they pulled out... well, I was a bit unhinged when I got back. so I grabbed the tequila and started making the margaritas. I was so lost in my head that I pushed the mix button before I put the top on the blender, and it went crazy. Got on the wall. Being the good little person I am, I went to clean it and, well, I sort of punched the wall in frustration. Broke through the plaster right away. A light went off in my head, and it didn't take long to find the sledgehammer. So that's why there's an impressive-size hole in the wall. I ran out of steam and needed to make another round. But instead of starting on the other wall on the other side between the living and dining room, I came out here. Figured I would need to chill out before the kids arrived."

"Shit."

"Yeah, that sums it up."

At least he chuckles and smiles.

I go to take another sip of my drink and make more noise than actually getting any this time. Before my brain even registers that I need a refill, Chains switches glasses with me and puts my straw in his cup but doesn't remove his. Not sure why, but I just grab both straws and drink heavily.

Why is my heart going crazy with the knowledge that I'm drinking from his straw? Can we say teenage crush much? God, I really need to get a boyfriend or something. This whole freaking out over every little thing the guy does is turning me into a middle schooler.

And let's be real. He isn't my first crush. I've had tons. Hundreds, even. So what? He might be the first one who actually talks to me or exists outside the fantasy world of books and TV shows. He also might be the only one who's all man and not a little boy from my younger days. And who cares if I see him checking me out every now and again? Even though he might be the only guy I've crushed on who might actually do something about it, that still doesn't mean I need to act like this.

"Probably doesn't help that you got to take care of two extra little ones, but you got saddled with a biker too."

"I don't mind the biker so much as the eating me out of house and home."

The look of self-reflection and shock on him has me smiling.

"Kidding."

He smiles but shakes his head and looks at his feet. "No you ain't."

I keep my mouth shut. I really am only half joking. His arrival and nightly fanfare made the budget shrink a bit. I can live off PB&J, as can the kids—not that we do that, of course. I made things last before with leftovers, but the man does not know what a leftover is. Or he's still in a prison mindset with eating and leaves nothing on his plate in case it's his last meal.

Okay, fine, I could have made him PB&J too. He would bitch and complain, I'm sure, but it would have stopped the money issue for a bit. But I didn't, and despite my head saying it was because he was *forcing* me to make him a decent meal, my heart knew differently. I wanted to win this guy over. He comes off all badass and shit, and he is, but then I see him with the kids. No one can be *that* badass and not have a heart of gold at their core when they let a little girl pretend they're her pony, and she gets to ride on his shoulders, and he makes the noises while they gallop away. So I splurged to impress him. I'm not a whiz in the kitchen, but I had a few jobs in the restaurant biz, and I picked things up. I ain't the best, but I can hold my own. And I wanted to show that off. It's definitely in my top five best features.

"Sorry." It's muffled, but I hear it. And I *hate* it.

"Don't. Don't say that. I don't want it. Told you this wasn't about pity or making you feel bad. You asked, and I told you. Want nothing but a 'yeah, that sounds like it sucks' from you."

He raises his eyebrows at me, his elbows on his knees as he looks over at me, waiting for me to deny it.

"Seriously. I ain't like most girls. Even odder than that." He nods in affirmation as he grabs his drink from my hands and takes a sip, looking out toward his club. "Been told I'm different all my life, and stubborn as hell. But I make my own way. I accept nothing from anyone. I work hard. If I screw up and get into a mess, I fix it and get out. Been on my own for a while. When people get involved, it usually ends up worse for them, not me."

I'm surprised he doesn't get a neck crick from how fast he turns to look at me head-on. "You going to explain that last part a bit?"

"Nope." I pop the *P* and grab a chip with a shit ton of salsa before popping it in my mouth.

We look at each other, waiting for the other to break. But it won't be me. Even if my stupid mouth has gotten away from me and I spilled more beans than I wanted to, I know when I've hit my limit. Even with all the tequila in the world, I'm not about to share the rest of my shit life. It ain't pretty. Worst part is I know he'll run away, taking the kids with him, and that's something I'm not ready for. I know I'm on borrowed time with them, but my time isn't over, not yet.

"Right, I'll let you have that for now." He stands to leave. I just watch, not wanting to move any more. Swinging that sledgehammer wasn't easy, and my muscles are screaming at my unintended workout. For once in my life, I don't have a slip of fear creeping up my back at being below a man standing.

"Maddy." He waits till he has my eyes to continue. "I'm leaving, but that doesn't mean we're done. Not with this conversation, not with the one at the hospital, and not with the one about us. You don't want me to fix shit, I get that, so I'll say what you want and move on, but don't expect me to say it more than once."

I nod, my heart rate increasing and not letting me do much of anything else. *"About us"? Fuck, that could mean so many things.*

"I'll let myself out and lock up. Stay here, drink your drink—or mine, since you finished yours. Watch the sky, or hell, the clubhouse. It's a hell of a view you got here. And, well, you had a shit day, and ah, what was it? Oh yeah, sounds like it sucked."

His smirk does a thousand things for me, but mostly it has me looking out at his clubhouse and smiling as I hear the door lock on his way out.

Chapter 9—Chains

"I don't know about this, man."

"Shut up. It'll be fine."

"You've been away for a bit, so maybe you forgot how to do this whole wooing thing. Chicks don't like to be woken up. Like ever, man. Sure, sometimes when you're licking their pussy, but even then they expect us to finish, and then they go back to bed."

I glare at Flint as I climb the stairs to Maddy's house. "I ain't wooing. This shit is club business. And why the hell wait? Besides, she tells me the kids get her up early every morning. She's probably on like her eighth cup of coffee by now." I'm so confident in my shit that I don't see any flaws in my plan.

"Hey, I tried to warn you, man." I see him hold his hands up in mock surrender from my periphery. The guy has no clue about my girl. I ain't waking her up. In fact, she's going to be delighted to see me. Can't wait to rub it in his face too.

I shake off his comments and knock. And knock again. And knock a third time, louder in case they can't hear me over the TV. I'm about to knock a fourth time when the door swings open and Mama Bear appears. Full-on Mama Bear. Maddy isn't there by the expression on her face. If looks could kill, I would flop on the deck, dead.

I give a side glance to Flint, who takes one look at her and then me, snorting his laughter as he backs down the stairs and goes to talk to the guys. Yeah, I really don't want an audience for this.

"Hey, Maddy—"

She doesn't let me get any further than that. Surprised she even let me do that much, honestly.

"You have any goddamn idea what time it is?" Okay, so my confidence is shaking even more. "I thought we had a nice little talk last night."

I take a step back as she raises her hands above her head. Don't think she'll hit me, but I ain't really sure about much right now. I obviously got this arrival wrong.

"Hell, even a freaking understanding. But apparently not. 'Cause if we did, you would not be here waking everyone up on my day off."

"Day off? Thought you didn't work." I'm trying for laughs but see I'm missing my target, and bad.

Her scream is more of agitation than in volume. "Of course I don't work. I meant with the kids. And before you say anything, yes, they are a job and one I love, but a freaking job of hard work 'cause the little suckers suck every energy cell out of me. I used to be a nice person in the morning." She groans. "Okay, maybe nice isn't the right word, but I was better than this. Now I need like three cups of coffee to even see past my hand. And today is worse since you forced me to drink last night."

"Forced?" I raise an eyebrow at that. Pretty sure I was the one being forced to drink a fruity drink. Not that it didn't taste good, because it did. I'm even willing to have more if she ever makes them around me again. Not that I would ask... or tell the guys. Go into the slammer drinking whiskey from the bottle and come out wanting margaritas with frilly umbrellas? Yeah, that would go over really well with them.

She breathes hard. "Fine, not forced. But you left, and margaritas don't reheat."

"They freeze, though."

"Interesting. I'll consider that next time." Her sarcasm has my eyes rolling, but I can't keep the chuckle away as she continues. Don't think she really thought it was a possibility. "I've never seen that. Of course, I'm never able to let a full batch go to waste. So I drank last night, and you know what I love about the kids this morning? That when I woke up at six, expecting them to be up, they were still asleep. I even went as far as wanting to text you a thank you 'cause I know it was all due to you working the energy out of their system. So my poor head, which is aching right now, was happy to lie back on the pillow and sleep. And that's why it's my day off, 'cause I *was* sleeping in."

"It's 7:30 a.m." Not sure why I feel the need to keep stating the obvious. None of it is working for me, and it's more than apparent this is the true Maddy in front of me. One without a lick of caffeine in her system. You know you got it bad for a woman when even her rants and growls at you get you going chubs. Real bad.

"Yeah, it's sleeping in when you got kids. Like to see you party it up and wake up chipper every morning. Obviously your band of rebels here hasn't gone to sleep yet, as it's the only reason you're up this early, on a Sunday, and at my house, waking everyone up. Who knows how long they would have slept till? Eight? Nine? There were soooo many possibilities, and now I'll never know. So tell me, mister, what the hell are you doing here? What can I help you with? And if you ask for me to cook you and your crazy people anything, you got another thing coming."

"I come bearing gifts." I shrug it off as nothing, but I know I've hooked her. Even if she wants to pretend I haven't. Might not have been around much, but I've watched this woman a lot. And one thing I know is she's big on gifts. Never seen her get one before, but I don't think she would turn one down from how often she gives things out.

"Bribes? Really?"

"If it works." I shrug as I turn and grab the four coffees behind me, then turn back to her.

"What's this?" There's the perk in her voice I expected when she first saw me on her doorstep.

Note to self: show her coffee before I talk next time.

"Didn't know what you went for, so I had the guy make four different ones. Only know you drink a ton and you like a crapload of creamer." I can't hide the smirk when I see I'm no longer on her mind as she eyes the coffees before her. Doubt she even heard what I said. "Figure you can pick one, and then I'll let the guys have the rest."

Okay, that got her attention back up to me and glaring again. "Bribes work better if you don't threaten to take things away." She grabs all four and turns back into the house, leaving the door propped open. "Bring the food you have in the bag for the kids, and let's talk about why my yard has a bunch of bikers in it."

I turn to grab the donuts and catch Flint's eye, showing him my smirk.

"What the fuck, man? You said we would get coffee."

"What can I say? Lady doesn't share well."

"Now I know why you call her a bear," he grumbles and heads back to the boys. Probably to tell them they've been had and won't be getting the caffeine perk they were all hoping for when I got them out of bed this morning.

I walk into the house and see two sleepy kids, pj's on, hair standing up, watching TV. Teddy's at least sitting on the couch, but he looks more zombielike than anything else. Grace isn't any better.

"Grace, honey, sit back. Don't stand too close to the TV. You'll hurt your eyes, and your brother won't be able to see."

Neither kid acknowledges me, but at least Grace moves to the couch and sits by her brother to finish *Scooby-Doo*. Guess they still like that show.

Turning toward the kitchen, I see Maddy has taken the lids off all the coffees and is fixing each one to her liking. The last one didn't need any fixing, so she starts with it. I make a note of which one it is—the one I picked out from the list of shit on the wall at that coffee place. Happy to know I'm not a complete idiot, but also happy I had the guy fix it up to more than just what the sign said it was.

"How long they staying?"

No use in beating around the bush. "A while."

She nods and pulls out a big-ass coffee maker, not her usual single-cup one, and starts making the brew, I'm assuming for the guys. Even shit like *that* does things to me. Her talk last night had me thinking. And while I really got little sleep last night, I managed enough to let me know I was doing the right thing in my next move.

"Last night you talked, and I listened and said what you wanted me to say. Now I expect the same thing, and all I want out of your mouth is 'Okay.'"

Covering her mouth with my hand, cutting her off 'cause I know that isn't what she's about to say, I step in close. "Nope, I said only 'okay' was allowed. See, you said shit, and it got me thinking. Want you to know, I don't pity you at all, and this isn't 'cause I feel bad. This is 'cause I need to do this for the kids—*my* kids. Flint is going to come in, and you guys are going to talk about plans for this house. The plans you want, not what some stupid buyer says. You're going to work with him, and then the guys are going to get to work doing just that. You can help all you want. It's your house and shit, but we'll get you back on track. Not because we want you gone, but because you want this, and this is our thank-you for watching over our family, mine and the club's family. Jennie might not have been near the club in years, but they still claim her as one of their own, and we take care of our own. You're watching the club's kids, so we take care of them too. Should have been doing that from the start, so I'm doing it in a way I know how. Got it?"

She nods, and with the water in her eyes, I take the chance and remove my hand from her perfect mouth.

"Okay." It's a whisper, but I hear it.

"Okay, I'm going to assume the only reason you gave in so easily is 'cause the coffee is good. 'Cause there is no fucking way you would do that. Unless you gave me the Sunday school version last night, and shit is a lot worse than I know."

She shakes her head, smiling at least. "No, you got the whole of it last night. And the coffee is awesome, which helps. Now, when it wears off, I might sing a different tune. I hold the right to change my mind."

"Right, well, let's get this shit done quick before you suck all that down too fast." Ain't about to push my luck this morning any more than I already have.

"Oh, I'm great at sucking."

The moment holds between us. I don't know if I should laugh or groan. The thought of Maddy sucking me off sets my dick digging into my zipper, hard as a rock and begging for attention. Her face just flames, and I realize laughter is not what's needed here. But she really needs to know the affect she has on me. If anyone else said that, I would know they already knew and did it on purpose. But the way her face is as red as a tomato and she's looking everywhere but at me, still standing there as brave as can be, I know it was an accident. Doubt she even noticed the sexual undertone till her own ears heard the words.

I pull on her braid. God, I love doing that. A jerk of it has my dick mirroring the same response. Another image flashes behind my eyes, this time of me pulling that braid to get her to suck me harder down her perfect throat.

I clear my own throat, more to dispel the image in my head than to get her to lift her eyes to me. "I'd be happy to be the judge of that."

I don't smirk, 'cause I ain't teasing. I got it bad for this chick. Not sure why my chest hurts every time I'm close to her, but ain't denying I get a hard-on for her. Case in point.

The kids complicate things, but they don't have to. We can be adults about shit like this. Hell, I slept with the vamps at the club before getting locked up and could still talk to them after. Of course, a few got a little territorial, and some even made a catfight scene. I'm not the guy who gets off on that. Find it annoying as shit.

With the vamps, they know they're there for a variety of sexual tasks. A take-and-leave sort of thing. Maddy isn't that type of girl, but I could do an exclusive friend-with-benefits situation with her. If she'll let me.

But the more I stare into her eyes, the more I know if I shack up with her, I won't be able to walk away. She isn't the type you walk away from. I just don't know if I'm ready for that kind of lockdown. I just got out of a place with a literal ball and chain on my feet. Not sure I want another one so soon. Or ever.

"Are those donuts, Uncle Chains?"

Teddy's voice breaks the connection, and I'm reluctant to let go of the hold I have on Maddy. Of course, she jumps back like she's touching fire before I can even hold her in place.

"Yup, little man, I got a few dozen. I'm a fan of the ones with cream filling." Yeah, I totally look up and smirk at Maddy at that one. I like my things creamy. I even chuckle at the scowl she tries to send my way, but it doesn't quite work as she goes all red again. Her mind's getting into my territory, the "constantly dirty even over simple things" territory.

"I like the jelly ones. When you bite into it just right, it pushes it out the back and looks like brains."

Maddy scrunches her nose. "That's gross. You're such a boy." Not sure how she does it, but even grossed out, she's adorable.

Teddy shrugs, but it's one of the bigger smiles I've seen on the kid, and even Maddy's all smiles.

"Can we eat in the living room?"

"Yeah, as long as you put them on paper plates, and you get a few with sprinkles for your sister."

"Did I hear donuts?"

Flint and the rest of the guys poke their heads around the door. Wonder how long they were there. Wouldn't surprise me if they didn't send Teddy in first to clear the way. Especially since they were there this morning when I bought the damn things. No use in pretending they had no clue since I did promise them there would be food when I convinced them all last night to take this job at the last minute.

"Yeah, have a few. Coffee is just about done. Help yourselves to mugs by the fridge. Cream and sugar are already out. Just put it back when you're done. I'm going to get ready for the day."

Maddy walks toward the door, stops, and turns back to the group. Not sure she realizes that half a dozen pairs of eyes are glued to her ass. She might have slept in a thicker shirt that wasn't as see-through as the last one I caught her in, but the shorts are damn short. When she walks, bits of her delectable ass hang out. I have half a mind to punch the guys for looking, but damn, the woman is fine. Can't tell someone *not* to look.

As long as they don't touch.

If anyone's gonna do that, it's gonna be me. Not that I'm sure it'll ever happen, but I already called dibs. And everyone needs to know that.

"I'm just going to get my coffee." Despite that she still holds the one she favors in her hand, she puts the other three in the tray and takes all four cups back to her room.

I can't help but laugh my ass off at the sight of Flint's shocked face.

"Well, fuck."

"Told you she wouldn't share."

"Yeah, brother, but do you?" His look's a challenge, and I note that most of the other guys are keeping tabs on the conversation, even if they aren't openly obvious.

I hold his stare for a long time. "Not this one."

"Noted."

Well, shit. Guess that seals the deal for me. And from the smirks on the guys' faces, looks like I'm the only dumbass left who didn't know it.

Am I that obvious? Does Maddy know? Doubt it. Girl's only focus is the kids, and coffee, and I really have no idea which one is the higher priority.

"Okay, so who's the foreman? Who am I dealing with?"

Maddy is definitely not like the rest of the chicks the guys—me included—are used to. She doesn't take hours to get ready. She doesn't come out to a house full of bikers with tiny clothes on to put her best assets on display. Nah, my girl literally throws on jeans that have more paint on them than threads holding them together, a ratty black tee that matches the pants, and even work boots. Took maybe three minutes, but she's a sight for sore eyes. She might think the clothes are nothing, but they mold to her figure being so well worn. She's not about to let them work on her house without getting her hands dirty. She's the total package.

"That would be Flint," I tell her.

Flint extends his hand, giving her his best panty-melter smile that's literally caused girls to drop their panties and hop on him to fuck right on the spot. "Hey, baby."

"Name's Maddy, not baby. And hi. Okay, I got the plans in the garage. We can go over them there since donuts and coffee have taken over the kitchen table. I've run over these plans with a contractor friend before, so I know it's not impossible. I've already determined what's load-bearing and that I'll need at least two beams added for the open concept since we're going all out on this thing now."

Flint can't hide the surprise and respect in his eyes, and I can't hide my own pride. I ain't going to deny, I like that she put him in his place right off the bat with simply voicing her name.

He nods in acquiescence and trails her out the garage door. I turn and follow them, intrigued by the plans she has for this place. And even if Maddy makes it clear she isn't interested, that doesn't mean Flint won't try again. Or hell, four or five more times.

"Where are you going?"

"Um, with you?" I'm confused by her asking. It seems obvious to me.

She shakes her head at me like a teacher would a student asking for the hall pass. "Don't think so. You're the one who brought those little ones sugar. You're on babysitter duty till that sugar is out of their system."

"What happened to just saying 'Okay'?" Though why am I surprised? Maddy's not the type of girl to let others decide for her. Well, not for long, anyway.

"Looks like the coffee isn't as good as you thought." Her smile is too sweet, even for her, but I just shake my head as I turn and go to the living room.

"Fine, Mama Bear." I'm not mad. Can't even hide my smile.

"Hey, Chains."

I turn back, noting Flint is no longer behind her, but the door to the garage is open.

"Thanks." She opens her mouth to say more, but she just shakes her head, does that small smile thing that gets me every time, and says, "Thanks," again before going out the door.

Yeah, I'm totally screwed. I wonder if the new ball-and-chain set at least comes in a color other than gray.

Chapter 10 - Maddy

"So...." Izzy says.

"So what?"

"Girl, the man has practically lived at your place for the last two weeks. You trying to tell me you haven't jumped his bones yet? Even if I haven't seen him, from the way you describe him, and the photos I dug up from his conviction, the man's damn fine."

I still haven't asked Chains why he was sent to prison. I didn't think it mattered before, but with the more time he spends at the house, and with the kids... and with me, I'm just too damn curious. Though anything short of murder probably won't affect how I feel.

Oh, who the hell am I kidding? I bet I could even live with murder.

Not that I condone it, but I'm that far gone for the big biker. My head will probably be smart and want to kick him to the curb, but my damn heart will twist it around and come up with a crazy reason, like it was self-defense, or hell, maybe the guy deserved it.

Chains might not be the sweetest guy, but I know he's a good one. Everything in my bones, in my soul, tells me he is. That I can trust him. And yet I hold back. Hold back my thoughts, my feelings, my past. Denying myself from asking questions about his own past. I'm dying to know, but I'm also afraid.

Fear has been a constant companion of mine. One I try to avoid, but it's there. Choking me so much that I can't breathe, but it keeps my head on a swivel. If you're always afraid, even if it's a small part, you stay alive. You think of the worst and plan for it. You also learn to live each moment as if it's your last. No regrets.

Except I can't live out my wants and desires with Chains. When I leave, he and the kids will continue on. They don't need me to tarnish anything between them before I go.

"Hello? Earth to Maddy. This is Izzy. Please squeak if the aliens have you."

"Shut up. I told you before. There are no such things as aliens."

"See, that's what they want you to think. Then bam! You're in a spaceship and being auctioned off for your organs that they eat."

"Ew, you're crazy. Got one for you. Maybe we're already on a spaceship, huh? Maybe they just have us in pods, and this is all a dream as they transport us to their new world."

I laugh outright, as Izzy is too quiet for her own good. Yeah, she's going to be thinking about that one for a while. She and that crazy sci-fi group she joined online. Such a nerd, but I love her.

"Fine, you win. But seriously, you zoned out on me for a bit. I've known you long enough to know a zoned-out Mama Bear means you're not thinking happy thoughts."

"Don't call me Mama Bear, and no it doesn't. I zone with happy thoughts too."

Her snort does not make her sound like the lady she is. "No, you don't. Seriously, Maddy, you okay?" Her voice gets low, like she knows any big noise might spook me. I'm not a talker about my feelings, but Izzy has been through my hell. She can relate with her own.

"I... ah... I'm okay. I think being so close to it all is throwing me, though."

"What do you mean?"

I shrug, even though she can't see me through the phone. "I don't know. I feel eyes on me, but it could be anything."

"Well, you have a badass biker following you around, plus kids. You're like a little biker family now."

"Funny. But it's more than that. I think my imagination is getting the best of me. Even thought I saw someone I knew from then."

"Who?"

I pick at the hole in my jeans, forcing myself to talk it out. "A girl from middle school. We weren't close. I doubt she would remember me even if it *was* her. Hell, she might not have been caught up in anything, just a rumor mill, you know? Schools are like that, right? Saying everyone is in the drug scene, even if it's not true. If she was part of the group who was involved with their organization, I doubt she is now. I mean, it was like, what, fifteen years ago? People change. I know I did. Not that I'm saying it was her. Just thought I saw something, you know?"

I'm rambling. Nothing good ever comes from my rambles.

"Maddy." She pauses long enough to make sure I'm with her completely before she continues. "Do I need to call Frank?"

I don't want to move. I don't want to reinvent myself again. I can't. It isn't just me I have to think about anymore.

"I can't." It's a whisper from my heart.

"Um...." Her lack of speech says volumes. She's never without a response unless she's hiding something from me. Then she gets quiet. Too quiet.

"Spit it out, Izzy," I growl, doubting I'll like what she's about to say. Last time she did this to me, I got kids. Not that they're bad, but it took a lot to get to where I am with them today. Not sure if I'm ready for more.

"I sort of already have him on standby."

Her squeaked response is not what I was expecting, and I doubt she even hears my reply, as it's barely audible. "What?"

"Look, it's not just about you. Like I said, shit was weird when Jennie died. Having all three of you together, I thought it would be smart to have the paperwork lined up if you needed an escape. If you *all* needed one."

"Izzy," I breathe.

She grew up with Frank in her foster homes. Not that his name is even Frank; that's just what he tells people. Izzy knows his real name, but she keeps it to herself, and that's why he's always willing to help her with the paperwork for when I need a new identity. It doesn't happen a lot, but enough that Frank has his own speed dial. He's definitely not a model citizen. He does crazy shit that's probably illegal, and the easiest thing is to create new identities, to include cards and documentation, at a moment's notice.

The fact that Izzy already started the process just makes me love her even more. She knows I'm not a grow-roots type of girl. With my past, it's best to keep moving and not get caught in one place too long. Only a few people are looking for me. Okay, only one. But he has more followers than the average cult, so I never know who to trust.

Except for Chains and the Hounds of the Reaper. They wouldn't be connected with my stalker's business. They might be bikers, and who knows if they're one-percenters or not. But even being around them in a limited capacity, I know they don't deal in that same shit my past is filled with.

"I... I can't tell you what that means to me, but I... I can't. It's only been two weeks, but Chains really has changed. I doubt I can leave with the kids and not have him follow me and bring down his own wrath on my head. Hell, he showed he cared for them the second he threatened to take them away from me that first day. And I... I can't leave them. Not yet."

"Okay, Mama Bear, but you let me know if you need me to make a call. No judgment, you know that."

It's more tradition than anything that I know she's smiling softly and nodding, just like me. We have this conversation a dozen times a year. We've been through this song and dance before; we know the usual ending.

"Even if it's just because you feel too cramped in a place that has too many nightmares," she continues. "You're too close to your old haunts as it is, so I know you're having them. Either way, I get it."

"Thanks, Izzy."

"No sweat. Besides, no matter how far you go, I'll find you."

I can't help but laugh at the ways she singsongs that last bit. Of course she will. No doubt about it. She's a stalker on a whole other level.

"Noted. I got to get going. I hear Chains pulling up, and I need to get dinner on the table."

"Ciao, baby!"

A lot of things have changed in the last two weeks. Izzy wasn't lying. The guy is here more than at the clubhouse. The kids have gotten completely comfortable with him, even the others who help on the house. Chains even takes to riding his bike over now. Don't even need my security video to alert me; I can hear the sound from miles away. And it totally does something to me, forcing a shiver of pleasure to ripple through me each time I hear it.

"Nah, man, I got dinner tonight with the kids. Yeah, I know. Yeah, okay. Fuck you too." Chains hangs up the phone with a smile as he walks into the house without knocking.

I *also* have changed in the last few weeks and don't always lock the door anymore, except at night. With the amount of people coming in and out these days, it just makes sense.

"Problem?"

"Nah, just guys giving me shit about poker night."

"Poker night?"

"Not really poker. We all get cleaned out by Flint, but it's fun till someone gets pissed and throws a chair. Then it's hilarious."

"Sounds like a party. Why don't you go?"

"Don't feel like it." Even the half shrug says he doesn't care, but I've gotten able to read him easier over the last few weeks. He wants to go; hell, even I can understand that. I literally signed on the dotted line to watch the kids 24/7, but there's no reason for him to miss out on a few fun times with his buddies. He was in a cell for five years; the man deserves time to hang with the boys.

"You should go." I'm not trying to force the matter, but I really am fine with him going.

"I said I wasn't interested." His eyes glint as if he's expecting me to test him or something.

"Chains, it's not going to look bad if you hang with the boys. Seriously, one night off won't kill anyone." I smirk. "Well, maybe it will. Not really sure how wild your parties get."

He graces me with a small smile and tugs on my braid. Another thing he does that zings right through me each time he does it. He nods in acceptance. "Okay, Mama Bear."

Yeah, that does things to me too.

"You know..." He takes a step forward, and instinct has me backing up. We do this dance till I bump the hall table.

I look back to confirm I didn't knock anything off, but as I turn back to Chains, he's closed in on me more, going as far as putting his hands on the table to block me in.

"Maybe you should come out too," he finishes.

"Me?" It surprises me that my voice keeps squeaking that high.

"Sure. When's the last time you had a night off?"

"Ah...." I got nothing.

He leans in a bit, and my neck strains up and away, but he just moves his nose right to the part where my neck meets my shoulder and breathes deep. He almost purrs from smelling me, and I lock my knees at the sound and feeling his hot breath on me. Thank God I took a shower thirty minutes ago; I doubt he would purr if he'd sniffed me then.

"I wouldn't mind seeing you away from the kids. Maybe have a few more drinks together, see where the night leads us."

Yeah, definitely a squeak coming out of my mouth at his last words. Never had a blatant proposition like Chains just gave me. Fuck if that doesn't have me squeezing my legs together so he can't smell my arousal.

Doesn't help that his lips are brushing over my skin with each word he speaks. It's not a lot, just a feather's touch, but it's sending my body into a fit of shivers that I'm sure he's noticing with the way he keeps doing it.

I totally want to rock his world, or him mine, but I still don't know if that's the right thing to do. There are too many things in my head, too many things I'm keeping from him for me to actually go over the edge. Fantasizing, even flirting about it, is one thing. Doing it is another.

I hesitate, which is good, because the kids running in from outside to claim their daily time with their uncle gives me the excuse not to answer as he gets pulled away. But the lingering look he gives me lets me know he saw I didn't say no either.

We've been playing this cat-and-mouse game for a while now. I know I'm dying to see where it goes, and with everything Chains throws at me, I know he is too. I doubt we can keep this going for much longer before one or both of us crack.

Dinner is uneventful, but I'm happy Chains doesn't rush through, even if he can have the night off. I'm not saying I can tell him what he can or can't do, but I enjoy having him here. I like that he stays longer and helps with bedtime. He even helps with the dishes when I do bath nights.

"You want me to do the dishes?"

"Nah, I got it. You should get going. Don't want to miss out on that poker fun." Okay, I'm acting lame, but I've been off since he caged me in. I've felt him in the room the entire night, even when I wasn't looking at him. Feeling his eyes on me constantly has me fidgeting nonstop.

"You sure? I know tonight's bath night. Or maybe you can rethink my offer and come with me. I can get a prospect to watch the kids, you know."

"Um, no, it's okay. Anyhow, I wanted to go over some new ideas for Flint tomorrow. I was thinking about maybe redoing the kitchen as well since we're already taking out a few walls and really opening it up, you know? So yeah, I'll, um, I'll do that. You go have fun. Next time, okay?"

I have to say no. It's not just about a quick night in the sheets for me. It's more. Feelings are involved now. I don't know how, but they got there, and they aren't leaving.

Never had a one-night stand before. Don't even know how to. I've done the "felt up in the back hall by some random guy" scenario before, but that just made me feel gross, especially since they never called. I won't be able to deal with a one-and-done with Chains. It'll crush me. Even if it's a multiple time one-and-done, I don't think I can handle it with him.

As I watch him climb on that sexy beast of steel to head out, I wish I was that type of girl. The type who just runs and jumps on his bike and goes where the night takes me. Who doesn't think about the morning conversation, or what it means if he doesn't call right away. One who can hold her head up high as she holds her panties and shoes in her hand and hails a cab at 6:00 a.m. The type who leaves a guy's place and doesn't need to remember the address 'cause she doesn't expect to come back. The type who lives in the moment, free of doubt and worry.

My past is complicated as it is. I've done everything in my life that's let me live as free as I can because I still feel a cage around me. I don't think a one-night stand can liberate me. I completely doubt it can. And that much faith on one night of sex is a lot of pressure. Probably another reason I'm not jumping in with both feet.

My thoughts continue to linger on Chains' words as I give the kids their baths and do each bedtime routine with them. Two hours after he left, I'm still wondering if he meant more than just a quick hump and dump, or if he even meant that at all. He could literally have just meant I need time out with other adults. I mean, I bailed on him the last time he asked me to stay and meet his friends. I've met a few since the renovation started, but being in a completely social setting differs from a working one. Even if we do have some fun and it isn't all work.

"Girl, if you keep saying no, one of these days he isn't going to ask you anymore."

Now I'm really in trouble. Talking to myself only happens when I hold myself back. And that's exactly what I'm doing with Chains. It would be too easy to fall for him. And that will only lead to problems I don't need or want.

I look over the dishes. *Ugh.* This is my least favorite part of the renovation. I decided the dishwasher needed to be updated, so we removed it and already gave it to another family the club knew who needed it more. But the one I ordered is delayed, so that means hand washing only for two more weeks.

Looking over the dishes, I groan at the mere sight. It wasn't an elaborate dinner, just grilled fajitas, but man, it appears to have doubled in dirty dishes since last I looked. Probably doesn't help that Chains used like four different knives to cut up the steak that Grace complained was too big to eat. The fact that she can fit a cookie four times the size of the meat into her mouth is beside the point.

Chains was insistent that it wasn't a big deal. It was sweet seeing a big guy move around a kitchen, trying almost all the knives I own till he went for the biggest one, more for size factor than practicality. Which I mentioned, but he just said the other three didn't work. I think he secretly just wanted to try the new Japanese knives I bought the other day. They are pretty sweet. And sharp. And blue. Yeah, Grace picked them out for the color, and I agreed. Color was all that mattered.

Nevertheless, I have more dishes than I want to wash, but they won't get done on their own. I plan to change out the kitchen sick tomorrow and need it cleaned out.

Starting the water, I move the dishes around, then feel a buzz from the phone in my back pocket.

Yup, totally forgetting everything, I focus on the phone, hoping, stupidly, that it's Chains. If he asks me again, I'm pretty sure I'll cave and have him come back to pick me up. I'm that weak for him.

But it's not a text. It's an alert from my security system. And as I watch the feed, I hear the rumble of motorcycles.

Multiple.

And from the patches I see on the screen, they aren't Hounds of the Reaper.

They're Devils Damned.

Chapter 11–Chains

"**F**uck, Flint, you cleared me out again. Between you and sending the vamps out, there's a problem with poker night. Not sure who thought this was a good idea. Those bitches can be exhausting, but after losing a wad of cash, I sure could use a distraction in the form of *T* and *A*."

I chuckle while Bass continues to moan and groan as he stomps around like a child, yelling the entire time to God and country, or just to those inside the clubhouse who can hear him and don't care. The guy wouldn't last one night in the joint if a few hours away from pussy has him acting like a little kid sent to bed with no dessert.

"I'm just happy Christy is fucking gone for once." I groan at the thought. "A night without that cunt begging to lick my balls is what I needed."

"Yeah, that bitch has been all over you for a while now. Even heard her brag to the other vamps the other day that she's going to be your old lady." Domino grunts as he tosses his empty beer into the trash can on the other side of the pit.

I snort at the possibility. "Fat fucking chance. Made the mistake of doing her again after I got out. Ain't about to dip my dick in something like that a second time. I make mistakes, but I don't make them twice. Well, not recently anyway."

"Not sure why you're turning *that* away. She has talents, if you know what I mean," Casper chimes in, handing us fresh beers as we stand around the fire pit. It isn't a blaze, but it's got a few embers that seem to have drawn us in to watch.

"Ain't interested."

"Is what you're interested in a brunette with a signature braid?" Bulldog's sly grin isn't as sly as he thinks. And I really want to punch it off his face.

The rest of the boys chuckle, and I just tell him to shut up. Everyone knows I have it bad for Maddy, and everyone knows to stay ten feet back from her. I made it clear as fucking crystal. She's off-limits to the club till I make my move. And it's coming.

The way she looked at me when I caged her in at her house tonight has me thinking she's ready. No one looks that *willing* when propositioned if they ain't interested. But I saw the doubt too. She thinks it'll be a onetime thing. It won't. Made that decision a while ago now. Not sure she would be my old lady, but I'm willing to give it a go. I'm even willing to bet every motherfucker here their losses to Flint that she's going to be. It's the timing that's the unknown.

I also want to make sure she says yes because of me. No one else.

I'm a selfish bastard. I know if I say the kids are tied to the old lady status, she'd say yes in a heartbeat. But I want her to say yes despite that. I want her so completely out of her mind for wanting me that she claims the status before I bring it up, letting *me* know she ain't leaving for nothing. 'Cause the girl's a flight risk. Her comments, the house on the market, her constant traveling past, she's not one to lay down roots. And fuck me for wanting to do that. With her.

Damn, when did I turn into the fucking girl in this relationship?

"Hey, Chains!"

My name echoes out the back door of the clubhouse and filters down to the group of us "losers" who decided fresh air was better than seeing Flint fleece the other boys out of their cash.

"Yeah?" I bellow back, not even thinking about moving away from the group.

"Flint's looking for you."

"Motherfucker," I mutter under my breath. The boys laugh. "He's gotten worse since I've been away."

"Yeah, he's like a whore who wants her payment right now. Do yourself a favor next time and come strapped with the cash you plan to lose, then walk away. IOUs aren't what they used to be. Once Flint has one, he gives you a few hours to get him his winnings, then puts on an interest rate, and that shit gets damn pricey."

"Say what? And Law lets it happen?" Our prez used to only put the interest on those we loaned out to, not our own brothers.

"Who do you think gets the interest? I mean, the money goes to the club and gets dispersed as needed, but shit, the interest rate they put on IOUs is worse than a used car lot. No offense, but I'd rather the club get the extra cash out of the jobs we have, not just me stocking the bar, if you know what I mean." Domino's got a point, but I still don't want to pay up. Well, not yet. Flint can wait five fucking minutes.

"Ha, sounds like you had that experience before."

"Fuck off, Bulldog." Domino sneers, but it's Bass who wraps his arms around the glaring man to pipe up for him. Best part of the brotherhood is that we've got each other's backs, even against one another.

"You weren't laughing six months ago when you had to cough it up instead of buying Princess that bike you said you would—"

Laughter filters through the group as Bass shuts up Bulldog clean, but his look of retribution has Bass zipping his trap.

A siren blares from the speakers we have set up for music around the property, followed by "Incoming. I repeat, incoming. We got a F-91. Repeat, F-91."

The boys drop their drinks and race to the front of the club. I follow but have zero fucking clue what's happening.

"What the fuck's going on?"

Bulldog is parked next to my baby as he pulls out his gun and checks it. "A break-in is happening at a family's house. Flint installed the system about three years ago."

"Chains, take this." I turn and catch what Law throws me. "Comms with Flint to relay what's going on while we're on the road. Two-way communication, but keep the chatter minimal so we can hear what he sees. Prospect, get the van. We got kids involved." He turns away from me as he says the last part, and a chill races through me.

Who the fuck has kids? I've been away for so long, and I know some of my brothers, but there are new ones, and fuck if I don't feel for them for having kids being involved right now. Don't care who it is; they'll get the best from me.

I slide the earpiece into place and hop on my bike, not caring about the helmet. Other bikes are already pulling out when I get connected to what Flint's barking out to everyone.

"Three assailants have pulled up. Bikes ain't ours, and neither are the Glocks in their hands. Vests say Devils Damned."

Fucking Devils Damned.

"Entry points yet?" Law shouts as he opens his throttle up.

"No idea if others are around, still scanning, but see no one else in the area currently. Goddamn assholes got some balls on them. They have no fucking problem pulling right up to Mama's house. It's a one-way trip. These bastards should know this is our turf by now. No one comes into our goddam town like this—no one."

"Any sign of the cubs?"

Mama? Cubs? They better not be saying what the fuck I think they're saying.

"Negative."

"Wait, who the fuck's place is this?" I question.

Flint pauses, and Bulldog gives me a look as he rides next to me.

"Fuck, Chains, I swear I was only gone for a second," Flint says. "The prospect was watching the feeds, and nothing, and then I took over, and fuck. I messed up, man. I tried to talk to you, sent the prospect to get you, but shit went south quickly."

"Who the fuck is it?" I'm screaming as I ride with the brothers down the familiar roads.

"Mama Bear. It's Maddy's place. Sorry, Chains."

I grip the shit out of my handles as I speed up to Law, taking over his spot in front of the pack. He lets me 'cause he knows it isn't a debate. It's also where I should fucking be. That's my woman in trouble. My kids.

"Shit. Damn, Chains, your girl's awesome."

"What happened?" Law barks 'cause I'm too lost to say anything.

"She just double-barreled a Devils Damned as he walked up the porch. Didn't even open the door. Your girl is smart—shoot first, question later."

I grin in reaction, knowing she's as badass with the gun as I thought, but then it falters as Flint keeps talking. "Now what's happening?" I ask.

"She got off two more shots, but the others are returning fire."

"She hit?" I have to know. I say it rough like I don't give a shit, but I'm stealing myself for the worst of it.

"No." One word and I feel like I can breathe, but then fucking Flint just has to keep talking, and I'm back to holding my breath again. "She took cover, and the two got into the house."

"Where are the kids?" They better be all right. Not sure what the fuck is going on, but if it's Devils Damned, it ain't good.

They're worse than the scummiest bastards I've ever met, and I've been to prison. They deal with drugs, guns, sex, and kid trafficking. We've tried more times than not to take them out, but they rarely venture this far north. They stay near the Mexican border, linking with the cartels down there. We always have eyes on them. They're the only MC in the south that causes this many problems for anyone.

Hounds of the Reaper ain't a bunch of fucking Boy Scouts, but we all have some sense of right and wrong, and the need to eradicate those who are fucking plagues on this earth and send them back to hell where they came from. That's the Hounds in the name. We track down those who deserve it. We have the mighty Reaper on our backs, and he gives us the need to bring him the souls he wants. That's about as poetic as the boys and I get when we talk about the club's name.

"I don't know. Can't find them on any of the surveillance you had me install. I took a leak, so she could have moved them to a bathroom or shit. I don't know. I didn't put cameras in there, and the only way I can tell where they went is if I rewind the feed. Dammit, Law, I need to get updated equipment stat. This shit ain't going to work anymore."

"Cut the sales pitch and keep the current view. Have eyes open in case you see something. Is Domino with you?"

Thank fuck that Law can think right now. I'm a single-track mind, focused only on getting to the house.

"Yeah, he's watching out for them, looking at all the feeds while I follow Chains' woman. Fuck!"

"What?" This secondhand report isn't doing it for me. *And why the fuck is it taking fucking forever to get to her place?*

"A Devils Damned snuck up on Maddy and pulled the gun away from her, tossing it out of reach. Shit, the man just fucking hit her. She's backed up against the sink. She... well, fuck me sideways."

The surprise in his voice has me growling in response, but it's Bulldog who barks out this time for him to tell us what the fuck is going on.

"Damn, Chains' woman is badass. She just sliced the shit out of her hand on a knife, I think. She got pushed against the sink one moment, and the next she's yanking something out of her hand and stabbing the dick in the neck. He's spraying blood all over the place, and Maddy is covered in it. Fuck, that's a lot of blood."

"Dammit, man, stop with the chick talk and give us something we can focus on. Is Maddy still being held by the guy? Where the fuck is the other guy? You find the kids yet?"

I should probably take the time to thank Bulldog for talking for me. God knows I'm not good for anything but killing right now. But fuck, we are brothers; it's already known that I appreciate each of them.

Just as I think that, I can hear Mama Bear in my head telling me I should say something nice when this is over. Fucking woman's in my head, and instead of her screaming at me to save her, she's telling me to be kind.

"Yeah, sorry. Shit, um, no sign of the kids still. Fuck, I lost the other guy too. Maddy's good, though. From the way the guy with the knife sticking from his neck is twitching on the ground, he's done. She's running toward the back hall to her bedroom. Bet that's where the kids are."

I try not to smile, but I can't help it. She's a mama bear through and through. I breathe a sigh of relief but should have known it would be short-lived.

"Oh fuck. Oh fuck."

"What!" The whole group of us growl it this time.

"The third guy, he bounced out of her room and just punched the fuck out of her. She's laid out flat but is getting up. Shit, he just kicked her again. Damn, the girl isn't going down. She knocked him on his ass. Get him, Mama Bear! You got it. Punch the asshole. Come on, woman, do it again. What the fuck are they doing now? Hey, Domino, can you tell wh—Shit."

Silence.

"What?" This time, it quietly slips from my lips. From the way he said, "Shit," it can't be good.

"Ride fast, man. Just ride fast."

My veins freeze up. Flint is the life of the party, even on surveillance duty, he keeps up the banter and the play-by-play to keep us all in it. He isn't known for anything but a good laugh. But this isn't the *normal* Flint on the line right now. Or at least not a part of him I've heard in a long time. Only when shit has gone so far south does *this* Flint come out.

"What the fuck is going on?" My heart is about to come out of my chest, the sense of foreboding heavy on my soul.

"Jesus, he's... man, he's gonna rape her. He's fucking trying to rape her. Get there, Chains. Get to our girl."

Fire bursts through my veins and pours into my bike. I'm not the only one who shoots forward at that shit. I'm already breaking every law and some physics with the way I'm forcing my bike to go faster and taking turns that have the rest of the group slowing a bit to be safe, but fuck it. My family's in trouble right now.

I hear the house before I see it. Not sure if Maddy did it on purpose or one of the Devils Damned, but the music is blasting so loud I can't even hear myself think. But I don't need to think. I already know where my target is. I've walked in and around this house more in the last two weeks than most people would in a year of owning it. Mapped out each camera I had Flint install for security. Marked all the entry points, which aren't many, but I checked and double-checked them.

The music dulls out the noise of our bikes pulling up, but we still fan out, not taking chances that there are only three Devils Damned.

I rely on my brothers to have my back. They always have. Going to prison wasn't because I took one for the team. It was because I was *part* of the fucking team. Just because I'm a Hound of the Reaper member, I got popped by a fucking DA with a need to make his name. Didn't matter if I did the crime or not; I was a bad guy and thus had to be put down.

But they're stuck with me. They had my back then, even when they could have walked away and washed their hands of it. But brothers don't do that.

And that's what we are. I would die for these boys. Each and every one. Even the new ones I don't know. If they wear the patch, they earned that.

Just like I knew every motherfucker getting off their bike right now would lay down their life for me and mine. And this place is mine. The kids are mine. Even the house, since I put my blood and sweat into it. And so is the woman inside being assaulted by a piece of shit who isn't even good enough to breathe the same air as her.

I grab the Glock tossed to me as I take the porch steps two at a time, not even sparing a glance at the body still pouring blood out on the deck. The door's wide open, but I still check behind each corner before proceeding. My heart's screaming at me to race in and save my girl, but my head, thank fuck, is still in play.

That's till I come to the hallway and see the motherfucker tearing off her pants, her shirt already ripped open.

Yeah, my brain's off now. I see and hear nothing but seek and destroy.

I roar as I run toward them, knowing I can't fire a shot without possibly hitting Maddy. I knock the fucker off her with a full-fledged dive into his chest. The gun goes wide, and I roll with him till I get him on his back. He's stunned for a moment, and that's all I need. I sit on him, putting every ounce of weight I have to force him to stay where I want him. He isn't even fully on his back before I take my fist to his face.

Again. And again. He bucks and tries to get me off him. He's a big fucker, but I'm bigger and determined.

He laid his hands on what's mine. Dared to touch *my* girl. He will die, and I will give him that death.

His lame attempts to punch back only make me chuckle. I zone in on the blood, creating a masterpiece on the hardwood. Focusing on the hole I want to force into the face I'm beating. Nothing's going to stop me. Nothing.

"Chains."

I ignore my brothers calling my name. Don't care what they say. This Devils Damned needs to pay. His soul's going to be claimed by the Reaper tonight.

"James."

I want to say it's the softness in her voice. That it calls to me to stop. That the mere sound of hearing her lets me know I can stop and that she's okay. But it isn't. It's that she called me by my name. Not my club name, but my name—my real name. No woman has done that since I joined the club.

No, it's the fact that her saying my name turns me the fuck on, and I lose all interest in the scumbag below me. That's why she's it, why Maddy will be my old lady one day. Something that simple, and I focus solely and completely on her.

Chapter 12–Maddy

I say his name 'cause he isn't responding to the others. I say it once, maybe not more than a whisper as I try to grasp everything that's happened.

I was attacked. I was *fucking* attacked.

I shot someone. I actually pulled the trigger.

I think I even stabbed a guy, but my brain is bouncing from one thought to the next so much that I can't grab on to a memory long enough. It happened so fast, so freaking fast. I was doing the dishes, and then the phone chimed, and that was it.

I didn't even have time to call Chains for help. By the time I hid the kids, they were already on the porch. I didn't even think, just aimed for the door and fired. From their cussing, I think I hit someone. No victory there, just a need to keep firing till they were gone and off my property.

But they shot back, and that was fucking scary as shit. I trained to shoot. Trained how to aim and pull the trigger. I have zero knowledge of what to do when they fire back.

I hid, and by the time the bullets stopped coming in, I could only think about reloading my weapon. Fucking hell, I'm stupid. So stupid. I trained so much, but in reality, I didn't train as hard as I should have. Should have gone to paintball school or something. Should have set up real-life scenarios about what you do when they come in the house and your back is turned.

I took a few self-defense classes, but nothing like I should have. I knew this would happen one day, but I was a fool to think it wouldn't be like this, with guns and everything. Just thought he would find me, and I would run. I'm good at running. Great at it. I can outrun anyone. Just ask everyone who's ever tried to be more than a friend. I can run so fast and so far away, so quickly.

But running wasn't an option tonight, and when the guy grabbed my gun and backhanded me to the point that it threw me to the other side of the kitchen, I knew I was fucked. I really thought that was it for me. But as I turned to look at him, my hand slipped on the counter, and I fell into the sink behind me. I wanted to hiss in pain, to curse Chains seven ways from Sunday for using so many damn knives at dinner, since being sliced in the hand was my reward. But instead of it being a curse, it was a thank-you from the house, no doubt pissed that I brought this to its door. So I reacted. Guess my body wasn't done with fighting, and it grabbed the knife and just stabbed it in the guy's throat.

I know I did it, but it felt like I was a puppet. My body was reacting, but my mind was huddled in a corner, crying and rocking. It felt like hours flew by as I stood watching myself stab the guy, but as the blood sprayed on my face, it was the slap I needed to get the hell out of there. I needed to get gone. Needed to get the kids and get the fuck out. I survived the gun and knife, but my assets were my feet. Needed to use them to get us all out, 'cause God knew I wouldn't survive anything else. I'd already used up any luck I had.

I ran to the bedroom, wanting to get the go bag I'd packed and left in the closet when I moved here. It isn't much, but it would get me and the kids out of the state—hell, out of the country if needed.

But I didn't get there.

The feeling of arms wrapping around me has me pushing back, fighting off the unwanted touch. I scream in agitation, and I'm released instantly, which has me rolling back and huddling in on myself.

"Jesus, baby, it's just me. It's me, Maddy. It's Chains."

"She did the same thing to us, man. Give her a minute. She was just seconds away from having his thing between her legs."

"Fucking hell!"

I hear his voice but don't look up. I can't believe I thought he was the same man who assaulted me. Chains has been in my dreams more times than I can count. I want to have those arms wrapped around me, daydreamed about it more than a normal girl should. But it's too soon. Everything feels like the clammy hands that pushed away my clothes. The ones that kept hitting me till I was too drained to put up enough of a fight to keep them off me.

I look down, seeing how exposed I am, but I'm still too lost to know how much time is passing as I try to make sense of everything going on. The weight of warmth hits my back, and only then do I look up and see Chains wrapping his leather jacket around me. Treating me like Grace, helping me lift my arms to put them through the armholes, even going as far as zipping up the front.

I swallow hard and don't hold back my tears. His warmth, feeling him wrap his strength around me, even if I can't handle his hands on me just yet, knowing he's there, giving me what I can handle, it's enough.

I finally pull myself back to see what's going on, or at least to listen enough to get the gist.

"Law confirmed no one else is on the property. Just these three."

"I want the one still alive enough to talk to be taken to the hole. Get rid of the others."

"Ain't our first rodeo, Chains. We got this. Place won't even look like they were here once me and the boys are finished."

"It better, or it'll be me you have to deal with, not your boss, Bass."

"Roger that. Any luck on the kids?"

"No. They ain't in the bathrooms or Maddy's bedroom. Those were the only places without cameras."

"They aren't there." My voice is the strongest thing on me right now, and I'm more surprised than the rest of them.

Chains, and I think I see Bass and Bulldog, but I'm not trying to look too hard, turn to look at me as if I've grown a third head. They either didn't know I was still there or just didn't think I was back from the la-la land I was visiting.

"They're in my room."

Bass is the one to shake his head. "Sorry, Mama Bear, they ain't there. You think they went out the window or something? Was there another Devils Damned here? Could they have taken them before we got here?"

Now it's my turn to look at them oddly. "I put them in my room."

"Maddy, the boys just looked in there. They ain't there." He points behind him, and I just shake my head.

"That's not my room. That's Aunt Jan's. I just sleep there now. But that's not my room."

Silence.

Chains lowers to sit on his heels, pushing a strand of hair behind my ear. The need to rest my face in his palm is so strong. I know his touch; I know it can soothe me, even if my head is still wondering if he could hurt me just like he did the person attacking me. His words are soft, but I can appreciate the tenderness he's showing me right now when I bet he's dying to confirm they're okay, that they're unhurt. "Okay, Mama Bear, where's your room?"

I move to get up to show them, but it hurts too much in... well, just about everywhere. I let out a groan and a grunt and fall back on my butt. Chains is there quick enough to grab my forearm, slowing the instant descent to a manageable one.

"Wow, you move fast." I stare at him in wonder. I must look like an idiot, marveling at this after everything.

He gives me a small smile, and the guys still standing all chuckle.

"Only when it matters, baby."

I have no idea why my mind goes to the dirty side, but it does, and I feel hot. Like way too hot. But I'm not taking off the jacket. It's the only thing covering my breasts since my shirt is split in half and hanging down like a cardigan. At least I pulled up my leggings, but I want out of them. They are too tight on me and I still feel like I'm exposed.

"Where're the kids, Maddy? Where's your room?"

"The pantry by the garage door."

Chains nods to the boys, and they run that way, but someone yells back in confusion, "Nothing's here but canned food."

Chains looks at me for an explanation, but I don't have the energy to shout. "The carpet on the bottom. Tell them to pull it up."

"Check under the carpet."

From the noise, I know they found it. I should be ashamed, but I'm not. After everything going on, showing these guys that I used to live under the kitchen isn't something to shy away from. Thank God I still have it. I have no idea what I would have done with Teddy and Grace if I didn't. I thought they were here for me, but from how the last guy.... I shudder from the memory. His words as he tore at my clothes, pawed at my skin, and bruised every part of my body had my mind reeling in those moments that I was just extra. That I was the throwaway thing, not them, as I had always assumed would be the case if I was found.

"Chains! We got them. Man, you need to see this."

I grab his arm, though I'm not sure why. Maybe out of fear of what he'll think of me after he sees my past. Maybe 'cause I know it will only lead us to a conversation we should have probably had from the start. One that will reveal that I'm not as safe for the kids as I like to pretend. One that will have him pull away even more so than before.

But as I hear Grace's voice float through the house, fear for myself is gone. "You need to cover their eyes. They can't see this. Teddy will take it worse than her. And... and please don't let them see me like this. Get me up. He... he won't understand. He'll think I'm hurt, like his mom."

"What are you saying?" I can feel the rage he's holding back from my words.

I shake my head, but I don't dispel his worry. "I don't know if she was, or if he ever saw her get knocked around, but the nightmares. Sometimes he wakes up screaming things about her, about Jennie, that make me think he might have seen her hurt, and it affects him. I don't want him to worry about me, and he will. He's got a big heart, and I don't want me halting the little progress he's made in becoming a somewhat carefree kid."

"There she is. There's the Mama Bear I know." His praise brings a shy smile to my lips as I look away. I really am a mama bear with these kids.

He shakes his head but smiles. He leans in and presses a kiss to my lips. A quick one. Too quick. Not enough time for me to taste him. Not enough time for me to feel the heat of him on me. Only enough to realize it happened before he's standing and slowly getting me to my feet.

I hiss but keep my bottom lip firmly between my teeth to keep from making any other noise. Chains gives me a minute to breathe through the pain before moving us slowly to the front door. And it's all him. My feet might be on the ground, but there's no weight on them. I could walk if I wanted to, but my brain and body are finally on the same track and recognize Chains isn't here to hurt or harm but to help. And if the gorgeous, badass biker wants to carry me out of my house, I'm not going to say no.

His jacket is still on me, and I breathe him in and sigh as I let him take more of my weight. It gets to the point that he just lifts me in his arms. I don't care anymore. I'm tired and hurt, but I'm safe. Safe with Chains.

I can hear the kids' voices, and I wiggle to get down, but Chains just holds me tighter.

"They can't see you. The boys are blocking you from their view. General is with them, looking them over."

"Why is a general here? You guys military?"

It feels good to have him laugh as I'm in his arms. "Some of them were, but not that kind of general. Think surgeon general."

"So a doctor? Why not just call him Doc?"

"We tried, but he said no." He shrugs but shows no sign of being burdened by my weight. And ladies, I ain't a spring chicken. Don't think anyone has ever carried me before, not even to pick me up to sit on a table to make out or anything. Not that I imagined that with Chains or anything.

"You can do that? Turn down a road name?" I really need to get a biker "how to" book. I'm basing everything I know about the club off Google and TV shows. God knows how much truth is in both.

"Not usually, but it happens. General claims he's more badass than a normal doctor. He also had a friend he called Doc in the Army and doesn't feel right using that guy's name."

"That's sweet."

This laugh is more of a grunt, and I can't tell if he's thrown by my statement or maybe jealous. Is it bad that I hope its jealousy? Not that Chains has anything to worry about. Even if General's somehow hotter than him, which is impossible, Chains has something that no one else does.

He has a way to my heart.

Not that I know if he would use it to get in, but he has it. Doesn't have to do anything but show up and it's in his hands. I'm not going to tell him; it's too soon. He doesn't need to know yet. That, or that I would stay if he asked.

But as I look him over while he helps me crawl through the passenger door of the van, I know it won't be long before I'm biting my lip for a reason other than pain.

Chapter 13–Chains

The look in Maddy's eyes is exactly what I need out of her right now. I see it all: trust, desire, love.

I know she doesn't want me to know or see it, but it's shining bright. I cherish it, and it's the only thing I'm focusing on so I don't kill that last Devils Damned who had his hands on her. The need to kill is strong, but I'm holding on to Maddy. She might think I saved her, but she's saving me. I can't go back to jail. I refuse to.

When I was first sent there, I didn't have a reason to stay out. Other than the club and my bike, I had nothing to keep me away from the four walls. But now, with her and the kids, I have more than a few reasons to keep my ass on this side of the law. Not that the boys would let me go back. Bass wasn't lying. I know they'll have this place clean, removing any trace of the Devils Damned. But still, why not hedge our bets and just kill the fucker?

Wait till we're in the hole and I can beat him into the ground, at least. We'll just lay some dirt over him when we're done before we move on to the next. Because there's going to be more. This act means war. The Devils Damned will pay, and they'll pay in the blood of their club.

General moves out of the back of the van, giving me the first glimpse of the kids as we switch places so he can take a good look at Maddy.

"They're good. No signs of trauma. Kid said Maddy had him and his sister watch some *Scooby-Doo* on their iPads the whole time." General's voice is low enough that those in the car miss what he says when he passes me, but I get it.

Mama Bear to the core.

I look in, and Grace is all smiles. "Hi, Uncle Chains. Do we get to go spend the night at your place? General said we get to come home with you guys. It's like a real sleepover. You think Princess will be there? Do you guys want to watch *Mulan*? Or we can watch *Frozen*."

This little one has me wrapped tight around her finger. My smile isn't forced but natural. "Whatever you want, baby girl. I'll ask Bulldog, but Princess might already be asleep. It's pretty late, darling. Maybe tomorrow she can stay with us."

"Okay." And just like that, she's back into the movie she must have been watching the whole time the attack was going on.

I move my eyes to Teddy. He's stoic but looks like he's ready to give his report. Damn, this kid really needs to have some happy times. I pray this doesn't set him back.

"Hey, buddy. How you doing?"

"I was going to call you. Maddy put us down there and gave me the phone. Told me to watch two episodes, and if she hadn't gotten back by then, I was to call. But I was only going to give her one episode. I've seen these episodes before, so I know what happens. And Maddy taught me how to read time, and I set an alarm like she showed me for when I watch games on her phone. She only lets me watch for ten minutes before I have to go outside. But I set it for three ten minutes.

Every time I'm around these kids, I learn more and more how amazing Maddy is. How many foster, or actual parents, teach a six-year-old how to tell time? Few, I bet, as it's hard to teach kids unless you have the patience of a saint.

"You did good, little man."

He looks down at that and shakes his head. "No I didn't. I failed."

"Failed? Teddy, you did the only thing that matters. You kept your sister safe. That was your only job, and you did that."

I lean my head down so he can see my face, even if he doesn't lift his own. "You did good, little man. Real good."

"But... but I didn't protect Maddy. She got hurt." Tears well in his eyes, and I pull him into a hug as much as I can with him buckled into his car seat already. The guys must have moved them from her truck to the van when I was carrying Maddy out.

"No, little man, that's my job. And trust me, she won't get hurt again. I won't let her." I lean him back and look him in his eyes. "*We* won't let it happen again."

He nods and burrows in a bit before I pull back. "Let me check in with the guys, and then I'll follow you all back to the clubhouse, okay?"

"Sorry, Chains, but I'd rather get her there sooner if you're going to be a few more minutes. Need to do a few more tests."

It doesn't take a nurse to understand what General's saying. He wants to see how bad Maddy is hurt in areas that can't be seen with clothes on. He might not have been raping her when we got there, but she may have already had parts of her used before I was there to stop it. She isn't one to complain, so if she's hurting, she won't say it, especially with the kids nearby.

"General and I will take them now. I'll take a few of the boys with us too. The rest of you can follow up after." Now it's Law who's giving me a secret code. I need to see what's in the house. The grave look on his face tells me more than anything else.

I nod, kiss the kids' heads and promise to see them soon, then move to the passenger door. I don't understand the feeling of need running through me. The need to be with her, to make sure she's a hundred percent. But I know I'm not a doctor. I've looked over her enough to know she's alive and will live long enough for me to stay as long as I need to. I know this, and yet I hesitate.

"I'll see you soon." Leaning in, I give her a quick kiss, just like last time. I can't *not* claim those lips anymore. So much has happened in the last hour, but one thing has been happening for a while. Tonight's events just cemented it. Maddy's my woman. I don't have time to claim her like I should, not now, especially not in front of the kids, or right after she was attacked. She deserves more than that. She probably deserves more than me, but I'm a selfish bastard, and I won't let her get away. Not anymore.

I nod to the prospect, who starts the engine. My eyes linger on the dazed look on Maddy's perfect face that's already showing signs of bruises and at least one black eye. "I'm entrusting my family with you, Prospect. It's a fifteen-minute drive back to the compound. It's the most important fifteen minutes of your life. One hair is hurt on their head and you better run, 'cause I won't stop till you're dead. Get me?"

I ignore Maddy's gasp. Don't know if it's from the threat I gave or that I called her "family." Don't know and don't care. She needs to see how far I'll go to care for her, even if it's from my own people. I know she won't get the fact that I claimed her. She might not understand it for a while, but she'll see it. She'll see it in everything that happens from this point on.

I shut the door and step back to let half the group that rode up with me encase the van in full protection as they drive toward the compound. Not till the last brother crosses the threshold do I turn and head into the house.

Bulldog's on the porch and turns to keep in line with my steps as we head to the kitchen.

"Get someone to pack a bag for the kids and Maddy," I tell him. "They ain't coming back here till this place is clear."

"Already on it. Got the kids' stuff packed up and a few of their toys. Figured you would rather be the one to get your woman's clothes than have me or Bass do it."

The thought of either man touching material that holds Maddy's goodies has me balling my fists. "Thanks," I grunt. Yeah, I'll get Maddy's things. My woman won't have anyone touching her stuff but me.

We meet Bass at the pantry door, and he gives a nod. "Casper's already down there. Don't think there's enough room for more than that."

I eye Bulldog, but he just gives me a chin lift. "Seen it. I'll do another look over the kids' rooms and make sure I got everything, then head back and get them settled. Come find me when you get back."

"Thanks, man." I feel a weight settle in my stomach. This isn't going to be good. I knew it the moment Maddy said the place she sleeps isn't her room.

The carpet is already pushed back, and if I wasn't looking for the hidden room, I would have missed it. There's about three feet of a lip inside the pantry, and the carpet lifts to reveal a hatch that pulls out, allowing stairs to come out from the pantry door. If the flap isn't lifted first, the access to the stairs isn't available. The space is like from a movie I saw about World War II, with bomb shelters in houses.

Despite the age of the house, the stairs don't even squeak as I descend. The space is vast, but only if you kneel the entire time. Only place to stand is right by the stairs. Wires are exposed but there's lighting throughout, though I wish it wasn't.

"Jesus Christ."

"Yeah." Casper gives me a minute to look around before he points out his assessment of the area. "Took a few pictures and sent them to a friend. He says from the drawings on the wall, you can see a progression in age by the art style, going from stick figures to elaborate structural pieces. No windows that I can see, but it's vented. This might have been an old bomb shelter or something. Should have been a basement, but you can tell they didn't dig deep enough to lay the foundation more than a few feet below ground level, or maybe they did and just filled it in. Won't know till we get a few guys down here in the morning to check things out officially. May have been originally used as a pantry or cellar before she started living down here."

She.

There's no denying it. The pictures, the small photos, and the bed on the floor with a few teen magazines on the table. There're even a few beanbag chairs formed into a couch of sorts.

Casper nods toward a small bathroom behind us that I missed when I came down the stairs. It's nothing more than the smallest toilet I've ever seen with a tiny sink on top, like you would find in an RV.

"Hey, man, the prospect called. They're secure at the compound now," Bass yells from above, but I barely take in his words, still trying to grasp what I'm seeing before me.

Why was Maddy living down here? Was it voluntary, or was she forced? I look but don't see any chains or anything that might have held her down here. So what had her so terrified that she chose to live beneath the floor? Was it her aunt? Was it something else?

"Why's the prospect calling Bass and not you?"

I glance over at Casper before I take one last look, memorizing everything as I go. "Guess he doesn't have my number."

"Or maybe he thinks you're going to kill him," Bass chimes in as Casper and I come up from the hole.

I just shrug. "Kid's got to learn when to stand up and when to protect. Don't give a shit that he called you over me as long as he got them there."

I move past them and head to Maddy's room. There's already a bag open on the bed, and I try not to spend any more time there than I have to. I've never been to her room—well, the place she sleeps. I've now been in both places she's called her own, and I feel I'm starting to really see her for the first time.

Maddy might be my woman, but there's still so much I don't know about her. There was always a shadow behind her eyes that called to me, a shadow I wanted to eliminate before. Now I *need* to. Never had a genuine relationship before. Have little experience with how one works. But I know one thing: if Mama Bear ain't happy, no one is. And that's what I want. I want Maddy happy. With her life. With the kids. Happy with me.

Probably should just do the typical guy packing and grab whatever's closest and put it in the bag, but I don't. I take longer than I should. I open each drawer, feeling the softness of the fabrics, only picking items I've seen her wear before.

We may not have known each other for long by any real time standards, but I know Maddy. I know she chooses comfort over fashion, and she makes it all look good. She'd rather wear worn jean shorts over leggings. She likes the thicker tank tops to the thin straps. Socks with a pattern or design over plain colors.

What I don't know is what she prefers for underwear. But she has a variety, so I choose what *I* like. What feels soft as silk and I know will hug her figure. Items I know she probably wouldn't choose for herself when she lives in a place full of rowdy bikers, but I want to know she has them underneath all her other clothes. Items that will tease my imagination throughout the day.

I'm actually surprised she has so many pieces that aren't just basic cotton. The woman has many mysteries, and I can't wait to discover all of them.

I zip up the bag and bring it out to strap to the back of my bike. Casper and Bass are already waiting for me to mount up. A sense of belonging and pride ripples through me. These are my brothers, and my family is an extension of their own. They take to the kids, and Maddy, like they're their own, and they watch out for them. Just like I'll do when they find their own woman and family.

The ride back seems quicker than when we rode out. Might be knowing that my family is safe and Maddy is finally where she belongs, with me and the club. I push away the agitation that I wasn't there to show her around, but there will be time for that. I might not be the first to show her the place, but I'll be there for all the other firsts and lasts she'll experience.

General is waiting out front smoking when we pull in. As I dismount and start unstrapping Maddy's bag, he walks over, and I get right to the point. "He hurt her?"

"Not in the way you're asking. Bruises on her face, a black eye, split lip, bruising on her ribs, stab wound on her right hand. But the guys tell me she did that to herself."

I nod in affirmation.

"No penetration, Chains."

I inhale slowly and let it go. Let it all go. Won't lie, the thought ate at me like a leech out for blood, sucking me down till General cut it off. Thank fuck for small favors.

That's what I needed to know. I needed to know what steps I would have to take with her. Maddy's my woman. I've put a claim on her, but I'm not an animal. Might have been locked up as one, but I won't act like one with her. If she'd been raped, I would have still stood by her. It would just have taken longer. But even if the ass didn't get his dick inside her, I know the effect of what happened won't go away quickly.

Maddy is nothing like the vamps walking around here. She's not a shot glass you take in one swallow and then walk away. She's a fine bourbon: you taste, you wait, and you taste again. You enjoy. And that's what I plan to do with her. No matter how long it takes, I will enjoy Maddy, every part of her. And if holding her hand and just giving her soft kisses is all I'll get for a while, I can live with that. No matter how long it takes, I'll wait. She's worth waiting for. Knew that the minute I rolled up on her place.

"Where are they?"

"Law put the kids in the bunkroom and is staying with them. Think they just inherited a granddad from the way he's hovering. Got Maddy in your room. Gave her a few things to help her sleep. She should be out for a bit."

"Thanks, man." I start to walk in.

"Chains."

I pause and look back. The hesitation in his voice is new.

"Bulldog filled me in on what you guys found. I had to take some blood from her." I wait for him to take another drag of his cigarette. "Want me to run it?"

Run it.

Her blood.

This is a typical routine for us. We run DNA all the time to figure out who we're dealing with. But that's usually when it's a person we don't know.

But what do we *really* know about Maddy?

What do *I* know?

She has the kids using an alias last name. That for the kids' sake or hers? She has a room hidden beneath the house she's lived in for God knows how long. Her words of "the life before" let me know she travels frequently. But it doesn't sound like leisure travel. More like running. But from what? Or who? Was the attack random? Was it because of me and the kids? Or was it about her, about her past?

I know she'll tell me. Know that to my core. I can get this information out of her. But how long will it take? She has secrets, and even if she starts talking tonight, will it be everything?

My heart is heavy as I nod at General. He doesn't need words; he gets what I'm saying.

Maddy will be my woman. But I need to know what's going on, and the club needs to be prepared for it. Now.

If we're going to war, we need to know what we're up against. The DNA won't tell us everything, but it'll get us a starting point for Flint to work his magic and get a background that can explain a few things. Things Maddy will clarify. When she's ready.

Whenever that is.

But as I open the door and walk through my home, I pray to whatever is out there that it's sooner than fuck. 'Cause we need answers.

I didn't lie to Teddy. Maddy is mine to protect, and if I have to, I'll even protect her from herself.

Chapter 14—Maddy

wake with a scream, pushing off the vanishing hands that had been holding me down in my dream. No, not a dream—a memory. I jump out of the bed I'm in to get far away from the memory but hit my hip on some furniture.

Where the hell am I?

I squint, but the only light is coming from the bottom of a closed door. Shuffling my feet toward it, I feel my way like an idiot. I know I'm at the clubhouse. I remember coming here, and General saying he was giving me something. But I honestly was already fading in the car, and I have no clue which room I'm in.

Finding the door, I clumsily feel up the wall till I find the light switch, then blink against the bright lights that hurt my head more than anything. Looking around, I see nothing that explains whose room I'm in, but I'm not above snooping. And I want out of these clothes. Chains' jacket is warm but not the comfort level I need right now. I need to feel cozy in my own skin.

Moving to the tall dresser by the bed, the one I must have hit my hip on, I pull open the drawers and smile. Chains. I smell his scent on the clothes. I should have known I'd be put in his room. A warm feeling goes through me knowing I'm invading his space. An even bigger flutter hits my stomach as I realize I'm about to go through his belongings to find something to make me feel safe.

It's poetry, really. Chains has done that to me since I met him. His presence and aroma alone hold the same power. Safety. It's a heavy scent, and I'm finally able to shake off the last of the nightmare memory.

Wanting to feel completely human, I grab a pair of his boxers, sweats, and a T-shirt that says "Hounds." I want out of everything that was ruined by my attacker. I want to feel safe everywhere, even if it's just a mental game with the clothes. I really want to shower, to scorch my flesh with hot water until it burns away the unwanted touches, but I need to check on the kids. A shower might be quick for some, but I know me. If I get into one, I'm going to crumble and won't come back up for a bit. Better to do that after I know the kids are safe.

Stepping out into the hall, I close the door behind me but make note that it's the third from the end so I can come back to it. The hall has wooden floors, whereas the room was carpeted, and I wish I'd put on socks as I pad toward the noise at the end.

A door opens, and I pause, watching as a woman steps out, tossing me a glance before she turns and heads in the direction I'm going. I look down. I'm completely overdressed if her lack of clothes says anything. She isn't inappropriate, nothing hanging out, but her shorts and tank barely cover her bits.

I don't know why I feel self-conscious. I was just attacked, almost raped—hell, a part of me says I *was* even if the asshole never penetrated. He started, and that's what matters, right? But instead of worrying about how fucked-up I'm going to be around guys and wondering if a single touch will send me into a screaming fit, I'm stuck in the hall wondering if I look okay. It's so fucking stupid, but she was *so* pretty. Like a model who walked off a magazine. How do I expect to get a guy like Chains to want someone like me, with all my baggage and then some, when he has that ready and willing for him when he's here?

Closing my eyes, I ball my hands into fists. I need a moment to get it together. I was just attacked. The kids were in the house. The last thing I need to think about is Chains. I need to think about myself and the kids.

Fortifying my resolve, I square my shoulders and march toward the noise. Fuck anyone who gets in my way. I'm on a mission now. Get to the kids and make sure they're a hundred percent okay. Everything else is just fluff right now, and I can worry about it later. Time to be my true self, bring out the mama bear in me and see to my cubs.

The hall opens to a large room with three other hallways leading off it. A quick scan tells me what I already half expected—the kids aren't in this room. But it seems everyone else is. No one is noticing me, so I take the time to look around. I recognize a few of the club members who work with Flint on the house, plus others I saw tonight for the first time. Don't remember anyone's name, so I'm happy to see they all have a vest with name tags. It makes things easier on my brain, which is still fuzzy.

I sigh in frustration as I notice my hair tie has finally broken, and my mass of hair is coming loose from my braid. With the static in the air, it makes it go everywhere. Fucking perfect timing. I can go through being attacked, but I walk into a room and the damn thing just gives up.

"Stupid hair," I grumble as I try to manage it, but I already know the only answer is to untangle the mass. Going as far as flipping my head over and shaking out my hair, I scratch my scalp a bit before standing back up.

Okay, so this is a major mistake. I sway on my feet as a dizzy spell combines with a pounding in my head and behind my eyes.

I feel arms grab me and force me to sit. Only when I take the water forced into my hand do I open my eyes—I had no idea I closed them—and see Chains glaring at me. I tilt my head to keep looking at him as I drink the entire bottle down, not sure what his deal is. Once the water is gone, which has ridden him of his glare, I make another attempt to wrestle the nest of hair around me.

"Fuck."

I pause in my ordeal to get my hair under control. That's not Chains' voice, and I take notice that several of the guys are staring at me.

I look down and back up. *Did I spill or something?* "What?"

"Jesus fuck, is she for real?"

The vest says the guy asking the weird question is Domino.

Chains grins. "Yup."

"Fucking lucky man. Fucking lucky as hell."

"Huh?" I'm so confused by everything Domino is saying. I shake my head as I continue to sit through the dizzy spell till it's completely gone.

"Maddy, what are you doing out of bed?"

Chains' words jar me from staring at his brothers, as I, along with everyone, look at him. So many eyes are on me now, but all I see is the powerful man who makes my knees weak and holds a part of me that wants to stand tall all in one.

"I need to find the kids."

"Jesus, woman, you need to be resting. General said he gave you something to do just that." He shakes his head. "Fucking hell. Casper, get General back in here to give her something else, 'cause what he gave her isn't working."

I freak at the thought of sleeping right now. The nightmare rushes back to my mind, and my skin breaks out in goose bumps. Springing to my feet, I grab his arm. "No!"

Yeah, I totally just made everyone stop talking. If I thought having eyes on me was bad, making the room go completely quiet is far worse.

I swallow the lump in my throat as I look at my feet and wrap my arms around myself. Shaking my head, I speak in a much lower voice, but I know most can still hear me just from the sheer silence around me. "I don't want to sleep. My... my mind goes back there. I'm stuck on the floor, and he's... he.... I can't sleep. Don't make me sleep right now, okay?"

"Okay." His voice is just as soft as mine, but when I look up, I see the fire in his eyes, and it makes me bite my lower lip in response.

I need to break the trance between us, mostly so everyone will go back to what they were doing. I turn my head left and right in a quick scan to figure out if there's a neon sign on the wall that points me to Teddy and Grace.

"Where're the kids?"

"They're down the hall in the bunkroom we use for guests. Don't worry. We got Laurie—"

"Who the fuck is Laurie?" I can't explain the intense rage that flows through me at hearing another woman is watching my kids. *Mine!* "If she's one of the ones the boys call vamps, she needs to get gone. I am not about to let some skank anywhere near my kids. I don't give a fuck if she's part of your club. I will literally die for those kids. Hell, I was willing to be raped if I knew it kept those pigs on me and not on them. So don't for a fucking second think I'm going to let that stand here. Tell me where the fuck my kids are right now, Chains, or so help me God, I will rain destruction down on this place like you haven't ever seen before."

"Lucky motherfucker," Domino says as he leaves me to glare at a chuckling Chains. I really don't give a fuck that I'm once again the only entertainment for the boys to watch. Those are my kids we're talking about.

"Why the fuck are you laughing?" I screech at Chains.

"*Law*, baby. Not *Laurie*. Law's got the kids."

I squint my eyes together, trying to remember who the hell Law is. "You just said Laurie."

"No, I said, 'Don't worry. We got Law *ready*.' What you didn't let me finish saying was he's ready to cover if Teddy has a nightmare. The kids met our president at the BBQ, and they've taken to him, just like he's taken to them."

Can we say overreact much? Way to go, Maddy. You just went from semi-cool chick to total freak. Okay, maybe semi cool is just me hoping, but they all know I'm crazy now. Crazy possessive over Teddy and Grace. And maybe I went a tad far about expressing my thoughts on the ladies they have hanging around here. I've never met them, and I'm totally basing what I'm assuming they are on the talk from male construction workers, movies, and one glimpse of a beautiful girl in a tiny outfit.

Fingers on my chin let me know I once again fell inside my head and cowered inward. Strong fingers lift and hold my chin till my eyes follow the movement and meet intense silver ones that swirl with gold fire.

"Let's get a few things fucking straight right here."

I already know what he's going to say, and I pray I can talk my way out of it before he speaks and doesn't have the chance to rethink his words.

I whisper to him. I know he can hear me, but I don't want others to watch me beg.

"Chains, look, I'm sorry I called them mine. I know they aren't, but I will treat them like they are. I call them that, but I know they aren't. Don't take that away from me. I'll do whatever you need, but just not that." Hesitating to say more when he says nothing, I lick my lips, and a small part of me fears that I made the biggest mistake. That I pushed him too far. But I would do anything for these kids. He needs to know that. Anything.

"Anything, Chains." I glance down, telling him with my eyes how far I'm willing to go. I'm not that kind of girl, and I don't think he's that kind of guy. I don't even think his club is. But I want him to know—I *need* him to know—how far I'm willing to go to protect them and be in their lives.

The attack was a wake-up call for me. The moment I was running around getting them into the hiding spot I used as a child, I realized how much my life has changed since they came in it. It's no longer just me. It's we—us. We're a family in my eyes. I think of them as mine, and I will protect them any way I can. Even sacrifice myself in ways I never thought I could for them.

"Shut the fuck up before I bend you over and start slapping the shit out of your ass to get you to listen."

My mouth drops open, but he grabs me behind the neck, and I freeze as he leans in close.

"Don't you ever, I mean *ever* fucking again say that shit. I don't give a fuck that you claim the kids. You should. They're as much yours as they're mine. But if I hear you say that you would do anything like *that* to protect them, I say fuck that. I get you're a mama bear, but you don't *ever* just lie down and take it. You hear me? You fight. You fight your ass off. And that includes me. Don't you, for one fucking second, think I would use them against you. If I do, tell the guys, and they will hold me down as you castrate me. You get that?"

I laugh at his words. No way would his brothers turn on him. I'm ignoring everything else he just said 'cause my head, and heart, can't take it.

But, typical male that he is, laughing at him doesn't go well, and his face gets mean. Like super mean.

I get why people can be afraid of him now.

"Hounds!" His voice bellows into every corner, every crevice of the complex. I see some members popping their heads out behind doors, others walking into the large room from the hallways I haven't ventured into yet. My eyes go wide.

Seeing this many men in one place is intimidating as hell, especially right after the night I've had. I lift my foot to take a step back, retreat strong in my nerves, but he shakes his head, and I'm rooted to the spot as I once again get lost in his eyes. His hand didn't even need to flex in a reminder that he has me pinned.

He doesn't take his eyes off me as he speaks to the others. "Do we disrespect women? Do we take what's not offered freely and willingly? Do we attach fucking strings to get what we want from them?"

"Fuck that."

"What the fuck is wrong with you, Chains?"

"Shut the fuck up."

The snarls rippling at him are surprising. Surprising in the venom in the voices and shouts of protests that he even mentioned that.

"And if one of our brothers does that? What the hell do we do to him?"

"We end him."

My eyes shoot to the one who spoke as Chains releases his hold on my neck and steps to the side to give me a better view. An older man than the rest of the group, but the gray in his hair and beard doesn't distract from the muscles below that are covered in black material and a vest of his own. One that says in clear and large print "President".

I don't take my eyes off him—his presence demands I don't—and I watch as he comes closer to me and Chains. I notice the others make room for him like a parting of the sea, but no one disputes his words. No one even gives any sign of rebuttal on their lips.

"You must be Mama Bear."

I nod, but my tongue is weighted in my mouth. Probably a good thing, since my mouth hasn't been making me any friends of late.

"We ain't like the ones who attacked you. We got honor. Not much, but we know when no means no. We also know when a string is attached, even if it's offered to us on a silver platter. We ain't saints, but we respect women—well, till they pull shit, and then they're treated like any man who double-crosses us. Sorry to say, but there're a few bitches who need to be put down. Hell, I can think of two we got hanging around here of late."

The boys around him chuckle, and that seems to break whatever spell he holds on the crowd. No doubt that he could wield it again at a moment's notice if he wanted to.

"Speaking of...." Bulldog steps up next to the president and nods to the right. I turn as well and look in their direction but see nothing.

"Jesus. Ruby! Get your ass out from behind the bar!"

I watch in fascination as the beautiful woman I saw in the hall earlier rises from her crouched position behind the bar, looking like a contrite three-year-old.

"What the fuck are you wearing?" Law's growl has *me* shivering and wanting to answer.

"Pajamas."

"Like fuck those are."

I can see the eye roll from here. "Seriously, Dad, I'm practically dressed like a nun compared to what's usually around here."

"Yeah, but you ain't a vamp, and you never will be. What the fuck are you doing out of your room?"

"I got thirsty. Relax, old man. If I had known the entire group would be around, I would have stayed put. Why the hell do you think I was crawling around trying to get some water? Think I enjoy being on my knees in this sticky shit? Does anyone even clean the floors back here?"

"Might learn a few things while you're down there," a voice pipes up from the back, but I can't see who says it. From the glare and steam rising off Ruby, she does.

"Fuck off, Kooper. I ain't about to get on my knees to blow your fucking ugly ass."

"Never fucking wanted you to. Just thought you could learn how to clean up after yourself for once instead of getting us to do it."

Oh, that hit a mark, even if I have no idea what it is. The girl's practically ready to jump over the bar top and throttle the guy.

Luckily her dad steps in—for the Kooper guy, not her.

"Get back to your room. We'll talk in the morning."

As she huffs back to her room, I feel about as small as I can be. Totally thought she was a vamp, not a daughter. Here I am, standing in a clubhouse, hoping they don't judge me for my past, and I'm doing just that. They probably already have some guys looking closer into it. My contact to keep my past hidden is good, but if someone really dives deep enough, they'll find things.

Maybe I should take Chains up on his offer to get General. I need a redo, and maybe with the right amount of mixed drugs, I can sleep without dreaming and wake with a clear head.

Maybe.

Doubtful, but a girl can hope.

The president shrugs. "Kids. No matter their age, they sure know how to make us both love and want to throttle them. Know what I mean, Maddy?"

I'm stunned that he knows my name, but I guess I shouldn't be. I accepted the group calling me Mama Bear, my unintended nickname that seems to stick no matter how much I protest. But to hear my actual name, well, that throws me a bit.

"Come on, I'm sure you want to make sure your kids are settled in. Don't worry. I had the guys clean the place before they put them in there. We usually use it for guests, but we only get a few, so it's turned more into Princess's playroom than anything."

I nod as I follow the president—Law, not Laurie. There's nothing about the guy that's feminine, that's for sure.

I try to ease my flutters on how they'll react to seeing me. I haven't looked in a mirror—mostly been hiding from one, really—but if I look as bad as I feel, it ain't pretty.

A warm hand on my back has me glancing to my left. The gesture is so natural for Chains, leading me along with Law. It's the comfort I need. He can feel my worry, I'm sure, especially when he pulls me closer to wrap his arm around my waist before dropping a soft kiss on my temple.

"We'll talk more later. Just know you're safe now. And they are too. And you look beautiful. You act like it's nothing, and they'll follow your lead. They're stronger with you in their lives."

I look up, confused by his statement.

"The boys kept tabs on them when I was away. Ask any of them. You're good for them. Won't change that at all. I've seen it from the way they act as well. They might be scared, but they look to you for guidance. Just be the Mama Bear I know you are, and they'll be fine."

"And what about everything else?" I whisper my fears out loud. I don't expect him to answer them.

"Leave it to me. I've got it. I've got you."

Chapter 15—Chains

Teddy and Grace are completely out when Maddy looks in on them. I told her it would be fine, but I'm actually relieved. I really don't know how Teddy will handle it. With the attack and waking in a new place, anyone would freak, and the kid's only six.

I didn't lie about them being better off with her, though. The guys can see the difference. Even I can, week after week. They're both more engaging with others around them. They don't flinch or shy away from the crowds anymore, or even my bike. And I know that has a lot to do with Maddy. She might not know, but I saw the books she bought, the stuffed animals and kid toys with motorcycles to help wean the kids away from their fear. She's perfect, exactly what they need.

Exactly what *I* need.

Getting her to leave them is harder than I expect, but I shouldn't be shocked. Her name is Mama Bear, after all. But Law insisting he isn't going anywhere helps. That and the fact that he plans to watch Westerns all night, a closet John Wayne fan, has her agreeing when she knows someone will be there if the kids wake up.

I still can't believe she thought I would let a vamp watch them. I know a few babysat for Princess before, but I've been away a while. Not one brother since I've been back has shown any sign of trusting them with a child. No offense to Bulldog and his choice, as the guy doesn't have many options for babysitters.

I'm still a little flabbergasted by what Maddy said. I doubt she meant for half of that verbal vomit to happen, and I know it was mostly due to panic. But her willingness to sacrifice herself, her body, to a Devils Damned made me pissed. Then she offered herself up to me. Never been that mad before. Not even when I was sentenced for a crime I didn't commit.

I was furious that she thought I would force that on her. I'm *still* annoyed that she thinks I would ask that. But I might be madder at the fact that she offered herself as a bargaining chip. Does she think so little of herself that she would offer that? Maddy has never once come across as the type of girl who had one-night stands. She isn't vamp material. But her offer to become one to keep the kids in her life? It makes me both mad and proud to call her my woman.

Talk about confusing as hell in my head.

I need to talk it out with her. We need to have a conversation—several, in fact. The window of avoidance is coming to a close. I'd hoped to do that when she woke up, wanting to be there to ease any issues when she woke in a strange place. But that was ripped away from me. And my plan to lead her back to my room and talk it out is also not going to happen. Not from the way she's yawning, or the way Bulldog's headed in our direction with purpose as we leave the kids and enter the common area.

"Flint needs you." His eyes trace to Maddy for a moment before coming back to me.

Shit. That means they already found something. Either about why the Devils Damned were there or something from Maddy's past.

"Go."

I can't believe it. I can't fucking believe how lucky I got with her. She was attacked just hours ago. She said she didn't want to sleep earlier. But here she stands, knowing I have to leave, and she doesn't even allow me to explain before she lends her support. Once again, she sacrifices herself.

So fucking lucky.

"Casper, get Maddy set up in my room, will ya?"

"Of course."

He jumps at my words, and I glare in his direction, the first time I've really looked at anyone considering Maddy's had my complete attention ever since she took her hair down. It's fucking amazing. I just want to wrap myself in it. The curls make me want to play with them and watch them bounce as I pull the strands out. I thought I had a thing for the braid, but this is serious dick-hardening material. And I doubt I'm the only one who thinks so.

"*My* room, Casper. Get that?" I growl, and the guy is wise enough to stop his skip step in our direction.

"Sure, man, I know when a claim is made."

"Good. Make sure the rest of the boys do too."

I turn back to my woman, whose confusion is evident in her wide eyes as she looks between me and my brothers. She has no idea what's going on, and I chuckle internally. She isn't going to like it. Not my feisty, independent woman. Doubt the idea of a claim will be seen as anything less than barbaric in her feminist mind.

Grabbing her by the neck, I don't give her a minute to argue before I give her a bruising kiss. A kiss that should be quick, but I'm half blind with the need to claim her in every way with the way the boys keep talking about it. There's no tongue, which is a pity, but it allows me to feel her lips still touching mine when I finally pull away.

I can't hold back my smirk as she continues to lean forward, as if following my lips, before she catches and rights herself. Her fingers hover over her lips, ones I want to press into again, but if I go back for seconds, I won't be coming up for air soon. A fact that is apparent to everyone.

Bulldog chuckles and turns around. "Let's go, Romeo, before you have Mama Bear on the pool table and give the boys another show."

Her face pinkens at that remark, and my wolfish grin shines. It would be a show for sure. But the boys don't get to see her, not like that. They'll only see how she looks after: after I kiss her, after I fuck her, after I make her come more times than Grace can count.

Knowing this makes walking away easier, and I'm practically light of foot when I enter Flint's domain of computers. The place used to be nothing more than a barn, but the boys and I fixed it up years ago to make the clubhouse triple the size of the original building. Top-of-the-line everything from gaming systems, original pinball machines, steel taps for the beer, and all the gizmos in Flint's little "cave of justice," as he calls it. He likes to think he makes the decision on what is justice and what isn't . He has the eyes with his cameras and his ability to hack most anything.

"What you got?" Bulldog never wastes time. One of the many reasons he's called Bulldog—he's bullheaded and like a fucking dog with a bone when after something.

Flint swivels in his chair to face us. "You ain't going to like it."

"Probably not."

"Ain't no easy way to say this, so I'm treating it like a fucking Band-Aid. Maddy Fox is really Maddy Taylor, born to Cindy and Mike Taylor. Mike was a cop and died in the line of duty. Cindy raised Maddy as a solo parent with some help from Maddy's uncle, Mike's brother. Another cop, one we know."

"Who?"

"Dwayne Taylor."

"Jesus motherfucking Christ." Bulldog continues going off in the background, but I'm left frozen to the bone.

"The same guy who...." I can't even say it.

Flint nods. "Yeah, the same one who got you locked up. But that ain't the worst of it."

"Fucking hell." I eye Bulldog. He's not taking this well. It's my fucked-up life, yet *he's* freaking the fuck out. Don't get me wrong, I'm all sorts of twisted up about it, but he isn't the one claiming a woman who's related to the asshole who planted evidence that got them sent to prison.

"Maddy has an arrest warrant out for her, issued by her lovely uncle himself."

"What for?"

"Murder. Guy claims she killed her mom. I've been doing some digging, but not much is popping up. I found a buried file from one of her mom's hospital visits with bruising that assumed assault."

"That from the husband?"

"No, happened after the guy was dead." The look he gives me lets me know he has a theory, a theory I can already see.

"You think dear Uncle Dwayne got handsy with the mom after his brother died?"

"It would match his MO. Ever since you got tangled up in his webs, I've been tracking him. Got a few guys watching him now and again. Guy is careful, but he's got a type, and he always leaves marks. Maddy's mom is a dead ringer for the type. Might be the one who got away, if you catch my drift. Guy can't get Maddy's mom anymore, so he goes after those who remind him of her. Theory only. No proof. We'll need to talk to Maddy to know more."

"When did this all go down? Would she even be old enough to remember?" Typical Bulldog, thinking about a kid's memory. He might be a lot of things, but the guy's a devoted father and sees things from a kid's perspective.

"Yeah, she would have been twelve. After her mom died, she just vanished. Might explain the hole in the house she claims was her room. From the pictures Bass took, I can tell it wasn't much, but then again, what does a girl of twelve need when she's hiding from a life sentence?"

"Any connections to the Devils Damned?" I'm reeling from information overload, but I need to think about everything, and that includes the club.

"Just what we know about Officer Taylor already. They supply him the drugs, and he looks the other way when needed. Rumor has it he's getting a few other things from them as well, like women and whatnot, but I can't find anything concrete on that. He might've used the connection he has with them to get to Maddy."

"This a 'take out a witness' thing or something more?"

"Not sure, man." He shakes his head and turns back to his computer to monitor some security feeds. We're on a semi-lockdown right now, and he still has other houses to watch in case Maddy isn't the only target tonight. "Too many variables right now. Honestly, with what we know about Jennie's death, I'm not taking anything off the table. What we know is she and the kids are safe. Not sure how deep the knowledge goes. Hell, it could just be a link to the club, and they're random targets. Don't know nothing for sure. Give me more time. Just thought you would want to know the connection, random or not."

Or not.

Yeah, that's going to linger with me for a bit. *Was Maddy put here for a reason? To draw me out? Or is it just fate that we both have a connection to the evil bastard?*

"Go see to your girl. We'll talk more tomorrow at Church."

I nod at Flint as I head out, but I doubt he even notices, already back to the screens he loves and typing away like a crazy person.

I can feel the side glance even before Bulldog asks as we exit the security room, "You okay?"

"Not sure, man. Got a lot going on up here, if you know what I mean." I point to my head, and he nods.

"It's a lot to take in."

I shake my head, both in wonder and disbelief. "That barely describes it."

"Yeah, man, I get it." He pats me on my back, more for a show of solidarity than pity. Guy would never do that; he ain't the type. But being there, having one's back, standing with a brother, yeah, that's the guy Bulldog is.

And he would get it. He's one of the closest things I have to an actual brother. We prospected together, even knew each other growing up. When I went into the joint, I was more than happy to have him take the VP patch from me. I know some MCs hold it for the person locked up, but the club needed to live on and survive. I knew the boys would always have my back and not forget about me—that's just the way the Hounds of the Reaper live their lives—but I didn't want the club to be tainted in that way.

186

So after about four months of arguing, he finally accepted the position. The guy wanted it, always wanted it. We'd both talked about coming up through the ranks when we first started with the club. We were going to run it. That was the plan. But that was years ago. I no longer want that responsibility. And now that Bulldog has Princess, he doesn't mind being in the second chair, but he has no desire for the first chair either.

"Want a drink?"

I should say no. Should go into my room and find out details that I both want and don't want to know. I know Maddy isn't double-crossing shit. She doesn't have that type of fiber to manipulate her way into Jennie's life, to get her friends involved so the kids would go to her. Doesn't know how not to put her heart on her sleeve. She wants to be tough. And part of her is. But not the part that could do this. She's connected to an asshole, maybe even a monster. But that's it. Just a connection. Not the reason for it.

So, even as I know with everything I am that Maddy isn't involved and doing this against the club, against me, I need a drink to process it. I know she's asleep, and even if she doesn't want that, she needs it. Me going in there will only wake her up. I want to be there for her when she wakes; she needs to know that not only is she my woman, but I'm also her man.

But I need a drink first.

A big one.

Domino's manning the bar and knows what to put up for us before we even sit down. I take a steady drink and just let everything sink in.

Maddy's uncle is the same man who had me locked up for a crime I didn't commit. Learning that he's been pinning false crimes on others isn't a reach, but learning he did it to his own kin is a new type of asshole.

I know Maddy didn't kill her mom. That's not even in question. Anyone could see she isn't a killer, not really. If she was attacked like tonight? Sure. But otherwise? It's not within her.

"Man, it's quiet around here." Domino rests his arms on the bar as he leans in our direction.

Bulldog nods. "Kind of nice. My place is filled with noise ever since Princess learned to talk."

"Isn't she like five?"

"Yeah, and it's been one loud time for the last three and a half years. Swear that girl went from screaming her head off to talking my ear off. Love her, but silence is golden for a reason."

"Guess that means you're happy the vamps still ain't around here either, huh?" Domino smirks as he grabs his own beer and leans against the bar again.

I appreciate the boys not trying to draw me out, just doing the normal bullshit talk. It's normal, and I need that right now.

"Fucking vamps. Half of them don't even know why they're here. Most just trying to get me to make them an old lady since I got the kid, and they assume I want to settle down or some shit. If I had someone I trusted enough to watch Princess, she wouldn't even know them. But they think it's some sort of fucking big deal when I introduce them to her. It ain't. Just letting my girl know which ones to look out for."

"You got a smart girl. She knows who's who."

"Yeah, but you know how it is. Women get manipulative. Vamps are bad, but at least I know what they want in the end. It's the civilian woman out there who I can't figure out. Ma tried to set me up on a date last week with a friend's daughter. Didn't take long into dinner before she was making plans for her and Princess. Like I somehow would want a woman to come in and take over my daughter's life. She's *my* kid. If I need help with her, I'll hire a fucking babysitter."

"So what happened? You kick her to the curb," I can't help but ask.

"Nah. Need someone to watch Princess on Wednesday when we got that beer run to go to."

"Fuck, you hired your date to babysit? Don't you think she'll get attached or some shit? Think you like her or something?" Can't tell if Domino is outraged or impressed. I'm thinking I might be a bit of both myself.

"From the way the woman keeps asking for my dick, probably. Figured I could get about two or three more babysitting gigs out of her before I let her go."

Our pseudo bartender laughs, making me smile a bit. "Cold, man."

"Oh, she'll get what she wants."

I look over then, no longer keeping my eyes on my drink but the man beside me. He ain't a big guy compared to some in the club, but he's got muscle, and he uses it to intimidate when needed. Long top hair that's slicked back, a trimmed beard and 'stache. Even a few tattoos that I can see and some I know are under his clothes. I know women go after him, but the guy is cocky as shit, and both Domino and I raise our eyebrows in question.

Bulldog sports a Cheshire grin. "She'll get my dick. I'll get a nice fuck out it, but then it's 'bye-bye, lose my number.'"

"Harsh, man." His words might say one thing, but the grin on Domino says he's just jealous that he has to work harder to get laid.

"No it ain't. These women claim they want to settle down, so I give them a taste. They play the part of mom for like five minutes, realize it ain't what they want, but everyone leaves on a happy note, and I don't have to deal with them returning like some of these vamps."

"That why you pulling a Chains on them?"

"Say what?" I growl.

"You know, just get head but nothing more. Ain't like it's a secret."

Bulldog shakes his head. "Nah, man, Chains was waiting to get his head around what he wanted. I don't know who I want, but I know it ain't any of these bitches. Just taking a break from it for a while. Unlike the rest of you dicks, I can go longer than twelve hours without fucking something."

"Sure, but why would you want to?"

We chuckle till my name is called, and we all turn toward Kooper, who's by the pool table. He ain't asking me to play but nodding to the hallway where most short-term residents stay.

Maddy. Standing once again solo on the cusp of the club.

Shit. I fucked up again. Twice she woke and I wasn't there for her. I'm fucking up this claiming before it even really begins.

"Maddy, you okay? Have another nightmare?" I'm off my seat and charging toward her, but she doesn't seem to pay me any attention as she looks around.

"What? Oh, no. Where's the kitchen?"

"You hungry?" Kooper has come over from the pool table. I look him over to make sure he ain't trying to make a pass at my girl, but his eyes are only filled with concern, nothing more.

"No, I promised Grace we would have muffins tomorrow morning. I wanted to make them now so they're ready when she wakes up. The girl wakes up hangry, and making them when she's already awake just leads to a nightmare. Learned my lesson from that last time."

"Damn, Chains. If you ain't making her your old lady, I call dibs. She's absolutely fucking perfect."

Kooper's words don't phase Maddy, but I smile in pride.

"Already did, brother. So keep on fucking walking."

He laughs and bows out gracefully for a big motherfucker.

"Domino," I call back to the bar, "make some damn muffins for my kids. I've got to get my woman back to bed."

Chapter 16—Maddy

'm not tired. I know I should be, but sleeping is the last thing I want to do. But Chains is right, I need to rest. I might not shut off my brain, but I'm sore all over. I know it's going to be worse in the morning—hell, worse for a few days, if not weeks. I just hope the bruising gets better sooner rather than later.

After Casper showed me back to Chains' room—which I needed because I totally forgot which one was his—I found a mirror. I knew it would be bad; I mean, the pain alone told me so. That was the first time I'd ever been in a fight. I'd always imagined what would happen if I was in one. I'd seen enough brawls at the bars I used to work at to think about it at least once. Got to admit, I always thought I would get in a few good punches, maybe receive one or two, but it looks like *I* was the speed bag a boxer practiced on.

Going back to Chains' room a third time, I remember where I'm going. Completely helps that I left his door open so I can find it.

"You guys really need numbers or something on these doors."

His deep chuckle settles over me like warm honey. "Yeah, there have been issues a time or two. Actually, pretty funny."

I huff. "Sure, when it's not you. Trust me, walking in on these guys thinking I'm going to lie down with them isn't something I want to see. Last thing I want is to fall asleep in the wrong room, or have Teddy and Grace get lost."

His grunt at my imagery has me smiling internally. "Yeah, don't need these fuckers thinking you're available or anything."

Not going to lie, his words, even if he doesn't mean for them to, make me feel wanted. He's kissed me a few times, but I honestly don't know what they mean. They could mean nothing more than a need to make sure I'm safe. Or hell, maybe it's some kind of adrenaline thing about the night's events or just a biker thing. I don't see many women around other than Ruby; I'm the only one here, it appears. Maybe that's it, just needing a willing woman or something. And I'm willing. Very willing. As long as it's with Chains. The other guys are great, but they aren't him.

No one is like Chains.

"I'm going to wash up. Get in bed, Mama Bear. I'll be back in a minute."

I move to his bed and try to get comfy again. It isn't hard. His bed is like a pillow, and falling asleep is easy. Staying asleep is the hard part. I pull the covers up to my hips but don't cover myself, not wanting to feel trapped. That's what I did the last two times I tried to sleep longer than a few minutes.

The bathroom door opens, and then the lights go out. The bed dips before Chains' scent swarms over me. I knew we would sleep in the same room, even knew sharing a bed was an option. He didn't even have a chair to sit on in his room. But what I didn't expect is for him to pull me in close and adjust me so I'm lying on his arm and he's wrapped around my back like a sweater. I'm completely immobilized, tangled with the man behind me.

And I love it.

I sigh with contentment and settle back into him. I should probably protest. Demand my own room. Even stay with the kids. Prove I don't need a man. That I can be independent and take care of myself, take care of the kids. But I don't want to. I've been doing it for so long that I know how to, but that doesn't mean I *want* to.

For once, I want to rely on someone. I want to lean on another and not worry. To feel safe without locking a thousand locks. Spend one night going to sleep *knowing* I'm safe. Not just telling myself I am but really knowing. And that's what Chains offers.

"Sleep, woman. I've got you."

Once again, the man can read me so well. He knows what I need to hear, and his words settle me so I can finally close my eyes and do just as I'm told.

First. Time. Ever.

The alarm goes off a second later. Okay, I know it's not a full second, but it feels like it. I groan, knowing I need to turn it off, but I'm too damn comfy. The beeping doesn't stop, and I don't want to wake Chains. I attempt to roll away, but his arms tighten around me.

"Where're you going?" His grunt has butterflies taking flight from the deep rumble that vibrates through me as he sticks to me tight. His warm breath sends goose bumps down my body. And I refuse to acknowledge that with each wiggle, I can feel hardness on my back. And I'm talking *male hardness.* As in... yeah, *that* thing.

"Turning off the alarm."

"Why did you set one?"

He lets me go. Well, sort of. I set the phone on his nightstand last night, so it's not that far of a reach. By letting me go, it's more he eases his hold on me but never releases it.

As soon as I set the phone back down, I'm pulled flush to his chest once again. I attempt to move away, but his arm tightens like a vise.

"Quit squirming."

"I got to get up."

"Why?"

"Um, the kids? Did you forget about them?" I turn my head to give him a look that hopefully reads "seriously," 'cause I really hope he's joking. But I don't speak grunt, especially without caffeine in my system.

"Relax. Law's got them. And if he doesn't, one of the other brothers will spend time with them till we get up."

"They ain't anyone's responsibility but mine," I huff as I cross my arms, acknowledging that I won't be released unless he lets me up. Don't know why I'm getting defensive about this. He's right. For once, I have help in the morning. I don't have to get up and be ready to go when they are. I can relax if I want to. Sleep in, even. But I don't.

His answering huff is all the warning I get before I'm flipped on my back with him above me, arms on either side of me, legs trapping mine in the middle of his. It's surprising as shit.

"Our. They are *our* responsibility." I can't tell if he's pissed at me again or what. My mouth keeps getting me in trouble since I've been here. Everything he says has me raising my hackles lately. I bite my lip to force myself to keep quiet.

"Even if no one else was here, I would not expect you to go get them after the hell of a night you had. If you want me to, I can get them, but I'm a hundred percent sure they're in excellent hands. But I also know you're a mama bear. Didn't call you that just 'cause I thought it was funny. It's who you are, to the bone. I get it, you need to make sure they're safe. You just had a night that would leave anyone questioning their safety, especially with kids involved. But trust me, even if you can't trust anything else, the boys will protect them with their lives. Each of them knows what family is, and each knows they're all I got left of my sister. I couldn't save her, but I and, by extension, the club will do what's needed for those kids. From taking a bullet for them to making sure they get muffins while watching cartoons. Few people get a village to actually raise kids anymore, but with the Hounds of the Reaper, think of us like that. 'Cause each of them will be as much in their lives as any uncle would be."

"I trust you." It's a whisper, but it's the truth. No matter what, I trust him.

His eyes bore into me, forcing me to say more.

"I trust them. I just...."

He nods in understanding as he locks eyes with me. "You just don't know us. Don't know what it means now that I have you all here. You don't know where *you* stand."

"Yeah," I whisper in awe. I didn't even know that was my issue till he voiced it. But it makes sense. Our deal was I take care of the kids till he finds a place for them. But if they're here, with him, and even have a big family to watch out for them, what do they need with me? Especially after it's apparent that staying with me isn't as safe as I thought. I should just let them go. They're safe here. No one will get through the club to get to them. No one will get past Chains. But I don't want to let go. Not yet.

"With me. You stand with me, Maddy." He brushes the hair off my face. His lips split in a smile as he runs his fingers through a few strands of my hair. "I love your braid, but got to admit, woman, that little hair flip of yours yesterday got me rock hard. And now, being able to run my fingers through it, I don't know if I'll ever be able to stop. Why do you always keep it up?"

"My mom used to braid my hair. It's what I do to remember her. And it's easy to maintain, especially now."

Don't know why I said the truth. I usually never speak about my mom. Never give anyone the real answer. And from the sober look Chains gives me, I ruined whatever moment we were having.

"I'm sorry about your mom."

I suck in my breath. He knows. He doesn't know everything, but he knows enough. I squirm, wanting to be anywhere but here, not wanting this conversation, but more weight settles on me. I look away, not wanting to see his perfect face. Not wanting to see the pity I'm sure is there.

"Tell me." His words are soft and unrushed as he continues to play with strands of my hair. He doesn't force me to make eye contact, which I'm grateful for.

I swallow the sand in my mouth, which has dried it out. I take time to clear my thoughts enough to tell my sad tale. I don't want to do this, but it's time. He needs to know.

"You once asked what my favorite show was. I said *Scooby-Doo*, but I didn't tell you why. My dad was a cop, which I bet you figured out." I glance at his face, and he nods once.

"We were a happy family, him, me, and my mom. Then it changed." I swallow the lump that always rises when I think about it. I never talk about this, but I think about it often enough.

"Dad was killed. I don't know the details—no one told me—just that it was while he was on duty. It wasn't until I was older that I learned it was during a traffic stop. No one caught the guy. Even if they did, doesn't matter. He's gone, and life took a turn for me and my mom. And that's when my dad's brother started coming around more." I can feel my lips turn to a snarl, and I'm surprised that it doesn't push him off me, or at least pause his petting of me. Then again, I look like shit, so my facial expression might be an improvement.

"It wasn't like he never came around before, but he basically moved in with us. I don't know what it was, but I never liked him. Think I just did what my mom did. She always hedged away from him, so I did too. We didn't ask him to stay, but he just never left, you know?"

I feel him nod but don't look at him this time. What's coming next already has my eyes watering even as I blink it back in hopes they don't spill over.

"I came home from school, and I guess they didn't know what time it was, or maybe he just didn't care. He was on her. My mom was crying, and her clothes were mostly off. I guess I made a noise, because they turned, and my mom started screaming at me. I froze, realizing my uncle was raping my mom, and I didn't think to stop him. I just stood there, rooted to the spot as she screamed. I don't even know what she was saying. It could have been to run, to get help, or even to help her. But I just heard the noise and watched as he continued to move into her, a sneer on his lips. I guess he figured she'd just lie there and take it at that point, didn't expect her to start fighting back, but she bucked him off. His pants were at his ankles, so he fell back on his butt. Then I was plucked out of my stupor and ran toward her. There was blood dripping down her legs. I pulled her to her feet and grabbed her arm to help her to the door. But as we got there, my uncle realized we could get out, and he fell on her. She pushed me forward to my knees, but she didn't do the same, and her head hit our kitchen table. It was one of the few things we had that my dad made for us. It was made from this tree that my mom had run into with her car." I chuckle at the memory, the only happy part of the tale.

"My dad was the cop on duty who found her. Mom said she just fell in love with him at first sight. Dad said he didn't want her driving anymore, so he figured it was best just to marry her and take her with him everywhere he went. As a wedding gift, he made my mom a table from that tree. Parts of the car were still imbedded in the wood, and it was the metal on the end of the table that my mom hit when she fell to the ground."

I look into his eyes, holding his attention as I make my declaration. "I knew she was dead right away. Don't know how I knew, but I did. My uncle and I were both in shock, but I was more scared about what he would do to me. Something wasn't right with him and the look he was giving me, like... I don't know." I shake my head, forcing the memory back. His eyes have haunted me for years, and I don't want to feel them on me anymore.

"I'm sure I've imagined it over the years, but I think he was madder that he didn't get to finish. He didn't look at my dead mom like it was a big deal. But then he crawled toward me, saying I was going to pay for that, and it was my turn. Don't know if he meant it was my turn to die or just my turn with him. So I ran. I ran and ran. My aunt was the only person I knew I could go to. I didn't have any other family. My mom had taken me to her place every weekend since my dad died. My uncle never came there, so I thought I was safe. It took me two days, but I made it to her house. She figured out immediately what happened, even if it took me a few weeks to talk about it."

I breathe through the pain. "She hid me from the beginning. My uncle put a warrant out for me, concocting an elaborate story that I killed my mom in a fit of rage, even going so far as to fabricate that I was a troubled kid even before my dad died. I couldn't dispute it. I was a kid, and he was a decorated police officer. No one was going to believe me. And my aunt was an eccentric. Lived by her own means, was more known for her flower-power status than anything. But she was loyal. And her loyalty was to my mom, and to me. After my uncle showed up at her place the first time, I stayed hidden in a closet, but it was close—too close. So she made the storage area below the house my room. I lived there more than I did above. We never knew who was going to stop by. If it wasn't my uncle, it was his friends, or his contacts. The house was constantly bombarded by random visitors."

He tightens his arms around me, a weird hug, but strength flows to me through him, and I'm able to continue my sad tale. "I lived under the floor for seven years. My aunt taught me most things, and we used her name when we signed me up for courses online. She dropped out of school when she was fifteen. I don't have any papers that say I graduated high school, much less college, but I did under my aunt's name, and all of it was online. When I was nineteen, we both decided enough time had passed for me to leave, but I couldn't use my real name. The warrant was still out there, so I called the only person I could."

"Izzy."

I look at his face and see only understanding, not pity. I mentioned her name a few times, and the man is smarter than anyone would give him credit for if they went on looks alone.

"Yeah. She has a friend who's on the other side of the law more times than not. She considers him family, and he got me the papers I needed to start a new identity. I moved away, though I always expected I would be back one day to visit. But it wasn't till I found out my aunt died that I returned. Didn't even go to her funeral 'cause I knew it would be a place my uncle would assume I would go. It's the hardest thing. Every person who ever cared for me is dead, and I've never been able to say goodbye."

"Not even your dad?"

I shake my head and turn away. "No, Mom didn't want me to be the news story. It was during one of those uprising times where cops were being killed more times than not, and the media had been on our lawn for a few days before the funeral. She didn't want my face to be the one they focused on and put that burden on me for years to come."

"I'm sorry, Mama Bear. I'm so sorry."

I shrug. I never know what to say when someone says they're sorry for the dead they never met. Doesn't make sense that they would apologize for not knowing someone.

We just lie there for a bit in silence, me not looking at him but feeling the heat of his eyes on my face. I'm in my head, and I need out. Talking about this sets me off. I can't control the tear that slips free, and just like a levee breaking, my entire face and body crumple. I cry, then sob, loud and hard. I can't stop it. Everything is going through me. I was almost like my mom. A man tried to take me like my mom. I would have sacrificed a part of me if I had to for the kids, just like I know my mom did for me that day. I don't know if it had happened before then, but I suspect it didn't. My mom was strong; no way would it have been any more than one time, and it was the one I walked in on. But I survived it. My mom didn't. And I'm alone, again. Always alone.

Arms wrap around my back and my head, and I'm rolled till I'm lying on Chains. I don't fight it, just cling as I wrap my own arms around his head and hold tight. He coos in my ear, soft words that only make me cry harder. It's as if he knows that I've never grieved for the losses I've had in my life. His words aren't for me to hush or even to tell me it'll be okay. He speaks calmly as he rubs my back in encouragement.

"That's it, Maddy. Let it out. You're safe. You can let it go now. Don't hold it in anymore. I got you. You're safe. It's okay, Mama Bear. Cry out your release. You're safe. I've got you. I will always have you."

Chapter 17–Maddy

I wake up to the feeling of fingers in my hair. I must have fallen asleep after I cried myself out. Like literally out. I doubt I have a single ounce of water left in my body. But I don't feel embarrassed about pouring my sorrows out on Chains. I feel elated. Sappy, but I feel like a weight's been lifted. I never grieved before. I've cried a few times, but nothing like that. I had it burrowed so far down that it took a while to get it all out.

"Sorry for waking you, but I can't stop touching your hair."

"Want me to cut it off for you so you can keep it?" I joke with my face still on his chest so my words come out muffled.

He pulls my hair slightly, and a zing of arousal goes through me. "Don't you dare cut your hair."

He lifts my chin so I can look at the determination set on his face, and parts of me get wet. Like really wet.

He guides his hand from my hair to my back, running over me as he holds me tight. "Like this too."

"What?" I lick my dry lips.

"You in my clothes. Knowing a bit of me is touching every inch of you."

I blush at his words. "Sorry. I had nothing else to change into."

"Don't apologize. I might take the bag I packed back to your place so you have no excuse to get out of them. Unless I take them off you."

I know he can feel my heart double its pounding. I would like nothing more than to do that, but I'm so nervous at the same time. Chains is experienced, and I'm, well... not at his level. He probably expects things I doubt I've done or even know how to do.

"But we're going to have to wait on that for a bit," he continues. "I got to get to Church, and I'm sure you want to see the kids."

I just nod. He smiles wide as he realizes I'm too stunned to move my body off him. "Come on, Mama Bear. You got kids to play with first before you can play with me."

"Right," I say and slide off him, but I'm not much more active than that.

He chuckles as he gets off the bed and moves around the room, pulling out his own clothes before he stares back at me, smile still in place as he sees me still sitting on the bed.

"The bag by the door has a few of your things. Didn't know what you would want to wear, so I picked a variety. If you want something else, let me know, and I'll get one of the boys to go get it."

"I can't go back to my house?" His statement has me back in the present and not la-la land.

"No, Mama Bear, not till we know what's going on. I want you and the kids here where we can protect you. No one messes with the Reaper's family and gets away with it."

"But I'm not family." I say it offhandedly, just correcting his words, nothing more.

He turns and stalks toward me, putting his fists on either side of my legs as he leans into my space. "Let's get this straight, 'cause I'm not going to have this conversation again. You are mine, Maddy. I've claimed you. You are mine. Teddy and Grace are mine. No one messes with mine. You got that?"

His words are strong. Steel. The question is rhetorical, and I nod quickly, his tone telling me he isn't allowing anything but acknowledgment on something he sees as a done deal.

My head is running in circles, trying to grasp everything he just said. Biker speak for "mine" means girlfriend, I think. So I'm dating Chains. But can it be called dating if we haven't had a date? Well, I mean, we have dinner together all the time. That's usually what happens on dates, right? So have I been dating him for months now and didn't know it? I'm confused and out of sorts with him so close. I can't get a full thought in my head.

It isn't until he leans close and seizes my lips that my brain goes blank. Completely and utterly blank. This is not a quick kiss. This is not like the others we've shared. It's intense. It's passionate. It leaves little doubt that he's claiming me, that I've been claimed by him. His mouth doesn't ask for entrance, just takes, forcing mine to open and let him in without even knocking. I'm trying to catch up, but I'm just a passenger along for the ride. I want to wrap my hands around his head, spread my fingers through his hair. I wish he would push me on my back and touch me everywhere. I want more, and I groan in discomfort when he pulls back to rest his forehead on mine. I'm panting in his face, but he doesn't mind as he does the same to me.

"I've got to get going. Come out when you're ready. I'll make sure the boys have coffee ready for you."

We share a lingering kiss, and then he's gone and I'm sitting in a puddle.

"Panties. Need to find new panties."

Or heck, I just need to get some on. The boxers I'm in don't keep much in, and I'm sure I'm a mess down there. 'Cause I'm definitely a mess in my head from that kiss and Chains' words.

I'm actually a little embarrassed that it takes so long to get out of his room. It didn't take long to get ready once I found the bag he'd packed for me, but it took a while to come to terms with the clothing he chose. They're not my normal frumpy, comfy clothes. No, not at all. Everything he picked is tight. Not tight as in not comfortable— 'cause let's be honest, I'm old enough to only buy comfy things—but tight as in all my curves show. Again, not a bad thing, but they'll continually make me think about him picking these out and expecting me to wear them. I'll feel his eyes on me constantly, even if he isn't in the room. And I'll feel conscious of my body in a way I've never been before. Chains makes every cell come alive in me so easily.

When I finally make it to the main room, I'm taken aback. I should have expected that last night wasn't normal, not if the number of girls walking around is normal today. I only see one guy—I think they call him a prospect—and he's behind the bar. When I move in his direction, he smiles big and puts a mug in front of me.

"Chains said something about keeping you caffeinated if I wanted to get on your good side."

"Smart man." I take a sip and force myself not to spit it out.

He winces. "That bad?"

I very noticeably swallow, which only makes the guy laugh more. "I've had better." I cough to get the taste out of my mouth. "Thanks, though."

"Sorry, not taking credit on that one. Pot's been on for who knows how long. I just put it in a mug. Blame one of the other guys for that."

I smile and laugh a little. Looking around, I notice I'm getting a few eyes but pretend I don't see them. "You know where Grace and Teddy are?" I'm totally not comfortable with the kids being around these women. *I'm* not even comfortable, and I'm their age, or maybe older. Can't tell with the amount of makeup they have on. I'm not a prude, but girls walking around with little on is not good for kids. I might not have had really outstanding role models growing up, with a hippy aunt and a rapist uncle, but I know what fucks up kids. And seeing a naked woman, or practically naked, trying to get fucked by a biker at any age below eighteen is sure to do a number on someone. And that's exactly what these girls are here for. I'm not even going to pretend I don't understand.

"Bulldog brought Princess before Church, and Domino took them out back to the playground."

"Wow, didn't know you guys had that many kids around here for something like that. Or hell, that even a bunch of bikers would want that around."

He chuckles again, and I notice I enjoy making him laugh. He doesn't get my blood pumping like Chains, but the guy is easy on the eyes, and his voice is smooth like whiskey. Young, but older than me. Maybe late twenties, early thirties if I was guessing. Built but not bulky, and rocking a fauxhawk. Even has a few tattoos on the side of his head to make it look more like a short mohawk. It really works on him, and if I hadn't seen and fallen for Chains on sight, I might be a little tempted to flirt and see where things could lead with this one.

"We don't, just Princess. But the girl needed a castle, and we were happy to provide her one a few months before you all showed up. And then Chains had us double it in size a week ago. Pretty sure that one is on you for putting it in his head."

"Showed up," as in came into everyone's lives. It's still so odd how familiar I feel with some of them and distant with others, but if they're a member of the club, I trust them. The guys, not necessarily the vamps giving me the stink eye as I chat up the only guy in the place, it seems.

"What's your name, by the way?" I ask.

"Prospect."

"Seriously?"

Another deep chuckle. "Yeah, we don't get a road name till we patch in or right before we do. Till then, they call us Prospect."

"What's your given name?"

"Sorry, but it's better if you just call me Prospect. Keeps us both out of trouble, if you catch my drift." He winks at me just as I hear voices from a set of double doors on the back wall and a group of brothers saunters into the large room.

I keep my eye out for Chains but try not to seem too eager. Okay, who the hell am I kidding? I'm a ball of nerves. It's only been forty-five minutes since we spoke last, and I doubt he wants to take back what he said in such a short time. But I still hesitate to run into his arms when I see him exit with Law and Bulldog, trailing the rest.

I especially don't want to when I see a vamp practically bounce him back with her fake breasts as she jumps in front of him and swings her arms around him, kissing him easily on the lips.

I don't think, just grab the mug and take a large gulp. My hand flies to my lips to keep me from upchucking the sludge in my mouth as I force myself to swallow. *Yuck!* I would profess my love to Prospect for the water he sets within reach if I wasn't afraid I would barf on him if I don't clear my mouth out first.

"Hey, Mama Bear."

I nod, side-eyeing Bass as he slides into the seat beside me. I hate myself for doing a quick glance to see that Chains is still wrapped up with the vamp, giving myself away.

"Ah, don't worry your pretty little head on that," Bass says. "She's just a vamp. Chains ain't about to let her impede your claiming. Besides, I have it on good authority that he only used her mouth, nothing more."

Never had water come out of my nose before. That one's new. But only Prospect seems to notice; Bass sure as hell doesn't as he keeps running his mouth. "That boy's been a saint since he laid eyes on you. Think he only fucked one girl before he switched to blows only. That's dedication right there. Loyalty."

I roll my top and bottom lip in my mouth and try not to make a noise. I have so much to say, but keep it locked down.

"Hey, baby." I hear Chains' voice and feel his head swivel in from the side to kiss my cheek, but I move away. Yeah, I'm not ready for those lips on me. Not even close.

"Maddy, you okay?"

I turn around on the stool and fold my arms across my chest as I raise an eyebrow, then pointedly look at the vamp who's pouting in the corner. He follows my eyes, and I can already see him thinking I'm some crazy jealous woman. And maybe a part of me is. A small part I'm willing to cop to.

"Don't let the vamps get to you, baby. They always service the guys after Church. They didn't realize I made a claim last night. I'll make sure they get the message soon enough. Only woman I want before and after Church is sitting right here." He smiles his megawatt smile, and I'm sure on any other girl, the speech and the combined hotness he's putting off would make them swoon and just drop to their knees. But that's not me. Especially since I've never given a blow job in my life. Ain't about to start now, not here, not with him.

As soon as he gets close, looking for that kiss he's expecting, I put my hand up and push against his chest. Not like I could really push the mega-man away, but he humors me and halts his movement. "Not going to happen."

"What the fuck?"

"You heard me."

"Seriously?"

I give him another look, and he just huffs. "Jesus, Maddy, they're just vamps. They're here for one thing. To get guys off. I didn't fuck them, just got my dick sucked. If it helps, I thought of you the whole time."

My jaw drops. "Are you fucking for real?"

"What? It ain't like I cheated or some shit. We weren't even together then. Besides, blow jobs don't even count even if we were."

I can't keep my mouth closed; it's just hanging wide open. I look to my left at Bass and I think a guy named King. They're nodding in agreement. I swing to my right, and I just see Bulldog shaking his head as he downs his beer and walks away.

I feel like a fucking fish gasping for air on dry land with how many times I open and shut my mouth. I can't think, but

I know staring at Chains isn't helping, so I swing back to the bar. Reaching for the coffee, even as Prospect tries to remind me, I tip the mug back and drink the rest, coughing and sputtering at the slime as I try to get clarity over whatever shit I just heard.

Blow jobs aren't cheating? He thought of me the whole time? What the ever-loving fuck?

I'm pissed. *So* pissed. But I really don't know if it's because I'm jealous that he used another girl instead of just coming to me or that he'd rather have been with them than deal with me before I was attacked. Or just the fact that I haven't had a decent cup of coffee in over twelve hours.

Looking up, I tilt my head as I glance at Prospect. He *has* potential. Very easy on the eyes. I like him and don't want him to get in trouble. But then again, I'm just pissed at any male in the vicinity, so tough shit for him.

"Did you know that green eyes are actually the rarest eye color in the world?"

"Yeah, my mama always said I was special, like her."

"Yeah, they're hereditary too. You know what else is hereditary that I just found out about when reading Grace a book the other day? Rolling your tongue. Had no clue."

"Really?" He eyes me skeptically, even looking at the others, Bass and King still to one side and Chains taking the spot that Bulldog vacated on the other.

"Yup. See?" I roll mine easily. "Can you do it?"

He does, and I smile. I then turn to Bass and King and get them to do the same. "Interesting," I murmur to no one in particular.

"What you doing, Mama Bear?" Chains eyes me closely.

I spare him a glance as I look back at the guys. "Just trying to figure out which one would be useful for a blow job of my own." Bass sprays beer everywhere, and Prospect barely moves out of the way in time. "Figured I don't have the luxury of experience or even getting recommendations like you might with the vamps, but if a guy can roll his tongue, he can't be all that bad. Just need to test which one would be good between my thighs. I shaved... everything, really, and my inner thighs are like silk, so I can't tell if I want a bit of scruff like Prospect, the clean face like Bass, or a full beard down there like that one." I point at King as I tilt my head in thought.

"Like hell anyone is getting between your thighs." Chains stands as if he really is going to challenge his brothers. Like he has a say.

I lazily look over at him. "Don't worry, hon. I'll think of you the whole time. It ain't cheating, after all."

"The hell it is. You're my woman. I claimed you, Maddy."

He's roaring, and everyone is looking, but I don't give a shit. I jump off my seat, going up to him and not backing down. Wish I had my shotgun with me right now.

"And when the hell did you claim me, huh? Last night? This morning?"

"Jesus, you've been mine since day one. Don't for one fucking second think you ain't. We've been dancing around this for a while. I just made it fucking official."

"Well, sorry to say, but I decline."

"You *what*? You can't fucking decline." He's sputtering and it's kind of cute, if I wasn't so mad at him.

"Well, I just did. I didn't claim your ass, so go get a vamp to suck you off. Think of me all you want, 'cause that's all you're going to be doing. And while you do that, I'm going to get coffee. Real fucking coffee, because whoever made that shit literally has never had coffee in their life."

"You can't just leave." He's seething now, and it only makes me grin more.

"Watch me. Better yet, watch Prospect, 'cause he's taking me. I ain't stupid, no matter what you think. I know I have people after me. Hell, they're probably just after the kids, but I ain't going to be dumb about this.

"And you." I point at Bass, who looks like a deer in headlights and will probably pee himself if I keep the attention on him for long. "You make sure Teddy and Grace aren't bothered by any of these vamps. They don't need to see sluts. They've been traumatized enough."

I turn and catch Bulldog's eyes. Yeah, no one is getting left unscathed by my wrath right now.

"You seriously bring your daughter here with these *things* walking around? I thought you, of all people, would know better. But you're just typical bikers. Shouldn't expect much different, I guess."

I see the fire behind his eyes, but I don't give a fuck. Livid doesn't even describe what I feel.

"Let's go, Prospect. Ain't waiting on your ass."

I don't look back, and no one calls my name, but I hear Chains threaten Prospect within an inch of his life if he lets anything happen to me. I also hear my supposed *man* tell King and another guy to follow us.

I live on the anger, let it feed my feet as I stomp to the SUV, the one that brought me here last night. I refuse to let the fact that Chains sent more of his brothers along with us to make me feel anything right now. I'm pissed, and I need time to think. Lots of crazy is going on in my head and outside my life that I've never had to deal with. Jealousy being on the top of that and wondering if I'll still have a man after all this is said and done.

But before I tackle that problem, I need coffee. Lots of coffee.

Chapter 18–Chains

"**A**nyone want to tell me what the hell just happened? I take a phone call from Ruby and end up watching Maddy stomp out of here faster than a bear chasing honey."

"She wanted coffee," I grumble to my prez.

"We got coffee here."

I shake my head as I sit back down. "Apparently not."

"Boy." I cringe as Law draws closer. I usually punch anyone in the face who calls me that, but with him, I feel like the reprimanded child I'm supposed to be. "I know you're new to this whole claiming thing, but we don't usually let them out when they've been attacked."

He talks like it's no big deal, when I know it's huge and he's being kind, which is odd. He usually would have no problem ripping off my head and spitting down my neck. Done so for far lesser infractions before.

"Why do you think I sent King and Casper?" I'm blunt and harsh. Two things I don't give a fuck about right now. I should be respectful. Law has earned that. Not just for being the president of the club but from me. He's been there, stepped in more times than not. Even treats me like a son.

"Saw that. Ain't enough. Had General and Kooper also tag along. We ain't been at war in a while, but when we are, we double and triple protection. Especially for an old lady and one who's got kids. Got me?"

I let my head drop between my shoulder blades as I nod. Shit, I could have really fucked up. I was mad but not completely idiot mad. I got some protection on her, but Prez is right. She needed more. Hell, I should be out there following her around.

"Now." He slides a beer in front of me. I'm not even sure who gave it to him. "Want to tell me how you fucked this up?"

"What? Why do you think it's me who fucked it up?" I pull up quickly to glare at the man next to me.

"Really, son? You going to pull that shit? When is it *not* our fault?"

"He said she was his from the beginning but that letting a vamp suck him off wasn't a big deal and it was legal in the eyes of the club."

I turn to glare at Bulldog, who's sauntered his sorry ass over to talk on my behalf.

Prez just chuckles. "Is that so? Guess she didn't take it well."

"Actually, she started her own job fair for a brother to do the same for her. Was even kind enough to say she would think only of him, like he apparently did with the others."

Now the two of them are full-on laughing, and I'm pissed.

"Fuck off. The vamps are there for a reason. If she's going to be part of the club, she's got to understand that. And it's not like I was going to go back to them now that I got Maddy. I ain't stupid. The woman pointed a gun at me within the first five seconds of meeting me. If I came home to her after being with another, she wouldn't even greet me before she pulled the trigger."

My supposed brothers are still chuckling as they drink their beers, and I'm not willing to be the only one with a sneer on my face. "Didn't see you telling her off when she made a point in your direction," I said to Bulldog.

"She went off on you too?"

I smirk as Law's eyes go wide, staring at his second-in-command.

He ain't laughing so hard now, is he?

I smile as Bulldog glares at his glass bottle. "Commented about me having Princess around the vamps."

"Ha, you chose right when you gave her her name. Seems like she's Mama Bear to more than just your two, Chains. She ain't wrong either."

I think Bulldog is more surprised than me, but we're both looking at the old man like he's crazy.

"Vamps have always been around." Bulldog rebuts.

Prez shakes his head as a sad smile spreads across his lips. "My old lady wouldn't have it when Ruby was young. Hell, we almost went seven years before we allowed them back in the club, and even then it was on probation. My woman would probably still have had them banned if she was alive today. But things changed when she died, and hate to admit it, but I lost a bit of myself when the grief took over. Let things get lax. Didn't even care if the guys brought the girls around. Didn't matter, 'cause Ruby was in high school by then, old enough to look after herself when I came in for Church. I actually expected you to bring it up, Bulldog, when Princess came along, but you kept your mouth shut, and I wasn't about to tell you how to raise your girl."

"Well, shit. You think it makes me a shitty dad that I didn't even think I could ask that till Maddy brought it up? I raised Princess knowing what a vamp was, thinking it was a norm, but damn. What kind of father am I that my five-year-old can tell the difference between a vamp and a lady from fifty miles out?"

"You're still a damn great dad. Don't doubt that for a fucking instant, son. We all see things the way we see them, don't know options are out there till someone else brings it up. Hell, even Maddy's aunt had choices, but she chose to have her niece hide in the dark for years. Don't for a second think you fucked up. Princess and Maddy had great parents and shit circumstances, but both are here and happy. Well, at least one is. Maddy's probably still mad at him." He chucks his head in my direction, and it breaks whatever solemn moment we had.

"Bring it up at Church. Tell the boys what you want. More than a few might back you if they know your reasons and know you ain't banning the vamps but just limiting their time at the club for certain days and times when kids ain't around. You got my vote either way you go. Think about it."

"Thanks, Prez." Bulldog nods as Law pats me on the back, more to use as leverage to get off his seat than anything else. The old man ain't heavy, but he ain't young, and we all need help when the knees start to creak when we sit and stand.

We nurse our beers and say nothing for a bit, both lost in our heads.

"You know you fucked up, right?" Bulldog says after a while.

"Yeah." I fucked that completely up. Who says the shit I spewed to a woman— *any* woman, but especially one they want as their old lady?

"You know you're going to be getting on your knees and begging before she'll be getting on her knees any time soon."

"Yeah. Any advice?"

"Haven't had many woman worth the effort, but if she is, and I know she is, saying sorry helps. Don't even try to deny it, but call it out and get it done fast. Otherwise, it festers, you know?"

I nod in understanding.

"Also, probably a good idea not to let any vamp hang on you for, like, ever. That woman was practically planning how to scratch the eyes out of the sluts who attached themselves to you when we got done with Church. Now that Maddy knows what the others have done with you, doubt any of them are safe. Help keep the club out of a police investigation, will you, my man? Keep your woman occupied and not looking to kill anyone. We already have enough dead bodies out back. We don't need to dig any more graves for a bit."

"Don't worry, brother. I plan to keep her well entertained for the foreseeable future."

By the time Maddy gets back, it's past two. I know every place she went, thanks to the guys keeping me in the loop with texts, but I'm surprised as shit by the amount of stuff she's unloading from the SUV.

I saunter over and say nothing, but she's already glaring at me.

"Don't give me shit. Things needed to get bought if you expect me and the kids to stay here for a while."

"Yeah, but I didn't expect you to buy the damn store."

"There's still stuff I can go back and get," she warns me, but I smile at her threat. She can buy whatever the fuck she wants as long as she brings it here, to me.

"You guys have shit for coffee, so I needed to stock up. And the kids needed something to do other than sit at a bar all day."

I love the fact that she's mad as hell at me still but not enough to take it out on the kids.

"Also noticed your phone charger was shit, so here." She throws me a new cord as she stomps off with enough packages in hand to trip over. But I see a visible red cup in her hand, too, so I know the world would literally have to tip over if she's going to be spilling her coffee.

I gather the rest—well, the ones the prospect doesn't get—and kick the door closed as I follow them into the clubhouse. When I arrive, her bags are already on the pool table, taking over whatever game was in place between Bulldog and Domino. But neither seems to mind.

"Noticed Princess had a hole in her jeans. Here, take this. And these too. Don't give me that look. They were on sale, so it was stupid not to buy her clothes."

Yeah, Mama Bear to all.

"And here. Got you an e-cig. If you're going to be around the kids often, you ain't going to be smoking like a chimney. Ain't telling you to quit, just asking that you don't do it by them, and if you do, it ain't nasty smelling." She throws a few items toward Domino, who's as wide-eyed as a cat on a high ledge with no way down.

I just follow, knowing she's headed to the kitchen and is going to need the Keurig I'm holding. I smile my head off in pride, watching as she passes out a few things here and there to the guys. She's been here a millisecond and noticed so much in such a short time. She may have seen a few of the guys working on her place, but I know she didn't get to know them. Not well enough to buy them things. Guess that changed.

I'm not jealous. Jealous would mean I fear her leaving, and I don't. She could have done that. She literally could have walked out that door for coffee and never come back. But she didn't. She bought coffee, not only for her but the five guys with her, refusing their money to pay. Then she went shopping and bought stuff for the rest of the brothers.

"Seriously, man, you fuck this up, and there's a list a mile long willing to step in for you."

I look around the room and see my brothers all giving me the same look that echoes Bulldog's words.

"Ain't about to."

I step into the next room, pausing at the door, watching her ass as she bends over, searching through the last of her bags.

"You about done in here?" I ask.

"Almost."

"And what about our argument? We done with that too?" I put the shit I'm carrying down and lean against the doorframe that leads into our industrial-size kitchen. The club is big, so it's no surprise the kitchen is too.

"Don't know. Never had one before." She keeps her eyes on her task. Childish, sure, but it's kind of cute on her as well.

"An argument?"

She shrugs as she turns away from me to put the coffee in a cabinet she'd already cleared out and started calling her own. Guess she doesn't have any problem making herself at home here. It warms me seeing this bit of settlement from her. It bodes well for us.

"I've had them before, but usually when I had one, it meant I was getting too attached, and attachments weren't really my thing. Doesn't help when I'm trying to lie low, so I never saw the end of an argument, unless you count me leaving as ending one."

"You planning on leaving at the end of *this* one?"

She shrugs again, but at least she looks over her shoulder at me.

I saunter over to her slowly, not rushing this. I know this is a deal breaker, and I don't want to mess it up—again. I turn her, moving my hands up her arms, using my fingertips to brush her hair out of her face. She hasn't put it back in a braid yet, and I'm enjoying having the right to touch her like she's mine. 'Cause she is.

"I fucked up. I get that. Never had a girl before who I cared about more than what happened in between the sheets. Going to fuck up again knowing me. But don't leave. Not now, not later. You're scared. I get that. This is new for you: the rules, the club, all of it. But don't doubt us, because I won't. What I said was shit, and I know you won't let me get away with saying it again, so I won't." I tip her chin up a bit to see her beautiful eyes. "I also won't be going after any vamp. I may have used them before we were together, but that was just it. A use that is not needed anymore, 'cause I got the girl I want. No one else. You get that?"

She licks her lips and nods. I think I lost her somewhere between me saying I fucked up and that I didn't want anyone else. She's staring at my lips, nothing more. I see the desire swirling behind her eyes; she can't hide it. We might argue, but it's all just foreplay of sorts for us. One I like.

"Where're the kids?"

I smirk, knowing exactly what she's asking and why. "Law's got them watching a movie. It's a long one, and they just started it."

"Um, maybe you and I should talk more. Get it all figured out before we tell them." It's damn cute that she breaks eye contact with me to look at the fucking tile we have in here. Borderline adorable how I see a blush on her cheek. My woman wants me but has no idea how to ask for it. Fucking fantastic. I'm tired of the vamps and prior girls who tried to goad me by flashing skin and saying blatantly obvious things. Some were as subtle as "I'll suck your dick if you want." Yeah, I wanted. But that was then. That was the easy chick with no strings. I want the strings now. And I don't want easy.

I want Maddy.

"Ain't nothing to say. They already know you're mine. But if *you* need more convincing, think it would be better to do it in my room with not so many eyes."

I drag her toward my room, but only because her feet don't move as fast as mine, and I'm not letting go of her hand that I took as soon as she said she wanted to "talk." *Yeah, like speaking is actually going to happen beyond me asking her if what I'm about to do to her feels good.*

As soon as my door shuts behind me, I push her against it, my mouth claiming her lips, her moans of pleasure filling the air as I let my weight press against her. I clench her hand in mine as I bring it up to the doorframe to rest beside our faces as the other goes to her hip, squeezing her, enjoying the firmness of her curves below my hand.

I can't get enough of this woman. Knew being with her would be explosive. I want to take my time and savor every inch of her, of this moment. But I can't stop myself. I need more.

I pull her away from the door, spinning us both. Before I let her fall onto the bed, I yank off her tank top, and then my brain sputters for a full thirty seconds. Seeing Maddy on my bed, hair in a million directions, shirt off, just in a bra and jeans, it does something to me.

Time slows as I push her gently back onto the bed. She goes back to her elbows and watches me undo her pants and pull them off with her socks and shoes.

Only then do I stand and take in the vision on my black sheets. "Fuck, baby, you're beautiful."

I can tell her movements are from her being shy, not from a wanton woman who knows how to get a guy to focus on her legs that slide over each other in a come-hither way. I feel the devil that sits on my shoulder smile.

This is going to be fun.

Maddy isn't like the vamps. She won't just moan to get me to think she likes something. She'll do it 'cause she's into it. I know she isn't experienced like the girls I've bedded before, and that's a fucking turn-on. Bulldog was right. Knowing I'm the only brother to sink my dick into her honeypot sets me off.

I pull my shirt over my head with one hand as I unbutton my pants with the other. I don't take them off, not yet. Still need to make penance for my sins. I still need to make sure Maddy knows I'm sorry. I need her to know that I'm the only brother for her.

I crawl up the bed. Her breathing is labored as she watches intently. Leaning down, I kiss her knee, enjoying the fact that her leg tightens in reflex. I guide my nose along her leg, moving to her inner thigh, then out again. No pattern, and it drives her wild. I'm not too far behind either.

When I reach her center, I just breathe her in as I bury my face between her legs. Her back bows as she reacts to such a simple thing as my face between her thighs. It lets me know she's ready for more, and I'm done with this slow shit. I pull her panties off and drop my mouth on her the instant they fly behind me.

Her body shudders as she writhes below me. God, she tastes amazing. I don't go down on a lot of girls, and never a vamp. I know what dicks have been there, so I ain't a willing person, even though I demand that of them. Or I did. Before Maddy, before Mama Bear came into my life. I'm not a novice, but I ain't known for my pussy licking, though you wouldn't know that by looking at her.

I glance up as my tongue dances around her clit and see her head thrown back, twisting her hair in ways that make me want to grab it and twist it on my own. I want her eyes on me, but I don't want to stop eating my snack. So I play dirty.

I nip her skin enough for her to come back from the edge to draw her wide eyes to me, but as soon as they're on mine, I suck her entire nub into my mouth and keep sucking as I push two fingers into her at the same time and reach for that spot only women have.

Her hands find my head, and I love the pull she gives my hair. She ain't directing me, just holding on for dear life 'cause I'm sucking the pleasure right out of her. I continue to suck and plunge my fingers in, but I know by the look in her eye that she's so close but can't go over.

I scrape my teeth across her sensitive clit once, and it's the gateway she needs to go over to oblivion. I lose her eyes as they roll back in her head, but I don't mind. I got to see the look as she passed over, and it's worth the five years I was in prison. She's worth everything.

I untangle myself from her, running the back of my hand across my lips as I crab-walk up her body. She doesn't even give me time to ask for a kiss before she's taking one, not caring about her taste still on my tongue. Hell, I think she likes it even more with the way she's moaning and rolling her hips into me as our tongues touch.

"God, Maddy, I need to be inside you. I need you baby. Let me in." I barely get the words out; she ain't letting me come up for air, and I ain't all that willing to let go of her either.

She holds me as I kick my pants and boxers off. As I line up, she pulls back and stares down between us, watching me palm my dick and glide it between her lips but not in yet. I raise my head and look at her.

"You've done this before?" she asks.

I nod.

She giggles. "Good, 'cause I haven't."

Chapter 19–Maddy

I don't know why I spoke. It's not like I don't know Chains isn't a virgin like me. The guy oozes sex from a ten-mile radius. But I'm nervous. There's no going back for me on this. Not that I fully expect my first time to be with my one true love or anything. Or even that Chains is that person. It's the one thing I've held back from giving to the world when it took everything else from me when I wasn't ready.

But I'm ready now. Even if Chains and I don't work out, I know I won't regret letting him be my first. But I'm still damn nervous that I'll get it wrong somehow. I know it's basically impossible to do, but hey, it's my first time. Everyone's nervous their first time.

But I shouldn't have said anything. Not by the way the blood is running out of Chains' face.

"You're a virgin?"

I bite my lip and nod.

He moves off me fast. Like superfast. Like he's going to catch something I have if he doesn't vault away.

"That a problem?"

Apparently so. I've never seen a person dress so quickly. Okay, that's not entirely true. The guy pulls on pants sans underwear. Grabs his boots and forces his feet in without socks, then snags his shirt without putting it on before he's out the door so fast it bangs closed.

Wow, okay. Not the reaction I was expecting. I mean, I get it's a bit of shock, but outright running away? Yeah, that never crossed my mind.

I'm too stunned to even cry. Which I know will be the easiest thing to do, but I'm confused. My heart is still in overdrive from the possibility of him seconds away from being inside me. Seconds away from making me a woman.

The AC kicks on, and the air freezes my naked body. With more shakes than I want to admit, I get up and go back to the bag of clothes to find comfort. Nothing is baggy like I need right now, but I have no other choice. I'm holding back the wild thoughts in my head about what it means that Chains left so fast. I know if I choose to put on his clothes, he'll find me. In a ball. Crying my eyes out. Days later.

I put my hair in a braid and feel a small sense of relief when I find a sweater in my belongings that I'd missed on the first look through this morning.

This morning? Has all this happened today? God, so much has happened in twelve hours—hell, in the last twenty-four.

I know I'm made of tough stuff. I watched my mother be raped and then killed and still got myself to safety, for fuck's sake.

I need a distraction, and spending time in Chains' room isn't what I need. I find the kids, and thankfully, Grace has already lost interest in the movie and perks up when she sees me. Focusing solely on her and Teddy, I ignore the rest of them. I don't ask about Chains. Pretty sure everyone saw him run out on me, so no need to ask. Besides, their looks of pity, which they suck at hiding, give it away.

I hate to admit that, as I try not to look at anyone else, I find myself occasionally looking around for him. The day keeps growing longer, and still no sign of him.

I try to keep my mind busy, but he's in the back of it. Always.

I've never been to a clubhouse before, but I have a feeling it's not usually this quiet. I'm not sure if it's because of the attack on me, the truth about my past, which I know Chains told his brothers, or that Chains left me here after first his claiming and then our fight and then our attempted make-up. The looks I feel are constant, but no one voices them. I have a feeling that everyone knows where Chains is, why he left. I know they aren't laughing at me, but I feel like an insect, or maybe an animal in a cage. Everyone looking, pointing, seeing the virgin in the crowd.

When others turn in for bed, I don't go back to the room I slept in the night before. It doesn't seem right. Chains said I belong with him, that he'll take care of everything, that I can lean on him. I know it was silly to believe he was speaking truth. I keep the manic laugh from bubbling to the surface. Who the hell knew being a virgin would set him off enough to leave and probably regret his words? If being an old lady is anything like marriage, which I think it is from the Google searches I've been doing all day, then it's safe to say the marriage is off. Can't be an old lady without sex, and Chains made it clear we won't be having any of that.

I settle in on the couch in the room adjacent to the bunkroom the kids are in. A look at the clock tells me it's 1:00 a.m., so I prepare for what's coming. And like clockwork, I hear the wail and then the patter of feet pounding on the floor before I see Teddy race out of his room.

"I'm here, Teddy. I'm here." I stand so he can see me, as the room is only lit by one lamp on the side table. He races to me and throws his arms around my middle.

This isn't the first nightmare, not even the first one when he's sought comfort from me, but this is the first time he talks before I can probe him to tell me.

"There was a fire. I couldn't get the door open, and you weren't moving. You just laid there on the ground."

I hug him tight and sit, pulling him into my lap.

"Shh, honey, it's okay. It was just a dream." I let my rocking calm him for a bit before I start in on the normal routine we have. "Now tell me, what was the room like?"

He shrugs. His typical response.

"Is it closed off like this room?"

He looks around and nods.

"Did it have any windows?"

He pauses in his inspection of the room as he thinks and nods slowly.

"Well, if the door isn't working, what could you've done to get me out?"

"The window?"

I nod.

"But I can't break it."

"But you have friends who can. Do you really think any of the guys here wouldn't break through the glass and get you out?" I rub his back as he looks at me with earnest.

"Yeah, and they would also break down the door." His smile is infectious.

"Exactly. And you know what would happen after that?"

He shakes his head slowly as he leans on my shoulder.

"Well, then your uncle Chains will get so mad at me because then I'll have to go buy all new things for you. And he'll be upset 'cause I'll use his money. And when I'm done buying you everything, I'll get a coffee for me."

"Yeah, a big one."

I feel him relax into me, and I just hug him tight, kissing the crown of his head.

"It will be so huge we could use it as the house. In fact, we'll buy a house shaped like a coffee. And then I can have coffee all the time. But you'll have to learn how to make it for me, because I'll only want to watch cartoons and drink coffee, and I'll be too busy to get up to get my own cup, so you'll have to do it."

"What? No, you will. You'll have to get *me* the coffee." He pulls back from my chest and points at me like I'm the silliest person he's ever seen. I'll take it.

"You? Oh, so you think you're all grown now?"

"Yeah!" His laughter is contagious, and I can't help but join in.

"Come on, back to bed. And in the morning, you can get me a cup of coffee as I draw up our new coffee cup house." I grab his hand and lead him back across the hall.

"What? No. You're so silly, Mom."

I pause at his bed as he climbs into the top bunk but pretend I don't hear it. I don't want to spoil this. I know I'm not his mom, never could be. But him trusting me enough, it's all I can do not to burst out crying like a baby.

He likes me. He really likes me.

"I know. Now sleep, honey. Night."

"Night." He rolls onto his stomach and grabs the stuffed green crocodile I bought for him at the store. He isn't a big stuffed animal kind of kid, but I had to buy it for him. It called to me, and Teddy's willing to make it an exception for himself.

I move back to the room, fully intent on watching my show, but Casper is sitting on the arm of the sofa, opposite of where I sat with Teddy.

"Never seen someone approach a dream like that before."

I shrug, feeling uncomfortable at being watched and evaluated. "My aunt did that when I had nightmares. She couldn't always come down when I woke up, so she taught me how to go through the dream afterward and find a way out, or a flaw in my brain. Then it had to end on a good note. That was her thing, always end happy. She hated sad things, didn't even finish certain movies. Like *Titanic*. We always ended it after the sex scene. I had no idea the boat sank until like four years ago."

He chuckles, and I settle into the seat as he sinks into his side as well. "Might have to try it."

I want to ask what his nightmares are about, but I don't. I have enough going on in my own mind; don't need to add more.

"He'll be back. He just needs time."

I don't ask who he's talking about; it's pretty obvious.

"He didn't need to leave."

"No, probably not. But for him, he needed to get his head on straight. Couldn't do that here."

With me.

Its left unspoken between us.

I change subjects, not wanting to think about it anymore. "Any other news?"

I had finally gotten up the nerve earlier at dinner to ask Law about what was going on regarding my attack. I wanted to know if I was the one being targeted, if it was from my past, or because of what's going on in my present. Was it the club that brought the Devils Damned to my doorstep? Jennie and the kids?

I only got that the club was looking into it. I'm hoping if I keep asking, someone will let something slip.

"No. We got a few feelers out, contacts asking and listening around. Nothing concrete. It'll take time, though. And trust me, the Reaper's Hounds won't let that transgression go. No one attacks the club, family included. And don't think you aren't."

"What?"

He moves his eyes away from the TV to look dead-on at me. I've been watching him the whole time, but this is the first time he really looks at me. And I got to admit, having his attention is not something I want. There's a shadow about him, a cloud that hovers. I'm not scared of him, but I don't want to be on his bad side. I can tell he would not be a person to have as an enemy. Okay, none of these guys would be, but there's something darker in Casper than the rest.

"Family."

A weight settles in me. It's not entirely uncomfortable, but it's heavy. I've never had someone who thought of me as family since I lost mine. Izzy and my aunt were all I had for so long, but then I left, and Izzy and I became distant. She's the kind of friend you can be separated from for years and then get back together, and it's almost like no time has passed.

We both have scars on our pasts that make it hard for either of us to trust another person. We bonded over that, but it also keeps a small wall between us. A wall with a window down that we talk to each other through, but it's still a barrier. Don't know if either of us knows how to be completely open with another person. I sure as hell don't. I thought I would learn with Chains, but I think my schoolgirl crush has run its course.

I settle into the couch, groaning as I adjust.

"Sore?"

"That's an understatement. I don't get it. I was fine this morning." He grunts at my response, so I concede as I glance at him sideways. "Okay, not completely fine, but I didn't let it bother me."

"No shit. Think we brought half the store home with us."

"Didn't see you complaining as you downed that second cup of coffee, buster."

A saccharine smile crosses his lips. "And it was the best one I've had here."

"No shit. The stuff here isn't coffee, just snail sludge." I shiver and shake off the gag from thinking about that vile taste that I forced down.

He barks out a laugh. "Yeah, Law makes it. He knows it's shit, but it keeps him awake, he says. Noticed you weren't tired at all after that cup."

"Not sure you can say it was because of that."

"True. I think I counted four more cups you had."

I can feel my lips tip up in a smile. I have a terrible addiction to coffee, and no, I don't plan on seeking help for it. "Try seven."

"Fuck, you are a hard-core caffeine junkie. Think we need to get General to give you a patch or something."

"Nah, not a patch, but I wouldn't say no if you found him to get me some more meds. My face and ribs are killing me."

"Oh shit, I actually came in here to give you these." He pulls out a bottle of pills from his jeans, and I don't even ask what they are before I gulp them and half a water bottle down.

"General was looking to give these to you, sorry. My brain gets away from me sometimes. He said it should help you sleep as well."

"Don't care about sleep. Just want to stop hurting."

He breathes deep, and I know his next words are from sympathy, not pity. "Sorry, Mama Bear, but it's going to take time. I take it you never been in a fight before?"

"No, this was my first and hopefully my last."

"Yeah, well, think of a fight like working out."

I roll my head toward him, barely having the energy to do that. "Meaning I'm going to have to keep doing it to get better at it?"

His roar of laughter has me smiling. It doesn't cause the flutter in my stomach like when Chains laughs, but it's nice to know I'm still funny.

"No, just the whole sore muscle part. Like working out, the first day isn't too bad. Or at least it isn't for me. I can do almost anything that first day after a fight. I'm still sore, but the more I move, the better I am. When it gets later in the day, and then hell, the next day? Well, shit, I can't move, and I'm wailing and grumpy from being sore everywhere."

I nod in understanding; it makes sense. "Yeah, once I got back from shopping, I plopped myself in a chair and haven't been up much since you all helped with Teddy and Grace. Didn't see a need, but now I regret not stretching or something. Not that I think I could have stretched out the parts that hurt. Damn, that guy really kicked my ass." I move to ease some pressure off my hips. The guy held me down, and I twisted so much before he got my pants off that my whole middle is bruised.

"Yeah, but you did all right too."

I huff as I roll my eyes. "Pretty sure Chains did good. I just rolled on the floor crying."

He grabs my wrist. It's not tight, but as I attempt to move it out of his hold, he tightens it and doesn't let go. I move my eyes to his face in question.

"Don't. Don't play the victim. 'Cause you ain't. You're a survivor. A hell of one from what Chains said. You went up against three. Not one-on-one. You have no training, no experience. But you took them all on. You shot first when most girls run and hide and wait to be found and rescued. Even if we weren't there, you would have stopped the third guy. From what you said last night, I know you were completely willing to let it go all the way with him, but I doubt you would have just let him walk away after. Ten to one you already planned on how to kill the guy when he pulled off you."

Tears prick my eyes and stay glued to my lashes as I attempt to blink them back. "I had another gun. A small thirty-eight under the mattress."

He smiles easily and loosens his hold on my wrist but doesn't let go. "Of course you did, Mama Bear. 'Cause that's the type of girl you are. You ain't a victim. You're not one who just lies there and waits to be rescued. No, not you. And Chains gets that. He may need time to deal with his own shit, but he sees you. He sees who and what you are. Just give him time to get his head out of his ass."

"And if he doesn't?"

"I know about half a dozen brothers who will man up and take his place. Myself included."

My breath hitches as his fingers softly slide down my wrist to my fingers before moving completely away. I'm sure I'm hyperventilating. I've had a few guys hit on me over the past few years since I left my hole in the floor. But the guys here are intense, and I know it's not just pretty words to get me to sleep with them. When they speak, they mean it.

I choose not to say anything. What *could* I say? So I settle into the pillows and stretch out as far as I can without touching Casper. I don't want him to think I'm taking him up on his offer. While tempting, especially since I know he wouldn't run out on me, he doesn't make the butterflies sing and fly in my stomach like a certain dumbass with long, beautiful hair I want to grip tight as I kiss his perfect lips do.

I try to focus on the movie, but the pills draw me under, and soon the pain is gone and all that's left is darkness. I'm used to it, since I've lived in it for so long. It's home.

Chapter 20 – Chains

"**Y**ou're an asshole. You know that, right?"

I grit my teeth as I come into the TV room across from the bunkroom. I'm not pissed at what Casper says, nor do I disagree. But seeing Maddy's feet on him and her sleeping soundly next to a brother has me wanting to punch the shit out of him. But I don't 'cause I know I have no right. Not after I ran away like a little bitch.

"Yeah." I run my fingers through my hair as I sink into a seat opposite them. I don't get comfy. I can't. Only having Maddy in my arms will do that for me.

I look her over. She seems restful, and as I take in every dip of her curves, I also see every bruise. They've become more pronounced in color since I last saw her. They've been showing on her since she got them, but now they seem to have doubled to the point that Maddy's black and blue with splotches of creamy skin.

As she shifts in her sleep, I follow her movements. Especially her legs, which scissor together and then flex on Casper's lap as he lays his hand on her ankle to settle her.

"We going to have problems?" My eyes lift slowly. I don't enjoy fighting with my brothers, but I will. For this woman, I would even burn the place down if I need to.

"You going to leave again?" He challenges me with a raised eyebrow.

"Jesus." I stand and pace in front of them. "She's a virgin. Her uncle's the same guy who locked me up. What the hell did you expect me to do? It's like a fucking repeat of a movie, a sad, fucked-up movie about me. Too many things are the same."

"You saying you can't trust her? Think she's setting you up like the last one?"

I rub my hands roughly over my face. "Shit, man, I don't know. I just know it's a damn coincidence, and I fucking hate those."

He nods but doesn't let my bull slide. "You need to talk to her. Tell her about your past, just like you made her do."

"I didn't make her do it." I'm defensive. Technically, she offered up the truth, but I wasn't going to let her leave my room till she did. So, I didn't demand it, but can I really say I let her tell me, or did I just take the opportunity that presented itself?

"You're right. 'Cause this woman isn't like the one you're comparing her to. She isn't about deceit to hurt others. She hides things to keep herself safe. And when she needs to, she shares. And now it's your turn. Man up and share. Share it all. Your past, your dreams of the future. Even your damn feelings if you have to. But this is the last time the club's going to stand by and let you fuck this up. You don't get another chance. If you fuck up again, one of us will grab on to her, and we won't let go."

I nod solemnly. Yeah, the club would have no problem with that. I might be a brother, but if it comes to choosing between a woman like Maddy and me, I'll lose every time. Don't fault them for it. It's the right choice—the smart one.

With grace only a man with sniper skills has, Casper eases off the couch, making little movement to stir Maddy as he gets up and leaves the room.

I stare at the woman who's captured parts of me I thought were lost forever. A woman who shows me every day what self-sacrifice is. One who's been through her own hell and has climbed out of the hole. Fuck that, she climbed out and built a life on top of it.

I move to squat in front of her. She put her hair back up in her signature braid, but a few strands came loose to float around her beautiful face. Even with the bruising, she's the prettiest woman I've ever laid eyes on. I brush the softest strand across from her face and smile. She doesn't know I'm here, and she might even think it's someone else, but she moves into my hand. I know it's pretty arrogant to think she knows it's me and does it because *of* me, but hey, I'm a selfish kind of asshole.

I can't keep my lips off her any longer. Since I had a taste of her hours ago, even if my head is fucking up what's between us, I crave her. I lean close and kiss each bruise on her softly. I start with her eyes, then each cheek, and finally her lips. I linger as I feel her wake and return my kiss.

"Hey, gorgeous."

Her eyes flutter open and light up for a second, then dull. I did that. Seeing me did that.

Shit. I got a lot to make amends for. First things first, though.

I move my arms under her and lift her easily. She doesn't wrap her arms around me like last night when I carried her out of her house. That's okay. I know she needs time. And I plan to give her what she needs. But not space. We've both had enough of that.

Only a few brothers are up, but none of them stop me as I carry Maddy to our room. When I got back, I expected her to be there, and when she wasn't, shit, it did things to me. Panic. Twice I've felt panic over this woman. If that isn't a sign that I need her in my life, I don't know what is. Never felt that way for anyone not even my own family, which sounds like shit.

When I became part of the club, we drifted. It wasn't a complete drift apart, but there was water between us. Then when my parents went, I hardened myself even more. Jennie was always welcome here, but she had her own battles to fight. Addiction was one of them. I supported her as much as I could and was damn proud when she got clean. Then she was pregnant, and before I knew it, I was locked up, and she was dead. I mourned my family. Fucking went out and just lit the world on fire in my own way. Got locked in solitary for two weeks after I heard about Jennie's death. I don't even know who I fought that day, just kept swinging. Because that's what I know: rage. I can live with it; I can control that. But panic? It's entirely different. Unlike rage that makes me want to lash out, panic grips me with its icy fingers and I feel trapped. Caged. Vulnerable.

I kick the door open and go to lay my old lady on the bed before I turn to close and lock it. She doesn't move to take off her clothes to get comfortable, so I do it for her. She doesn't protest, just watches me. Her shoes and socks go first, and then I try my luck and slowly pull her jeans off. I will my dick down—it ain't time for that—but it sees her creamy skin and has a mind of its own.

I don't even ask her to sit up, but she accommodates me enough to lift first her stomach. then shoulders off the mattress enough for me to pull her sweater and shirt off. She's lying in just her panties and matching bra. White. Virginal. Sexy as fuck.

A part of me is still scared as hell that she's a virgin, but that's my shit to deal with. My past. A past I need to share with her. But despite that, I can appreciate what's before me. What she offered on a fucking platter.

I turn and go through my drawers until I find my favorite shirt. Gray with a motorcycle on it. Okay, it also has my name on the back of it. A charity event we did years ago. I know it's soft as shit and will feel great against her skin. Skin that's still marred black and blue. And yes, it's a subtle way to have my name on her. What? You think I'm bad enough that I would go as far as tattooing my name on her ass?

Hmmm, not a bad idea. It would let everyone know she's mine. Interesting. But it's too late. Jumper went home, and I ain't having anyone but him mark her beautiful flesh. So a shirt with my name is what she gets instead.

For now.

When I go back to her, I notice she hasn't moved. She's still on her back, legs slightly parted and bent, hands haphazardly beside her from where they rested when I took her shirt, hair still in a braid. I sit on the bed and turn her to the side slightly, enough for me to get at her hair. Pulling out the hair tie, I run my fingers through the braid till it's all separated.

I play with it some more. Not for my sake but for her. I can feel the worry drain out of her. When I see her finally relax and roll back a little into me, I breathe a sigh of relief. It's not much, not where we were, but it's a start.

"Sit up, baby."

She does, facing away from me, and I unclip her bra and slide the straps down her shoulders before pulling it off her. I run my fingers through her hair once more. I can't help it; it's the softest thing I've ever touched. I keep going, my fingers gliding down her spine. There are only a few bruises back here, and her skin is so smooth. A tilt of her head to the side gives me half her face. She isn't saying no, but she isn't looking at me. I can't tell if desire is in her eyes, and I won't rush this. I grab my shirt and put it over her head, and she threads her arms through it.

"Lie back down, Mama Bear. Going to get a shower, and then I'll be back." I don't know why I continue, but the hitch in her shoulders tells me I need to say more. "I went for a ride. Didn't know I went too far till I was in Nebraska. Bulldog said he needed to get back to Princess, and when we turned to come back, he got a flat. Spent more time than I wanted to on the side of the road." I hesitate, but I know I calm her when she hears I only went riding and had a brother with me. I know what's running through her head. All day the topic has been sex, so no doubt she thought I was with someone, especially after I ran out on her.

"I'm glad you guys got back safe." It's mumbled against the pillow, and her face is turned away, but it makes me smile. Yeah, we're going to be okay. I mean, I still need to grovel a shit ton, but we'll make it.

"Me too. I really didn't expect to be out that long. Maddy?" I wait until her head turns and her eyes catch mine. "Seriously. Only meant to go for a ride to clear my head. Nothing more."

I watch her swallow, then nod. Breathing another sigh of relief, I turn, walk into the bathroom, and start the shower. I crack the door, more so I can hear her if she needs me. I know General gave her meds to help her sleep, but I don't know if she'll wake from a nightmare. She didn't last night when we finally drifted off together, but I'm not there to hold her. Not yet anyway,

I shed my clothes and step in, feeling the steam before the warmth of the water rains down on me. I'll never go back to prison for this shower alone. Every bathroom in this place was upgraded while I was locked up, and this one is no different. It's got one of those rain head things, and it's fucking amazing. You don't get that in prison. Hell, you share time with other males, and I've seen more dicks than I ever wanted to for a straight guy.

A sound behind me startles me, and I jerk my face out of the water, ready to strike. Memories of more than one guy trying to settle some crazy vendetta in the shower against me or the club rush to the forefront of my mind.

"Sorry."

I blink out the water, trying to understand what I'm seeing.

"I should have realized this was a bad idea with your, um, your past and all." She bites her lip, and my dick goes from flaccid to rock hard.

I don't speak, not willing to fuck up this second chance. She's naked as the day she was born, and my eyes roam every part of her. This is the first time I've seen her girls with nothing covering them, and I'm not disappointed. I'm zoned in on them, in fact. I can't take my eyes off her cranberry-red nips and silver-dollar areolas. I need to taste them. The small part of my head still freaking out will just have to freak the fuck out, 'cause I'm not about to stop what's coming next.

I snake my arm around her waist and pull her close, going straight to sucking on her nipple. I pull it in my mouth, run my tongue around it. Bite it. Nibble it. Savor it. Her hands are in my hair, not controlling me but moving with the way my head goes. I almost shoot my load at how good it feels when she scrapes her nails along my scalp.

Her moans have me shifting my need from tasting her skin to wanting to know what she sounds like when she screams my name. I move to her mouth and hold her head as I part her willing lips and secure myself to her. I trail my other hand between her legs, needing to know she's ready for me. She needs to be, 'cause I'm a second away from exploding, and I want to be inside her when I do.

She's wet, but I don't know if it's enough. She's a virgin, for fuck's sake. It's going to hurt even if she's sopping, like she is. I don't want to cause her any more pain than what I've already done, but I know I can make it better.

"Please."

Fuck yes, and thank you fucking God.

"You on something, baby? I can get a condom, just don't have one here right now."

"I'm...." She licks her lips, her breaths fanning my face. I love it. "I'm on the pill."

I'm clean, won't risk that for her. And I know the pill ain't always worked. Where the hell do you think Princess came from? I should ask if she wants to double down on safety, but I don't. Call me any kind of bastard you want, but I know Maddy's my old lady. She's it for me. She'll be the one who carries my kids. And since I know this, I don't think twice before lifting her against the wall by her thighs. I take one second, mesmerized by seeing my cock close to her virginal walls, before I plunge in to the hilt.

Her cry of pain fills the room, but I hold still. I'm not coming out of her. No fucking way. She feels too good. Too right. Perfection.

"Chains." Her voice is strangled, and I see tears leak from the corner of her eyes.

"Shhh, baby, shhh. I got you. I always got you."

She tries to wiggle in my arms, but I won't let her up. I know her body needs time to adjust, and then we can get past this and into the good stuff. The really, *really* good stuff.

My kisses land on her face, her neck, her shoulders. They're a contrast to my punishing strength holding her on my cock. They're soft and cause goose bumps to pepper her skin. When I lean low and suck on her tits, I know the pain is less, that her mind can focus on the pleasure. She grips my hair, and this time she pulls me in the way she wants me. And I let her.

For now.

When her moans ricochet off the walls of the shower, only then do I pull out. Slowly. She shivers as I go till only my tip is still in. I chance a look down. Blood, it's there. Not much, but enough to know that she really was a virgin. I felt the barrier break; I felt everything. Like that her smooth pussy clenches at me and only me. Maddy has never been with a man, and seeing the blood, knowing the truth, it doesn't freeze me like last time when she told me. It doesn't throw me into a need to run far away. Fuck that. I never felt this need to take, claim, mark as my own. She's mine, and I'm hers. Her first. Her last. Just hers.

I tilt my hips till I'm back in fully, groaning at how wonderful it feels. I continue to pound into her, forcing her to take everything. But by her moans and thrashing of hips to meet mine, I know it's no hardship on her part.

"Never... it's never been this good. Fuck, Mama Bear, you got me harder just being inside this silky pussy. I'm never leaving. Shit, this feels goddamn amazing. Tell me, tell me you feel the same. Say you want my cock buried in you all the time, that it makes you complete."

She just moans and tips her head back, revealing her entire throat. I latch my mouth on her, licking and biting her, which sends a gush of her sweet juices around my dick. Fuck, I love that I can feel everything. I went bareback once as a kid. Thought I was tough shit back then. I walked around like a cocky motherfucker till the girl said she thought she was pregnant. Thank God it was a false alarm. But never again. Not till Maddy. And feeling her walls clench around my dick has me grinning and pounding faster. I'm about to feel her explode. I know she's close. And I want that. I want to feel that and see her face contort in bliss as I push her over.

"Be my old lady, Maddy. Be mine. Claim me like I claimed you." I pull back enough to move one hand away from under her thigh. She doesn't fall; her legs just tighten to hold on more. I move my fingers to brush over her clit, and I look at her face as I pinch it just a little. Just enough pain. She goes off from my harshness, and I'm not surprised as she does. Just at what she says.

"Yessss," she replies as if that's the only thing keeping her grounded, and if I didn't have such a hold on her, she would have flown away. Hips bucking and holding my dick like a vise as her shoulders are the only thing now resting on the wall, everything else curved out toward me. Her hair is a mess, both wet and dry, sprawled out and wild. Face covered in bruises, but I don't see them, just the beauty that's her.

I didn't expect her to answer. She didn't seem like the type to speak during sex. And I love dirty talk. I know it gets girls—or shit, Maddy—hot as fuck. And I wanted to push her over, letting her know it was more than just sex with her. But her response has me doubling down, wanting to go over with her. It won't take much, 'cause I'm close too. I want her lips, but her tits are right in my face, and I'm not about to say no to these puppies. I lean down and suck one deep, causing a quake in her as she comes again. Which is fucking perfect, 'cause I'm lost now. I keep moving my hips as I release in her, loving that my cum is coating her walls, painting them white.

Slowly, I release her tit, and she slumps back against the wall. I move my hand from her clit, which had been a constant strum between her first and second orgasm, to the back of her neck, pulling her close so I can latch on to her lips. She's wild on my mouth, as if still in the throes of passion. But we slow it down together till I part our lips and rest my forehead to hers, sharing the air between us.

"Let's get cleaned up and then to bed, Mama Bear. The kids will be up soon."

Some would think that the mention of the kids, of responsibility, would put a cloud over what we shared. But I know my girl, and from the soft smile on her lips, it's exactly what she needs to hear. Teddy and Grace found their way into her heart, and she isn't letting them go.

I can only hope that she lets me in there as well. She might not love me yet, but I know I'm starting to. Hell, I might already be. It ain't hard, and I'm not scared of it. Not anymore. Just scared I'll be the only one between the two of us.

Chapter 21–Maddy

Having Chains dry me off, taking extra care to collect each drop off my skin, is a complete contrast to what happened between us just minutes ago. I knew sex wasn't going to be the sweet, soft way they make it out to be in the movies. I especially knew Chains wouldn't be the type. But I don't regret it. Hell no. What we had was explosive.

More than explosive. World-changing. Mind-boggling. Earth-shattering. And it put something back together in me that I didn't know was broken.

I'm not an idiot. I know one round of sex doesn't make things change for most people, but it does for me. It might not mean Chains and I are soul mates, or meant to be, or whatever. But it makes me realize there's good out there. There's amazing in the world.

Even if I go out and sleep with hundreds of men, I know I won't find that same feeling with anyone else. Chains did something when we came together. He was in tune with me. He forced me to live through the pain and see a light at the other end of the tunnel. A light that was bright and warm, and shining through all the darkness that's been clouding my eyes, and my heart, for so long.

I blush as he leads me into his bed and under the covers. I've never slept naked. Never. But it's definitely different. Not in a bad way, as the sheets are smooth and cool on my skin. And I'm honestly not even feeling the parts you can see. My soreness is internal, an ache I won't take back.

"Don't get shy on me now, Mama Bear." His chuckle shakes a laugh out of me as he wraps both arms around me and pulls me flush to his back.

Of course Chains would pick that up as I attempt to curl in on myself so he can't see my nakedness. Now that we've left the shower, being naked with another person is new territory. Very new territory for me. Guess other than being an old lady, this is something I'll have to get used to.

I meant it. When I agreed, I meant it with everything I am. And not just because I was experiencing my first orgasm "from coitus," as the books call it. I'll be his as much as he's mine. But talking about that is too much for me, so I go for an easier topic.

"I'm not shy, just don't know what to do with my hands."

"Did you just quote a Will Ferrell movie line?"

I glance over my shoulder at him, his expression flabbergasted. I smile slowly as I shrug.

He chuckles at my movie reference and flips me onto my back.

"Oh, I'll show you what to do with them." But he surprises me, and instead of going for round two, the bastard tickles me.

I scream for him to stop, but I can't get enough breath in to belt it out. "Stop... stop. I'm going to pee. Stop." But he doesn't, and I wiggle so much that I really do think I'm going to leak on the bed. So I go for the big guns, then wish I didn't.

"I'm still mad at you."

Yeah, that has him stilling. He breathes deep, nods a few times, and then rests his forehead on my stomach.

"I know."

I comb my fingers through his hair. He might say he likes mine, but I'm addicted to touching his. It's a different texture than mine. Coarser, like it hasn't been washed in days, but not greasy. I like it.

"You want to...."

"Talk about it?"

I nod, and from his deep inhale, I know he feels it from where he lies on me.

"No."

A surprised bark of laughter leaves my lips. I really don't expect anything but the truth from this man. He rises and looks me dead-on. "But I will."

He bounces up, and it forces me to roll into him as he steadies one hand on my hip and bends to rest his head on the other as he leans above me.

"You ever have that friend of yours, the one who set you up with the kids, check out why I was in prison?"

"I didn't ask. I know she did, but I didn't ask." Stupid, I know. But I don't regret it.

He flashes a quick smile before he continues, squeezing my hip a bit as he goes. "I was arrested and charged with sexual assault."

I open my mouth on instinct to break in and ask about forty questions that spill into my brain in 2.5 seconds. His finger halts my lips from opening farther. "You once said I was only to listen. Now it's your turn. Questions at the end, Mama Bear."

Reluctantly, I nod.

"I was sentenced to ten years, but once I found out about the kids, I had the lawyers work hard, and I got out early. The club must have paid a shit ton, 'cause we got a damn good lawyer who managed to get me out without parole. He was a million times better than the first one. But that was probably the motivating factor, since the first guy just fucked me and took the club's money. The claim was for sexual assault, rape, but I didn't do it. There was DNA, which was mine, 'cause I had sex with her, but that was it. Everything was fucking consensual. I don't deal with that shit, and neither does the club. Club even has strict bylaws that if we find out about it, the guy's patch is stripped and he's sent walking. I wasn't about to risk my club for an easy piece of ass. But a few winning actors and the DNA, and my fate was sealed. The girl claimed she was a virgin and I stole that from her. And this is the kicker—she told me she was one when we hooked up. But she lied. There was nothing virginal about her. Boys even followed up on her after I got locked away— a few interesting conversations, should we say—and we learned the truth. She *had* been raped, but not by me. Some other asshole did it and then forced her to pin it on me, saying he would tell her churchgoing parents. The boys would have brought the evidence to court, but as luck would have it, the girl mysteriously vanished, and we never found her. Or should I say the body? I know she's dead. The asshole doesn't leave witnesses."

He takes a break and runs his hand over his face, giving himself time. "No witnesses but you."

My breath hitches.

"I forgot to say, at my trial, there was a deputy who was up for sheriff. He really pushed for the trial, spinning the jury and judge up each time he gave testimony, as he was apparently the one the girl went to see to report the supposed crime. But that's Officer Taylor. Good old Officer Dwayne Taylor."

I'm trying not to freak the fuck out and really make sure I hear him right. *Is he saying that...? Could he mean that...? Is it the same...?*

"Your uncle ain't a saint, sweetheart, and I'm sorry I didn't tell you sooner that I knew him when you told me your story. It was shitty of me, but I wanted to spare you from my past. I realize now that was shit, and if we're going to make a real go at this, I need to know the bad about you, and you need to know mine."

I can't breathe. Can't fucking breathe. I don't even hold them back, just let the tears pour from my eyes.

"Jesus, Maddy, I'm sorry. Shit, I knew this would be bad. You regret it, don't you? Shit, of course you do. I don't fault you. My past is fucked-up and that's just the topper on the cake. I bet you want out, and shit, baby, I'll give it if you want it. I won't be able to fully for a while, but I'll try. Maybe we can just take it slow first, see if you can forgive me for this, and then we can move on from there. Maybe one day you can let me in. I'm so sorry." Panic is on his face, in his voice. But it's the instant sadness that comes from his eyes that has me pulling it together a bit. Not much, but a bit.

It's my turn to hush his mouth with my hand, planting my full palm over it 'cause I know he'll continue talking over just my fingers pressed to his lips.

"No. No regrets." I shake my head. I could never regret him being my first. Never. "Not with you. I'm just sorry. My uncle destroyed my life, and he did it with you too. If I'd been stronger, if I'd forced myself to go through with taking him down, you would never have been tainted by him. You would have *had* a life. It's me who needs to apologize. I took five years of your life." My voice breaks at the end as I pull my hand from his mouth to bite into to hold back the tears.

"No, baby, no. You did nothing."

"I know," I wail on a sob. I cover my face with both hands so he doesn't have to see me, his biggest screwup of all.

He pulls me in to him, hugs me as I sniffle into his chest and his warmth. "Hush, woman, hush. Your mouth is about to get me really upset. You had your own demons to fight with him. I ain't mad you didn't go after him. Grateful, really. 'Cause he would have killed you. Just like he did the girl who framed me, just like he did your mom, and just like he did with a dozen others. No, baby, you didn't take five years off my life. He did. It was you who gave me my life back." He pushes my hip to roll me back so he can look at me.

"You hear me? I would still be locked away, having not known my niece and nephew. I might have been let go early, maybe, maybe not. But I know that not one other person would have taken in two kids, claimed them as her own, then let an asshole like me barge in and allow me to spend time with them. Only you would have spoken sense to me that I wasn't doing enough. Only you would have gotten under my skin to make me itch to be better. For them and for you. That's what you did. That's what you can take credit for."

God, this man. This beautiful, scary ape of a man. He doesn't always get it right, but when he does, I'm liquid goo. And my damn heart is making up his room inside it. I can practically feel that bitch moving furniture around so he'll be comfy for a very long time there.

I take a breath, rub my hands down my face, wiping the tears as I go, and chuckle.

"What's so funny now?"

"Two nights in a row, all I seem able to do in your bed is cry. I'm pretty sure I'm the only woman who can say that about sleeping with you."

He smiles before he sobers. "Once. Only once since being arrested, in prison, and getting out was I with another woman. That first day out. But it felt like I was cheating on you even then. Had to have you in my mind to get off. I knew that was wrong, and until I could get you out of my mind, I couldn't fuck another woman again. Won't lie, I had a few girls blow me to let steam off, but that was before I decided I wanted to claim you. Hell, even then I was so pussy whipped I really did think about you to get me off each time."

"When was that? When did you decide it was me over them?"

"The day I showed up with coffee and the boys."

Okay, so maybe I should still be pissed. Maybe I should still feel betrayed. But I'm not. The guy went five years without sex. Hell, it could have been longer if the time between his arrest and trial took a while. And when he did, he had known me for all of five minutes, since I know I was his first stop after prison. After meeting me, he fucked one girl. A girl who was just a body as he was picturing me. And the blow jobs? Again, we weren't even friends for a long time after we met. Just 'cause I was fiddling with my nub solo didn't mean he had to too. When it counted, when he made up his mind, he was mine. All mine.

Cue the melting.

"I thought of you too." He tilts his head, and I can feel the burn in my cheeks. "But I used a battery boyfriend to help me out."

The smile I've grown to love seeing on his face returns with a vengeance, and I squirm under his predatory gaze. "Oh really? Tell me, Maddy, how often did you change the batteries? How often did you imagine it was my dick gliding into those silk walls you have? Wishing it was me fucking you over a plastic toy?"

I gulp down the dryness in my throat. "A few times."

"You won't be needing it anymore. Understand? You have an urge for dick, you come find me. Ain't about to let my old lady go without, unless we're playing a game to draw it out."

"People actually do that?" I'm shocked. I mean, I read about it, sure. But it was in a book. Most of that shit is to make the reader crave the imaginary boyfriend between the covers. Seriously, no guy goes down on a girl as much as they do in the books. It's not possible. Okay, I really have no experience in that department. I mean, it happened a few times before Chains, but even Izzy said she rarely gets it. Of course, the blow jobs are hinted at and requested often. That's one thing the books get right.

"Yeah, baby, they do. Don't worry, the outcome is worth it. But I don't think we'll play that game, at least not for a while."

Morbid curiosity makes me ask rather than really wanting to try it. "Why?"

"'Cause I haven't gotten my fill. My need to have you, to see you coming is my new favorite addiction. If I withhold that from you, I'll be denying it from me. And I'm a selfish bastard If you haven't figured out yet."

"Oh, I know."

His soft chuckle eats at me, causing the butterflies to take flight in my stomach. Well, that and the press of his hips as they lower on me and buck against me so I can feel him hard as stone. "Oh you do, huh? Then you probably already know that I ain't done with you yet. Not by a long shot."

I like playing this game. This one of us pretending we don't know what's about to happen next. It's the best foreplay I've known, getting me slick with arousal. "There's more?"

"So much, baby. So much more." He kisses me deep and hard, and I grab on to his shoulders tight.

I want to crawl inside him and take up residence. He's everything I want in a man, even if I have no clue what that is. Sure, he's strong. A complete badass. Sweet to kids. I have no clue about old people, but he's nice to his president. I think that's more out of fatherly figure and club respect, but I'll take it. It's his kindness and inner strength that really do it for me. Never had anyone look out for me, offer to be my white knight like he does. He knows my demons and doesn't run from them but to them. With a bike between his legs and his brothers at his back.

He rolls us easily, and I'm sitting on top. I lean up, absentmindedly rubbing myself along his dick that's snuck between my folds. We both groan in pleasure as I run my hands across his chest and map out the scars beneath my fingers and the hard planes of his abs and pecs.

"Fuck, woman, ride me. Ride your old man."

He says it like it's my choice, but it's not. Not that I'm complaining as he grabs both hips and lifts me enough for his dick to stab at me. But I take it from there and glide my fingers around him, then push him toward my entrance. I should take my time caressing his beautiful dick, but I want it in me more than just having it in my hand. Later. Later I'll memorize it with my hands and mouth. I've never given a blow job, but even if I suck at it, I can just go back to the thing that works.

Sex.

'Cause that's something we both do well together. Another groan and moan fill the room as I impale myself on him. My cry is longer than his. I'm still new at this, it being my second time after all, and in a new position, I swear he's breaking in new parts that he didn't reach in the shower. And I'm sore, but I'm not about to let that stop me.

I still and feel my walls clench around his cock. I need a moment. Hell, I need two.

"Oh my God, what did you just do?" My eyes fly to him and then to where we're joined. He ain't moving, not his hips anyway, but he does it again, and I feel his dick jump in me.

I'm in awe. I had no fucking clue they can move their dick like that. It feels good. Really good.

He's looking at me closely, analyzing me. Biting my lip, I lift hesitantly, only a bit off him before coming back down. He lets out a breath and grips my hips in encouragement. I do it again and again, going farther up his dick each time till it's almost out of me before I slam back down. It's fantastic.

One hand stays on my hip to keep me there, but the other slides up to my breasts and pulls at my nipple. I lean into his hand and push mine back to rest on his thighs as I bounce more on him. Fuck, his touch feels amazing on me.

I whimper in protest but don't stop my rhythm as his hand travels down my stomach before he goes to my clit and moves two fingers over it as if a vibrator was directly on it. It's a whole new sensation, and I jerk forward to rest my hands on his chest. I rise and fall on him. I shiver, shake, bounce. I'm close, so close, and then I'm lost. Gone, flying high.

I barely register that his hand moves off my clit before he pulls me down to him as he lifts his hips and fucks me hard with me still on top. I'm still coming when he goes off on his own and fills me once again. Feeling his release sets off another trigger of shivers as a mini orgasm shakes through me.

He's kissing me everywhere: my head, my eyes, my lips. This guy is getting dangerous. If he's not careful, I'm going to fall for the selfish bastard and never let him go.

Never.

Chapter 22–Maddy

'm glowing. I know I am. Can feel it on my skin. And I can't stop smiling. Literally. Can't. Stop.

When Chains woke me, I was so lost in slumber land that I had no clue where I was. Even had to ask.

"Got to get to Church, Mama Bear. Figured you would want coffee."

"Church? Is it Sunday?"

I can still feel the warmth of his chuckle at my confusion.

"Remember, that's what the boys and I call it when we speak without others around. Shouldn't last longer than an hour. Figured you would want to walk me to the door and give me a kiss goodbye."

Realization slowly creeps in. "Coffee. I'll go with you for the coffee."

"What? No kiss?"

"Kiss? No, you need to be punished."

"For what?" His deep chuckles send a zing to my core, a part that I'm so very aware of today.

"Being too good at... well, what we did." I know my cheeks are heated as I look at the bed. We had sex, and not just once in the shower and once in the bed. No, when Chains said he wasn't done with me, he wasn't kidding. We had more sex than I knew people could have in one night. And I still don't know how he's so fucking chipper and full of energy. I'm pretty sure I drained every drop out of him.

"You mean sex? Baby, that wasn't me. Never been like that before. That was you—all you." When he crawls over me to lock his lips with mine, I think we're going for another round. People have quickies every day, right? But he pulls back, taking the covers with him.

"Hey, give those back. What time is it? Like six or something? I might get a few minutes sleep before the kids get up. You go to your little meeting thing. I'll find my way." I curl into the pillow but the smack on my ass—shit, I forgot I'm naked—has me sitting up straighter than a pole.

"Come on, hot stuff. I know you need your coffee. It's after ten, and you're making me late."

"Ten! Where are the kids? Why didn't my alarm go off? Why the hell didn't you wake me earlier?" I run around his room like a crazy person putting on clothes. Okay, so I throw things all around, effectively claiming the space as my own as I search for suitable clothing.

"Damn, we really need to get you sorted. Love seeing your shit mixed with mine, but not this much. I'll clean out a few drawers, and you can pack the rest of that shit in the closet. The alarm didn't go off because I turned it off. And don't start glaring at me, woman. *You* finally stopped harassing me for more dick around five thirty, so I know you needed sleep. Law took them over to Bulldog's ma's house this morning. And yes, before you even ask, I trust her. She's nothing like my gran, actually takes care of Princess a lot, so I know she can do it. Well, that and we had a prospect go with them. So relax, woman. Put some clothes on, and I'll get you set up at the bar with a large cup of coffee."

"It better be big," I grumble, but I feel it lose some edge.

"Don't act like you're mad. Or at least when you do, try not to smile."

"I'm not smiling," I protest but reach up to touch my face.

He walks over to me, pulling on my hair, which causes a glorious ache between my legs. "Yeah you are, and I ain't being cocky when I say I'm glad I put that on your face. You deserve to smile like this every day, all day."

The man knows how to put the butterflies in flight, that's for sure. His words pull at my heartstrings, and I don't feel embarrassed at all for my face.

Or my glow.

We walk into the kitchen hand in hand—how cute is that—and find Casper pulling out an enormous cup from the shelf and starting the coffee for me. I smile in appreciation as I look over at a few of the brothers who are gathered close, all with coffee cups in hand.

"Seems I converted a few of you."

"Nah, we always live on this shit. Just never had good coffee here. Had to go to the diner a few miles down. Think you just saved the club a small loan a month for bringing this in," Bulldog mentions offhand as he walks into the kitchen, grabbing a mug and waiting on mine to finish.

"Think we might have to get a few more if you guys drink the stuff as fast as me. Not sure if I'll be saving you money then."

"We?" Flint smiles like a devil's on his shoulder, but I just keep my grin in place as my coffee is handed to me and I sip at it. No doubt he's hoping to stir shit between me and Chains, but I'm too happy to do anything but shake my head at his antics.

I sigh in happiness; these guys know how to make a girl feel welcome.

Strong arms gently pull me back, and I don't even have to look up to know it's Chains.

"Teddy gave the boys a tutorial on how you take your coffee in the morning before he left. Said if you ever get frowny to just make you a cup and wait about five minutes before asking for something, and then it's a yes."

Both Chains and I chuckle at Casper's confession. "And what do you want?" I ask. "Need me to tell a vamp to get out of your bed or something?"

"Nah, they've already left. New rules and all."

"New rules?" I turn in Chains' arms, and he just smiles down at me as Casper keeps talking.

"Yeah. With family, and now old ladies, back in the club's life, vamps are restricted to Friday and Saturday nights only. Even have to get their asses out by five. If we bring a girl back to the club, same rules apply."

I glance at Bulldog, surprised he took my words so literally.

He shakes his head as he drinks his coffee. "Don't give me that look, Mama Bear. Been a long time coming. Besides, Chains backed me up, and the boys fell in line."

I turn back to Chains so quickly, my hand wobbles, and I spill coffee on it. A small gasp escapes at the burn.

His pinched lips say so much. "Dammit, woman, can't you go a few hours without hurting yourself?" He takes my coffee from me and catches a towel someone throws his way.

"Did you really back him?" I'm too shocked to feel the burn more than that initial contact.

"Why do I need a vamp when I got an old lady keeping me up all night with her sweet pussy?"

The boys chuckle, but my jaw's on the floor, stunned he said that. But I shouldn't be. He's a biker, after all.

"Where the hell is everyone?" roars through the place, and I'm more surprised the rafters don't shake than to see Law yelling for the boys.

"Come give your old man a kiss, woman, and stop making us late. Got Church."

His words say he's late, but his lips take their time and stay locked on mine for so long, I have to grab the counter to keep from falling when he finally releases me. With a wink, he's gone, and so is everyone else.

I don't know about you, but when I get a decent cup of coffee, freedom to do as I please, and zero responsibility, I find the nearest comfy seat and Pinterest the crap out of my phone. You might not call it relaxing, but seeing new ideas for house makeovers gets me all gooey on the inside. If I get bored, HGTV is always my next stop.

But my plans are waylaid when I step out of the kitchen and realize I'm not alone. They also stop dead in their tracks as we eyeball each other, both dazed to see someone else. Well, at least I am. But the more I look, I wonder if the shock isn't because another person is here but because *I'm* here.

"Do you know me?" I ask.

The woman schools her face quickly. "No. Should I?"

"I think you do."

"Bitch, please. I don't know who you are, and I don't fucking care. Obviously it's you who doesn't know me, and that's *your* problem, not mine."

"You're wrong. I know you."

I watch fear shiver across her face.

"You're a vamp."

"Head vamp, and you better start addressing me with some respect, or I'll have whoever let you in here on his knees, pleasing me while you watch."

I laugh. Her response is so unexpected that I can't do anything else. I shouldn't be surprised. The girl is dressed like the queen of the vamps, if vamps have a dress code. Tight jeans that allow me to see her hoo-ha through them. No bra under her pink shirt that stops just below her boobs, cut off one shoulder. I literally see the things swinging as she moves. And her hair? She has the whole queen beehive going on in her fake platinum hair with the bump at the top that I guess holds her crown. But it's missing—probably broke when she was last on her back. And her makeup? Well, she obviously doesn't know that having that much only ages a person. Catty? Probably. Do I regret judging her? Nope. 'Cause while she claims not to know me, I *know* I know her.

"Don't think you'll laugh long when you realize you won't be coming back here. This is my place, not yours. So pack your shit and get out."

"Yeah, no." I sit at the bar and get comfy. "Think I'll stay. In fact, it's you who needs to be leaving. Curfew and all."

"Curfew? What the fuck you talking about?"

"Club made a change. Vamps only allowed Fridays and Saturdays and got to be out before the sun rises. Think it's so no one can see that you all don't look that great in daylight hours."

"Where the fuck did you hear that shit? A prospect? Sorry, sweetie, but they don't know shit."

"No, from my old man."

"You? An old lady?" She crossed her arms and squares her stance to look at me as if she's talking to a child. "With who?"

"Chains."

Now it's her turn to laugh. I just shrug and drink my coffee. If I'd known Chains from her side of things, I would laugh too. Hell, I'm still trying to figure it out. I mean, we've known each other for a few months now, and then I got attacked and bam! We're in a relationship. Odd, yes. Regrettable? Fuck no.

"Oh, sweetie, you really are a dumb cunt." She wipes the laughing tears from her eyes, and I clench my fist. Okay, I don't like how she said that. "That man doesn't do old ladies. He may make you think that, but no. You ain't his old lady. So I'm going to do you a favor and let you get gone before they get out of Church so you don't have to make a fool of yourself when he comes to me after. 'Cause that's what he does. All the boys do. They have Church, then find their favorite vamp and get off. Not side chicks. It's club tradition."

"Tradition has changed, it seems."

She steps closer, and I can feel her rage, if that's possible. "Listen, I ain't going to be nice anymore. Get gone!"

"This is you nice? Wow, what do the guys see in you to keep you around? Actually, don't answer that. I'm sure it has something to do with your mouth when you ain't talking. I'm not leaving, so get used to it. I'm actually trying to help *you*. Not sure of all the rules, but I know Chains won't like your type around when the kids get back. Not anymore. So leave now. We can pick this shit up on Friday when you're allowed back in."

"Chains has no problem with me around the kids. We did introductions before. He even said he wanted them to get to know the club. *All* of the club."

I tilt my head, reading what she wasn't saying. "You're lying."

"No I'm not!"

"Yeah, Chains would never intentionally introduce those sweet kids to someone like you. No doubt you met them, but

I bet it was you who went up to them and not the other way around. 'Cause even though you got this skank look down pat, you ain't stupid. You know Chains will do almost anything for the kids, and a woman chasing after him would need to be good with them."

"I ain't chasing anyone, sweetie. I'm the one being chased."

"By Chains?" I can't help but laugh that this chick thinks that.

"The man could have had any bitch when he got out of prison. The man is sex. Vamp or civilian, anyone. But he came to me. I'm his favorite, and he knows it. So let's clear this up real quick. You might be a flavor of the hour but nothing more. When Chains is ready to settle down, he ain't going to do so with some mama killer who probably doesn't know how to give a man like him what he needs. But I do. And you can bet that I'm going to be the old lady he claims when he's ready."

This chick's seriously delusional.

"You think you're being the faithful type by fucking all his friends? Really think he's going to want a woman who's had her cunt fucked by every asshole he knows and probably a few he doesn't? Think that's what Chains wants?"

She shrugs, and I'm mesmerized by the fact that her shirt is still hiding most of her boobs. It's like a miracle shirt that stays just this side of tease but not porno. "The man ain't a saint. And if you think he is, you're wrong. He's ruthless. He did time for assault. You really think he has a moral compass for cheating? Fuck that. He's hard and demanding, and I'm willing to share 'cause I know where I stand. But I know you wouldn't, and that's why you'll never cut it."

I take a deep breath. Really, I'm holding myself back. I've never fought anyone—well, besides the other night—but the urge to tackle this bitch is getting strong. And for once, I give in. I give in to the rage that's always been there since my dad died. Since witnessing horrors that should never even exist yet are a repeat memory. I do what Casper tried to convince me of the other night. I listen to my old man's words that are screaming in my head to fight. Not to run but to stay and fight the fuck back.

"Okay, now I get to tell you how much you just fucked up." I take a quick swig of my coffee, because it's damn good, and I ain't about to let this bitch make me waste most of it. "One, you know nothing about Chains. He comes off hard 'cause that's how the world needs to see him. Yeah, he went to prison for rape, but he didn't do it. Anyone with half a brain can see he ain't like that, nor would the club keep him around if he was. And if you don't know that and I do after only being at this place for two days, then you don't know the club as well as you think. You might put a dick to a face but nothing more. These guys are kind, and sweet, and sure, they like to fuck. What guys don't? But they keep you all around 'cause it's guaranteed pussy, a guarantee to get off by something other than their hand. I don't see any of you going up in rank. Not with this group. I know I haven't met them all, but they barely look at you all unless they want to get off. A man who wants an old lady finds her when he ain't looking. He seeks her out and sticks to her side, not 'cause she needs rescuing but because he enjoys being beside them and vice versa. And an old lady? She doesn't fuck the others. Even potential old ladies should stick to one guy, even if it's just talking and not spreading their legs. It's called class. Learn to get some."

"Fuck you, Maddy! I have fucking class, you bitch!" She stomps her foot as she screams at me, spit even flying from her mouth a little.

So classy.

"And that leads us to mistake number two. You know me. And I know you, Christy."

Neither of us speaks as she takes in what I said. I let her take a minute while I have another drink. The shit is superb, and I also need a moment. The blood pumping in my ears makes it difficult to focus. I'm so mad it can't even be put into words.

I watch as she crosses her arms in front of her, taking a wider stance. She's either about to play dumb or go raging catfight on me.

"So you know my name? Doesn't mean you know me."

Dumb it is.

"Yeah I do. You went to middle school with me before my mom got killed. Before that, your brother got caught by my dad for selling drugs. I remember seeing you at the precinct when my mom brought me up to see him one day. You were with your mom, who was drugged out also but sober enough to bail him out. My dad offered your brother an out, but he didn't take it. He OD'd a month before my mom died."

Her hand flies out to point at me, and I lean back. Not out of fear, I just really don't know where her hand has been. *Can you get an STD from finger contact alone?*

"You mean a month before you *killed* your mom? Don't think you're better than me. Does Chains even know you murdered your mom? That you pushed her against a table to bash her head in?"

I mentally pull back. *What did she just say? Fuck!*

"It was you." My voice rises like ten octaves in outrage. I'm so fucking stunned by what she said that I have zero calm left.

"Me what?" She moves back half a step, and I can see the fear on her face.

"You told them where to find me. I thought I saw you the day of the BBQ, and now I'm sure of it. You told my uncle, and he sent his friends to get me, didn't you?"

Oh my God, oh my God. It *was* me. It really was my past that forced all this. Foster mom of the year I am not.

"I don't know what you're talking about."

"Yes you do!" I scream as I jump off the stool. "No one knew how my mom died. No one. It wasn't even in the papers. You could only know she fell if you were told by someone who was there. What the fuck, Christy? I did nothing to you! Why the fuck would you tell my uncle where I was? Why would you do this to me?"

"You killed your mom! Killers need to be locked up and not shagging it up." Her false bravado flutters out as she looks around, realizing we're more alone than she probably wants to be with me right now.

"Seriously? You did this because you thought with me, gone you had a chance with Chains? How fucking mental are you?" I start pacing like crazy at this new information overload. "Why the fuck would you do that? Why the fuck would you sic that bastard on them?"

"Them?" She literally has no idea what I'm talking about.

"Them! The kids. That's why they were there. Not for me. They said I was extra. They went there for the kids."

"No, they said they wouldn't hurt them." She's so certain in her words. So positive that she's right and I'm wrong.

And it's the breaking point for me.

I lunge.

My rage hits the ultimate peak, and I want blood. I grab her head, pulling her hair, not really sure what the hell I'm doing but knowing I need to do something. She tries to pull my arms off her, then scratches at my face. I release one hand to punch her in the nose. I hit something based on the blood spouting out. I use my other hand and pull her to the bar as she stumbles along. I get to the bar top and just smash her face on it. Over and over, I keep smashing. I know she's clawing at me, but I can't stop.

She sent them. Sent them to hurt the kids. She needs to pay for that. Pay in blood.

Chapter 23–Maddy

I don't know when the guys come into the room, only notice when someone's pulling me off Christy. Once I release her hair, she slumps on the ground, crying and wailing.

"What the hell's going on?" No idea who's asking, but I bet it's Law. Seems logical since he runs this place, right? I can't tell who's who, as my eyes won't move from the piece of shit on the ground screaming for help.

"She's crazy, insane. She just attacked me. Killed her mom. She was about to kill me. God only knows what she would do to your niece and nephew, Chains."

I take a step forward, planning to end her measly life, but hands tighten on my arms, and no matter how much I wrestle, they don't let go.

"Easy, Mama Bear."

I look over my shoulder to see Flint holding me back, and I stop resisting. I trust this guy as much as I trust Chains. He isn't hurting me, just preventing me from hurting others. Even if they *do* deserve it.

"She needs to go, Chains. I know you think you know her, but you don't. I grew up with her. She's crazy!"

The bitch actually has the nerve to crawl her way over to my man and hang on him. I wiggle again, but the arms hold tight.

"That so?" He looks down at her indulgently, and I relax. He knows my past. That part isn't news to him, but her knowing me is. "What you got to say for yourself, Maddy?"

I narrow my eyes, focused on the slut who has a twinkle in her eye like she actually expects this shit to fly in her favor.

"Nothing other than this chick is seriously in need of a mental hospital. If you think for one goddamn second that just because you're all cuddled up to my man and he ain't pushing you off makes you better, forget that shit. Even if they do decide to believe you, know this. I don't give a fuck that you had them come after me. Don't care that you think you're Chains' old lady. But you better bet that I will hunt your ugly ass down and first cut off your fingers, then your tits, and then your used-up clit for even daring to bring harm to Teddy and Grace. And once I'm done cutting, I'll watch. As you bleed out and beg for mercy, I'll watch, as I'll have you tied to a bed, on your back, in your best position."

I'm seething. Snarling with rage. The grip on me loosens, but I don't move forward.

"How many you count?"

I'm confused by Bulldog's question as he looks at Casper.

"Three."

"Same as me. Anyone else have a different count?"

The rest of the guys shake their head, and I'm staring like they've sprouted trees from their heads. That would make more sense than the conversation I'm not completely in on.

"Chains?" Bulldog addresses my old man, who still has the skank clinging to him.

He shakes his head slowly as he looks at me. "Dammit, girl, why can't I leave you for any length of time anymore without you getting into something? I have half a brain to let General beat your ass. He doesn't like to redo his work."

"Fucking hate it, actually." The growl comes from my left, but I don't look over.

All their faces are stoic, so I'm clueless on how this is playing out.

"You broke the first rule, Maddy, about being at this club."

Shit. What? Don't harm a vamp? Is that really a thing? For the first time, I'm doubting myself.

"No blood on the bar." My old man's smile widens, as do the surrounding brothers'.

"It's a good thing she didn't open that knife wound. Would have made me redo stitches. Good thinking beating *this* shit with your other hand. Got a hell of an old lady, Chains." Only then does General come over and really give me a once-over before moving on with a nod of approval.

"Yeah I do."

I smile widely to match his.

"Wait, what?"

I sort of forgot about Christy for a moment there.

With a simple shrug and push from Chains, she falls on the ground, and I'll admit, I chuckle a bit. From the others chuckling around me, and her glaring at me, it isn't as stealthy as I'd intended.

"Three strikes and you're out. Get this cunt to the hole. I'll deal with *it* later."

A brother I don't know yet picks her up by one of her legs and drags her away, literally kicking and screaming. Another brother already has a mop out and cleans up the blood that dripped on the ground.

"You okay?" Chains walks up to me, and only me. Having all that male focus on me is something I ain't about to take for granted. My old man is amazing and I ain't letting go of him. Not unless he tells me to. Even then, I'll put up one hell of a fight.

I nod. "How much of that did you hear?"

"Actually, Flint had an eye on the cameras while in Church. You didn't really think I was going to leave you completely unprotected, did you? Even in my own club I watch out for you."

"Don't think you need to, man. She went full-on Mama Bear. Hell, you might have even dented the bar top." Bass chuckles as he takes my unused seat, even going far enough to take a drink of my cold coffee.

"Bastard."

"Nah, I knew my parents."

Chains laughs but tugs me close anyway, inhaling me. I shiver in ecstasy. Who knew a man smelling me would make my knees turn to jelly?

"Stay with the boys for a bit, will you? I want Flint to show me the cameras that got him running out of Church with the rest of us on his heels. He didn't give me much to work with and for once I'm regretting sound-proofing Church, but I knew it had to be about you. My old lady doesn't know how to do quiet."

"That's not true," I reply in outrage.

"Yes it is, sweet thing. We all heard just how many fun times you had last night."

While the rest of the guys laugh at Bass, I'm mortified. I had zero clue I make noise when I have sex. I don't even remember doing it last night with Chains.

A soft kiss hits my head before whispered words echo in my ear. "Don't be embarrassed, Mama Bear. Like knowing I can bring my old lady to peaks that shake the dust off this place. Fucking hard just thinking about how I made you scream. Give me an hour and I'll be happy to do it again."

I nod, 'cause what else can I do? I'm not about to say no. If vamps are basically willing to go to the enemy to get a girl from claiming them, then I'm well aware I got a catch. A mighty fine one, and he has a nice ass too.

A thing I have no problem ogling as he walks away.

Bass chuckles. "Try to keep the drool inside your mouth, woman. We just got done mopping up."

I roll my eyes. "Stop drinking my coffee and get off your ass and get your own. You know what? Get me one too. You drank the rest of mine, asshole."

"Better do as she says. You see what happens when she gets mad." Casper laughs as he pushes Bass out of my seat, who pretends to pout before he winks and walks away with my cup in hand.

I watch him and voice my concern out loud. "Think he'll actually get me coffee, or should I be worried he'll spit in it?"

"Nah, he'll get it, and just the way you like."

"Afraid of my wrath, huh?" I smirk as I take my seat again.

"Nah, Chains'. He's always been loyal. When he gives someone his pledge to be on their side, unless the bastard is dumb enough to turn on him, Chains won't back down from defending them. And if you can't tell, Chains ain't known for using his words when he gets mad."

"Let me guess, he uses a chain or something?"

"Ha, that would be funny, but no. He just beats the shit out of them, and the guy fights dirty. The joint just made it worse."

"So how did he get the name Chains?"

"His bike chain."

"What?"

Casper just laughs at my confusion. "He used to come around way before most of us were here. Always wanted to join the club, but back then, all he had was a bike—you know, the ten-speed kind. Rode it here every chance he could get. But the damn thing was old, and the chain always fell off. So he decided to always have a spare chain rather than buy a new bike. Carried one with him always. After he got patched in, the boys brought it back. Even gave him the chain he uses for his wallet as a 'welcome to the club' gift. And you can bet your ass that it fits most bicycles out there."

I smile at the love I hear clearly. The club's new for me, having what I always wanted. A family. Each person here is from a different past, and they all have different futures, but they're linked.

Like a chain. I laugh in my head at the sappy connection my brain is making.

A fresh coffee is placed in front of me, and I decide to trust Bass and drink it.

Perfection.

"What you learn?"

I look up at Casper, then flip my head the other direction as I see he's looking behind me. Chains is already back in the room and beside me. He pulls me into his hip, and I don't fight the comfort I find in his arms and the way he always seems to hold me lately.

"Christy put the hit out on Maddy."

"Fuck! No wonder you went all crazy on her," Bass pipes up from the other side of the bar.

I shake my head. "No. Like I said, it didn't bother me. I mean, yeah, I'm pissed about it, and I would have at least hit her over it if given another opportunity. But as soon as she started talking, I remembered what that one guy was saying as he held me down."

The shiver that racks me takes a moment to get through my system. The boys are nice to not demand I talk right away, but I feel their tension. Casper and Bass are in my line of sight, and it's clear on their faces that my attack wasn't something they condone for anyone. I don't have eyes on Chains, but I lean into him as he rubs my chill away, giving me the strength to know I have him and the club behind me.

"He made it clear I was a bonus. I didn't need to be alive, just gone. He thought he could take a few extra liberties before he killed me. It was his questions about the kids, kept asking where they were. Said I couldn't protect them forever. That not even their mama could do that, and I wasn't any better than her."

"Told you to stop thinking like that. You're just as important as they are." His growl rumbles through me, sending the last of my unease away completely.

I turn in his arms, not caring that we have an audience. "And I told you. I put the kids first. Always. So stop trying to change me, and I'll stop expecting you to stop nagging me over this. Neither of us is going to change, so get over it and deal with it."

I don't expect him to grab my face and kiss me senseless. I don't balk at it, not at all. It might not be completely appropriate with the audience, but I ain't about to tell him to stop.

"You'll need to cut that out unless you want to see my dick."

"Ew."

I pull back and look at Bass in disgust. He just shrugs. "What? I like to watch. Live and in person is better than twelve hours of porn anytime."

"And you've gone twelve hours?" I ask skeptically.

"Wouldn't you like to find out?"

"No, thanks. Anyway, I think we need to see if the Devils Damned or even my uncle has a connection with Jennie. Izzy mentioned something before, but with the way the guy mentioned Jennie, it was like he knew her personally and not just her name."

"Jennie would never have anything to do with a Devils Damned," Chains seethed.

"You sure? You mentioned you weren't as close as you wanted to be. When I met her, it took her months to even mention she had a brother."

"How *did* you guys meet? You never said."

Ain't like I'm embarrassed by it. "Counseling."

"No shit?" This from Casper, eyes wide as saucers at my confession.

"Yeah, it was one of those group things, like AA. It was for those who had loved ones killed by cops. I was there because of my mom. She was pregnant with Grace then."

"Fuck. I had no clue she did that. Do you think that's what happened to the kids' dad?" Chains asked.

Now it's my turn for saucer eyes. "You never met him?" Don't know why, but I always thought Chains and Jennie may have been closer than he let on. Guess not.

"No. Never asked her to come visit me during lockup, and when we talked, she changed subjects when I asked, so I just asked about Teddy. It took a while before she even told me she was pregnant again. Think it was about a month before she popped."

I can hear the sadness in his voice, and I just want to cuddle around him and support him. He might think I'm the only one who needs someone in my corner, but I bet he does too. The boys come with the club. I wonder if he ever had anyone to rely on without strings. I'm sure the guys would still stand by him, club or not, but I want to be the one he leans on when they might not understand the emotions going on in his head. They're guys, and sometimes they run from their emotions. I do, too, but I'm learning to deal with them to help Teddy and Grace. Maybe I can help Chains too.

"Hey." I glide my hand over his cheek till he looks at me. "She didn't tell me either. She was closed off from the world. Her love was for her kids and keeping them safe. Even keeping you safe in her own way by not putting herself in a position to be used against you. She loved you. You know that. Before you came into our lives, all Teddy did was talk about you. No way would he have warned me off getting attached when I brought him home that first night if he didn't know without a certainty that you were coming for them. And that would have only come from his mom telling him he could always count on you. And she was right."

He covers my hand with his and moves it to his lips, kissing my palm softly. "You can also count on me."

"Ditto." My throat is thick with emotions, but I hold it in as I whisper my response

"Damn, I want one." I hear Casper speak softly but don't pull my gaze away.

"One? Hell, I'll take two." Bass chuckles, but I can hear the sorrow in his voice as if he doesn't expect he'll be lucky enough to even get one.

"Hell, I'll just be happy if Princess turns out half as decent as you, Mama Bear."

I turn to look at Bulldog as he walks up to us, giving him an encouraging smile.

"She will. She's got you and the club to make sure of it. And I'm sure Grace will insist on having her around often enough that I'll encourage her as well. If that's okay."

He looks at me for a long time, and I'm not sure what he sees. He finally pushes off the bar and shakes his head. Leaning in to kiss the top of my head, like a father, or maybe a big brother would. Maybe that's what I gained from this club: more brothers than I ever thought possible.

"You're one lucky bastard, Chains. I'd be honored to have you in my Princess's life, honored. You don't by chance got a sister, do you?"

I shake my head while smiling. "Nah, just a crazy friend who's more blood than not. But she lives basically in another state, and I don't see you as the long-distance type of guy."

"You got that right. I'm going to go to Ma's and get the kids. You guys down to grill out and have the kids play out back?"

"Yeah, I'm sure they'll love that. I kind of kept them locked up inside yesterday," I say sheepishly.

"Don't blame you. Did the same with Princess. But we got enough brothers to watch our backs and keep them safe. That's what they'll have here—safety, always."

"Thanks. And thanks for changing the rules around here. Didn't mean to cause too much trouble."

Bass shakes his head. "You didn't. Things needed to be shaken up. All but a few of us actually like the idea of having this place be more for us than the vamps. Those bitches think they run this place just 'cause we let them stay after sucking us dry. The fresh air is nice. Hell, maybe we might even attract a few of the higher class, like you, Maddy. God knows

I'm not ready to settle down, but I'm sure a few of these old asses like the idea once they see Chains can do it and it ain't such a bad thing."

I'm surprised at his words, but it seems I'm the only one. I thought it would have been a fight to get the vamps out, but I'm happy to hear that no one is going to be mad at me for suggesting it.

The boys leave, and warm arms snake around me.

"Want to go take a nap before the kids get back?" Chains asks.

"I'm not tired, actually."

"Who said we were sleeping? Figured we could start our own code and get used to saying it before the kids get back."

"Right, okay. A nap sounds nice," I squeak as I feel myself getting aroused by each heated word on my skin.

"There will be nothing nice about what I'm going to do to you," he growls, causing me to shiver.

"Who... who said it was going to be *you* doing it?" I look back at him, lifting my eyebrow in challenge. There's something I want to try, and I'm just horny enough to attempt it. I rise from the chair and sashay away.

"Lead the way, Mama Bear. I'd follow you anywhere with a promise like that."

Chapter 24 – Chains

I lied to her.

I won't just follow her for sex. I'll follow her forever. It also helps that she has a nice ass to look at from this viewpoint.

No idea what she has in mind, but anything with her will be amazing. I need to come to terms with it. I've fallen completely in love with Maddy. And I ain't upset about it. I love that she's fiercely protective of my niece and nephew. I love that she stands up for them. Even stands up for me.

Flint showed me, Law, and Bulldog the feed. We put the entire place under video surveillance since we bought it. Other clubs might think they shouldn't watch their guys all the time, that it's a sign of distrust, but the club agreed. Everyone knows they're there. We ain't hiding them. It's more for shit like this than anything, when guests come in thinking they have more privileges than they actually do.

Hearing Maddy stand up for me had me going rock hard. But learning about Christy's betrayal, of me, of Maddy, of the club, it's unforgivable. She's lucky I don't just shoot her for putting her hands on my old lady alone, but I know we need answers. Like how the hell does she even know the Devils Damned?

I still need to work with Maddy, though. Love how protective she is over those she claims as hers, even me, but she needs to see that in herself. I know we'll argue about this time and time again. Might just be easier to make sure I'm always there to protect her, but even under my own roof, she gets attacked.

I shake my head. Now is not the time to think about it. Not when I have a beautiful woman, biting her lip and staring at me as I shut and lock the door.

I turn, expecting to guide her through this. We may have done the nasty a few times last night, but she's still a virgin in so many ways. She doesn't blush at everything, like I expect a virgin to, but then again, her childhood took away some of the innocence she should have had in her life. I like that about her past. Not that she went through it but that she had tough times and survived. It gives me hope that this is long-term for both of us. Club life isn't horrible, but it ain't easy. Shit happens, and a club member needs a strong woman to stand by his side through it all.

When I turn to face her, I jolt at how close she is. I was so lost in my own head that I didn't even hear her. This woman is already dangerous for me. Got me so twisted up that I can't focus on anything when my thoughts are on her.

"You're going to have to tell me if I get this wrong. I'm working off what I've read and seen in movies."

I'm confused till she undoes my button and zipper before she drops to her knees, taking my pants to the ground with her.

Not going to lie, I've dreamed about this. Fantasized. Jerked off more times than I can count to thoughts of Maddy on her knees before me. As I mentioned foolishly to her, I've even imagined it was her when I was with others. But unlike them, I don't tilt my head back and close my eyes. Don't force their head down to cover most of their face with my hand so I can hide who they are.

I watch. I move her braid behind her back, not wanting anything to obstruct my view. She's slow now that she's on her knees, and I don't rush this. She's never done this—she just said as much. Knowing I'm this girl's first—*my girl's first*—in so many things makes me happier than a lobster set free. I won't be able to give her a lot of my firsts, just one, my heart.

She pulls my boxers down, and from the way she jerks her head back, she wasn't expecting my dick to bounce up once it's released from its confines. I chuckle softly and rub her head in encouragement. She looks at me first and smiles, then at my dick.

She has no clue how much just having her on her knees, not even touching me, is doing to me. I'm so hard I'm sure I could hammer nails with it if needed. I'm even leaking, and when her tongue darts out to lick her lips, it only makes me leak more.

Leaning close, Maddy flicks the tip of her tongue up and collects my cum before it hits the carpet. It's a little touch, but now I'm shivering, and the air conditioning isn't even on.

Her moan at my taste has me moaning as well. She wraps her hand around me, and it's like a ghost hand, 'cause there isn't enough pressure for me to get off, but it feels amazing.

"Tell me. Tell me what you like. What feels good?" she murmurs.

"You do. Everything."

"Please. I want to do this right. I want to make you forget."

I slow my breathing and focus on her words.

"Maddy, look at me, baby." I wait till her eyes are on me. "No one, *no one,* can compare to you. Everything we do, that *you* do, is amazing. You don't need to make me forget 'cause I already did. You're my old lady, Maddy. You, just you. I might have a past, but I want nothing from it. I want you. Just you."

I wipe the tears that fall down her cheeks. Never thought I would get harder seeing a girl cry while on her knees. Sure, they slip out a few times from gagging, but these tears are from feeling accepted. From feeling wanted. From being loved.

She closes her eyes and gathers her wits. I love the strength in this woman.

"Okay, but I still want to know. I've... I've never done this. I want to make you feel as good as you make me feel."

"And how is that?"

"Like a queen."

I smile. Good, 'cause that's actually what she is. "Grip me tighter. I'll let you know if it's too tight. Go up and down. Feel how hard you make me."

She does as instructed, even rotates her hand a bit.

"Fuck, just like that." On instinct, my head goes back and rests against the closed door behind me as I feel her, but I quickly force myself to look back down at her. She's so fucking beautiful as she stares at my cock so intently.

"Now part those pretty little lips and take me in your mouth. Feel what it means to gag on your old man. I want to feel your throat contract around me. Swallow me down, Mama Bear."

I don't know how to be soft during sex, not really. She saw all my softness last night, and I was the bastard who didn't go easy when I slammed into her virginal channel.

Maddy is eager for this and doesn't hesitate. Like my need to be inside her, she doesn't just put the tip in but sucks down the whole damn thing. I bow back, not at all expecting her mouth everywhere. I have to pull out or I'll be done and miss out on all the joys of watching my old lady take my cock in her mouth for the first time.

"Jesus, woman, do you even have a gag reflex?"

"Did I do it wrong?"

"Fuck no, but you got to go slow if you don't want me going off so quickly."

She sits up straighter and smiles wide. Yeah, my girl likes knowing how close she can get me so quickly.

"*You* didn't go slow."

I look at her with narrow eyes. Her face is a bright ball of sunshine, even with the bruises still covering it. Some are fading, some are just turning to yellow, and others are getting dark purple. She's still the most beautiful woman I've ever seen, and she did that on purpose.

"You minx. Was that payback?"

She bites her lip but can't control it enough to stop smiling.

I stand straight and grab my cock at the base. "Oh, you think you're funny? You won't be laughing for long. Open up, my girl. I'm in charge now."

I hold my dick straight out to her and grab her head, but I don't force it. She ain't no vamp. Maddy's my old lady. Never had one before, but I ain't a complete idiot. A happy old lady is a happy life. I ain't about to ruin this experience enough that she doesn't want to do it again, 'cause that would kill me. She had her mouth on my dick for a second, and it was the most amazing feeling in the entire world. Scratch that. Being inside her was the winner of that cake. But this is a close second—a pretty damn close second.

She dips her head forward, and I thrust in, but I don't hit the back of her throat like I'm sure she expects. I pump slow and steady, the pace I want, but also giving her time to feel me inside. Her tongue swirls around, and I grip her head tighter. But I want to feel her hair through my fingers, not just hold on to her braid.

"Take out your braid, baby. I want to guide you how I want."

Her fingers are quick as they release the tie and unwind it. She even puts her hands behind her head as I keep up my steady rhythm, and my eyes latch on to how her breasts push out. It's a temptation I'm not about to be denied.

I move my hand just enough to grab both of hers and force them to stay on her head as I use my other one to push her tank and bra down and then cup her tit. It's fucking amazing having her fullness in my palm. I stop moving my hips, but my old lady keeps up the pace I set, moaning as I palm her and tweak her nipple with my fingers. When I pinch and twist a nipple, she deep-throats and swallows.

I let go of her hands, but she holds them there a bit longer, and I wonder if she likes the idea of being restrained. It's something we'll have to explore, 'cause that's sexy as fuck. When she does move them, they trail to my thighs, squeezing, kneading, gripping for support and release.

Her nails dig into them, and I relish the sting, as it only increases my arousal. I attempt to hold myself back. Don't want this to end; I never want it to stop. I grit my teeth as I continue to watch her, resting my hands at my side, not wanting to touch her anymore 'cause feeling her with my hands is an added pleasure. I need to wean off the release a bit.

Her hands travel up, one going to my shaft, the other to my balls. She is soft on them, green as to how a man wants them touched, but she runs her fingers around the sack, and I shiver to hold back my release. Shit, maybe she *does* know what she's doing, and the other women had no clue.

Her fingers grip me tight on my cock. It's tighter than before, but it's fucking amazing as she uses it to stroke me in time with her increased bobbing on my tip. Her tongue runs all around the head and then she deep throats and hollows her cheeks as she sucks. I'm lost. So fucking lost. She continues this torment, no pattern to alert me when she will change it up and it's amazing.

I can't take anymore; I need my hands on her again. My resolve has crumbled to nothing. I grab both sides of her head and grip her. She pulls back enough to suck on my tip as she pumps me tightly and looks at me.

Desire.

Trust.

Love.

I explode, looking at my old lady as she stares at me on her knees. It's a sight that I'll never forget.

I should have told her, given her a warning. I know vamps swallow, but most civilians would rather spit. Hell, Maddy is new to this; I should have pulled out and jacked the rest off in a sock or some shit. But my girl doesn't disappoint. Other than my groan as I let go, her name on my lips, she doesn't break pace. There's no sign that she took all of me except for me leaning spent on the door as she slows her movements and gives me soft kisses up and down my dick and then thighs.

I move my hands from her hair to her face, stroking her cheeks. Running my fingers gently over her, enjoying her attention moving from my legs to kissing my palm, my fingers.

"One lucky bastard I am. Never thought I would find someone like you, but don't think for one second I'm about to let you go."

"So, you saying you liked it?"

"Like it? No. Loved it, baby. Loved it."

"Really? Would you say it's the best you've had?"

"Baby, it's the *only* one I've had. Told you before, nothing compares to you. Now get your ass undressed and on that bed. I need to reciprocate, and then I'm going to fuck you before the kids ask where we are."

"Well, I hope you can get back in gear quickly 'cause it won't take much."

I take off my shirt and kick out of the jeans and pants still on my ankles.

"Did sucking your old man get you turned on, Mama Bear?" Fuck yeah, that's hot. Knowing she enjoys sucking me as much as I like getting sucked is like finding out that you get cake *and* ice cream.

She nods and looks over at me as she shimmies out of her shorts, then takes off her top and bra in one pull. I doubt she meant to be sexy, but fuck, it is. And the beast in me doesn't want to wait any longer to find out how wet she really is.

I take two steps and close the distance between us, pushing her over, grabbing and spreading her ass wide for me at the same time. Her cry of shock turns to pleasure as I dip my tongue into her honeypot. Fuck, she's soaked, and my face is already dripping after a few licks.

I don't give a fuck that I'm all up in her. It's amazing. Her taste is an addiction. I have half a mind to think it's because of all the coffee she drinks. There must be something extra special in her creamer or something to make her taste this good. No way this is normal. If everyone tasted this good, no bitches would complain about how little their guys go down on them but more about how they can't get them to stop.

I chuckle as I lick and suck. I have plans for Maddy and me. No doubt we'll use the 69 position more times than not if I have my way. Having both our mouths on each other will definitely make for interesting and intense orgasms.

I'm already hard again, but I promised her she would get off before I do.

I smack her ass hard, and she moans like I knew she would. My old lady likes it a bit rough, and that's just what I want to give. I'm not into the full-on sadism thing, but I ain't sweet or soft. A little pain just adds to the flavor of it all.

She gushes more into my mouth as I knead her globes. I inch up and swirl my tongue around an area I'm sure Maddy never even thought was a possibility for pleasure.

She tries to pull away, but I hold firm, growling as I continue to circle it with my tongue. I pull back as I peer down at her rosebud. I want in, and I will, but not today. We'll work up to it, and I'm going to relish training her to take my cock in her ass.

"Don't think you can get away from me. All of you is mine—all of it. Including this fine ass you got here."

I smack it again.

Once, twice, three times in rapid succession on each cheek. Then I sink back to my main course of licking up her clit before going farther. I push her over the edge as I inch a pinky into her tight ass. She goes off like a rocket, and I suck on her clit a bit more before standing and ramming my cock right into her coming pussy.

"James!"

The sudden intrusion has her calling out my name. Not many ever called me my given name in the bedroom. A few tried, and I cut that shit out quickly. But with her, with my old lady, I like it. I like that she knows who's fucking her, that it isn't just a club brother. It ain't just her old man—it's me. The man outside the club who's fucking her in my room inside the club. I'm one and the same, but there are two sides that I rarely acknowledge. But with her, I can be both. I can be what she needs. I know she'll need the club side more times than not, but the outsider side, she can have that too. She can have it all.

I keep my finger in her ass, pushing it farther in and moving it to match my hips as I jack into her. She's still coming. I don't know if she ever stopped and started again or if it's just lasting forever. I ain't complaining. Having her pussy grip me as it convulses has me rocking into her harder and faster.

It doesn't matter if it's seconds or hours that pass. Only thing that matters is hitting that edge. Getting to the point of heaven only Maddy can take me to. I come on a shout that I'm sure half the place can hear. Don't give a fuck, though.

My old lady also cries out, matching her scream of my name to her own. No way to hide what we're doing, not that I'm hiding it. Just hope the kids aren't back yet. Last thing I want is to have *that* talk with them.

Chapter 25–Maddy

Thankfully, Chains and I get our sexual lust out of us long enough to pull away from each other and shower before Bulldog gets back with the kids.

"Go on out. Going to talk with Prez for a moment."

I nod in assurance, but he leaves me flustered as he kisses my temple, then slaps my ass. Hard. It reminds me of what just happened, and I'm red as a beet, I just know it.

I slip out the back double doors and take my first good look around. I never could see the backyard from the front when I first came here. The combination of two garages and the *L*-shaped compound block it out. It's a huge spread that includes a large outdoor patio and eating area with about six picnic tables spread out. There's a fire pit with a decent pavement surrounding it so it doesn't just look like a place where beer cans get thrown after a party.

Don't get me started on the playground. With it being built for Princess, and now Grace and Teddy, I should have expected it to fit royalty, and it is. The thing has three slides. Three! I only had a swing set for the kids, but this thing has a rock wall, a tower, even one of those bridges that wobbles as they walk. It's more than just something you buy from a box. I can see the love the boys put in this thing. I even see wolves cut out to match the Hounds they have on their cuts. But unlike the one body with three heads the guys wear, the kids' playground has a cutout that looks like solo wolves howling at the moon. Hell, they even used tires to make a few swings look like motorcycles.

Not sure what was here before I mentioned something to Chains, but I bet it was mostly just the tower. And they did all the other stuff in a month. What will these guys, pseudo uncles, do when these kids want the big things? Hell, what does a birthday party look like around here? No doubt Bulldog has Princess's here. Bet my life that she has it here every year and will continue to till the day she dies, or moves.

I snort. Like Bulldog would let his girl out of his sight for longer than a few hours. Don't know the guy well, but I do know that.

I look around for him and only see the girl who hid behind the bar the other night sitting on top of one of the picnic tables. She nods at me, and I take it as my cue and walk over.

"Hey, Ruby, right?"

"Yeah. Nice to officially meet you, Mama Bear." She shakes my hand and pulls me up to sit by her.

"Thought it would be best to keep the kids outside till you and your old man got done screaming the doors off. Trust me, no kid needs to know their parents have sex." She shudders. "It's gross, and therapy doesn't help."

I laugh awkwardly. Can't tell if she's being serious or kidding. Not sure what volume I reach when I'm with Chains; I barely hear him with the thumping in my ears each time we have sex.

Sex.

I'm having sex.

"Stop it. No need to walk around like you're better than us 'cause you're getting hot sex and the rest of us ain't." Her growl comes off with a heavy dose of annoyance and an eye roll that goes from my face back to watching the kids.

I giggle at this. I was her like a handful of days ago.

"Sorry, can't help it." I really can't. Seriously. Who knew a girl's face could hold a smile for this long? I swear I'm not even trying. It's just natural.

"Yeah, I get it. That man is fine. Been raised around these bastards and consider most my brothers, but I ain't blind."

"Most?" I side-eye her, reading between the lines.

She tilts her head, narrowed eyes and pointed lips assessing me.

It's cute, since she's probably a few years younger than me. I may have been a bit out of it the other night, but I wasn't wrong. The girl is gorgeous. Now that I see her, I can really tell it's a natural beauty thing she's got going on. Her night trip for water was her thinking she was alone, no makeup or hair done. She was just a beautiful girl walking around in pajamas that were probably super comfy if I think about it.

But now that she's wide awake, I can't tell if she's putting up a wall or if she really is this badass-looking all the time. Then again, her dad is the president of an MC, and her family is basically a group of bikers, so maybe it ain't an act.

Her clothes scream pinup, with the dark blue corset and leather pants. And wow, her boots are laced up the front but have a heel of about six inches. I can't walk in anything over two. I really need to get some pointers if I ever want a chance of getting taller. Not that being shorter than Chains is a problem. He certainly has no problem lifting me to fit me where he wants.

Her skin is pale but not creepy-like. More like her skin is just alabaster and she isn't the sunbathing kind. Her makeup is heavy on the eyes, dark, and her lips are a subtle red. Wouldn't be surprised if the color was ruby red—kind of poetic, actually. You would think she would play up the big pouty lips and blush, but it's very subtle, which just makes me stare more at her.

And then I get to her hair. Last time it was in one of those handkerchief things that ties it all up. This time it's mostly down in a half pony of sorts. Her hair goes from black, to dark red, to bright red, to hot pink at the tips. Some looks to be in intricate braids while the rest just runs straight down. How much time does she spend on her hair a day? It's long as hell, touching the picnic table we're sitting on, and I wonder how many times she's sat on parts of it.

"Shut up. I like you. You busted up a vamp. That makes us BFFs, but don't start psychoanalyzing when we're just getting to know each other. Do that shit after a few bottles of tequila, will you?"

"How about margaritas? Straight tequila will get me dancing on tabletops."

Her laugh is lyrical and has me stilling to listen to it. "You sound like you're perfect for the club."

"Perfect for me is more like it." I startle, not having heard Chains and a few others walk up to us.

Ruby fake gags. "Stop, you're going to make me throw up."

Wrapping his arms around me, Chains chuckles as I lean back into him. I'll never get used to having someone to lean on. It's nice. It's warm and comfy too.

I look out at the kids and hold my breath. Teddy's standing on top of one level and is just staring at us. At Chains and me. *Fuck.* We never told the kids, and I know from the look on Teddy's face that he isn't for it. Maybe not against it but definitely not wanting to try it, like when I introduced him to Pop-Tarts.

I move to get up, but Chains pulls me back.

"What's up?" he asks.

I nod toward Teddy, who's still standing motionless as he watches us. I feel the group go silent more than hear it, then feel Chains slowly let his arms drop.

"Want me to go?"

I shake my head. "I got it."

I'm still new in Teddy's life. I might have been around longer than Chains, but he's known his uncle his whole life, even if it was just an image in his head. He and I have built a bond, but it's still new.

As I walk toward him, he takes the little leap of faith he has in me and meets me halfway after using the slide to get off the playground. He stands a foot away from me but continues to stare behind me, at Chains I'm sure, but I don't look back. I focus on him, because that's what he needs right now—all my attention.

"Hey, little man."

He hesitates but gives me a chin lift that I know he copies from his uncle. It brings a smile to my face. I want this to work. I've been on my own for so long. The need to stop carrying the world is within reach. It's just been me for so long, and now I have Chains.

I always feared that once I met someone, I would push them away. It was a fear based on reality, but with both Chains and the kids—and the club, really—all were forced on me. I didn't get a say, an out. Chains showed up and didn't leave. The club came with him. To an extent, I had a say with the kids, but not really. Izzy knew I would fall for them instantly; we have a connection in not having any family left. I was young when I lost mine. They're babies, and I doubt

Grace will even remember her mom. I know she doesn't know her dad. Doubt Teddy even remembers him.

"Why was my uncle hugging you?"

"Um...."

"'Cause she's his old lady."

Both of us turn to see Princess to our left.

"What's that?" he asks her but gives me the side-eye.

"It means they married."

"Wait, what?" Okay, this is news to me. I mean, I got it was a term for a serious relationship, but Princess has me thinking that maybe it's legally binding somehow.

Before I can even voice more, the little girl spouts out more stuff my old man left out.

"Yeah, she gets a nickname, and now she's part of the club. I an old lady too. That's why I get called Princess."

"Huh? Who you married to?"

"No one yet," she draws out like *we're* the crazy people here. "But I will be. Only girls in the club are vamps or old ladies, and Daddy said I ain't no vamp, so I'm an old lady. Want to be my old man?"

He shrugs. "I guess."

"Good, now we just need to get you a nickname. But I can't give you that. Only club can. I can ask my daddy to give you one. Or you can ask your uncle. I bet he'll give you one."

How the hell does a four-year-old know more about this than me?

"Princess!"

"Yes, Daddy?" Her face is pure innocence, but I know it's an act. Grace has pulled it on me several times before.

"You ain't allowed an old man. We've talked about this."

"You said I can't have anyone in the club. Teddy ain't in the club. I bring him in. He my old man now. Can we find an old man for Grace?"

"No," Chains and Bulldog both bellow, and I smirk before I turn back to the one who matters in this conversation.

"That okay, little man?"

He looks from me to his uncle and back again. Putting his hands in his pockets, he shuffles his feet as he watches them. "That mean you ain't going to leave?"

Taking a step closer, I kneel to his level and take a hand out of his pocket to hold. "Not sure what the future holds between me and your uncle. But no matter what, it won't affect you or Grace. I'll be here for you, just like I said that first day. I'm here till you say otherwise. Got it?"

He nods, and I realize I hate the seriousness of this talk, so I stick out my tongue, and he giggles. "Now go play. I'll get us some snacks."

He's off before I can finish my sentence, and I watch him play for a second before I head back to the group that includes Law, Ruby, Bulldog, Casper, Flint, and Domino. And my old man. Can't forget him, especially since apparently we're married.

"Everything good?"

I saddle up to Chains and let him drape an arm around me. "Yeah, he seems okay with it, but I think it's best we still watch him. Grace doesn't know what's going on, so she might have issues with it later."

"They won't, baby, and if they do, we'll talk with them and explain it again."

I nod as he kisses my temple, and then I ask the burning question.

"So apparently we're married now?"

I'm really good at getting this group to go speechless. They also suck at pretending not to listen in on other people's conversations.

Except for Ruby. She's full-on laughing. No pretending from her.

He eases back, knowing he left things out. "Not technically, but old ladies in the club world are sacred. Most guys marry theirs."

"Most?"

He shrugs as he puts his hands in his pockets, mimicking Teddy just moments ago. It's sweet, really, that they share the same mannerisms.

"Some don't. Just like some civilians live together forever and never marry. It's a preference thing more than not."

"I married mine. Woman wouldn't have it any other way." I hear the love in Law's voice as he speaks about her. "She was a hell-raiser, and if I didn't put a ring on it, you bet your ass she would have tattooed one on my finger as I slept."

Ruby grins. "Yeah, Mom was pretty crazy."

"Where do you think you get it from, darling? Ain't my side, I can tell you that."

I sigh in contentment. "Sounds like a hell of a woman." This is nice, talking with others, just shooting the breeze as the sound of little people squealing with glee floats on the air around us.

Law nods, pride clear on his face. "She was, and you should know, Mama Bear. You met her."

I'm just as confused as the rest of the group.

"Her name was Katrina, but we just called her—"

"Special K." He nods at me as memories flood back into my mind. "She was the one my aunt had drive me to Texas. We spent a week together getting me settled in. God, she never said she was part of a club."

"That was the point. Your aunt was just this side of crazy, so she and my old lady got along. Nothing that had people talking but enough that your aunt could trust her to ask a favor. I wish I'd dug in more into why my lady drove down south for a pair of shoes when she never wore the damn cowboy boots when she got back. But I didn't push, and I trusted her. I still do, just wish I'd asked so I could have helped a bit more."

"Oh no, don't say that. Your wife was amazing. She was the first decent person I met outside of my aunt. She took me in, taught me how to live on my own—hell, taught me how to live above ground. I even texted her a few times over the years asking random questions. Nothing too big, just things like a mama should know. God, I'm so sorry. I've always seen her as a stepmom." I'm bawling right now, and Law is tearing up, too, just like Ruby.

"She never made me feel like a burden, and we always spoke on holidays," I continue. "She even sent me a few birthday cards. It was perfect 'cause I felt like I had a home, but one no one could trace, one my uncle couldn't connect me to. I got nothing from my aunt, but your wife, hell, she saved me so much in those first few years. I always wondered what happened to her. I just figured she tired of me."

"No, she never did. She got cancer. Took her pretty quick about three years ago. She never said a word to me about you, not like that, but she mentioned you. I would see her texting and smiling, but she kept it to herself. It wasn't till the boys discovered your little hideout that it triggered a memory. My woman was good at goodbyes. I was the one who sucked at them. During her last few days with us, she wrote a few letters, mostly just her way of saying goodbye, sparing me those heart talks that I couldn't handle at that moment. Took me till last night to find the courage to read them. And that's how I found out about you. She thought about you to the end, I want you to know that. She may have never said your name, but I figured it out."

"I asked." Ruby's voice is thick with emotion. "I asked her, and she sat me down once and told me she was speaking to an angel. That's what she called you. A fallen angel who didn't know how to fly anymore and needed advice to keep the devil away. I thought she was just being silly, but it seems she wasn't. You really are an angel, Maddy. And I'm happy to call you a sister, 'cause you brought a smile to my mama, and that's all I wanted for her."

Her hug is a surprise, but I take it. I need the support as we both hug it out.

"Welcome to the family, Mama Bear. If you considered my Special K as your mama, I don't mind you thinking of me as anything but your dad. I'm sure he was a good man, but I would be honored to claim you as my own. We both would." He looks down at Ruby for confirmation, who's just a barrel of smiles and tears and nods profusely.

I have no words. What does anyone even say to that? I can't do anything but nod. Nod my head off, really.

I'm grateful that Chains turns me so I can crawl into him and shed years of tears. Years of anguish, sorrow, loss, loneliness. This man has given me everything. Absolutely everything. Even as I unintentionally ruined a part of his life, he still takes me in. Him and the club. They claim me as their own; they claim me as family.

The only thing I ever wanted, and now that I have it, I will do anything to keep it.

Anything.

Chapter 26 – Chains

After the heartrending moment that Law laid out, we all need a moment. Hell, I need a few hours to process it all. So do the rest of the boys. Knowing Special K helped Maddy just makes me love the dead woman more. She was a mama to all of us, so it's no surprise to know she did that for Maddy as well.

I love my club. Everything about it. Especially that we're a group that can go from strangers to family in days. Hell, minutes, really, after a story like Law's. I'm happy to see them claim Maddy as their own. Makes me happy to see her getting things she was deprived of from her own family.

I ain't got proof, not yet, but I got suspicions that Maddy's dad wasn't killed randomly. Ten to one her uncle did that too. He's dirty enough to kill his own brother; the guy is scum. I want his neck. Actually, I want Maddy to have it. I want to watch her squeeze the life out of that bastard.

Sick?

Yes.

Cleansing?

Fuck yeah.

I'm sure other guys don't want their old ladies near death and blood and shit, but Maddy is who she is because of it. I ain't about to take something from her she might want. I know the club's got things in the works, but I got to ask how far she wants in. We ain't most clubs, but we do try to keep things between the brothers when we can. When retribution is on the line, it gets blurred, and some people who might not otherwise know what goes on behind closed doors get pulled in.

Dinner with a few brothers turns out to be a semiformal BBQ. It seems the vamps getting kicked out for a bit actually brought a few more brothers around, and they hang out longer. Could be that, or that my sexy old lady is literally walking the line between picnic tables and getting to know everyone and offering to help get them what they need. I keep telling her they're grown-ass men who can get their own damn beer and food, but she just shushes me and keeps going. I ain't mad as long as these rat bastards know she's sleeping in my bed tonight, and every night.

Teddy keeps giving us looks when we kiss, but I think the kid is just trying to figure out his own feelings about Maddy and his mom. We've had a few talks, nothing too serious, but he's hinted about what I think his mom would think if he liked Maddy. I'm pretty sure it goes above like. If the kid is anything like me, he's head over heels in love and just doesn't know how he should feel.

Maddy is the mom Jennie would have been if she'd been allowed to. I have no doubt that Jennie was doing everything for them. And now, the possibility of a connection between her and Maddy's uncle gets me wondering how much more tangled up our two lives are.

"She's good, man. She's good for the club."

I take the Miller off Bulldog as we both watch Maddy go to yet another brother and have the guy gushing and blushing within two minutes.

"Yeah. You think you ever going to get one?"

"An old lady? Fuck no. Got one princess. Don't need another."

"Yeah, but that princess might need a queen to look up to."

"Not anymore. I'll just borrow Maddy when you ain't looking."

I punch him, but he doesn't complain. Nothing's broken.

Flint joins us a minute later. "What you two women doing?"

"Trying to convince this asshole that old ladies ain't so bad."

Flint shakes his head and laughs. "Fuck, I was just kidding. Get one old lady in the group and look at you all. Already gossiping like damn chicks."

"Not chicks. Still got my dick. Used it to fuck your mother last night."

I chuckle at Bulldog's quip before he turns that steel tongue against me.

"And what do you know about old ladies? All you did was claim one. And from what I can see, you've been in the doghouse more times than not since. Not seeing the positives here."

"That's just 'cause you ain't *seeing* it, brother. Trust me, old ladies have perks. Many, *many* perks."

"Pretty sure the club heard those. Seriously need to get your girl a muzzle or something. She even sounds like a grizzly bear when she's with you." Flint's trying to goad me, but I ain't taking the bait. I fucking love that I make my girl scream so much and she has no clue she's doing it.

"Nah, not a muzzle. Bet she would look good with a ball gag between her lips, though."

I smirk at Bulldog, knowing he ain't just saying that to get a rise out of me. Pretty sure the guy has more ball gags than socks, and he goes through a lot of socks. Not sure why he has so many, but he likes variety.

"Speaking of gags, Casper's down in the hole. He'll text once she starts talking. Don't think it'll take much."

Bulldog shakes his head and speaks for the both of us. "Still can't believe it was her."

"I can. She's had her eye on being an old lady since she crawled in here. Didn't take her long to set her eyes on Chains." Flint grunts as he drinks his beer.

"Damn, why didn't you say something? Would have stayed the fuck away."

He shrugs off my glare, not even showing any signs of remorse. "Thought you knew, man, and just shook it off. I especially love that she thought you would be all for her being your old lady as she serviced the entire club. Yeah, like you share anything that counts. Stupid cunt didn't think shit through."

"Yeah, but she didn't know us. I saw the tape. She has an opinion about us—about *all* of us. Glad to see Maddy gets it. Gets *us*." Bulldog ain't being shy with showing his respect for my woman. And the nod from Flint tells me he feels the same.

We all watch as she flits about a bit more till a ping goes off and Flint checks his phone. I don't have to ask; I already know who it is.

"Give me a minute. I'll meet you guys down there. Get Prez, will you?"

"Yeah, tell Maddy to keep an eye on Princess for me," Bulldog says as he follows Flint into the club.

I nod as I head across the field to my old lady. God, I love saying that, even if it's not out loud. The idea alone makes me happy. And so does the woman in question.

Pulling her back from talking with Domino and General, I spin her quickly before kissing her, giving her no chance to back out or protest. Not that she would deny me. Okay, she would, and the fight would be interesting and probably end up with me getting rock hard and then having to carry her away to get rid of it, but I have things that need to be taken care of, so I end the kiss.

"Got to go have a talk with a vamp. Watch the kids and Princess for me?"

"Sure. You want me to come with you?"

I love that. Fucking love that. She has no clue what a "talk" really means, and I know she isn't into violence. Unless it's protecting someone, which is what she's trying to do with me. But I've told her before, I don't need her to protect me. *I'll* protect *her*.

"Nah, I got this. Watch her for me?" I say to Domino.

"Don't need watching" she grumbles beside me, but I pay her no attention as I keep my eyes on my brother, knowing he won't let me down.

The boys know what I'm about to do; ain't no hiding what needs to be done. We only waited this long to get enough brothers in the area to watch Maddy and the kids while we have our "talk." We have no clue how much Christy is in league with the Devils Damned, and we aren't about to assume anything. More brothers means more protection for my family. Another word I love saying.

"Be back soon."

With one last lingering kiss, I make the break and head toward the hole. We keep it under the clubhouse, through a few series of tunnels. Most people think it's under the main area, but it's a few yards away, under a small garage we have at the back of the property. We don't go in that way; it's used as an exit only, and usually only when we're getting rid of the evidence.

The club isn't one to go on a killing spree, but we do what we have to, and most of the boys are from pasts that have death in them: gangs, the military, hell, even a few mixed-up police and lawyers tired of the jacked-up system. We aren't vigilantes, but we step up when needed and take out the trash when the law's hands are tied.

Like with Maddy. Don't even need to bring it to the table, 'cause I know my brothers will back me for spilling blood under our club's name.

The hole is just the name we gave for our own little prison. It's actually three separate rooms, but you never know how many enemies we'll have at one time, and the rooms aren't small. We can fit a few in each, hanging from the hooks above if needed. The torture devices in the rooms are more for looks than use. A few guys get off using everything, but I prefer the mental image. They have no idea what I'll use, and they see that I can do anything my evil mind imagines.

And trust me, I have several ideas for Christy, but the last thing I want to do is touch that bitch. I want to take a hot shower and skin my own flesh after being touched by her. But then I remember that about four hours ago, I was swimming in my woman's release, and I ain't about to wipe that off, so I focus on that being my cleansing, my own little baptism of the evil I had before her, and now it's nothing but sunshine and rainbow shit from here on out.

"Took you long enough," Casper grumbles, but I know he's just in his role of pissed-off brother right now. We all have to play it every now and again. Of course, the guy probably isn't acting. Having a betrayal like this, which could have been years in the making, has us all on edge.

"Ain't apologizing for enjoying my old lady's tight cunt. Her pussy wouldn't let me go, it's so fucking tight." I'm being intentionally crude. I want this bitch to get it, that she ain't it and Maddy is. Has been since I got out and always will be now that I claimed her.

"Must be nice to get a tight one. Getting tired of these used ones. Can't even feel them coming anymore they're so loose. Got to pull out and use my hand if I even want to get off." Flint's snarl has me smiling as I see the flinch in Christy's shoulder. Apparently he isn't just being suggestive.

"She talking?"

I don't ask her, don't want to waste my breath. And as predicted, she opens her big fat mouth.

"Chains, please. I promise, I didn't mean for the kids to be involved. I told them to leave them out of this. They were just meant to scare her. That's all."

"Scare her? You call assaulting a woman, shooting up their house, and then threatening to kill her a scare tactic?"

"No, they said they wouldn't kill her. Just scare her. She was going to live. I promise you that."

"You think she would have lived through a rape?" Maddy's strong, but I don't know if she would. Few people do. Oh sure, they still walk around, but there's no living. Parts of them die, and nothing can bring them back.

"I did." I don't know if she says it just to get a reaction from me or if it's the truth. Doesn't matter. The bitch is getting nothing but what's coming to her.

"Yeah, yeah, yeah, you got it rough. Blah, blah, blah." Bulldog ain't having it any more than I am. "Start talking about the things we actually care about. And in case you don't know, none of us give a shit about your past, present, or future."

"Now, VP, I care." Christy is too stupid to see the twinkle in Flint's eye. She actually smiles at him. "I care about her future. Want to know how much pain the boys and I can inflict before we cut this cunt loose. We even started a pool to see how many cuts she can take before she passes out."

Casper snorts. "Can already tell you that. Bitch didn't get past two broken fingers before her eyes rolled back. When she came to, I just threatened to start on the other hand and she started talking. Fucking pathetic."

The boys and I chuckle. No one enjoys doing this to a woman, even one like this slut. But we don't discriminate. A betrayal is a betrayal, and blood is required. It's the way of the Reapers' Hounds. We're playing a role here, but it ain't that much of an act for us. Vamp or not, a part of this club or not, a debt needs to be paid for her part in hurting my old lady.

"Tell me what I want to know, Christy. Tell me what the connection is and how the hell you got tangled up in this and for how long."

Instead of talking, she starts bawling.

"Jesus." Flint takes a few steps back to shake off the frustration that we all share.

"Better to get it out and over with, girl. The boys ain't patient, and if you have any chance of making it out of this with minimal damage, it'll help if you keep the tears at bay till after you talk." Law always was good with the ladies. He never touched one after his old lady left the world. Guy never saw a need to tarnish what they had. Said he got a hand and enough memories to keep him happy for three lifetimes.

She sniffs, but thank fuck, she actually starts talking.

"Met a few of them through my brother. He was a low-level dealer when I was in school. That's how I knew who Maddy was. Her dad busted my brother a few times, so the name was known in our house, and if my brother didn't sell enough, then that meant we went without food till he did. Mom just used what he had, and Dad left as soon as I was conceived."

"So, that explains how you know about Maddy, not the rest. Keep talking and keep the sappy details to a minimum, will you? Said it before, no one gives a shit. We all have shitty pasts. Don't make you who you are today. Only you do that." Casper exhales with a groan of annoyance.

She licks her lips, more to keep herself going rather than to entice. Might be the first time she ever did that without hoping it led to sex.

"When there's no food, you take what's there. Got hooked in high school. Got clean when I came out this way. But every time I go back to see my mom, I dip in. One time I dipped and didn't know it was no longer my brother's but the Devils Damned's. Didn't know they were cutting out the family discount, and I guess I partied too hard one night. Woke up at their clubhouse. No one said nothing, and I just got my shit and left."

"But you went back." No questions, just statements from Law.

She nods nervously, and she should be. "But you got to believe me, it was just for the parties. I didn't tell them shit about you guys. Never even mentioned the club."

"Yeah, but I bet they know what a slut you are. Bet they just let you feel like you belonged and shit. Never asking you for much, just kept giving you what you wanted, huh?" Bulldog's snarling his words, spit flying from his mouth.

She looks down as if ashamed, but fuck that. A look and a feeling of guilt aren't the price we need paid for this deceit.

"So you know the Devils Damned 'cause you're a drugged-out whore," I cut in. "And apparently you got a fucking hard-on for me, which, got to say, not even flattered about that. You were a lay, and honestly, only reason I remember it is 'cause the guys told me. That's it. Even before jail, not one goddamn thing about you is memorable. Not a one. So tell me what this has got to do with my niece and nephew. Tell me how Maddy's uncle is involved. And stop wasting my fucking time. I'm getting bored, and I'm liable to use my chain when I get bored."

I know the boys told Maddy how I got my road name, that I carried a bike chain with me all the time. What they left out was that it's my go-to tool. I always have it, and it fits in my hands nicely. Either to punch the shit out of someone, or for other reasons, the chain is just a part of me, like the road name itself. And Christy knows this. She's witnessed it a time or two when we got into a few brawls on the road.

"Her uncle is at the clubhouse often. Does the drugs and other stuff, and the boys take care of things when he gets in a mess. He thinks the kids are his. They ain't. I knew Jennie, partied with her plenty of times. Her guy was nothing like him, and they fell in love. He was a Devils Damned, though. Wanted out, and Jennie even got him convinced he could be a Hound of the Reaper. He didn't fit in with the Devils, not anymore. She knew who I was, and I was supposed to be the one who introduced you all. He got connected to their MC because of drugs, but once he met Jennie, he wanted out, and he got sober. They both did. Becoming a family was unexpected, but any asshole could see they were happy. They did well with the Devils Damned till Maddy's uncle showed up a few times. He set his eyes on Jennie. He didn't know she already had a kid when he met her. She didn't give him the time of day, so he had her guy killed, and then he raped her. She ran away after that, but someone must have seen she was pregnant and spoke up. He got psycho and said it was his. It isn't. She told me she was pregnant before her guy died, which was the last time I saw her. He wants your niece as his own, but once he found out about the other one, Teddy, he wants to train him or something. Take on his business, I guess, mold him in a way."

"My fucking sister was raped, and you didn't say shit?" I throw her across the floor, chair and all. It breaks against the wall, and she crumples to the ground. I take a step to deal out more, but Bulldog blocks me and pushes me off.

"Walk it off. We need more out of her. I'll take care of it, trust me."

I know what he's saying, but he can't have that. He can't take away my right to seek the revenge that's needed for my sister.

"No, you get the info, but *I'll* take care of it. Got me?" There's no challenge in my eyes. He knows I need this. I wasn't able to honor Jennie's death like I should have, but I'll make those pay who knew of her assault and did nothing.

He nods. I look to the others, and they all nod as well. They're pissed, and they'll deal out their own pain, but they won't kill her. No, that joy will be my own.

Chapter 27–Maddy

f you asked me a month ago if I would feel comfortable in a clubhouse, much less have a routine with Chains and the kids, I would have laughed right in your face. Hard, full-on, maybe even peed myself type of laughter. But that's exactly what happened.

The night Chains came back from dealing with Christy—because I'm not an idiot and knew exactly where he was going when he said he had to get shit done without leaving the property—he didn't beat around the bush. Said I couldn't go back home, and I said okay.

That was it.

I didn't balk about it. What good would it have done for me other than start another fight between us? And we did that already. We needed to do something new. Like me just accepting what he said and moving past my own issues.

If he says the area isn't safe, then it ain't.

It took another week before he finally came clean about what was going on in their little dungeon. I mean hole. Apparently calling it a dungeon is a no-no. Whatever. It's below the clubhouse, and I stand by my name for it. When I asked if they torture people there, he got quiet. I took back the question, 'cause I don't want him to lie to me, and I know he would. Just saves me from having to do the same if needed. I appreciate that from him, but I already know I would lie for this man. Hell, I would die for him, but that's a bit mental, and I don't want to tell him that. Mostly 'cause I really hope it never comes to that.

He told me what Christy told him.

I cried for him 'cause I knew he wouldn't. Couldn't. That isn't who he is. But I was that for both of us. I was the one who shed the release we both bottled up. Sounds fucked-up and crazy, but I cried out all the tears for the pain and torment Jennie went through, and for Chains never knowing that side of her. A side she held away from him, which probably hurt more than learning about the rape itself.

After, we both seemed lighter. Don't know if he just needed to talk it out or what. Just know that after that night, we had a connection. Beyond sexual.

And yes, totally about to do the super-duper sappy girl part now. It was almost like our souls connected.

Yup, that's right, I'm talking about souls here. Not sure if I would go as far and saying we're soul mates, 'cause I don't even believe that exists. But I do think we connected on a deeper level. And for us, a girl who can't connect with anything but coffee and a man who hasn't had a decent human connection for the better part of the last five years because of a crime he didn't commit, it was monumental.

And so was the sex after.

Okay, okay, the sex has been monumental every time. Each time I expect it won't be like the last time. And to a point, I'm right. It never is—it's better.

How is that even possible?

We've had sex every day since the first time. Well, it's more like we've had sex every few hours, really. Both of us are making up for lost time. Me from my own celibacy and him from prison, which is also a celibacy of sorts. I can never stop the giggle when I think about it. Guess we have more in common than we think.

And that's another thing we do—we talk. Not like total pillow talk and sharing our hopes and dreams, but we don't shy away from filling the silent nights. We also don't like a ton of the same things, and I'm okay with that. But he tells me things, things I bet most of his brothers wouldn't like to know.

I know about almost every brother's past, how they all got their road name. I still play along that I don't know; don't want them to look at me differently. But I get that Chains is doing this to make me feel like I belong, pulling me in with every detail that could connect me to the club and keep me here.

It took a while, but I convinced him to let Christy go. Killing her wasn't the way to go with her. It would be too easy, and he didn't need her death on him. He already carries too much guilt; he didn't need more if he regrets it later. I mean, I wanted to do it too. I really did. She's caused harm to each person I've cared about since my parents passed.

Jennie and I weren't close, but we were good friends for a while there, even if we didn't know our paths were so interconnected. But the kids had my heart from the moment I looked at them. And then Chains crept in and made himself at home. He set up shop in my heart, and I only noticed when I tripped over his shoes. He was sneaky, but he's got a place in my heart all to his own now.

I want Christy dead, but I know it's just anger talking. I lived with it for so long. Fear and anger were my best friends for more years than I care to count. Okay, they're still there till about five seconds after Chains kissed me. I mean, like really, *really* kissed me. My knees went weak, and then I let go of my fear and fell into strong arms that caught me willingly.

I don't want Chains to be buried in the anger like I was. I knew killing Christy wouldn't solve anything. Neither will letting her go, but if she's gone, then she's gone. Not a dark spot to deal with. The boys gave her plenty of parting gifts in the form of a few broken bones and a heavy threat that won't be given again if she ever steps on Hounds' territory again. Which apparently is vast and covers more than just Kansas. Hell, they got a group in Ireland. Who knew?

I sure didn't.

So, Christy's gone, but Chains still thinks it's not safe till my uncle is dealt with. Him and the Devils Damned. This is the part he doesn't share with me, and I'm good with that. I don't want to know; I like living in my pretend bubble that all my troubles are behind me and I can live happily ever after from here on out. Telling myself every day that this isn't a dream. That I really am waking up to my own sex god and get to touch and play all I want with him.

Till he ties my hands and says it's his turn.

Which I'm totally okay with. For a guy who was locked up for years, he's really good at sharing his toys, if you catch my drift. *Wink, wink.*

I can't help all this sappy shit. I'm smiling more than I ever have. I'm carefree, even. Hell, I'm not constantly putting my hair in a braid anymore. It was always more than just a simple reminder of my mom. More for the convenience and a shield of sorts. Easy to maintain, and if I had to get up and go at a moment's notice, I had no issues 'cause no hair got in my way. Apparently my few psychology classes are finally working; only took three years for me to understand and self-diagnose myself. Time I usually spend prepping and anticipating my next move in case I need out. But out is the last thing I want any more.

No, I want to stay. Stay with Chains, stay with the club, stay with the kids. Just stay.

"You keep smiling like that and I'm liable to squirt lemon in your eye just to see you squirm for a bit."

I choke on the lemonade I'm drinking. Bulldog's mom is tough as nails and mean as hell. Her only weakness is Princess and anyone Princess says is okay. Took me three visits, but I finally got the old bat to talk to me. Princess said I was okay on the first day, but the old woman didn't believe it, or just didn't want to be nice.

Which is fine. I've had more than enough happy moments of late to sit in silence and daydream about the sex I've had with Chains. Or will have. Every time I mention trying something I'm interested in from a book I read, he's more than accommodating. It's only been three weeks, but the best three weeks of my life.

"Told you to stop it."

I drop the smile like a hot plate. Something tells me this woman isn't joking.

"Which one did they say you belonged to?" Her eyes are beady as her face remains pinched. It's always pinched, at least around me. If Kathy Bates ever had a twin, one who was rounder and meaner, then Margret is it. She's older than I expected, and completely set in her ways. Her house is nice, but damn if everything has its place. I made the mistake last time of trying to take a book off the bookshelf that framed her fireplace, and boy, you would have thought I was stealing from King Tut's tomb. Apparently the books are for looking, not touching. Ever.

I look to Prospect, who's sitting on the porch steps with another newer member trying to join the club. He just smiles and shakes his head. We're inside the house, windows open, no way to hide what we're talking about. But apparently since they ain't in the club yet, prospects aren't allowed inside the house. Sort of wish I wasn't allowed in either.

"Um, Chains."

"Huh, figured that one would be a lifer like my Bulldog. Those two were thick as thieves for years. But I guess now that he got you, it won't be long till my son brings around someone sniffing to be his old lady. Do me a favor and scare off the vamps. I don't mind doing it, but by the time they all make the drive over here, they usually try to get my boy to drive them back into town. They should all just walk, you know, relearn, since all they do is lie around all day on their backs."

I stare wide-eyed at her, then look at the girls, who are both playing with dolls about six feet away. And we aren't being quiet at all.

"Oh, stop looking at me like that. They ain't hearing nothing they shouldn't already know. Ain't that right, Princess?"

Not sure if the little girl is paying attention or just acknowledging her name, but she looks at both of us and smiles wide while nodding before returning to the tea party their babies are having.

"Yeah, sure, I'll warn them. But got to say, none of them talk to me much. Not that I mind."

"'Cause you an old lady? Good, that's how it should be. You now run the roost, chica. Got to treat that position with respect or it'll be taken from you. I've seen it happen."

"Don't intend to lose it. Not for anything."

She looks at me, and I know she can see the fire in me. She nods in approval. "Just what Chains needs, no pushover old lady. That one needs someone to tell him when he's being a dumbass."

"Oh, I do. But it's not because of the old lady thing that keeps the vamps away. Pretty sure they don't want their noses busted."

"Now why the hell do they think that?"

"'Cause she did it to a vamp who tried to take her old man," Prospect yells from the porch. He might not be allowed in, but he's permitted to talk to us.

"You do that?"

I blush in response.

"Well, I'll be a monkey's whore."

"Nanna, that's a bad word."

"What word?" my sweet girl asks us all.

"Nothing."

"Whore." I cringe as Princess speaks over me. I already know what's going to come out of my sweet girl's mouth before she says it, and she doesn't disappoint.

"What's a whore?"

"It's like a vamp but outside the club. They can't be old ladies, and being an old lady is the best. They get to tell the boys what to do, and they *have* to listen to them."

"Really?"

"Yeah, that's why Daddy won't get one. Says I'm already enough, and he doesn't want one to take my spot. Says I'm enough of an old lady for him even if I'm just a little lady."

I roll my lips in and hold back my laughter. I look around, and I ain't the only one. Even the crazy old woman is hiding her smile. Who wouldn't love what this little angel is saying? She has the vocabulary of a sailor some days, the knowledge of an eighty-year-old woman, and the voice of a child. It's quite a package. Throw in a little doll she keeps referring to as her baby that plays tea party with my own little girl, and I'm almost to tears. It's a sweet picture. I almost don't mind her teaching my girl what a whore is. Almost.

At least she told her it wasn't something to strive for. Girl's got maternal instincts, it seems. Her babies will grow up to be good little old ladies.

I hear one guy yell something but don't register what's said as I watch the bookcase in front of me explode with paper and wood before I hear the shots. I dive for the girls and cover them with my body as I half run, half crawl to the kitchen, pulling them with me. I push the girls against the wall and look back into the room that was once a haven.

Bulldog's mom is bent behind the couch.

"Come to me, Margret. Get in the kitchen." I'm yelling, but there are so many bullets going through the walls that I can't hear myself speak. I feel the adrenaline and can't control the volume of my voice.

She takes a second, nods, and half stands just as the front of the house explodes and she's pushed back into the second bookcase. She falls, along with everything else. I can't tell if she's alive or dead, but I can't focus on that. The girls are screaming and crying, but I can't focus on that either. The door bursts inward and Prospect limps in, dragging the other prospect with him.

"Get down and stay down. They got grenades. Not sure how many. We need to go out the back. Bulldog's got a shed that's above a fallout shelter his granddad built. It's secure."

Another grenade goes off just at the front of the door, and Prospect loses his footing, dropping to the ground with his club brother.

"Shit."

From the blood coming off the kid on the floor, I know what Prospect is saying—the other guy's dead. I gulp and try not to get pulled down the dark hall of memory lane at seeing that much blood.

"Let's go."

I don't question. Not why we're being attacked or by who. Or that Prospect keeps shooting at someone behind us as we each grab a girl in our arms and run out the back. I don't think to ask why he's limping since he's running faster than me as the house continues to fall down around us with each shake of the wall. I don't even ask how this guy, who's maybe twenty-four, twenty-five if I'm pushing things, isn't freaking out but taking charge so easily.

Why question anything when someone is saving your life and knows how to? All I did was get us to the kitchen—*he's* the one getting us out of the house and to safety.

We run out the back door and down the steps. I don't see the pristine lawn, or the roses that must have taken years to nurture and prune to get to look like perfect balls standing on one stem, almost like lollipops. I don't care that the shed is painted to match the perfectly trimmed house that's now a pile of rubble behind us. I just focus on the door just head. That's all that matters.

We're more than halfway there when Prospect's steps falter and he falls to his knees, Grace going down with him as he holds her tight. I race to catch her and then see the blood covering his pant leg.

"Go. Get inside."

I want to protest, that I'm not the kind to leave people behind. But it's not just me I have to think about. Princess is clinging to me like a monkey, and I have no choice. I grab Grace's hand and turn to run the last of it, then stop.

A man I've never seen before is holding a gun on us and is standing right by the shed. His club vest isn't *our* club's.

"Move and we start taking the limbs off the girls. Job is only to take you all in alive. Nothing was said about keeping you all in one piece."

Grace clamps on to my leg, and I hold her against me as best I can while still holding Princess.

"Touch them and die, scumbag," I seethe.

"Ha, by who? You? Don't think so."

"I ain't down and out, just assessing, asshole. You really think the club is stupid enough to only keep two eyes on club property?"

"That's exactly what I think."

"Think again. We ain't like your little tea groupies. Each one of us was born to kill. You might play at this on the weekends, but we live and breathe with the Reaper. I suggest you get a head start now, 'cause I will enjoy slitting your throat."

"Don't think so."

No other warning before the Devils Damned shoots Prospect. I scream as he falls onto his back. He ain't moving, and my eyes are blurred with tears.

The asshole lifts his chin at me. "Now, let's get this party moving. We got a family reunion to get to."

I stumble along as another two Devils appear from nowhere, or I just didn't notice as my entire world of fear crashes in on me. My uncle found me, and I'm about to destroy another person's life because of my failures as a child. But instead of going to prison, the girls are about to meet a monster who's haunted me for years. A man who's about to become their own boogeyman.

As we get into the van they have parked out front of the now-demolished house, I hold both girls as close as I can. I have no misbeliefs; I know we won't be together the entire time going forward. So I offer the comfort I can give them now and hope it'll last through whatever hell we're all about to go through.

"Don't cry, Mama Bear. My daddy will find us. Him and your old man are coming. You'll see."

I love this little girl. She isn't mine, but I will claim her. I love her optimism, and I try to smile through it all for her.

"I hope so, baby. I hope so."

I tuck them both in under my chin and close my eyes as I wish for something that's never come true before.

I wish for a knight to come rescue me from my nightmares, just as I did as a kid. Maybe, if I'm lucky, he'll answer my call this time. If not, then at least I'm used to being denied that happiness. But I will do whatever I can to get these girls out. Whatever I can.

Told Chains more times than not, if it comes to the kids or me, I choose the kids.

Each. And. Every. Time.

Chapter 28 – Chains

"**Y**ou ever going to stop smiling?"

"Nope." I laugh at my response as Bulldog and Flint just shake their head at Casper's question.

Why would I? I'm happy. For once in my life, I got it all, and I'm happy as shit. I also know how lucky I am to have found all this. And scared shitless that I'll lose it. I'm relatively young, still in my early thirties, and most don't make long-term goals in club life. It's called that for a reason, 'cause you're in for that long. Which isn't as long as most people expect.

We deal mostly on the legit side of the law, but we get tied into things easily. Either from past brothers who get us connected in some area or another taking on shit we shouldn't be into. Most of the brothers are like me, would rather stay on the outside than get trapped in. And if that means we don't make money the easy way, we're all for it.

We got bars, auto shops, even a tattoo joint. We're invested in two strip joints, but we keep out of it, mostly. Not our fault most of the girls there end up being vamps for the club. That's just an added perk. Well, not for me anymore, and I ain't missing anything. My woman's got more moves than any stripper on a pole.

It's hell keeping everything running, and occasionally we're in the loan business. But only for those who can actually get us the money back. We ain't a charity outfit, so we get our money back or we collect in a variety of forms.

Mostly IOUs. You'd be surprised how often those come in handy.

Which is something we might need to do sooner than later. While I'm happy with my life with Maddy, I'm also antsy to get the shadow off our backs. Her uncle is a problem, and we need him gone. Problem is, no one's seen him in a while. We got people looking in his area, but nothing. Guy ghosted right after the attack on her house. Same thing with the Devils Damned. They've been lying really low. They're mostly out of El Paso, but they've been moving farther north for years, claiming parts of Oklahoma, and if I were a betting man, Kansas is next on their list. Rumor is they're connected to a few key cartels in Mexico and want to expand all the way north. And if there's one thing America is great at doing, it's providing highways that get you from one end to the other, with several convenient side roads for those who want the scenic route. How accommodating we are for the drug and other illegal trafficking going on.

"Okay, Uncle Chains, what next?"

Little man is taking after me, and got to admit, I'm digging it. And despite the shit I'm getting from the guys, they also enjoy having him around the shop too. He's only six, but the kid loves to tinker and watch me work, or any of the guys. And I'm pretty sure all of my brothers have taken Teddy in like he's their own kid with the way they're showing him everything. And the kid is sharp. He doesn't do much but hand me tools and listen, but he already knows the difference between most wrenches, and I know a few choice brothers who still have no clue, even after being paid to work here.

"Get the crescent and see if you can tighten up these bolts for me."

The kid beams, then literally flies on his toes to get the tool and get to work.

The boys and I chuckle. Man, it's good to have such a high-spirited kid around the shop. Hell, everything has been amazing. A few boys complained about the vamps after two weeks of them not being around as much, but a friendly reminder that they can visit them on their own had them shutting up. Vamps are good for a fuck. Going to their place to get laid makes them think it's more, so the boys shut up since no one wants to be tied to them. But I do know they keep them plenty occupied when they're allowed back in on Fridays and Saturdays.

During those times, a small group of us keeps the kids occupied, switching off on the babysitting duties. Actually, Ruby's taken them a few times for slumber parties at her dad's place. Law has taken grandpa duty extremely seriously and would rather be with them than watch all the brothers hook up. Man's never taken a chick since Special K passed.

Man, I still can't believe Maddy knew her. Every time we talk, things are said, and it makes me think we were almost fated to be together. Too many coincidences that lead to us being tied together today.

Some of those ties suck. Getting locked away because of her uncle, yeah, that's a big one. But I don't put that on her. She had nothing to do with it. Even if she had come forward, it would have been a miracle to get a guy like her uncle locked away.

And let's be honest, I ain't no Boy Scout. Prison wasn't ever *not* a contender for me. I didn't go military like most of my brothers did after they got out of high school. I just came here. Made sense, but it gave me no way to grow up. Love the club, love the life. But not till I was locked away, with my thoughts and no one else to help me, did I learn to grow up. Not saying the military did that for everyone, but I can see the difference between a man who learned the hard way about killing before being killed compared to a man who kills to protect what's his.

The club trains you to protect it, protect your brothers, protect your family. Honor the name. That's something the club gave me early, and I learned quickly. And that's what a few of the brothers new to the life are still learning.

In the military, they learned to kill or be killed. There were rules they had to follow. They couldn't simply just protect; they had to sit and wait it out till their own life was on the line. That hardens a man, but it also teaches him to grow up, to realize that while a team is what we all want, when you're on your own, you need to think through it all. You might be one man, but you need to think like a team of six, see all the angles.

Prison taught me that. Well, it taught me to keep my head on a swivel. The club's respected, but there's always some asshole who wants to make his name known, or just wants revenge on the club for something. Who the fuck knows, but they always seem to find me.

I can handle a brawl. The club taught me how to fight, and how to fight dirty. I fucking rule the ring when I come in. But being the last one standing in a prison just gets you sent to solitary, and that shit sucks. As much as I like alone time, that shit killed me when I was locked away for days, sometimes weeks at a time. So I learned to think like a team, see the enemy coming in all directions, and I did what I had to do to survive the attack, or I attacked first and then got gone.

Five years I was locked away. I missed a lot, and I'm glad I'm out, but, if I'm being honest—and I really fucking hate with this topic—I miss parts of prison life. Sounds crazy, don't it? But I do. Not really miss, but I appreciated one point in prison that I don't get here. Solitary. Yup, you read that right. Prison is loud all the time. Club life is no different.

Those first few nights out, I woke up in sweats, thinking I was back there because it sounded the same. It would freak me the fuck out and always took a bit for me to remember I was out. I was lost in my head more times than not those first few weeks. Needed the solitary, and you'd think that getting on my bike and cruising would do it for me, but you'd be wrong. I lost five years of club life, and the boys lost five years *with* me, so I was never alone. Which just made me think of prison more, since in there, you always have eyes on you no matter what.

I knew thirty seconds after meeting Maddy that she would be just like a warden. Hovering, always watching. But the more I went over, the more she let up, and I felt like I could breathe—really breathe. Falling for her was the simplest thing, and with her doing absolutely nothing, she gave me the solitary I needed that I didn't get at the club. It was just enough for me to regroup. It never got to the point like in prison, when I went crazy with the quiet. And it wasn't so much the volume but the quiet life. Kids aren't quiet, so I guess it was more about not having eyes on me that I learned to appreciate the solitary confinement that I missed.

At Maddy's house, the kids were always playing. Sure, they asked me to join in, but they weren't eyeing me to see if I would do anything. Their eyes were just on the toys. And Maddy, well, I have to chuckle at how many times I *wanted* her eyes on me, but she tried to avoid it at all costs. That was till I claimed her; now I get her eyes any time I want.

Took me a day or two, but having her wrapped up in my arms every night, it's also calmed whatever beast was inside me and now I never wake up freaking the fuck out. I know where I am. I can smell and feel her before I'm ever really awake.

Prison is a distant memory with Maddy in my arms.

"Now what?"

"Damn, kid, you're making the rest of us look bad. Better take a break before Prez sees how productive you are and gives you a job."

I smirk as Teddy squares his shoulders at the praise Flint's sending his way.

"Flint's right, little man. Let's take a break. Go get us some waters, will ya? Think Maddy even left us a few snacks."

Yup, my old lady even packed me and the kid treats in case we get hungry and she isn't around to offer to feed us. *Did I get lucky or what?* I know it's more for Teddy's sake than my own, but I'm not about to turn down some fruit snacks. Who the hell knew they were so good?

"What time you want to pick up the girls?"

"You mean, what time do you think is a good point to stop punishing my old lady?"

"Hey, spending time with my mom ain't a punishment."

I don't answer or look up. We both know it is. Only one that can tolerate that mean bitch is Princess, and occasionally Bulldog.

Bulldog snorts. "Fine, but she *should* expect some punishment after the shit she pulled."

"You mean when she painted the girls' nails? How the hell is that an issue?"

"You ain't a single dad. I was hoping Princess would never discover that shit, or at least not for another ten years. But now she's all about the pretty things."

"She was always into crowns and dresses, man."

"Yeah, but she never made *me* do the dressing-up part before. Now she throws a freaking fit if I don't play the part. All 'cause your old lady painted their nails, and then they all got dressed up and played together. Now my girl is trying to put nail polish on me and even asking me to wear her fake jewelry and shit."

Flint busted out laughing. "Fuck, I need to teach Princess how to work a camera. I need a picture of you all dolled up."

"Laugh it up, Flint, I'll sic her on you next if you keep that shit up. And I'll help."

The threat ain't empty. Bulldog is massive, and despite Flint being able to take out his own army if faced against one, he won't be able to throw Bulldog off. Especially if the man has an agenda, and nothing like sweet torture of a fellow brother is better than that.

"Hey, little man, you got enough?" The boys and I chuckle as we watch instead of helping as Teddy comes back in with about five waters and what appears to be an entire box of fruit snacks on top of them. It's amazing the balancing act he's got going on there.

The sirens going off, followed by Domino's voice coming over the intercom, has Teddy dropping everything, just like the rest of us.

"Code F-12. I repeat, we got a fucking F-12. Nanna's house."

I don't think, just run and grab Teddy, then head for the club parking lot like the rest of the brothers. I have no idea what an F-12 is, but the last time sirens went off, it was bad, and I know this involves Maddy again.

"How the fuck do they know where my mom's house is?" Bulldog bellows, and I can hear the fear in his voice. We don't have many on hand; it's a Tuesday fucking morning, for God's sake. But it's enough. You don't become a Hound of the Reaper without the ability to hold your fucking own.

I pass Teddy over to Domino, who's waiting with open arms. "Guard him with your life."

I turn to get on my bike, but the little man grabs my sleeve and holds tight. I see the fear in his eyes even if he can't ask for what he wants.

"Don't worry, buddy. I'll get them back. Stay with Domino."

"I want my mommy."

I give him a quick kiss on the forehead, then race to my bike. I push down the feelings at Teddy's words till I'm on the road, leading the pack with Bulldog. No one fights us for the lead; it's our families on the line. Even if they aren't part of the club, those women make and break us. If something happens to any of them, it'll be devastation for anyone they touched. Which is the whole fucking club and then some.

I'm not sure why, but as we race across town, my thoughts turn to Teddy and what he said. He hasn't mentioned Jennie at all since I moved them into the club, and I don't think he meant her when he said he wanted his mommy. He could only mean Maddy.

I'm not upset at all that Teddy thinks of her as his mom. Jennie's been out of his life for a while now. He might not even remember her; I have no clue how kids' minds work. I also have no clue how much time she spent with him. If she was as connected to the Devils as Christy claimed, Jennie might have distanced herself from him early to keep him safe.

She did what she needed to do to keep her kids alive. I plan to do the same, especially since I decided a long time ago to claim them as my own. Don't care if they call me Dad or not, but I have the club's lawyer looking into ways for me to make it official in the adoption process. I just hope Maddy's okay with the fact that I told our lawyer I wasn't going to be parenting alone. Don't know if she expected kids in the long run, but she's going to get them. She made that deal, even if she doesn't know it, when she agreed to be my old lady. Don't think she'll mind; the girl's basically calling them son and daughter now as it is.

I keep my mind clear and focused as we round the curve, and then we see the smoke over the trees. I should have asked what the twelve stood for; might have been more prepared for what we find when we finally pull into what was once a driveway that had about two acres around it.

Demolished.

Destroyed.

I look to my brothers and see they're equally stunned on their bikes, and they *know* the code. Slowly, Bulldog rises off his bike, then the rest of us. This is his place, his mama's. He wasn't raised here, but he bought his mom the land years back when he saved enough to get her out of the trailer park they lived in.

"Spread out."

I know from the tone in Law's voice that he's telling the brothers to look for bodies. Either the ones who did this or the people who should have been inside.

"Found one."

"Who is it?" Prez shouts but moves no closer.

Casper and Atom roll a body over. "Our new prospect, dead. Gunshot to the chest. Whoever blew this place did it after they got rid of our boy."

"Keep looking." The growl in Law's voice lets me know retribution is coming for a loss of one of our own. Even if the kid wasn't a full patch, he was here as a representative of us.

Bulldog and I stand with our prez on the outside. If they're anything like me, they don't want to go in. Not that there's a door. The entire structure is on the ground. Nothing but a few half walls are standing.

Nothing survived, and there's more than a chance that no *one* could have either. I swallow rapidly, trying to clear the lump in my throat. I've lost a lot in my life: family, freedom, justice. But I refuse to lose Maddy and Grace. I won't make it without both of them. I'm strong enough of a man to know my breaking point, and losing them, or Teddy, will do it for me.

"Over here! We got something."

The three of us carefully move over the stubble just as Atom removes some debris from where he's standing.

"Mom!" Bulldog exclaims.

"Call for an ambulance," Law shouts to anyone who isn't close, getting shit done while Bulldog's and my worlds crumble around us. "Get hold of General and get him to be on staff when she gets to the hospital."

"Where are the girls? Where's Princess? Who did this to you?" Bulldog's words are harsh and rushed as tears run down his face.

He grabs at his mom's hand that reaches out to touch her boy, and I bite my lip to keep my own tears at bay. I want to demand answers, too, but I see she's too weak to do more than breathe right now.

Turning away, I look at my feet, searching for what isn't there, moving item after item in my way as I scour the house to find any trace of my girls.

"Prez, back here."

I run to the back with Law, leaving Bulldog and Atom to wait on the ambulance.

"Jesus." I let the curse slip from my lips as I see our other prospect holding his chest as blood flows out over his fingers. Casper is doing a basic field dressing, but I have no clue if what he's doing is helping or if it even matters.

"Girls. Devils Damned. Van."

With each word he says, a bit of blood trickles out of his mouth. And as each word crosses his lips, my world shrinks to only one word in my head.

Vengeance.

Chapter 29–Maddy

They never blindfold us. They don't need to. Not only are the van's windows blacked out, but I also have two terrified little girls clinging to me and at least two guns on us the entire time we drive. I already know where we're going, and I just pray Chains knows as well.

Or I thought I knew. But we've only been in the car maybe two hours before we pull off and stop. It takes at least three on a good day to get to my old hometown, which is where I was certain they were taking us. It makes the most sense in my eyes. As far as I know, my uncle is still the sheriff there.

But as they open the doors and drag us into a trailer park, any hope of rescue is squashed. No way will the club find us now. I have zero fucking clue where we are, and other than those who brought us, I see absolutely no one. I doubt this is the clubhouse linked to these guys, though I'm just guessing. It's just the four who came with us. So if we aren't back in my hometown, and we aren't at the Devils' place, where the hell are we?

"This way."

Don't know why they even say anything, 'cause it's not like they aren't already dragging us around with them. Thankfully, the girls can walk on their own and I don't have to carry them. Of course, they're still stuck to me like glue, and I won't have it any other way. I have no clue what's going to happen to them, but I'm pretty sure I can guess what will happen to me. And I really, *really* don't want them to be next.

I know my uncle is sick, and the company he keeps can't be any better. Forcing themselves on a child is probably not that farfetched.

The ground is mostly dirt and rock, and I stumble along as the girls take small, cautious steps, and the guy at my back keeps pushing me. I really want to turn and say something, but I don't think it'll get me anything other than a smack to my face. My mouth gets me in trouble with my old man a lot, but it ends in sex with us. Not sure how it'll end if I open it now to these guys.

"Get up in the trailer."

I hesitate to glance back at the voice that says it, and I'm given a minor relief as he nods to which one he's talking about. We've already passed about five, and I see a dozen more, even with it being dark. Only a few porch lights are on; most of them seem to have been smashed rather than merely turned off.

I'm not sure I want to know what the trailers are used for, 'cause it can't be good. Nothing about this place screams that it can be anything other than a giant nightmare that reeks of fear and death. Who knew you could smell death, but I swear I can now.

It's too dark to tell the color of trailer we're being ushered into. There are three steps up to a smaller porch, but at least it has a light on. It only illuminates a brown door, or what looks like brown now; I swear I can see white under the dirt. The rest of the trailer is covered in darkness, and all I can see is that the color of it must be dark as well.

We enter at what must be the end, because as I look ahead, I see it's long, with nothing but a bed and broken furniture. Lots of broken furniture. A couch is mostly ripped open and slanted down. A table is just flat on the ground, legs poking out of it to look like a squashed bug. Chair parts are pushed against the walls, but there's nothing big enough to use as a weapon, nothing that will be useful.

Glancing toward the bed as we're shuffled into the middle of the room, I swallow the lump in my throat as I cover the girls' eyes and force their heads against my legs. Empty handcuffs hang on the rails of the bed with a mattress that's more stained with a red color than anything else.

The click of the door has me turning to see we're alone. I don't move to check the lock; it would be useless. I take another look around. There really is nothing for me to protect me and the girls. The only light is the one directly over our heads, a single bulb that illuminates more than I want to see. More than the girls *should* see.

I sink to the ground, which might be the only clean spot in the whole place. Either from debris or *other* things. The bed is completely a no-go, and I don't know if the couch or table was used for... let's just say "certain activities." I pull the girls up on either leg, and they curl in more, almost as if they know how disgusting this place really is.

"Think my nanna is okay?" Princess murmurs.

I bite my lip and try to keep my voice steady when all I really want to do is shake in fear. "She's a tough old bird. Nothing can keep her down."

God, I hope I'm right.

Lying might not be the best thing, but it's all I've got right now.

"They hurt Prospect. Will they hurt us?" Princess sniffs but doesn't show her tears.

My Gigi is quiet as a mouse, and I pray to anything out there that these girls will be okay.

"I don't know, baby girl."

Hours pass, and I strain to keep awake. I'm grateful that both girls are finally sleeping; didn't take long since their little bodies have been through so much. I'm completely uncomfortable, but I don't move, don't adjust. They need to feel some sort of peace. God knows what'll happen next to us.

We haven't been given food or water, and I've held each girl over the potty, but there's no TP and no water to wash our hands. I wasn't about to let them sit on anything in this place. Everything smells and looks ten times worse than what you can imagine.

I know I'll have to do the hover dance soon, but I don't want to be away from the girls. There was barely enough room for one of us in there at a time, and I don't want to be occupied long enough that someone comes in and takes them while I'm stumbling to pull my pants up.

A noise from outside has me tensing a second before the door opens.

"Uncle Dwayne." No use in pretending we don't know each other. He looks exactly like he did the day I ran, which is a direct reflection of my dad. Which might be the worst of it. They looked so much alike that my dreams had turned often to thinking it was my *dad* trying to kill me, not my uncle.

"Hello, niece. I've missed you."

He walks in, not alone. Two others are behind them, the same two who drove us here. But I pay them no mind. My uncle is all I see.

I bet some would call him handsome; my dad was. Dark wavy hair parted on the side and a clean jawline. His face is round but his eyebrows bushy, making his eyes more noticeable, as they sink in more than most. Dark eyes, almost black, which I bet he loves to say match his soul. My dad had kind blue eyes, ones you just stared into and felt like smiling as they were the same shade of the sky when the sun shone on a summer's day. But unlike my dad, who gave a full-fledged smile, my uncle only smirks. It's the smirk that haunts me.

Saw a special on Ted Bundy once. Not sure why I watched it, but I was drawn to the way they caught him. I liked that part, not the rest. And especially not the part when they showed him smirking. It's the same one my uncle always has. The kind that just makes you sick on the inside, that brings a chill through your whole body, and you want to go take a shower to get rid of it. Yeah, that was my first, and *last*, true crime show ever. I have enough demons without learning about more. I can just be happy reading the ending, you know the part, where they say the guy was arrested and killed? Yeah, I like that part.

While I can't take my eyes off my uncle, he has no problem skating his evilness over those in my arms. I tighten them around the girls, hoping I can use what little luck I have to keep them safe.

"Take her."

It's quick, and I should have expected it, but I didn't.

The guards rush me before I can even think. The girls wake when I'm pulled up, forcing them to fall off me. They scream in alarm from the jostle, then after seeing what's going on. They're scared, shouting and crying, but it's Grace who makes me want to run over and protect her even more.

"Stop! My uncle will hurt you. That's his old lady."

I hold back the tears that want to flow freely. She was so stoic before, but now she's fighting for me. I can't love her any more than I already do.

Her view of the world has changed so much in the last few months, but she learned one thing. Guys like Chains don't like their women getting hurt. Otherwise, they're the ones doing the hurting.

"That right?"

I can hear the smirk in his voice, and I can't fight the shudder that goes through me. Not liking that his attention is drawn to my girl, I fight, screaming and kicking. The girls try to help too but get knocked back by my guards as they easily push them away. I still as I watch Grace get knocked to the floor so hard that she doesn't get back up.

"Don't hurt her! That's my daughter, you asshole!"

I'm used to his rage, but I'm flabbergasted by his words. *Does he really think Grace is his?* She looks nothing like him. Even I look a bit like Dad. Not much, but enough if you looked at our pictures when we were the same age.

He stomps over toward the Devils Damned who still has a hold of my arm, grabs the man by the neck, and twists. I turn my head away as I hear the crunch, closing my eyes to keep my brain from seeing what I'm hearing. I try to do the same for Princess, but I don't know if I can hide something like that from her as the guy falls hard on the floor.

I didn't expect it, and I want to weep for their loss of innocence. Grace might not have been awake for it, but Princess heard it all. And from the paleness of her skin, I don't know how much longer before she breaks. How much can a little girl take in such a short time? I only saw my mom die after being raped. She witnessed her friend get shot, her grandma fall before her house collapsed on her, and now this. Who knows what else will happen once I'm out of this room? A room that screams of pain.

A small squeak helps dislodge the hand squeezing my heart as Grace moves, rising to sit beside Princess, who runs to her quickly and holds her hand.

Just as I take a breath of relief, my hair is grabbed at the top of my head and I'm pulled backward, and I fall on my ass. I crabwalk back with one hand on the ground and the other on the hand holding my hair. It fucking hurts, and I let out my cries of protest more than I ever want the girls to see.

I'm forced out as the girls are left in the room crying, and a dead body is *still* in there. I'm pulled down the stairs outside as I hear my uncle talking to someone. "Clean up the mess in there, but don't let those rug rats out."

I must be in shock, or else my uncle really thinks Grace is his daughter. That's the only reason he would try to "help" her. But my shock is quickly pushed away as fear grips me again when I'm pulled along with my uncle, twisting and turning around paths of the trailer park till we find one he likes. Then I'm yanked up the stairs and thrown inside, the door shutting behind me. But I'm not alone this time.

The force of being thrown in has me stumbling to my knees in front of a chair. When I look up, I see there's a person tied to it. Clothes ripped off and head bent awkwardly, but I know who it is. Christy. Looks like she had more than the Hounds of the Reaper to fear.

"Thought you would want to see the other person you caused to die—seems that's all you're good for."

I swallow hard and shake my head. This isn't what I wanted. Not for her. Not for anyone.

"You get people killed, and I'm always left unsatisfied," he taunts me as he walks behind me, pacing.

I don't look at him. I can't. "I didn't do this."

"Yes you did. By getting tangled up with the Hounds, you forced my hand. I know you knew I was looking. You should have just come back. I could have even forgiven you if you brought me my daughter."

I jerk my head to the side to glare at him, not even sure if he can see me in the dark room, but my fear is turning to anger. "She ain't your daughter."

"Tsk, tsk, always the troublemaker. Of course she is. Jennie and I were together."

I snort. "You mean you raped Jennie after you killed her old man."

He seems to enjoy our banter, not even showing a change in voice as he continues. As if he's talking about the weather or some shit. "He was just a boy with a crush on something that was mine. She was mine, just like Grace is."

"You're wrong." I say it on a gasp of air, a plea for him to not take such a precious thing that's all light into his world of darkness.

He finally faces me, standing beside the dead woman, even going as far as resting his arm on her shoulder to lean on. I flinch and look away. The disrespect he shows the dead is appalling. "Ain't wrong. Even Christy confirmed it."

"She lied!" I cry.

"Why would she have any reason to lie?" He twists his head to look down at her, as if he really thought the body would answer him.

"Why would she have any reason to tell you the truth? She would do anything to save herself."

"Well, didn't work." That smirk is back, and his eyes travel over her, even going as far as lingering on her exposed chest.

I swallow the bile but don't think I can do it again. I'm really getting sick, and I'm not faking it. "Fine, take a DNA test. You'll see she isn't yours, and you can let her go. I swear the club won't come after you if you do that."

"You say that like I fear your club. They're just boys with toys." He shakes off my words and stands up straight, away from Christy. "Now, the Devils Damned are the real ones you should be worried about. The guys know how to get shit done and how to keep their fucking mouths shut. You're in bed with the wrong side, sweetheart. But don't worry. That's all about to change."

I have nothing to say. Obviously, I disagree on who should be afraid of whom. Chains isn't about to sit back and let this rest. Even if I die tonight, I know the Hounds will come and take the souls for their Reaper. It's who they are. But there's no reason to fight on this, and it might be the advantage my guys need. If my uncle is too stupid to think they aren't a threat, he'll make mistakes, and they'll act on them.

"I wonder if your cunt will be as tight as your mother's. For an uppity bitch, to this day, I haven't fucked another woman who didn't remind me of her. Of course, that's probably because you interrupted us and then ran before I could finish. Had to get off with her, and it wasn't the same doing all the work."

His change in subject has me blinking in response.

Did he just say he fucked my mom's corpse?

I'm going to be sick. Total chunks are about to come out of me. I know I'm going to throw up. The other trailer wasn't clean, but no dead bodies had been left in it for God only knows how long. I gag, but nothing comes up since I had very little to eat that morning.

"Throw up. It won't bother me."

"I'm sure it won't, you sick fuck. You probably like to have sex with dead people too." I say it to piss him off, nothing more. Okay, maybe I want some sort of confirmation that I didn't imagine what he said. But the smile spreading across his lips has me shivering in dread.

"Your mom was special, wasn't she? Tightest cunt I had in a long while. Even dead, I got off twice with her. Never thought I could, but you ran out on me, and I had no one else close."

Yup, that did it. It's been a while since I threw up bile only, but it isn't enough. I keep heaving, hoping to puke up the image he implanted in my head, but it's not going away.

I ignore the door opening; now is not the time to make an escape. That'll come later. I might put myself in danger in place of those I care about, but I'm not about to just sit here and take it like my mother did to keep me safe. I'm going to fight.

It might seem like I did the last time someone attacked me, but I'm different now. I'm an old lady. I am a tough bitch. It's in the name, the self-proclaimed bylaws I imposed on myself when I found out who I was.

I channel my inner Special K, the woman who I saw as a mom to me. She would assess the area, think it over, and then react. That's what she did whenever I came to her with a problem. She always said reacting instantly wasn't always the right way. Sometimes you need brains to get you through a situation, not just muscle.

Like Uncle Dwayne used all his life.

"President wants a word. He's getting sick of picking up your mess and having the Hounds of the Reaper on his ass all the time."

I don't look up from the floor. My bile is better to look at than those around me.

"If he wants free passage to deal that shit around here, he'll keep to the terms. I look the other way when you deal that shit, even pin it on a few when needed. You all just have to cover my back when I ask. Ain't a hardship. And don't act like you all ain't benefiting from my whore takeaway spot."

I know I should be more worried than I am with the way they keep talking like I'm not here. They ain't even concerned that I can hear them, which lets me know they think I won't be talking to anyone about it.

 "Whatever, man, just get on the phone. I'm not about to get my ass chewed out for the shit you did."

My peripheral vision catches my uncle move from in front of me to the side as another pair of shoes comes into view.

"What?" I can feel the agitation rolling off my uncle with just that one world. He hates being interrupted. I would know.

"What is the fucking problem? It's just one. You got a hundred more, can even recruit if need be. Not my fault your man got shot. What did you expect when you send someone up against another club? Even if they are pussies like the Hounds, they ain't about to sit and take it like the cunts we got here, so don't go bitching to me about losing a man. I lost years away from my child that you all couldn't find till one of these cunts came talking."

A beat passes before he continues. "Sure, man, do whatever the fuck you want." He turns to the other guy in the trailer. "Here, your precious president wants to talk to you now."

He's pacing again as the other guy talks too quietly for me to hear what's going on till the end.

"Right, got it, boss. Yo." My uncle pauses his pacing, so I guess the other guy is talking to him. "Prez says this is our last deal. We're done after this. Not even your whore trailers are an appeal with the amount of heat you're bringing down on us. Did you even know she's an old lady? Taking a kid is one thing, but old ladies are territory we don't want. That'll bring the entire club, and the other chapters, if we don't let her go."

"Why are you all scared of them? They'll never find this place, or her, after I'm done. Even then, this place is wired to look like a fucking gas fire, remember? No bodies, no evidence. So stay the fuck out of my way. Go fuck one of the cunts around here and just relax, man."

"Whatever," the guy grumbles.

He leaves a minute later, and I'm left alone with my nightmare. But I don't care. My thoughts are on my old man. The fear of him getting hurt, of the others getting hurt, makes my own fear seem like a small pea under a mattress. Not noticeable at all.

"You won't win this. The club will come, and there's nothing you can do that'll stop them. They're smart and calculating. They'll see your traps, and they won't fall for it." I look up at him and glare, my eyes filled with all my hate for the years of pain I've dealt with because of this man.

"Oh yes they will. They're nothing but a bunch of has-beens." He takes two steps, grabs my hair, and pulls my head back to stare down at me. "They haven't had to fight for anything in a long-ass time. They'll just roll over and take it. Much like you'll do if you know what's good for you. And don't act like you aren't planning to run. Your mama had that same look in her eye when she thought she could get the upper hand on me. But look how well that worked for me."

"Fuck you."

He smirks. "You know what? Run. Struggle. Hell, fight my ass. I've grown accustomed to it, and it actually gets my dick real hard when I finally sink it into the pussy. Like catching a fish. The fight is half the fun. But don't worry. Your pussy ain't the only place I'll be sticking my cock. And once I'm done with you, I'll let my friends have a few turns. I'm all about expanding the love between them and me. They get the freedom to expand this business, and I get all the cunt I want."

"If you get it for free, why the hell do you keep going after what you can't have? Or are the 'free' the throwaway kind? Devils Damned know you're a sick fuck and only get their leftovers or something?"

"I get what I want, when I want. And now I want you."

He falls on me, but I'm ready for him and thrust the heel of my hand into his nose, breaking the fuck out of it. He lets go of my hair for a second, pushing me back on my ass. I react and kick out my leg, catching him in the chest as he holds his nose.

My luck runs out as he rears back and smacks me clear across my face. I see more dark spots than I want to as I cling to staying awake and not passing out. I'm sure that's what he wants as he grunts.

Pounding on the door only has him grumbling as he starts taking off his clothes. Another knock at the door has him shouting, "What?" He ain't stopping as he hits me again and again.

"Boss wants you."

"Tell him I'll call him back," he mumbles as he tries to pull my shirt up.

"Tell him yourself. He just rolled up." The door opens, and the same guy comes in but doesn't spare me a glance as I look to him to get some help.

"Fucking shit. Cuff her to the bed. I'll deal with her as my victory for dealing with *your* boss."

Chapter 30 – Chains

"**W**here the fuck are they?"

"We can't find them." Flint doesn't flinch at Bulldog's bark as we walk into his security room. Guy refused to go with his ma. He knows Atom and Bass will be with her, and General won't let anyone near her but our people.

"No shit." Sarcasm is my only companion that's decent. It's that or full-on rage.

Flint glances at Bulldog before turning his head back to the screens as he types away. "Is your girl wearing her birthday present?"

"Oh, Jesus, I hope so." The hope in his voice has me looking between the two of them, trying to understand what I'm missing.

"What present?"

"I got her a bracelet last year."

Flint is the one who elaborates, 'cause a piece of jewelry means shit to me. "And while she might see it as something shiny, I see it as a tracker."

"You track your kid?" I eye my friend and VP.

He gives me a hard look in response. "You got a problem with that? Maybe you should too."

I match his volume, and before you know it, the entire club can hear us yelling. "Well, of course I'm going to start tracking them. You keep the guy's number?"

"Fuck yeah I did."

Best part of the brotherhood, no one even bats an eye at us screaming our heads off at one another. It's a guy thing. No real venom, we're just both pissed that neither has a head to pound, and yelling beats throwing fists at one another. We need to save our rage for those who took our girls.

"Okay, it's coming up now... shit."

"What?" we both bark.

Flint just shakes his head. "It looks like it was damaged."

"How?" Bulldog demands

"You see this? Both should be green to show it's working, but only one is on."

"What the hell does that mean?" Bulldog's panic is not helping my own.

"It means I can track her, but only if we're within a twenty-mile radius. Must have been damaged during the explosion or something. I can only get a direct hit on her if she's within my radius, and hate to say it, man, but she ain't."

Fuck.

"Can't you do something? Look at cameras or check satellites or some shit?" I'm pulling at strings, seeing if anything will click for our computer guru.

He shakes his head. "We only have cameras on the house, and I only got it till they exploded, so I could only see they arrived and then nothing when the place went up. As for satellite, I don't have the access to get old footage. I can only hack into the live feed. But...."

"But what?" Law growls as he enters behind us.

"I think I know someone who does."

We all look at one another and wait it out. Flint's the only person in the room who has an ounce of an idea on how to work the stuff in here, so we give him time to figure things out.

"What are you waiting for? Fucking reach out, man." Okay, maybe Bulldog's done with the waiting. I am, too, but he voiced it first.

"It's complicated." He shakes out his hair with his hand as he rolls his chair to look at us three dead-on. "They don't just do shit for free."

"I'll pay whatever they want." The desperation is clear in my friend's voice.

"It's not money, man. It's usually higher than that. I've never directly asked for something like this, just heard and interacted with them on the dark web. They do crazy shit I hear, but the price is steep. If we go to them, we need the backing of the full club. This ain't a one-man thing."

"You got it." Prez nods once to solidify his statement. "Whatever is needed. Hounds of the Reaper never turn their back on family, and we're always in it together. Don't even need to vote on it."

"Thanks, man." I speak for the group. But the more I look at the man before me, I don't see another brother, or even a president of the club. I see a pissed-off granddad who's on the same side as Bulldog and me. And he'll do anything to get them back.

"Okay, give me a second to reach them." Flint's already tapping away before he speaks, and I'm grateful he ain't taking his sweet-ass time.

Time still seems to drag as we watch him hack away on his computer. His warning about reaching out should scare me, I'm sure, but nothing scares me more than a life without Teddy, Grace, and Maddy. Nothing.

—HELLO DAVE—

"Why the hell they calling you Dave?" I know shit about hacking, but I know Flint's name ain't Dave.

"It's a joke. They think they're funny or some shit." Flint grimaces before typing as he speaks. "Need a favor."

—ALL BAD BOYS DO—

—IT'LL COST YOU—

It's fucking creepy watching this. Not like a normal chat. As soon as one line flashes on the screen, it stays visible for about twenty seconds before it's gone and another flashes, or just a blinking line that lets Flint know it's his turn to type.

"What's the price?"

—DEPENDS. WHAT'S THE FAVOR?—

"Satellite feed for the last two hours till now."

—SAME LOCATION?—

"No, initial location is twenty miles west of Manhattan, KS. An explosion happened, and we need eyes on it and to follow those who left the location."

The pause this time is longer than before, and I ask, "What's taking so long?"

"They're calculating the price. Never seen it take this long."

I glance at Flint for a second before my eyes go back to the screen, not wanting to miss anything.

—PRICE: THREE FAVORS—

"What are they?"

—TO BE DETERMINED LATER. WE RESERVE THE RIGHT TO CALL UPON ANYONE IN THE HOUNDS OF THE REAPER TO COLLECT. DO YOU ACCEPT?—

"Fuck!" I take notice of Flint's reaction and probably should be wary but then look to Bulldog.

"Accept, jackass." He's all snarl.

"Look, three is a fucking lot." Flint turns to us, pleading for us to understand. "Last time I saw one of these, the price the guy had to pay was killing his best friend. He even got caught, and rumor was these guys were the ones who set him up for the cops to collect."

"What the fuck?" Am I really willing for the club to go down that road? For Grace? For Maddy?

Fuck yeah.

"Yeah, man, these guys aren't to be messed with. Shit is fucked-up for them. Not sure I know the details, but the debt ain't good. I've never seen them go this high on the favors."

"Do it, Flint. I'll take the heat when the time comes for them to call in the favor and we have to do what's needed."

Never been prouder to call Law my prez than right now. Sure, he stood by me when I got charged and locked up, but this is different. He's putting everything on the line for us to get our girls back. I could never repay him for something like this.

"You ain't taking it alone, old man, I got your back." Bulldog glares at our leader.

"Me too," I chime in.

"Well, all right, then." Flint goes back to his computer. "We accept."

—YOU SHOULD HAVE WAITED TO TALK IT OVER MORE WITH YOUR PREZ—

Sweat beads at the back of my neck.

"Why?"

—WE DON'T HOLD FAVORS OVER OTHERS WHEN KIDS ARE INVOLVED. CONSIDER THIS A GIFT. WE HAVE REDUCED PAYMENT TO ONE FAVOR. WE WILL BE IN TOUCH. C8—

"What the fuck is that?" I growl.

Flint spares me a glance before he accepts the incoming file. "That's how they identify themselves. C8 for Crazy Eights."

Watching the video that's part of the file has me fisting my hands and swallowing down vomit at the same time.

We had eyes on Nanna's house, but they were on the house itself, and they were the first thing to go with the grenades. But the angle the Crazy Eights are showing, it's almost like they had drones on the entire time, the clarity is so clear. We watch as the replay shows two SUVs round up and stop just off the perimeter and below trees. No wonder the prospects didn't see shit; these guys were hidden. I count four grenades being thrown, but after the first one, they keep firing at the two on the porch. I watch one prospect go down instantly while the other falters, dragging the other through the door. The prospects are still shooting, and at least one attacker goes down. Then nothing as more of the house crumbles till we see two people run out the back, carrying both girls.

"Oh, thank fuck."

We knew the girls were safe, at least from the house attack based on the remaining prospect's report. But seeing and knowing is something else.

What little hope we had ends as we watch the prospect fall, pushing Grace to Maddy seconds before he's shot. And then the nightmare comes as I watch my girls being pushed into one of the SUVs.

It takes another minute for the other tile to upload. This one looks like a grid that keeps going in and out of size till it finally stops and the image pixilates, becoming clear, and the van is seen again. Not sure how much time passed, but the van ain't moving, as it's parked by a trailer park.

—HAPPY HUNTING :)—

"Call everyone in. Who else is out?" Law is calm, another reason he's president. He can easily compartmentalize his rage, unlike some of us.

I'm some of us.

"Ruby is getting picked up now. She was signing her lease," Flint calls out as he checks a few of the other feeds to confirm none of the other places we own are hit.

"Shit, I forgot about that. I still don't like her living so far away." Can't fault the guy. I doubt I'll be any better once Grace tries to leave.

"It ain't that far," Flint says offhandedly, but neither Bulldog nor I speaks.

"Anything that's out of my house is far," Law growls.

Ain't that the truth.

Flint just laughs, solo.

Bulldog's parting words are echoed by us all as we leave Flint to work. "Have a daughter. You'll see."

We walk out to the main hub, and every brother I know is there, strapped and ready to go. Thank fuck for this brotherhood. They've stood by me more times than I'm willing to count, and they're about to do it again. I nod at a few as I walk with Bulldog, accepting their desire to fight for me and mine.

Okay, let's be honest. Casper said it before that the club was done stepping up for my fuckups. And letting Maddy get taken, that's on me. I should have had more men on her. Should never have let her leave the compound till I was a hundred precent sure the threat was over. Doesn't matter if we all thought Nana's place was secure, I should have done more.

But the brothers checking their gear are here for their family. Princess and Grace are the daughters that half these guys want, and the other half already claimed them as their own. And they're all here for Maddy. My old lady won over every fucker in this place in less time than it takes for a tat to fully heal.

"Let's load up." Law doesn't need to make a speech about what's coming. The boys know the score, and we don't need to waste time on our plan. We got a long-ass ride to get it figured out with Flint running scenarios right now to suggest to our prez.

He's a good man, a better leader. He knows his word is law, but he ain't an idiot and takes suggestions. Especially from a guy who used to run the ops for a select agency that Flint refuses to talk about, but we all know. Guy's a genius and sees all angles when given enough intel. When he isn't, guesses are made, and more times than not, he makes the right call. It's the missions he was given bad intel on that cause his insomnia. Reliving every man and woman you lose because of orders you gave is a heavy burden. I've seen weaker men fall apart or just quit and end it all. Shitty world we got, folks. Don't for once think it ain't.

"Prospect wants in," Jumper comments when we pass him as we head to the door.

Prez doesn't even break stride. "Dumbass is still being stitched up. Fucking miracle he ain't dead. General better make sure he laces his meds to keep his ass down. Don't need a stupid play on this just 'cause his damn pride is in the way."

"Actually, he left the hospital and is on his way here."

We all stop and stare at Jumper, who's brave enough not to backtrack like a few others do when faced with us three. We ain't small, and we ain't happy.

"Dumb motherfucker," Bulldog grumbles, but I just shrug it off.

"I don't know. I think I might start liking the guy."

The door flies open with enough force to bang off the wall, and we watch Ruby strut in, glaring at everyone, with a limping Prospect behind her.

"Who the fuck wants to explain to me why the hell I'm just learning my sis was kidnapped?"

I smirk, but it's Law who smiles wide. "Silly girl, why the hell would I tell you sooner than now? You're liable to go off on an insane rescue attempt."

"Nothing insane if it works."

"Keep wishing, sweetheart. You ain't as tough as you think. Leave the job to those who can finish something, huh?"

Kooper's always an asshole, but it seems since I was locked away, he got a special itch to rile up the club's original princess. Ruby's the daughter of the prez, and she took the role, and the responsibility, with ease. Girl was born to lead, and she's badass, in looks and mind. I once saw her stab a guy in the dick for trying to grind on her after she told him off. But apparently an extra piss hole isn't something that scares Kooper.

"Fuck off, Koop. No one talking to you. Go back to playing your video games, and let the world move on without you."

"Both of you shut it," Law shouts. "I ain't got time for this shit. Ruby, you're staying here. And don't for one fucking second argue with me. Need you to watch Teddy. Boy is scared shitless."

While Ruby sulks away, dismissing us all to find my little man, who I know has been hiding out in the bunkroom, holding his stuffed alligator and watching *Scooby-Doo*—all in honor of Maddy, mind you—Prez points to the asshole who should still be in the hospital, now leaning over a chair about ready to pass out.

"You get on the phone and call Atom. Tell him to get General to write you a script or some shit. You are to sit and fucking not die. We already got one dead prospect tonight. I ain't about to lose another one because you're too stupid to stay in the hospital."

"I can go with you."

Law puts his hands up, silencing the kid before he really fucks up. "Already told you what the hell I want you to do. Don't fucking make me repeat myself or you're out. Don't give a shit if you spilled blood for our kin tonight or not. You disobey, you're out. So sit the fuck down, guard my girl, and don't get blood on anything. Still don't know how you ain't dead. You were bleeding too damn much, and it's only been a few hours since we got you to the hospital."

He mumbles something, but I'm a dick enough to force it out, "What you say, boy?" Back talking will not be put up with, especially to our prez, and especially with the mood I'm in.

"Said it wasn't that bad. Passed out from the concussion of the first explosion. Blood that was coming from my mouth was a cut lip, and nothing vital was hit when I was shot. Looked worse than it is."

"Huh. Maybe we should call you One-Cut Pass. You know, one cut from your mouth and you pass out."

He looks pissed at Kooper's comment, but Law is the one to dismiss it. "I ain't saying all that, and we still don't know if this dumbass will make it through. Sit your ass down and keep your mouth shut if you know what's good for you."

The kid listens and sits. Okay, he falls onto the couch, but at least he's down and is already on the phone as the rest of us head out.

As we mount up, once again, I lead the pack. Flint is in my ear, watching live feed of us the entire way, telling me which way to go and how far south till we get there. The Crazy Eights hooked us up better than we initially thought, as the feed they sent us was also live. Flint can work a full grid on how many we're talking about. But he has yet to find our girls, and the feed doesn't cover the entire area. Just three angles, front, back, and a west side. It's not perfect, but it's better than going in blind.

We stop three miles north and take it by foot. The main road comes in from the east, so we hope that's the only area where they expect an attack—like the one they're about to get.

The Hounds of the Reaper are about to do what we do best.

We're gonna reap some souls tonight.

Casper and Kooper claim one for each of them, as they easily take out the two Devils Damned walking the grounds when we enter. It's silent and quick. A pity, really, as these assholes deserve time in the hole with me, hanging from a hook and nothing but me and my chain keeping them awake.

With one last glance to our prez, we split up in our four groups. King and Jumper keep a few brothers to cover our backs and keep our exit open. Kooper and Domino's group go hunting for any idiot wandering around. Prez takes Bulldog and another to find the girls. Me and Casper go hunting for my woman. It was quickly decided that I needed a chaperone, just in case this goes south quicker than we planned.

I know Maddy's uncle is behind this, and I got business with the bastard. Have no clue why he picked me to take his fall, if only because it was a simple thing to do or to get me out of the picture with Jennie. No doubt he knew of our connection. Wouldn't put it past the guy. He's an asshole but a smart one if he has yet to be caught.

Or maybe I'm just getting my reward from the Reaper himself. He didn't want to fault me this honor of squeezing the life out of someone who hurt every woman in my life and knew I would take the most joy from it. Boys have no problem with me killing the guy; they just want to make sure I don't get locked up again. I don't need someone to keep me in line, more like I need someone to make sure I get *back* in line when the time comes. From the way the boys and I were talking on the road, this place is going up in smoke once we're done with it. Cops will come, and if I'm left enjoying myself too much, there won't be any place for me to go but back to jail.

And I can't have that. I got a family now.

Yeah, I'm all about the fucking picture-perfect family image.

Chapter 31–Maddy

'␣ve fantasized about waking up handcuffed to a bed before. Even recently, but that was just because Chains put the idea in my head after a particular night of dirty talk. The idea of being chained up while he had his way with me got me so hot I was coming from his words alone.

But after this, I think I'm over the fantasy.

Way over it.

I remember my uncle saying something about putting me on the bed and then nothing. I can't open one of my eyes much, and from the headache, it doesn't take my slow brain long to realize someone put me to sleep. A fist to the face will do that.

Thank God I still have my clothes on. I know I was out, but I feared what would happen once I couldn't fight back. It would have been what my uncle wanted most. I also doubt he'd be that considerate to dress me up again after he raped me.

I need to get out of here. Need to find the girls. Warn Chains not to come. Or just let him know not to come without an army.

My uncle thinks the boys are lax, and maybe they were, but I saw the fire in them after Christy betrayed them. It burns through them all. They're coiled tight like rattlesnakes, just waiting to strike.

Fucking hell, Christy. I can still see her slumped body when I raise my head to check the trailer is empty apart for us two. She must have given them Bulldog's ma's address; it explains how they found me and the girls. The boys have been tight-lipped on everything, and it was the only place they let us go to with so little of an escort.

Chains even went as far as cutting out shopping after he had the talk with Christy in the hole. But that could also be because of the small mound of toys I kept buying each time I was out of the clubhouse. Come on, kids need toys, and there's nothing but video games at the clubhouse. They're too young for those.

The Devils Damned could have either been watching the clubhouse—which I doubt we would have missed with the number of cameras Flint has around the complex, even twenty miles out—or they could have been watching Princess's grandma's house. It had cameras, I'm sure, but I doubt to the same extent the complex does.

I hold in the hysteria that's about to bubble up. Margret hated being watched, but I bet Bulldog will be a million times worse after this.

If she got out of it.

Dammit, I need to think positive. Isn't that what they always say? Think positive during a bad situation? Not sure how thinking is going to get me out of here, though. Known all my life that my thoughts did shit for me. Actions are key. And I need to take action now instead of thinking about shit that means nothing if I don't get me and the girls out of here.

This trailer is much like the last one I was in, but the bed frame is an old brass one, even going as far as having slight detail on the poles. This place must have been cherished by someone at some point, before it was taken over by my uncle. Or—I gulp past my unease—before he took the owner from it.

The bed in the last trailer had only a single bar for the frame. This one has a top bar that runs the length of it and four thinner ones going vertically that reach the base. And apparently I'm not the first person who's been here. The bars are warped from the amount of force others have willed on them as they tried to escape.

I know I'll cry for those lost souls later, but right now, the single tear that slips its confines is from happiness as I see that there's enough of a break in the weld of one of the thin vertical bars to slip one cuff toward the end of the bedpost. Only on my right, and not enough to be free, but it's in the right direction.

I contain my excitement, what little there is. I'm not free, but it's hope, and that's what I need to focus on, to cling to. Any hope is better than just dreaming, right?

Pulling my right arm to me, as far as it'll go in the cuff, which ain't far at all, I bite my lip to keep me from crying out as my skin splits against the metal. I refuse to give up. If one of these bars gives way, then another could too. I just need one arm free, and then I can figure out what the hell to do. I'll still be cuffed to the bed, but with one hand free, I have a better chance. A fighting chance.

One last pull has blood running down my forearm, which is the only give in the whole damn thing. I slump back and hit my head against the bar behind my head, again and again. I push back one more time with a bit more force, and I feel a give in the bar, just a minor movement in the top one. I look to my wrist to see if it's free. Of course it isn't, but I have a new idea.

Wrapping both hands around the top bar, I hold tight as I use my entire weight from my back to my arms to push against the smaller bars. I move my feet to lie flat on the bed as I continue to push back, taking steps closer to my butt as I crabwalk another step back on the bed.

It might be in my head, but I swear to God the thing moved a bit.

I rock, really giving it a running start in the position I'm in. I'm driven by my sense of freedom, barely glancing at the door on the far side of the trailer. The bed squeaks, but it's still a few inches away from the wall, so it isn't hitting it.

I bite my lip and take one huge push to the wall, keeping my feet in a backbend position, putting everything I have into the bar. Almost my entire 135 pounds are pushing on these rusty bars, and they finally give.

A little too much.

The entire right side breaks off, along with two vertical bars on that side. My weight worked for me to get the shit disconnected, but I really didn't think it through, as my ass is hanging off the bed, and I'm folded like a fucking taco. Knees are down on the bed, my ass is being poked, and each time I try to jackknife up, my back is sliced open by a rod that didn't make a clean break. My left arm is still attached to the remaining bed frame, and my shoulder is fucking straining.

I chance my luck one last time and force the remaining energy I have to lift my ass back on the bed. I get it up for a second, but then the same amount of force I used to get up has me slamming back down. My left shoulder is pulled from its socket as I fall straight into a rod that cuts into my skin as I slide down it. It can't be more than a few inches, but it fucking feels like I got rammed clear through. I react without thought, screaming in pain.

And that's where my luck ends, because, surprise surprise, I apparently have a guard on the door.

I squeak out a scream as he grabs my leg, and, with more force than I think is possible for anyone, I'm thrown back on the bed. Another scream as the metal is torn out of my back and my shoulder is jarred again. Everything fucking hurts so much, so I won't be able to fight for long. I ain't giving up, but I already know I'm weak.

"You fucking bitch, what the fuck do you think you're doing?"

I kick at the guy, but he ain't skinny like the last guards. I barely move him. He's massive, probably never missed a meal in his life. He uses his weight, pushing my legs off him, and then just sits on me before he punches me twice in the tits.

Who does that?

"Fucking whore. I'll teach you how to welcome a man into your bed."

"You ain't a man." Okay, so my mouth really has no filter and never knows when to stop. Now is not the time when I only have one hand loose and the guy weighs as much as an elephant. He's going to break my legs from sitting on them alone.

"I'll show you just how much of a man I am."

I freak as he rips my shirt down the middle. Memories of last time flash before my eyes, and fear cloaks my skin. I won't be as lucky as I was before.

"My uncle won't like it."

The words taste foul on my tongue as I say them, but at least the fat hippo on me pauses. And that's all I need. I've been holding the bed rail with both hands, mostly to keep me from jarring my left shoulder any more than it is. But the fat ass doesn't even notice that one cuff is dangling loose, and I use it.

He glances at the door, probably to make sure my uncle isn't standing right behind him. That's the type of fear he brings to anyone, the fear that he's there, right behind you, ready to attack. Okay, that might just be *my* fear, but from the way this big guy peeks behind him, I might not be too far off thinking I'm not alone in it.

I swing my right hand toward his head and tilt my wrist, forcing the empty part of the cuff to catch him in the eye. Bull's-eye. Blood is already dripping from the cut, and from the way the guy yells, you would have thought I poked his eye out. Okay, maybe I'd hoped to, but he didn't need to come back at me like I killed his puppy.

He was meant to grab his eye and get up or roll off the bed in pain. I mean, I hit his eye. Ever get poked in the eye? That shit hurts and has me rolling around like a baby. Apparently, this guy didn't get the memo on how to react. Or maybe he's more badass than me, which I refuse to believe.

He reaches up to touch his eye—for like a second. It's already closed tight, and with only one eye to see out of, he punches me in the face. Again and again. I've been punched before, and recently, but this guy isn't like the last one, He ain't doing it to get me to be compliant. He's out for blood. *My* blood.

The hits keep coming, and I scream and kick my feet, but it doesn't help. I can't move my legs much, even though he moved up to sit on my upper thighs, so I can only half fight back. I'm trying to push him away with my right arm, but it just keeps getting batted away.

I'm losing this fight, and all I can think about is how pissed Chains is going to be. He'll think I gave up, that I put myself second. But I'm not. I'm trying with everything to put *us* first. I'm fighting with every part I have. For the childhood that was taken from me. For the hole I lived in most of my life. I'm fighting for the family I lost as a child and the one I've gained so quickly. I have kids now, a father and sister, even a man. And not just any man, but *the* man. The man I love.

I'm fighting for that love, for the future I'm supposed to have. Not the one of me dying on a bed and being used afterward by God knows how many men in this place. I refuse to let my body be used one last time by anyone but *my* old man.

With a spout of energy that spears from the need to prove I'm fighting back for my man, our love, I buck my hips and throw him off me midpunch. I don't know enough about physics to understand how I did that, as I'm not that heavy, but I'm sure I just reached superhuman strength. Or he was never expecting it, and he was at such an awkward angle from beating the shit out of me that it worked in my favor.

I move my legs under me and try for all that's holy to ignore the fire that's taken over my arm. I can barely move my body, much less my left arm, but I try. The pain is beyond what I've ever been up against before, and I'm crying as I move off the bed, holding my arm with my other hand. I see no way to move the handcuff off the bedpost, but I yank on it anyway. The bed scrapes toward me, and more pain, if that's even possible, shoots up my weakened limb.

I can hear my guard; I know he's close. His grumbles are adding panic to my attempts to break free. I'm screaming at myself, but I'm sure nothing is coming out. Fear has a hold of me, and my feet are frozen as my right arm pulls frantically at the cuff on my left arm that's limp.

A hand in my hair has me screeching as I'm pulled back on the bed, flat on my back. The face I look up at reminds me of the hatred I see in my uncle's eyes, but unlike the creepy interested look he gives me, this fatso is just a red face. Anger and hate are all the emotions he shows—might be all he has with the way he wastes no time circling his fingers around my neck and squeezing.

His thumbs are pushing down on my windpipe and I know I'm about to die. I can feel it, but I still fight. I thrash, I punch, I buck my hips to get away. But each movement just spurs him to push down even harder as I make my own indent in this used-up mattress.

Happy times filter in the sides of my eyes, memories of pleasant moments, but I push them back. I refuse to die. Not now, not yet. I have things to do. A man to love, girls who need saving. I have a life that finally needs to be lived, out from under the shadow following me.

The blackness that's creeping in, I can't push that away like I do my life flashing before I die. I fight it, but it's for nothing. It creeps in slowly, or maybe it's fast. Time has no meaning right now, only that I'm fighting to see light, not darkness. I've lived in it for so long, I never feared it, only what's coming with it.

No more breath is coming from my mouth anymore. My limbs are moving at a snail's pace of fighting compared to what they were before.

I don't want to die. The only part of me I have left is tears. Tears that leak from my eyes, making things blurry as the world fades to black.

Then nothing.

Chapter 32–Maddy

Nothing but relief. The hands are no longer on me, and I'm waking as a zombie from being buried, gasping for much-needed air as I rise quickly to sit up. I blink but see nothing, which is fine 'cause I can't focus on anything but getting air into my lungs. I'm still panting for more, but the noise from behind me breaches my mind that someone else is in the room as I look over.

Casper enters my line of vision but quickly fades to the periphery as he kneels in front of me and touches my skin. I shrink back, but not enough to prevent him from checking on me, just enough for him to lessen his touch. But I don't look at him, not even when he tells me to or when he tries to turn my head. I can't.

Chains has my attention. It's horrifyingly beautiful watching him attack the hippo who was trying to kill me. I should be ashamed, but watching him protect me in this way, it's sick, but I swear I love him even more for it.

My eyes miss nothing. I track each punch. Each kick. Even the chain he wraps around the man's neck and pulls tight on both sides.

Huh, guess it wasn't just to fix his bike after all.

They're both facing me, with Chains holding the chain behind the guy's head. Our eyes lock for an instance, but I don't look away. I want him to know I accept it, this part of him.

He isn't violent, not with me, not with the kids. He does this because someone touched what was his. I get it. I would do the same if I was strong enough.

When Chains squeezes the last of the life from the hippo, the body slumps to the floor, and only then do I turn my gaze to Casper, who's quickly pushed aside.

"Are you okay?"

I nod at my man, but the tears and the tremble in my lip don't prove it.

"Dumb question."

I would have laughed at Casper's remark—I mean, he isn't wrong—but I hurt. Everywhere. And now that my man is here, I really don't want to put on a tough guy act anymore. I want to be taken care of. I need it.

"Shut it, Casper. Fuck off for like two seconds." I ignore the way my face feels like it's being scraped as Chains pushes my hair off my bruised face, brushing my tears away with more gentleness than we have time for, I bet. "Mama Bear, you with me?"

His whispered words have more tears rushing over their threshold. I can hear the anguish, the trial in his voice. He was scared, maybe even terrified by the way his mind probably filled in the unknown blanks of what happened since we last saw each other.

I just nod. I hurt everywhere, but he's here. He's really here. I could fly if he wanted me to.

"Okay, let's get you out of here."

He goes to pull me up, only then noticing my arm still attached to the bed. The click of the metal on the antique frame has Casper moving quicker than I knew anyone could. He examines my attachment, as well as my arm, concluding what I already knew.

"Dislocated. We need to set it or she'll be in a lot more pain. And we got to do it fast. We couldn't have been the only assholes on this side who heard her scream that last time."

They move around me. At first I don't get what they are going to do, but then I do.

Fuck, this is going to hurt.

The gunshot has me jumping as the handcuff link is broken, but the jolt pulls another scream from my lips.

"Need you to be quiet for me, Mama Bear, okay? We need to set this, and it fucking sucks balls, so I need you to help me."

They give me no real time to process one thing before they move on to the next as Chains sits on my right and covers my mouth with his hand. I grab a hold of it with my free hand and just squeeze tight. I'm not an idiot. I know we're playing with the Reaper on when others will come in. We need to be quick, but we also don't need to make more noise to keep the luck from evaporating on our side.

I don't even get a count of three before Casper lifts my arm and pops my shoulder back in. I scream, but it's muffled. A sound I'm sure these walls have heard before, but while those girls were being held to keep the screams at bay, I'm being held to keep others away.

I scratch at his hand and arm, but he doesn't let up till we all hear the noticeable pop and then I'm feeling great. Okay, not great, but better than I was.

"That's my good girl."

He moves his hand away, and I nod, but I'm panting again as I'm helped to standing. Once again my shirt is torn, but it's for the best, as the boys use it to make a sling. I really didn't expect all this from a motorcycle club, so color me surprised by how awesome and useful their skills are. I have a million questions in my head, mostly how they know so much about field dressings and shit, but I only voice one.

"The girls?"

"Law and Bulldog are looking for them."

"On the other side, I think. A trailer with a light on the outside, brown door, dark color trailer. Had one small window in front. Others were sealed."

Chains nods, and Casper is already talking to someone. I don't see a phone, so I guess they're either using telepathy or some cool listening device.

"Let's go." Casper tells us before he takes a step towards the door.

"Not so fast."

Can blood freeze? 'Cause I swear mine did hearing my uncle's words. We're three against one as I notice he's alone, and we have others here if Law and Bulldog are around. But I still tremble. I still curl in on myself. The fear I've had of him my whole life doesn't vanish after one night, no matter how ballsy I feel about the last time I spoke to him.

We should have expected this. I mean, anyone should have, especially me. My uncle isn't one to talk. I witnessed it like two hours ago, but I'm still surprised as hell when he just shoots Casper with no other warning.

Fuck!

I scream and instinctively cover my mouth with my hands. I watch as Casper grabs for his leg, falls back, and smashes his head on the bed frame, then stops moving altogether.

Why is there always so much blood? My mind is playing tricks on me, and I get flashes of my mother lying by the bed before I see Prospect, then Casper. I'm losing it. I'm really losing it. There's a part of me that's still here, but there's also a part that's locked in fear, and I swear to God, I'm seeing my own body lying in that blood.

The air beside me changes enough for me to look over and watch as Chains rushes my uncle. The guy is certifiable, as he doesn't even hesitate to go head-to-head with a guy with a gun. But from the way my man uses his chain to knock the Glock out of my uncle's hand, maybe he ain't as crazy as he looks. Maybe. Jury is still out, as the idiot doesn't go for the gun but does some sort of macho boxing thing.

Do we even have time for this?

My guy is getting in more punches than my uncle, especially since his chain is still wrapped around his hand like a boxing glove and breaking skin with each punch.

The trailer rocks as a noise ricochets around us like a hundred lightning bolts striking at once.

"Yeah, asshole, those are my brothers, and by the sounds of it, they're pissed at waiting. You better hope Domino didn't bring all his explosives. The guy loves the colors when shit explodes."

Wow, okay, Chains definitely left out a lot about these guys. I really need to get to know them better. Maybe we can play twenty questions over coffee after this is all done.

Yeah, I'm still not all here, I think my brain is on a permanent vacation from the crazy around me if I'm planning fucking coffee dates.

"It's over." My man's growl has goose bumps spreading over my skin.

"It's never over. I can pin this all on you like last time." My uncle thrashes, but Chains has him on the ground, and there's little he can do from the looks of it.

"And why the fuck did you do that? I didn't even know you, for fuck's sake."

"Isn't it obvious, you stupid motherfucker? Jennie was going to tell you. I had to get you gone. She was mine. But at least she left me a part of her."

"She left you nothing. Grace isn't yours. And she never will be."

Chains pulls his hand back, and my uncle takes the opportunity to flip them and uses the momentum to get on top. The sick glee I can see on his face as he forces Chains' hand down around himself, choking himself out at the odd angle, has me cursing myself. He faked us out. Of course he did. The guy's smart, wouldn't have been preying on others for so long if he wasn't. And we fell for it.

The noise coming from Chains isn't right; I can hear him wheezing, and I'm scared what it means. I look around, seeing nothing but the bed and Casper. His foot twitches, and it's enough of a movement to jar my memory that I ain't as helpless as it seems.

I run to him, glancing more times than I should back to what's going on at the other side of the trailer. The gun they used to shoot my cuffs is lying beside Casper, which is good 'cause I couldn't move him even if I had to, not with my arm in this sling. I grab it and try to focus on the steps I forced myself to memorize on how to handle one of these. Thank God someone was looking out for me, as the hammer's already cocked, and the safety's off.

Standing back up takes a lot out of me; my balance is completely off, and my eyesight's blurry. Using the bed to push myself up with the gun in my right hand, I stumble to my feet, then take a few more steps forward to the two still on the ground. I don't know how much time I have, how much time Chains has, so I shoot.

The first shot has him falling on Chains, but he doesn't completely falter, so I keep going. Taking a step closer each time, even as Chains pushes him off and he rolls to his back. I'm right on top of him when I fire the last bullet in the gun in his head. But I don't quit pulling the trigger. I can't. I have to make sure he's dead. That he's gone. I have to end this. End the pain, the fear, the agony he holds over me and others. It has to stop. *He* has to be stopped.

"It's done, Mama Bear. It's over," he whispers against my skin as he presses his head against mine. One hand comes up to pull the gun down and away, and the other holds me to him as I just stare down at the lifeless body before me.

My uncle's dead.

A groan at the back of the trailer, followed by another explosion, brings our little moment to an end.

"We got to get out of here."

I just nod. What else am I supposed to say?

"Casper. Fuck, man, you alive?"

"Barely." Another groan, but this one ends with a chuckle from both men as Chains quickly puts a tourniquet on Casper's right leg.

"Come on, you big baby. You can lean on me while we get the hell out of here."

"What the hell is going on?" Casper rasps as Chains pulls him up and takes most of the weight from him as they limp toward the front door, me following.

"Brothers got bored."

He just nods like this is normal behavior.

Before we exit the trailer, Chains pushes his brother to the wall to hold himself up and pulls a gun from Casper's waistband, cocking it and handing it to me. "Take this, Mama Bear. Need you to hang on just a bit longer. Then you can freak out, and I promise I'll hold you through it all. But right now, we don't know what's waiting for us outside that door, and everyone needs their head on a swivel. You get me?"

Even with Casper groaning, I know both men have their eyes on me. The thought of having comforting arms to fall apart in and not doing it on my own like usual has me perking up a bit.

Breathing deep, I check the safety is off on my new gun. "I might not let you up for a while."

Casper chuckles, and a soft smile covers my man's face. He leans forward, giving me a quick peck, but it's enough to curl my toes. "Wouldn't have it any other way."

"Okay, enough of this Hallmark bullshit. Someone give me my sweetheart back."

Chains snorts. "Seriously, dude, you need to get a girl. Who the hell calls their gun that? But here, you need to reload this thing. Maddy used the full clip on your 'sweetheart.'"

I get an eyebrow raise from Casper at Chains' comment and just raise my good shoulder in a shrug. Not really sure how to respond to that. I mean, it's the truth, but it wasn't like I missed. No, I got that asshole every time.

"Damn, I really need to get an old lady." With a shake of his head, Casper leans to his left, pulls out a new magazine from his cargo pants, and reloads. "Take this." He hands another gun to Chains.

Damn, how many guns does the guy have? And why does Chains have nothing but his signature weapon?

So many questions.

"We got a plan?" Casper and I look to Chains. Of the three of us, at least all his limbs are working.

"Bulldog and Law must have found the girls. Only way they would start blowing shit up—or else Domino started work early. We go back the way we came in. No way we can do much to help but get our asses out of here before we become as flat as what this place is bound to become."

A nod is all I get that we're moving before Casper throws an arm around Chains' neck and Chains wraps his arm around Casper's waist. They run from the building in the best three-legged race I've ever seen in my life. Seriously, there is zero tripping, and it's not like the ground is smooth. The rocks made walking difficult before, but with each explosion, the ground is shaking, and debris is flying. I'm keeping my eyes open for what's going to hit me, but also for anyone I should be worried about.

We don't hide in bushes or shadows, just flat-out run to what must be the place they're talking about. A few things go by me, and I look left to see it's not debris but bullets. I fire back as the guys shoot in various directions. I aim even as I run, but I have no clue if the people I'm aiming at are going down because of me or if someone else got them.

I don't care enough to find out, as it's takes everything to keep up with the guys. I won't last much longer if we keep up this sprinting, but the alternative keeps me putting another foot in front of the other as I stumble along, firing randomly in the direction of people who keep aiming at us.

I haven't been counting my bullets, but I know I'm close to out. This isn't like a video game; I can't reload each time I put my arm down and pull it back up.

We round a corner, and I chance a glance behind us and see five guys lining up to take aim. I pull the gun up to fire first, but I watch each man drop in sequence instead. I look forward and see the best-looking cavalry I've ever seen as a row of Hounds of the Reaper stand before us, each armed and covering our backs.

Seeing them all is the motivation I need to push forward, knowing it's almost over. I keep going, and thank God, because the explosion that comes next pushes me off my feet as the fire at my back warms my skin and I fall to the ground. I'm in so much pain, but I look back and see the place is now one giant fireball. If I believed in dragons, I'd swear one just ripped this place apart.

No, not dragons. This was the Reaper's work. Hell is burning just a few hundred yards from me, taking the souls his Hounds have left for him. I finally get their club name.

I'm pulled up, and I whimper in pain a second before I'm released and pulled into another's chest. His smell calms me as I'm lifted in a fireman's hold and carried away from this evil place. I see the brothers staring at me, a few nodding at me, and I just give a small smile in response.

We run for a bit more till I see a van a second before the door is opened for me. As soon as it is, I force my way out of my man's arms, finding the last burst of energy I have and race to my girl, crying as Grace runs out and into my arms, followed by Princess. I'm hugging and holding them, all of us sobbing as we embrace. We made it out; we survived.

Warm arms cover one side, then another, and I see it's Chains and Bulldog. They give us all a quick hug while pushing us into the waiting vehicle.

With a peek out the open door, I realize the entire brotherhood has circled us as we shed our grief for the hell we went through together. It was only a few hours, but it was enough to say we're survivors, and this will impact each of us in our own way.

"Flint says the cops are on the way. We got to get moving, gents." Law's voice is low enough to not scare the girls but firm enough to get us all moving.

I glance at him and nod as I let Chains help buckle both girls in the van.

"Happy to have you back, little girl." I blink the tears away as Law kisses my head before he closes the van door and walks to his bike.

Chains hops into the driver seat, Bulldog in the passenger. I would rather have him in the back with me, but I bet they didn't really bring enough to ride all the bikes back and have two in the van. At least he isn't far enough away that I can't reach him. If he rode his bike right now, I swear I would insist being on it. But I also need to be with Grace and Princess. Both are leeches, and I am too with them. I really thought I would never see them again.

I'm in and out as we drive the few hours home. The girls have cried themselves out, and the sirens are no longer a distant sound. The boys are quiet for a bit but finally start talking. Not always to each other, so I assume they have communication with the surrounding bikes, the ones that have caged us in as we drive.

"Man, seriously can't thank you enough. If it wasn't for you being crazy overprotective of Princess, I don't think we would have found them in time." Chains ends it with a chuckle, but I know it's forced. Both men are trying to hold it together for the other.

"Yeah, well, this ain't the first time Princess has been taken."

"Say what?"

I'm fully awake from my man's tone alone. I'm also completely in shock as I smooth down the beautiful brunette locks of the little princess lying on one side of me.

"Her mom, for like three hours. The longest hours of my life—ill today. This girl ain't going out of my sight for nothing. Don't care what the boys say. She's going to be with me at all times. Only way I can protect what she's got."

"What's that?"

"My heart, man. My fucking heart and soul."

I catch Chains' eye in the rearview mirror.

"I hear that, brother. I hear that."

Chapter 33 – Chains

I swear my body has its own timer right now. A Maddy timer. Every thirty seconds I'm looking at her. I need to know she's all right. Seeing her being choked out, cuffed to a fucking bed? Fuck, that did shit to me. Real shit.

I'm not as bad with Grace, but yeah, she isn't allowed out of the room yet either. I'm not sure if I'll ever let her go. But the way her brother is hovering and constantly holding her hand, I think he and I are in the same fucking boat.

Also helps that my brothers are as protective as the rest of us. They ain't arguing about the kids still being awake. They ain't bitching about anything but keeping voices low and watching the princess shit that Bulldog had on as soon as we got back to the clubhouse. He was a thinking man for sure, 'cause the first thing we did was have General do a full check on each. And with the shit we feared to have happened, cartoons on to distract while he did his little tests had them focusing on that and not freaking at the questions he asked.

Even Maddy pushed off the zombie feel, which I'm sure she's riding high right now, to make sure the girls are okay. I know they'll need to talk to someone. Watching people die, being put in a situation like that, it does crazy things to adults. Kids bounce back, sure, but they'll still need to be watched and have counseling or therapy. And I'm going to be there. For it all. Whatever Grace needs. Might even think about getting it for Teddy, too, because I'm damn sure that kid has gone through his own ringer. Just 'cause kids bounce back doesn't mean they should have to.

And Maddy.

Fuck.

Whatever that woman needs, she'll get it. Everything.

She already has my heart, my soul. From the way she looks at me, I *know* she knows that. Still need to say it out loud. Still need her to hear the words. Shit, I've been silently telling her I love her since I called her my old lady. Probably before that. As soon as "Mama Bear" came out of my mouth, it was my way of saying how I felt without sounding like a lovesick fool that first day. Which I was. I would be crazy not to fall for a girl like her after five seconds of looking down her barrel.

I've been sitting behind my girls the whole time as they sit on the couch facing the big-screen. We rarely have anything on but sports or some shit, but we also don't usually go to war in a matter of hours. And that was what tonight was.

Law got on the phone once we got back and called the Devils Damned VP. He might only be second in command, but he's the one in charge or branching shit out. It would be on him for shit this far north of his club's territory. He wasn't happy he lost men, but the fact that we blew up the place speaks to the amount of power we have at the ready. I don't expect this will be the last time we'll hear from them, but they agreed to back away, as they were sick of the hold dear Uncle Dwayne had on them anyway.

General puts one last bandage on a minor cut on Grace's knee—fucker even has fairy princess ones to give out—before he catches my gaze. I know what that means. We all know, no matter that her injuries were the worst, there was no way Maddy was going to go first. But now it's done. Princess told us what happened after Maddy was taken. The body was moved out of the trailer, and the girls went to the far corner and sat together till Law and Bulldog found them, after we relayed the description Maddy gave. Thank fuck they were too stupid to move the girls to another trailer.

I hurry to my girl and just lift her in my arms, not letting her get a word in beforehand. "Teddy, watch your sister, will you? I want to have General look over Maddy real quick. Domino, King, watch my kids."

I tighten my arms as my girl struggles to be released, and I'm enough of an asshole to put a bit of pressure on her shoulder to quiet the words I know she's about to spout. "Hush, woman. You waited long enough. They got nothing that can be fixed right now. You hovering ain't going to do anything but just delay your own needs, and I ain't letting you suffer anymore. Now shut that mouth and accept that it's your turn, or I'll smack your ass as General checks you over. Won't even care if he sees your sexy ass when I do it."

I hide my smirk as my old lady stops fighting but huffs and glares ahead. General just laughs outright as we head to his room. He doesn't stay here often enough, like a few of us, but he's got a place stocked for when he pulls doctor hours at the clubhouse.

Putting her on the exam table, I take up space by the door, cracking it to hear if my name is called but still providing enough privacy for the three of us. General quickly cleans her up and gives her a proper sling. We took the cuffs off a while ago and put a zipped sweater over her; it was the best we could do with her refusal to be treated until last. I would have pushed it earlier if I hadn't thought she would have flat-out refused medical help, which I know General would have been honor bound to accept. Damn asshole is more noble than any biker I know, especially with medical rules and patient wants. But then again, he also has no problem using some interesting cocktails to loosen a few lips when we put people in the hole.

I stay back, out of the way, but I categorize every mark, every question asked and the response. We haven't had our time to talk yet. General's questions about how things happened and where things hurt is new information I'm gathering and storing and will use to beat every fucker who even thinks about looking sideways at my woman.

I hear a knock and poke my head out as King appears. "Bulldog's taking Princess to bed. Where you want yours?"

"Put new sheets on my bed and get them settled there for now. Mama Bear and I will be there in a bit. General's almost done."

Thank fuck for my brotherhood, my family. God knows I couldn't do this alone. Not that I don't know how to make my bed, but shit, knowing stuff like that can be taken care of for me so I can focus on other things is fucking awesome.

I turn back and watch as General throws his gloves away before he pats me on the back and walks out, shutting the door completely as he goes.

I take my position in front of my old lady and look her over. More bruises. More bandages. At least she's in a T-shirt now, probably more comfortable than the hoodie. I'm miffed that it ain't one of mine, but it's a new one from the club's swag, so I ain't too upset.

"Need anything?"

She breathes out a laugh as she pushes her hair back from her face. "Actually, this is going to sound weird as shit, but can you take my bra off? I hate sleeping in one, and I'm about five minutes away from passing out."

"Hell, darling, you know I love getting you out of your clothes." I smile as I pull the blade from my pocket. I ain't about to have her lift her arm any more than it needs, and taking off the shirt and bra the normal way would do just that. Looked painful enough watching the first time; ain't forcing her to do it again so soon.

Walking around to her back, I push up the shirt and cut the straps before pulling it down and tossing it in the trash can.

"Bet that's not the first one to wind up in a trash can in a place like this."

Her attempt at humor is cute, but I know it's just a ploy to push off the tough emotional shit we need to talk about.

"First one cut for that reason."

She just nods as I move back to between her legs. One hand goes to her thigh as I cup her face with the other, and she just nuzzles in.

"Ready to fall apart yet?"

A solo tear slips from her closed eyes, but she shakes her head instead. "Nope."

I lean in and kiss her forehead. "We got time, baby. We got all the time in the world." She nods but says nothing more. "Come on, Mama Bear. Let's go snuggle with the kids and pass the fuck out."

With another nod, she pulls back and lets me help her step down and walk out toward our room. It ain't just mine anymore but ours. Just like everything else.

King is at the door, and Domino is inside reading a Dr. Seuss book. Got to admit, didn't even know we had kid books around here. Then again, Maddy's been shopping since she moved in, so no doubt it's from one of her impulse buys. Girl can't stop buying to make up for things. There might be a problem there, but I don't care; as long as she doesn't make us go broke, I'm good with it.

Domino leaves, and we settle in. Grace is in my arms, and Teddy snuggles as close as he can to Maddy. Think he's afraid she's going to leave just like his fear for his sister.

Yeah, therapy for the whole damn family. Maybe even me.

Nah, fuck that.

"I love you, Maddy," Teddy says.

"I love you, too." Her whispered words draw my gaze to her as she tries to hold the tears in. "I love you all."

Her eyes travel to Teddy and then Grace, who just smiles and mirrors her words. I grab her hand across them, linking our fingers.

"And we love you." I hold her gaze.

Tears flow freely from her eyes as she nods continuously. I just smile as I rub my thumb over her knuckles in solidarity.

This might not be the big revelation every girl hopes for, but it's perfect for us, for me. We're a family, the four of us. Each person a part of the whole, and our hearts are just like that. I know Maddy never would have loved me without my niece and nephew. And I know I couldn't have met a woman like her without them.

The scream that rips from her mouth also rips my soul apart. I hate that she's going through this, and that it's only the beginning. But I'm here for her. I'm here for it all. And for once, I'm here for her when she wakes up in our room.

"Mama Bear, wake up. Come on, babe. It's just a dream." I move her closer to me, squeezing lightly so she feels the difference of what has her in her dream and that I got her in real life. I kiss her temple as I rub her back, my words whispering through the room.

Her breath evens out, and her good arm reaches up and pets my chest. It's the only acknowledgment I get that she's with me. Guess I was expecting some big jolt or something like you see in the movies, but that ain't my girl. She takes on the world with grace and deals with her nightmares with a calmness I would be lucky to have.

"Where are the kids?"

"Law came and got them early. Think he needed some grandpa time with them but claimed it was for breakfast. We aren't the only ones who's got a soft spot for them."

She nods but doesn't raise her eyes to me. And I hate that.

I lift her chin, and her eyes follow slowly till I trap them with my gaze. "How we doin', Mama?"

Tears fall down her face at my words as she shakes her head back and forth, but at least she isn't looking away.

"Talk to me." It's a simple command, one I need followed. I need to know where she's at mentally, how I can help her through this.

"I killed my uncle." Her voice is soft, so soft I would have missed her words if I wasn't reading her lips.

"You protected yourself, Mama Bear. Protected me and the kids, and God knows how many other women who would have been taken there. You saved a lot of lives last night. Don't for one second think you didn't do good."

This time when she shakes her head, it's not in defeat but to shake the tears away with vigor.

"No, I—" She takes a shuddering breath, and I just move closer to her, lending her my strength. "I don't regret it. The man was evil. He deserved to die. But... what kind of person does that make me? I'm happy he's dead. Happy I'm the one who killed him. I feel nothing but joy knowing he's dead. What kind of fucked-up person am I?"

It's my turn to shake my head, "You're not fucked-up. Well, no more than the rest of us. But especially not for wanting him dead. He was a sick fuck who deserved everything he got. Actually, he probably deserved a round in the hole for about a year and *then* death, but beggars can't be choosers." My attempt at humor has her placating me with a quick smile before she pushes out of my arms.

"I know what you're doing, but nothing you say will make this better. I'm a monster, Chains. I wanted to kill that man for so long, and now that I have, I just want to do it again. I'm sick. Hell, maybe we're more alike than I thought." Her eyes widen. "Fuck, what's going to happen to me? I can't be around the kids. No way I won't do something else one day. You better put me on the first bus south and then forget about it. Shit, get one of the boys to lock me in the trunk and just drive me away someplace and chain me up."

I can't help the smile she brings out in me. My old lady ain't crying anymore, but she definitely is acting crazy. I wouldn't have it any other way. She isn't worried about the mark on her soul for taking a life, but she fears she has a taste for it and might act on it again and take it out one of us.

That ain't happening.

For one, she's too small to get anything by one of us.

And another, she's too protective of those she loves to do anything more than give someone an accidental paper cut when she hands them a package she just bought them.

My smile quickly fades as I watch her pack. "What the fuck are you doing?"

"Didn't you just hear me? I'm a monster. I can't be here, be near you or the kids."

I take two steps forward, grab the duffel bag on the floor she's been stuffing her clothes into by the strap, and throw it across the room. "You ain't leaving!" Her craziness is no longer cute. It's pissing me off now.

"Don't you listen, you dumb ape? I'm saving everyone by leaving. I'm just like my uncle! I killed and enjoyed it! Who the fuck says I won't snap and kill again, huh? What if... what if I hurt someone?" She looks down for a second before she looks back up at me with fresh tears on the horizon. "What if I hurt the kids? How can you even want me around them right now?"

"Oh, baby." I move quickly and pull her against me. "You ain't a monster. You *took out* one. And don't for one second think he didn't earn the title. You ain't a monster, Mama Bear. You're a Hound of the Reaper. You're a part of this club more than you ever were before. We take out the bad so there's good in the world, and you helped with that. You ain't like him. You ain't cold, manipulative. You don't take pleasure in causing pain—unless it's to my credit limit."

I kiss her temple as she giggles at my joke.

"Be happy if you want. I ain't taking the kids, and you ain't getting rid of me. You have my heart, Maddy, my whole damn heart. Never had a girl take it before, and I ain't about to let you toss it away 'cause you're scared. We'll get through this, but we'll do it together."

She tilts her head up to give me a soft kiss before pulling back. "I love you, too, James."

My smile turns from joy to wicked at her words. "Damn straight you do. Now get naked."

Her eyebrow quirks, but she shimmies out of her sleep shorts.

God, I love this woman. Not just because she follows my commands—of course that's awesome and hot in its own right—but because of her strength through everything thrown at her. She's the most beautiful woman I've ever seen, with pale pink little panties and my club's logo on the shirt that's too big for her. It teases me, as I know she's braless, and her nipples peek out from behind it, but it's the only thing comfy we got right now with her arm still in a sling. She has more bruises, cuts, and bandages on her body than any woman should have to deal with, and she'll never have them again. I vowed last night as she was being patched together by General that it would be the last time she saw him in that room.

I wrap my hands on her hips and take steps backward, moving her with me. "You don't think I'm going to let you get away from me without putting my dick in your pussy after we said, 'I love you,' for the very first time, did you?"

She rolls her eyes. "How romantic you are."

"Yeah I am, baby, and I'm all yours." My thighs touch my bed, and I let go of my old lady long enough to pull off my shirt and toss my shorts to the ground. As I sit, I pull her panties down as well. My dick is begging me to just have her crawl on top and sink in, but my mouth is watering for a taste. I lean in and lick along her lips, growling as she grips my hair so quickly to hold on as my hands clamp on her hips to prevent her from moving to hurt herself. And because I'm just enough of an asshole to like to control how I give her the pleasure and how she takes it.

"Chains, please."

Her soft words, her begging, get me every time. I can't deny her. I can't deny her anything, even if I wanted like an hour of her in my mouth. She tastes fucking amazing, and the fact that she's completely mine, and I'm hers, just makes her sweeter to eat out.

"Sit on my cock, baby. Take your old man for a spin, and then I'm going to fuck you."

I move back enough to lie in the middle of the bed, guiding her with me as she adjusts and sinks down on me. Her small wince as I buck makes me feel like a prick for wanting this when she's injured, but then she moves and I forget it. The ride is slow building, Maddy does nothing but rock back and forth. Usually I can't get off like that, but fuck if my heart ain't exploding with my love for her.

Don't know how long we stay like this, but when we do come, we're together in that too. Fuck, if it isn't perfect. I know I sound like a pussy, but as I lean up and hug her close to me, I don't give a fuck. I have the woman I love in my arms, she's my old lady, and now she's a Hound of the Reaper.

Life is fucking perfect.

Chapter 34–Maddy

Two Months Later

"We ain't getting a dog."

"Maddy, we need a dog. The kids want a dog. I want a dog. Hell, everyone even says we need to get one before having kids."

I laugh at that. "Chains, we already have kids, in case you forgot. They say that so you can see if you're ready for the constant hourly attention required for a kid. I think we got ours covered by Thing 1 and Thing 2."

"Yeah, but what about Thing 3?"

"Think you need to read Grace that story again. There ain't a third."

He comes up behind me and wraps his arms around me. "Not yet. But we can start with the dog, see where it leads. I'm thinking we might have a whole group of them by the time I'm done with you."

"What?" I must have misheard him. I mean, he can't be saying what I think he's saying. But then again, his hands are all over my stomach.

He nuzzles my neck, laying sweet kisses there as he lowers his voice, sending shivers coursing through my body. "You heard me, woman. I want kids. Lots of kids. And with you, in case you didn't get that part either."

I can't breathe. So many things have happened in the last few weeks. This is all so crazy, and I'm not doing great with holding on to shit. My therapist—yeah, I got one of those after Chains and half the damn club insisted—says I have commitment issues. That being tied down is my way of feeling trapped in my tiny underground hole.

No fucking shit.

So instead of the breathing exercises she recommended I do when I'm like this, I just go bust out walls till I feel better. And Flint and his crew of mongrels have no problem letting me come on to their construction sites to do it—as long as I bust out the ones they want, that is.

I pull myself out of his arms as I gather the rest of the paperwork I need. "Stop with this shit. You know I'm already freaking out today. You can play this joke on me after I sell the house."

Yeah, so apparently even though my world stopped the moment I met Chains, nothing else did. The bank still had the deed to my house, and they were still within their right to sell it if someone came knocking. And apparently someone did seven weeks ago. The sale was on condition of a few things they wanted added. I was such a wreck that I had Chains handle it all, and I really haven't been back to that house since. I never knew how much I wanted to keep that place till it was taken from me. Now I feel lost, and my itch to run is growing at every turn.

I ain't leaving. It's just an itch. I have a family, and Chains—I have it all. And his minor declaration is putting me into shock. I mean, we haven't even discussed marriage. Then again, I'm his old lady, so I guess we already are? I'm still confused by a few things in club life. I'm learning fast, but with no other old ladies around, it's hard to talk through some things. Ruby and Princess are great at giving me tips and whatnot, but it ain't the same.

I love Chains, just hate that he sprang this on me. We got the call yesterday that they wanted to do the sale today, and I've been freaking since I got the message. But my old man? Not one bit. He even looks smug. Bastard. Probably expects me to move in with him now. I mean, I would, but he still doesn't have a place. And I might like the clubhouse, but I'm not moving in full time. Mostly 'cause I'm tired of the guys telling me they can hear me all night. I still don't think I make that much noise during sex. The teasing is fine every now and again. Daily? Annoying as fuck. Especially since I know several of them are just as bad as me, and yeah, hearing them doesn't make me wet. Makes me gag. Distance is best.

He just chuckles at me, but thank fuck he lets me off the hook—for now. I know I ain't got long before he starts talking about it again. The guy is like a dog with a bone once he gets something in his mind that he wants. Thank God he wanted me.

I smile till my ass is spanked, and not in the fun way. Of course, it does send a zip of pleasure through me, but I turn my head and glare at my old man as I rub out the initial sting.

"Let's go, Mama Bear. Kids get out of school soon, and I'm not about to be last again to pick them up."

"Don't look at me. Last time we were late was because of you."

"How was *that* my fault?"

"I told you not to come back all greased up. You know I can't resist, and I bet you did it on purpose from the way you had no problem letting me in the shower with you to help you clean up."

"Oh, baby, I know you can't resist. I also like getting you dirty so I can clean you all up, licking my way as I go." He's close again, moving in to me with that heat in his eyes that turns my legs to Jell-O.

"Just stop. We start up and we'll be late to everything, and I ain't about to let Bulldog have more ammo against me. Damn man just *loves* airing all our shit to everyone." I storm out of the room, my man laughing behind me as we go.

"Of course he does, babe. Princess is making him do all the girly shit now that you showed her. Even caught him wearing a fucking princess crown at his house when I went there the other day to drop off club property. Guy's forced to do as his little lady says, and he knows he can't tell her no, so you get the brunt of it. And your smile tells me you do that shit on purpose, so quit your whining and hop up on my bike, woman."

"I wasn't whining."

He just shakes his head before we ride out to my place. I mean my old place. It won't be mine much longer. We take his bike, as we don't expect this to be long and know we should have plenty of time to get back to the club to get his truck before we get the kids. Maybe I can convince the man to give me some happy time if we sign this really quick. I'll probably need a boost to keep me smiling after this.

As we pull into my drive, I already see changes to my home. Guess the new owners wanted the front spruced up a bit, so many more trees and flowers litter my property. It was pretty vacant before, so this really adds to it, but it's a shock. I grip Chains tighter, knowing I'm freaking out over the tiny things. Tons was changed on the inside. He tried to show me the plans once, but I just couldn't deal with it, though I know it's a lot.

He pats my hand before he gets off the bike. Turning to me, he cocks an eyebrow behind his shades. I take a steady breath, then grab his outstretched hand and let him pull me off his bike and toward my home that isn't mine anymore.

As we ascend the stairs, I take in the extended porch that goes out on the left into an octagon with a small sitting area all set up. The door has been changed, too, but I know that's from what happened the night of my attack. Maybe I should be scared to go inside because of what happened last time I was here, but I'm not. I got my man holding my hand tight—obviously he knows how willing I am to just start running away right now.

If I run, I don't have to sign, right?

As he unlocks the door, I take another look around. "Are we early?"

"No."

"How'd you get a key, then? Thought the bank collected them from the crew a few days ago."

"They let me keep one so I can get us inside to sign the papers. I promised to leave it once we signed it over."

I just nod, taking in the house as we walk in. It could be true for all I know; I've never sold or bought a house before, so I have no idea how it works.

It's so different and yet the same. Most of what I envisioned is here. Open concept, large kitchen, huge island. I go left first and see the kids' rooms aren't much different, even still decorated for a boy and a girl. The guest bath has been extended for a double vanity with a linen closet, and they even put a chute from that bathroom directly to the laundry room. There's another small opening on the opposite side, which I gather is from the master bedroom. Okay, that's pretty awesome, but I'm not telling anyone that I actually like the new owner's ideas.

My aunt's room is a complete change. They must have knocked out the back wall and extended it, as the room's almost double what it was before. The king-size bed fits nicely in it, as does the freaking fireplace. It's gas, but even so, the bedroom has a fireplace in it. The bathroom is freaking awesome. Double sinks, separate shower and bath, and both—yeah, you heard right—have jets. Marble countertops and subway tiling. It really is beautifully done.

The kitchen has a ton of cabinets, even one of those that goes floor to ceiling. But when I open it, I'm surprised, as it leads into another room.

"What the hell?"

"It's a pantry."

No shit, sweetie. I just roll my eyes at his Captain Obvious moment.

"But this place had a pantry." It's a big change, and I again secretly love it, but it's a change, and I'm freaking out a bit.

"Come on." He grabs my hand, pulls me over to the old pantry door, and opens it.

I breathe fast, seeing the shelves that were there have been replaced with stairs. I can't move down them till Chains pulls me with him. They aren't too narrow, nothing like how I used to get down to my crawl space. But this isn't my old room anymore.

Once we get to the bottom, I take in the transformation. We're lower than my room was. It's not a vast area, but it's large enough to hold some arcade games and french doors that lead out to the side of my property, which I must have missed from the outside.

"How is this possible?" I'm not into construction, but it doesn't seem feasible to build a room under a house without moving the house.

"New owner wanted to know how far down it went, so Flint had one of his guys drill into the concrete. Thing was just a huge fucking concrete slab. We found the original plans and saw the place had a basement all along, but someone filled it in. We just cleaned and cleared it. Over there is another bath and a guest room or office. We didn't go deeper than that—would have really dug into the backyard—so we focused on this side, making a small hill and leaving the rest."

"Wow." Not the most original word, but it's all I got. And I don't even sound enthusiastic about it as I just move to the french doors and look out, my arms wrapped around me. "I wished so many times to see the outside when I lived here. I drew pictures of trees and flowers and pretended I was looking out windows as I crawled from one area to the next."

He lets me soak it in for a bit before coaxing me back upstairs to sign the papers. Ones I don't even read, just sign in three spots, each marked with a "sign here" sticker. I do it quickly, ready to move on and try to forget the home that kept me safe from my past and brought me to my future.

When Chains grabs the pen from me and signs too, I raise a brow. "Why are you signing? And why are we the only ones here? I doubt they expect us to know what we're doing."

He rises as he folds the papers and puts them in his back pocket. Okay, now I know something is up, 'cause no way can you just fold legal papers. *Can you?*

"I'm signing because we need to get the process rolling for the legal adoption, and the judge says we had to. We're alone because why the hell would I let anyone else in my house?"

"Wait, what?"

He smirks. "What part did I lose you?"

"Um, try all of it." I'm deadweight standing, so it's easy for him to grab my hips and put me on the counter, making us eye level.

"I want you and me to legally adopt Teddy and Grace. We're already a family, but I want to make it legal so no one can take them away from us. And I bought this house because I knew you could never move out of it without losing a part of you."

I think he's smiling, but honestly, it's blurry. So many tears are falling from my eyes, I feel like a freaking broken faucet.

"Maddy, I ain't going to ask you to raise my kids. I ain't going to ask you to move in with me. And I ain't going to ask you to *have* my kids. I'm telling you. You're my old lady. You're the thing that makes me rise with a smile, and you put one on me each night—well, your mouth and pussy do that—" I hit him, and he chuckles before continuing. "But you're also the one who shoulders my burdens and takes things on and fights for me. You're the woman I want to show the kids, and our future ones, what it means to be, and to have, another half. I know you're itching to run. I've been seeing it for a while. But I bought you this house so you can stay. And I made you sign the papers to keep you here."

I can't help but shake my head as I bark out a laugh. Of course the manipulative bastard would trick me. Not that I wouldn't have signed if he asked, but this works too.

I take a deep breath as I rub my eyes and cheeks clear. I take him in, really take him in. He's a felon, even if he's an innocent one. It's a mark he'll always have. He has as much baggage as I do, and he comes with an entire group with issues of their own. But if there's one thing I am, I'm a girl who's up for a challenge. And he's one I'm more than willing to take on.

"Kiss me, old man, before I cry again."

"I'll do more than kiss you," he growls as he pulls my head to his quickly. We eat at each other's lips as I wrap my legs around his hips and his hands fly to my ass to squeeze before he rocks into me.

Yeah, we are so going to be late getting the kids.

Worth it.

Epilogue – Chains

"We need to branch out." Bulldog pulls all eyes at Church to him. "I want to build the beer business up now that we got a solid hold on a few things. Think it's time to go wide. Devils Damned also tried to take us out, and we need to expand our level of play too. Others need to know we aren't just for looks."

I chuff inwardly at that. "I think I can speak for most of the boys by saying we want more in a fight. It sure as fuck satisfied an itch I didn't know needed scratching."

Grunts of agreement come from all around the table.

"More?" Flint looks up with a twinkle in his eye, the kind that usually gets the boys into fun times. "I can get us more. I follow the web enough. There're a lot of people out there who want some help."

"Like the Crazy Eights?" Law side-eyes him skeptically.

He shrugs as he leans back in his chair. "Sure, them too. But there's enough out there that we can share with the Eights for those asking for help."

"Ain't worried about our skills. A lot of us played that game before and helped the wrong person. Innocents still died, and the wealthy got rich. Ain't about to get more shit on my conscience than what's already there." Casper's words float around the room as the group thinks collectively.

"Boys, that's why it is so great to be a Hound. We pick, and if we get double-crossed, we just deal with it the Hounds of the Reaper way."

I laugh at Flint's choice of words, and it seems to pacify the others. Casper even goes as far as smiling, something he rarely does when mentioning his past deeds.

"All in favor of both points Bulldog brought up?" Law asks.

The gavel, which looks more like an upside-down scythe than anything, bangs on the wood table as we voice our agreement.

Looks like the Hounds are going hunting and expanding.

"When's your old lady heading over?" Bulldog asks.

I take the offered beer and drink a bit before I answer my VP. "Soon. She wanted to check in on her friend one more time. She acts like Izzy ain't a grown woman who can't move by herself, but whatever."

"Ha. You can fake the grumble with some other asshole who doesn't know you."

"Don't know what you're talking about, man."

"Right. She ain't my old lady, but even I know how much having a friend close means to her. And you might like to pretend you run that house, but the boys and I know you're carried around by the balls and basically just do anything she wants as long as she smiles about it."

I shrug. He ain't wrong. "A smile and a blow job, that is."

"Man, you can get one of those from any girl. Not telling you to cheat, but no need to get your balls gold plated and strung up to mount around her neck."

I give my friend a long, hard look. "You need an old lady."

He glares at me as beer drips down his chin from the way he jerked at my words. "What the fuck, man?"

"Seriously. Vamps might be good with their mouths, but trust me, man, nothing beats knowing you got a good woman behind you. And hell, sometimes she's the one leading the charge."

"Got a woman."

"You got a princess, not a woman. Which is apparent by the way you been so bitchy lately. You might get laid, but you ain't getting what you need."

He scrubs his hands over his face. "It's this damn expansion of the beer and keeping eyes on Princess. I need to do both, can't stop the need for wanting it to be only me, but I got to admit I'm getting thinned out, brother."

"Maddy's always volunteering to watch your little girl, so why not take up the offer? I know what losing her did to you, especially with it being the second time. But you know I don't like Maddy out of my sight either, so why not let the club step in and help? We family, right?"

"Yeah, man, we family."

"Good. Now go get your costume on. Your princess is going to be pissed when she comes out of the back and sees you out of it." I can't help smiling wide. In typical fashion, his daughter demanded he go as her king. And not just putting on a crown and calling it a day. I'm talking full-on ruffled sleeves and jacket like in the Disney movies. So fucking funny.

"Fuck off. Who the fuck decided family night and Halloween was a good idea?"

"My old lady is who."

"Of fucking course. Where's your costume?"

I pull out the red nose and put it on. "I'm a clown. Family is doing a circus theme. Even got Teddy to dress up like a motorcycle stunt guy."

"Well, that's actually kind of cool. What are the girls?"

"Gigi is into animals, so full-on lion, and Maddy is typical Mama Bear-style lion tamer."

A whistle behind me catches our ears, but Bulldog scans the crowd. I don't need to look when I know what kind of woman I got coming to me soon.

"I think she's more like a ringleader with that outfit."

"Huh?"

I turn in my seat and see the seas parting. The brothers better get the fuck out of the way as my old lady comes in and walks over to me. There's a very cute lion holding her hand, a cool kid with a motorcycle jacket and shades on her opposite side, but they only get a glance from me. No, my eyes are square on my woman.

With it being family night—even if the family part is only till nine and then Ruby babysits the group at her dad's place with about four brothers on protective duty—she's dressed for anything but PG-rated fun. Her heels have to make her toes stand on points from the height alone. The fishnet stockings hug her toned, sexy legs, winding all the way up before hiding beneath a bodysuit. One that's super tight and doubles as a corset.

Bulldog's right—nothing taming about my lady as she works the ringleader hat and sparkly tailored jacket in the standard circus colors of red and yellow for the big top. Sexy as fuck is what she is, and she's all mine.

"Nice costume."

"Shut up." She smiles before I slide her onto my lap as the kids scamper off to wherever the fuck they go when they notice me and Maddy getting close like this. They don't mind—I can tell from the easy way they call her Mom and me Dad—but they don't like to watch.

She turns in my lap, talking to Bulldog. I pay them no mind, willing my cock to stop poking at her ass as I take in the outfit up close and personal. I focus on my task to keep my dick at bay, at least for a bit longer, as I reach into my vest and pull out what I need.

I lean over and rest my left hand over hers on the table. I slide the ring on her second finger from the left and take my beer back to finish it.

I wait for it. And I wait some more. I look at Bulldog, who just grins, making me glare. She didn't even look down at the damn thing. I slam the bottle on the table and still not one goddamn reaction.

"What, you ain't going to say anything?" I growl at her back. Don't know why I'm pissed other than I didn't expect this fucking reaction, or lack thereof.

With an innocence that can only be mastered from playing it up, she glances back at me. "Say what?" I give a pointed look to her ring, and she just shrugs as she looks back at Bulldog. "What? My guy got me some costume jewelry for my costume."

"That ain't no costume anything. You know how much it cost?" I laugh it off. She has to be kidding. Right?

"Why would it cost anything? It looks like a cheap piece of junk."

I think the shrug she gives and the refusal to look back at me is what really has my teeth grinding down. "Woman, that is an engagement ring"

"Then why did you put it on my finger?" At least she turns enough to lock eyes with me. It ain't what I was after, but the way she's acting, I'd be lucky to even get this much.

"'Cause I'm asking you to marry me?" Does she really not get this? What kind of woman *doesn't* get this?

She does this adorable head tilt—well, on any other day but today I would think it was cute. Now I'm annoyed as fuck 'cause I'm messing this completely up, and I know I've got the entire room's attention.

"Yeah, no."

"No?"

"No."

"What the hell do you mean, no?" My outburst damn near stops the entire place.

"To all of it. It ain't no engagement ring." Again I get her back.

"Yeah, the hell it is. Cost me fucking more than half my new ride. Trust me, it is."

"Can't be."

Her sass is about to get her ass smacked if she keeps this up.

"Oh yeah, and why's that?" I ignore the fuckers around me, knowing more than a few are smirking at this exchange. All of them knew I was going to do this tonight, and they all gave me shit that she wouldn't accept me. Hence why I didn't ask. But it doesn't look like my "oh so clever" plan is working any better than the shit the boys said she would say.

"'Cause you didn't ask me anything. If there's no question, there's no engagement, and thus this is just a shiny piece of metal."

I cross my arms, leaning back and adjusting her a bit on my legs. "I ain't going to ask you, 'cause that would give you a reason to say no."

Her smirk as she looks back at me has my dick going full mast. He loves that smirk she gives out. "Think so?"

"Know so. No woman as decent as you would willingly chain herself to me."

"Oh, Chains. Funny choice of wording." She turns and sinks back into me, leaning more on my chest than anything else as she cups my jaw. "So what, you think I would just accept it and gush over it as a thank-you even if I wasn't consulted? Don't think so. I'm not better than you. I would be lucky to have you in my life—anyone would. But I'm still a woman, and asking is the right thing to do. You might be surprised at the answer."

I take a moment to think it over but don't need long to weigh my option. "Nah. I ain't asking." I uncross my arms and pull her closer to me. "You would just say no now to prove a point. But it doesn't matter."

"Doesn't matter, huh?" She giggles more in surprise, I bet, than being ticklish.

"Nah, you're already tied to me even without the 'metal,' as you call it."

"Might as well return it. Could get a decent chunk of change for it." Her smile could stop a man from breathing, and I love that I put it on her. We're so not on point for this conversation like I wanted, but I love the fact that she's enjoying herself enough to smile like that. Would do anything to keep that smile on her face for the rest of my life.

"Oh, you think Teddy and Grace, and *my* house, are the ties keeping me to you?"

"No, but they help." She smiles quickly before she thinks on it for a bit. "Then what is it?"

I sit up straight and tighten my arms to keep her close to me as I lean in to her, pushing her hair away from her ear as I whisper, "My baby inside you."

I hear her gasp as I nuzzle her neck with my nose and enjoy the shiver I cause. "You know about that?"

"You really think I don't know everything about you, woman? You make my heart beat. You're the reason I'm here. You changed my life for the better, and you can bet your ass I watch out for the things that make my life better."

She turns to me and kisses me quickly to prevent the tears from crushing over her lids and ruining her makeup. A habit she's formed, and I ain't complaining. "I love you."

I kiss her once more before pulling back and holding her gaze. "I love you too. Marry me, Maddy. Not 'cause you got my kid inside you. Not 'cause you've made the world shine for my niece and nephew so much that they claim you as their own. And not 'cause you brought life back into a black soul like mine. Don't say yes 'cause you know I would follow if you left, that I would chase you around the world if I had to. Say yes 'cause you want to. 'Cause you *want me*."

She melts into me. "I always want you, Chains. Always." Her kiss is light before she pulls back and says the one word I need from her. "Yes."

"Hell yeah." I lean in to kiss her, sealing the deal she can't take away, but she stops me with her fingers between our lips.

"But."

"What do you mean, but?"

"We can't tell Izzy I'm pregnant."

"Why not?"

"'Cause I promised her my first kid."

C8

Connecting...
Confirming connection is secure

//: Window has been established and set as secure for 20 seconds. Report...

Local area assessed. Roots planted...://

//: Any sign of target...

Negative...://

//: Tick tock

Connection terminated

Bulldog is now available!

Click here to buy now!

To sign up for the monthly newsletter and get a copy of LAW, a free novella just for joining, click the link below.

Sign me up for the newsletter!

Thanks for Reading

Thank you for reading *Chains: Hounds of the Reaper MC (Book 1)*. If you enjoyed this book and would like to give back to the author, please consider writing a review! Reviews are a tremendous help for authors. So if you were moved and enjoyed this book enough to write even one sentence of encouragement, it would be a huge boon.
Review Here or
Go to www.SJROWE.com to get started!

Also by S.J. Rowe

**Titles in The Cain and Abel Series
(only available in Kindle Unlimited currently):**
Marked for Seduction
Marked for Deception
Marked for Protection

Titles in The Hounds of the Reaper MC Series:
Chains

Bulldog

Flint

Mad Max

Coming Soon:

Gator

Please enjoy the following exert from the first book in the Cain and Abel Series: Marked for Seduction

Chapter 1

Well, it looks like we have a success on our hands."

Maliki continued to scan the area ahead of him as he spoke into his earpiece. "How so?"

"Easy. No one is in a body bag, and we've only had to break up four fights. Given what happened last time we tried this, I say we're in for a happy ending." Even though they were separated by fifty feet, it was easy to see Eddie's shrug from Maliki's post in the crowd.

Maliki continued to scan the area as memories of the last gala plagued his mind. It had been a nightmare, for sure. It was the first time Primes and the Fallen had tried to be civil to each other after the Treaty. Maliki didn't have to be a rocket scientist to realize it would end badly. Putting two groups in a room together and telling them they were now all good friends after they'd been fighting each other for over five thousand years had its limits. The initial body count had been smaller than expected, but it was still a scar on their history. Maliki was glad the Council had waited almost a hundred years to try it again—not only to let cooler heads prevail but also to ensure the Loyalists were placed in a better position to handle the situation. Of course, it also helped that both sides had quadrupled their security to keep the pretense that everyone was getting along.

Another scan confirmed all of Maliki's men were in position and alert. He didn't so much mind working on his night off from the training facility; he only minded the dress code. He felt like a monkey in a suit. He stretched his neck again in hopes of loosening the noose around him called a bow tie. He could barely move in the thing; how was he supposed to break up anything if the damn material was holding him in?

Maliki glared in Eddie's direction at the sound of his laughter through the earpiece. Eddie, another Prime trainer, was born for wearing suits. He moved with a grace and ease that only came from being around royalty, neither of which Maliki had, nor done. He was made for battle, not dress-up. Give him military gear and combat boots any day over a suit jacket.

Grabbing a flute glass off the passing waiter's tray, Maliki downed the champagne as if it were water.

"Careful, my friend. Your obvious discomfort is showing."

"Obvious, huh?" Maliki set the glass down on the table beside him. "And here I thought I was hiding it so well. Jesus, I hate these things. Why didn't they go to Jayden's compound to host this event?"

"You know Jayden doesn't have as much manpower as we do. And I think they wanted a neutral location, neither side having a strong foothold. I'm just happy they chose this place. The others they were looking at were out of state. At least it won't take longer than a couple of hours to drive home. Besides, in case something does happen, I think Sir Orrick wanted to have the holding cells available at the nearby training facility."

Maliki knew Eddie was right, of course, but he didn't have to like it. It was true, Jayden's facility was for small groups of thirty or less, not for three hundred plus. Moreover, it was considered Abel territory, although Jayden was a Loyalist, a Peacekeeper between those of Abel and Cain blood. Jayden's place was similar to all Loyalist compounds, protecting those of Abel and Cain blood by blocking the use of their specialized abilities. That just wasn't possible on the training facility's grounds, where all new Primes learned how to survive in a world they once thought was a myth.

Maliki ran a hand through his buzzed hair in frustration. "Yeah, Sir Orrick was right. The best place for a fake peace party is here. The area is large enough, and with the added rookies we brought in, we have enough security in place. Besides, I doubt the Fallen King would have ever agreed to let us host the event at his place."

"He might agree, but I doubt his protection detail would. You know how Lakays are. No one goes near their king without a signed memo from God himself." Eddie snorted as he continued to scan the crowd from his position by the entrance.

A slow whistle sounded through Maliki's and Eddie's earpieces. "Anyone see the blonde in the long black dress? Not sure which side she's on, but I would be more than happy to do a pat-down on her."

Maliki scanned the area where Jeremy, another Prime trainer, was stationed and noticed a blonde walking in his general direction.

"You talking about the one with the slit halfway up the side of her dress?" Eddie asked as he also eyed the beauty, making her way toward the back entrance.

"Not sure about the slit, but I can tell you the back of the dress is doing all kinds of things to me."

"What back of the dress?" Eddie asked as he squirmed in all directions to get a better look.

"Exactly, my friend. The dress practically points to that fine ass that's shimmying away from me. Permission to investigate? I'm assessing a possible threat."

Maliki barked with laughter. "The only threat you're assessing is how quickly you can get your dick wet. No, stay in position. You have two rookies at your flank who know nothing about how to handle a Fallen member if words get heated."

Maliki continued to follow the beauty and was pleased to see she was stopping for a drink instead of exiting the facility. The dress had a single slit on the right that went up to midthigh, revealing beautiful creamy flesh that mirrored the skin on her back. It was high at the collar in front, exposing nothing, but the backside was utterly bare. The idea of innocence from the front and devil be damned from the back set Maliki's blood pumping.

Despite that her hair was styled neatly around her face, Maliki was still blocked from seeing all of her. Grinning, he started his approach.

"I, on the other hand, have no rookies with me and need a break. Eddie, take point. I should be unavailable for fifteen minutes."

As Maliki got closer, he noticed the blonde's high cheekbones, plump lips, and curves that seemed to be accentuated almost tenfold by the dress. He now truly knew the reason why Jeremy wanted to investigate.

"Make that thirty."

Taking up his new position, Maliki took his earpiece out after hearing Jeremy's curse and Eddie's laughter.

About the Author

After traveling the world as a child, S.J. Rowe has found a home in the southwest with her husband and two kids. She continues to visit exotic destinations around the world with her best friends, and when she is home, she splits her time between watching baseball and singing in the car. To unwind, she enjoys a good cup of coffee while curled up watching Star Wars.

Contents

www.ingramcontent.com/pod-product-compliance
Lightning Source LLC
Chambersburg PA
CBHW050852210726
48290CB00004B/1194